The Next Cell

A NOVEL

David A. Davies

DAPCON PUBLISHING

10 9 8 7 6 5 4 3 2 1
Printed in the United States of America

LCCN 2018912217

ISBN 978 0 9974727 2 1

For more information on *The Next Cell* and the author, visit:
www.davidadaviesauthor.com

Editor: Julie Scandora
Cover Designer: Dapcon Publishing
Interior Design: Paul Salvette

Also by DAVID A. DAVIES

THE POTENTIAL
MASK OF DECEIT

Ellen
Happy Reading
Enjoy !

David A. Davies

FEAR MAKES THE WOLF BIGGER THAN HE IS.

GERMAN PROVERB

FOR MY PRETTY LADY

ACKNOWLEDGEMENTS

First and foremost, I thank my wife, Patty, for her continuous support, love, and understanding, without which I could never have completed this and many more of my projects. A special shout-out and thanks to my editor Julie Scandora who once again kept me on my toes and put up with my 'interesting' writing style. Thank you also to beta readers Stacy Nelson and Lawrence Kane for allowing me to test the waters and also thanks to Nathan Rees for his expertise.

CHAPTER ONE

Khvajeh Baha od Din, Northeastern Afghanistan

THE TWO INTELLIGENCE OFFICERS sat in the rear of the Toyota Land Cruiser, gripping the handholds as tightly as they could while the off-road vehicle bounced its way from one pothole to another. It should have been only a short ride from the helicopter landing site to the ancient town on the banks of the Panji River, but the road, which resembled more a dirt track with sporadic portions of tarmac, was extending the promised one-hour drive to an almost two-hour teeth-clenching, bone-jarring, ball-busting ride from hell. If any of the passengers in the vehicle had a complaint, it went unsaid as each dealt with the discomfort in his own way.

As the landscape began to change from the dry, arid wasteland to the east, pastures of green, lush farmland sprang up from the west, which provided the town its means of income and employment for the citizens who were not otherwise engaged in the army of the Northern Alliance and under the command of General Ahmad Shah Massoud. The driver and translator for the group announced that they were over the worst of the rattle ride and assured the travelers that they would be at their destination within the next fifteen to twenty minutes. On entering the outskirts of the town, the two intelligence officers released their death grips and began to straighten themselves up as the trail became an actual road.

An American security officer riding in the front passenger seat held a Glock 23 with both hands pointing the weapon down to the floor and out of sight. With an AR-15 wedged securely between his seat and his door, he dialed up his level of awareness and scanned the area in front of him. To the casual observer, the man in the front seat looked relaxed, but to the trained eye, it was evident that the man was all business and in no mood to talk about farming, culture, or local economics. He was a trained killer, and his job was to protect the two officers sitting behind him. A second security officer sat in the rear compartment behind the two intelligence officers and had the same automatic rifle but held his firmly in his hands. He too kept the weapon from plain view and was conducting the same exercise as his partner but looked out of the rear of the vehicle and began to take in the sights and, without being too paranoid, saw danger with every person, every object, and every building.

When the Toyota entered a traffic circle in the center of the town, a pickup truck with four armed men pulled in front of them. As they exited the circle, a second pickup truck, this one with a heavy machine gun mounted on a tripod on the bed of the truck and an equal number of men moved in behind to form a three-vehicle convoy. Nobody in the Toyota stirred, as this was the welcoming party they had expected. Nonetheless, the westerners still felt uneasy as this show of security drew more than a fleeting glance from the locals, especially since the shiny new Toyota with dark-tinted windows advertised that strangers were in town.

The small convoy laboriously wove its way through busy streets, which were awash with traders, farmers, soldiers, men, women, playing children, and vast arrays of cattle and fowl, each headed in one direction or another, meeting and separating, buying and selling, confronting and negotiating. The Afghan market town was a symphony of chaos that had survived hundreds of years without the need of a conductor or ruler to instill order or make sense of functionality. If the visitors had traveled down the same streets fifty years prior or did so fifty years in the future, the same scene would be painted with little change as the town ebbed and flowed with the passing of the seasons, the sporadic but bountiful harvests, the killer droughts, and the unending conflicts that afflicted and benefitted the country of Afghanistan throughout the centuries.

As the din of the center subsided, the three vehicles began to pick up some speed leading them to the edge of the town where the tarmac once again grudgingly surrendered to dirt roads and potholes large enough to conceal small children and animals. Death grips were once again the order of the day, and inward curses were suppressed as the small convoy negotiated the rough landscape while teeth and bone grinded and crunched over every rock and stone. Although the road in front of them ran straight as a die, the convoy peeled off to the left and towards the outer suburbs of Khvajeh Baha od Din where the town met the Panji River, the confluence to the Amu Darya that separates Afghanistan from Tajikistan, Uzbekistan, and Turkmenistan. The only other thing on the road behind them was a brown, cement-like dust that permeated every possible human orifice and every conceivable mechanical device. It hung in the air for a few seconds as the convoy twisted and turned and then swarmed after its prey, giving no respite to man or machine. Only when the convoy slowed to a crawl did the dust settle as the lead vehicle maneuvered its way slowly around an obstacle in the road, an entrenched T-55 Soviet-era battle tank, its barrel pointing ominously down the throat of anyone who approached.

With the tank disappearing in the rearview mirror, the visitors were greeted with the next impediment in the road, a checkpoint sandwiched between two elevated bunkers, each of which was fitted with heavy machine guns. Suspicious Northern Alliance soldiers looked down on the three vehicles as they approached, but a small makeshift barrier barring the road was raised by a sentry to allow passage. Crossing over the threshold, the visitors entered the stronghold of General Ahmad Shah Massoud and began navigating their way through narrow streets towards his headquarters that lay on the banks of the giant river. At first, progress was slow as the convoy was hindered by other military vehicles and Alliance soldiers who had equal missions of importance and were not interested in foreigners and hurried about their business without a second glance to the strangers in their midst.

When the group of three vehicles escaped the bustle, the road in front of them dropped drastically down a steep hill and into a scene of serenity and beauty. Before them lay an oasis of lush, green vegetation that stretched for kilometers before them with stunning views of the glacial waters and the distant snow-draped mountains of Tajikistan. Here, the houses were two or three stories high and neatly aligned with the street. Most were well kept and maintained and were detached by walls and gates or by neat lawns, flower beds, and brooks of gently flowing water. It was easy for the westerners to gain an element of ease in their new surroundings; however, as they approached the fast-flowing waters of the great river, the convoy took a sharp turn into a walled compound and back into reality as another T-55 barred the way forward, causing each vehicle to come to a complete stop. Fifty pairs of veteran soldiers' eyes zoomed in on the spectacle.

The driver, not knowing that all his passengers had been here before, stated the obvious with a cheery note, "We are here."

As everyone was about to alight from the Land Cruiser, the lead security officer holstered his pistol when he caught sight of an unarmed man rushing towards the vehicles, which he assumed was an aide or assistant to the general.

On exiting the vehicle, the security officer was taken aback and surprised at the sight of a big puff of brown and black smoke, which was followed by an explosion coming from a large squat building to the front of them. His instincts took over, and he took cover behind his still open passenger door. As he was popping his head up to see what was going on, he drew his pistol from his holster. Every one of the soldiers around them automatically drew their weapons to the ready position and searched for the cause of the explosion. As they did, a man on fire came screaming out of the building that was now burning furiously.

The security officer grabbed one of the gawking intelligence officers who was standing behind him and screamed at the top of his lungs, "GET BACK IN THE CAR! GET BACK IN THE CAR! LET'S GO! LET'S GO!" As each of the westerners followed the command and dove back into the vehicle, the security officer looked back to see what was happening to the injured man who was now being chased by a soldier with a Kalashnikov. The soldier let rip a burst of ten rounds into the man who fell head first into a bush. Instead of getting away from the man on fire, the soldier approached closer and shot another burst into the prone lifeless body, but before he turned away, he spat on the man. The security officer tried to tune the image out and concentrated on getting his party out of harm's way, but screamed as loudly as he could to the driver, "GO, GO, GO!" The driver didn't need any more convincing and screeched the Toyota back out of the compound and on to the road where he managed to turn the vehicle around and point them in the direction from where they had initially come.

It had been almost two hours since the party had left the compound of General Massoud. During the ride, each speculated and discussed openly what had happened and what they saw. The security officer was concerned with the man on fire. Someone mentioned that it was probably a mercy killing as the man was so overcome in flames that he probably would not have survived his injuries; however, the security officer saw it differently. One bullet is a mercy killing, emptying half a magazine of 7.62 mm into a man is murder, and to spit on him afterward, that was contempt. One of the intelligence officers suggested that they turn around and find out what was going on, but the security officer adamantly objected stating that they did not know if there was an ongoing internal dispute at the compound or it was an attack of some kind. Whatever the reason for the blast, they did not need to be there to be blamed for something they didn't do. The best course of action in the opinion of the security man was to exfiltrate per the predetermined emergency plan back to the helicopter and regroup across the border to Tajikistan.

After another forty-five minutes of bone-jarring discomfort, the Toyota finally turned off the highway and headed once again towards the river to their final destination. Again, the road dropped sharply, this time coming off the arid plains and towards the lush banks and crystal blue waters of the Panji. The team now relegated to failure for the day were in a somber but relaxed mood knowing somewhat reluctantly that they would probably have to make this same journey again and very soon. The two intelligence officers were both silently ruminating about possible scenarios, causes, and effects, while the two security officers were juggling with thoughts of safety, security, and logistics. The driver, a paid contractor, seeing only dollar signs, was more than happy to run through the whole exercise again and still again if need be.

As the vehicle navigated the final bend to the helicopter landing site, each person in the Toyota sat up ramrod straight in his seat when the group saw a number of pickup trucks and multiple men with guns surrounding the chopper. The driver slowed his approach, but as they got closer, they could see that their pilot and co-pilot were on their knees being held at gunpoint. The security officer in the passenger seat screamed for the driver to stop. The noise of skidding wheels on gravel and the cloud of thick brown dust drew the attention of the gunmen whose new focus became the intruding vehicle. A staring match ensued for a few seconds as nobody uttered a word or made a move. The stalemate ended only when one of the gunmen pointed an AK-47 at the Toyota and motioned for the interlopers to get out of the vehicle. Before the security officer could coach the driver on his next move, the contractor panicked and rammed the vehicle into reverse and hit the gas. When the driver attempted to look over his shoulder out of the rear of the vehicle, the gunman opened fire and killed him with two shots to his head.

"GET DOWN!" the security officer yelled, but the shattering of glass and the spray of blood was all that was needed as an invitation for the passengers to find cover. Without much hesitation, the security officer grabbed hold of the steering wheel with his left hand and contorted his left leg over the center console. He rammed his left foot down on top of the dead driver's right foot, hammering down the accelerator to regain motion, and then looked over his left shoulder towards the rear of the vehicle. His line of sight was hindered by the dead body and headrest, but he didn't care; his objective was to get moving and get out of the line of fire that had now intensified as enemy rounds started peppering the front end of the Toyota. Realizing that his limited vision was hampering their escape, he needed to spin the vehicle around to face forward. He pushed the accelerator down for more speed and attempted a J-turn by aggressively spinning the steering wheel hard left, which forced the front end of the Land Cruiser to rise slightly and lose traction enough to bring the front of the vehicle around 180 degrees. Just as the front end started to move to the right, the security officer felt a sharp sting on his right shoulder which almost forced him to lose control. Through sheer grit, determination, and will to survive, he saw through the pain and focused on getting the vehicle facing forward, but as the Toyota spun around 100 degrees, the front right wheel caught on a boulder flipping it over violently first onto its right side and then onto its roof.

Within a few seconds, the gunmen descended on the upside-down vehicle, guns at the ready and prepared for further action; however, there was no need. Nothing stirred in the vehicle. But as one of the gunmen first looked in the driver's seat, he was confused to see two bodies so close to each other. Then as he tried to inspect further, a set of hands appeared from the rear of the truck followed by a mumbling and incoherent cry for help. The gunman called his comrades for support and immediately grabbed the pleading hands and began to drag the captive out of the wreckage. By the time the gunmen retrieved the survivor and unceremoniously dumped him at the side of the road, a call came out that another was alive.

Richard Nash, deputy director of Operations, CIA, bloodied, battered, and bruised began to make a move to see what was going on outside his confinements but was invited to remain in place by the barrel of an AK-47. When he looked up at his captor, he recognized the thick black beard and the black turban and succumbed to the fact he may have just been captured by the Taliban.

Chris Morehouse was awake, but he did not have his eyes open. He searched the inside of his eyelids to warm up his senses before a body check. He had a swollen lip, and his right shoulder was aching. When he raised his left hand to touch his bearded face, he found crusty blood around his lip and nose. Then his finger jabbed his right eye by mistake, which made him flinch as it too was puffy. Satisfied that there were no other upper injuries, he began a scan of the rest of his body, which was sound; however, there was a weight at the end of his feet, which he could not identify. Knowing only that he was back in the United States, he was still uncertain of his surroundings. He remained quiet and let his senses continue sending messages. The inside of his mouth tasted like he'd eaten five large pepperoni, garlic, and triple-cheese pizzas washed with copious volumes of Guinness and Baileys chasers. His nostrils, although partially clogged with dried blood, let in a faint waft of coffee to confuse him more. He dared open his eyes, and when he looked down at his feet, he saw and felt the heaviness of a large cat sitting on his legs and staring intently at him.

"That's Mango."

"What?"

"You're in his spot."

"Oh, sorry . . . Mango, didn't mean to intrude, old chap." Chris got himself into a seated position on the leather couch that he couldn't remember occupying.

"He usually sits on the couch when I'm getting ready for work."

Chris moved cautiously so as not to disturb the orange tabby cat too much. Still, it looked on him with disdain and loathing, ready for a fight. Chris knew when to back down and decided not to make any sudden moves. He was not a fan of cats.

"How are you feeling?"

Chris turned his head to see where the female voice was coming from, "Um, okay, I guess."

"Coffee?"

"No, thank you, I don't drink the stuff." He slowly spun his feet around to the floor, dislodging the feline, and began to take in the strange environment that he found himself in. "I'll take a glass of water if you have one."

The place that he was in looked to be a small apartment. Directly in front of him was a small kitchen, off to the left was a door cracked open enough to reveal a bathroom, and to its right, another room, which he assumed was a bedroom. There was a door at the end of a small hallway, which, by the look of the locking mechanisms, was the outer door. *Okay, that's where I go out, but how the hell did I get in?* he thought.

The girl made her way over to him from the kitchen and gave him a bottle of water. She was wearing medical scrubs, which fortunately for him bore her name tag. She looked at his eyes and saw that he was reading her name.

"Thanks, Sandy."

"You're welcome." She paused and stood in front of him with her arms folded across her chest. She could tell he was confused. "You don't remember last night, do you?"

"My hangover tells me no, but I should be polite and say I do."

She tensed at the cheesy reply, "Well that sounds like a bunch of crap. You either do or you don't."

"Sorry, Sandy, it's a bit hazy, and I kinda ache, you know?"

"I'm not surprised." She moved back to the kitchen and continued to bustle around.

As he tried to drink the water, he winced as his upper lip protested the proximity of a foreign object. He managed to take a few sips and then bore the pain to take a longer drink. As his pain subsided, he placed the bottle on the coffee table in front of him and did a further review of his circumstances. He was still fully dressed, except for his boots, which he spotted near the front door. But his belt and the top button of his jeans were open, which surprised him. "Um?"

Sandy followed his gaze and smiled a little. "It's okay. I didn't take advantage of you, just tried to make you comfortable."

"So we didn't . . . ?"

"No, Chris, that is not why I brought you home. You were just having a bad night."

Chris was mystified. *She knows my name!* He rubbed his forehead and rolled his heavy eyes around in their sockets. "Thanks, but can you fill me in on some of the details?"

"New Park Tavern," she answered plainly.

He nodded remembering going into the pub.

"You were drinking by yourself, you'd had some fish and chips earlier, but you were slowly getting hammered."

"Oh," he managed, embarrassed.

"Except for a few locals, there were two guys playing pool. One of them had his girlfriend hanging around, but otherwise the bar was empty. It was a quite night."

A blip of memory surfaced. "Yeah, bit of a flirt, if I remember right."

"She was trying to bait you into a conversation to piss her boyfriend off for ignoring her."

"Oh shit."

"Well the boyfriend sees what's going on and tells you to mind your own business. I'm being very polite with my verbiage, by the way."

"And I told him where to go, not so politely, I suppose."

"Yes, you could say you had some colorful language, all the better with a British accent." She smirked at the memory.

"Where were you in all this?"

"Behind the bar, about to call the owner and his baseball bat."

"Who hit whom first?"

"The bigger of the two guys hit you with a pool cue. He was aiming for your head, but you somehow dodged it, and it hit your shoulder."

"And it went sideways after that, right?"

"You took some pretty heavy blows from those two guys. I'm not surprised you don't remember too much. Here, come and get something for the pain."

Chris got off the couch slowly, and Mango almost sprinted to where Chris had been sitting and let out a hiss signaling he had won his territory back. As Chris made his way to the kitchen, he tucked in his shirt and buttoned his jeans. "How did I end up here? I assume this is your place?"

"What can I say? I'm a sucker for sob stories."

He stopped mid-stride, astonished, surprised, aghast. His brow furrowed. "Say what?"

"You started pouring your heart out to me about someone called Pam."

"Oh shit. Really? I'm sorry," he said, truly feeling remorseful. "I didn't mean to bother you with that. Sorry," he repeated.

"Don't be so hard on yourself, Chris. I'm sorry that she died, but you never told me how."

Chris breathed a long sigh of relief. *Jesus Christ, what the hell did I tell her?* he thought and then said, "Sandy that's not me, really. I'm not the guy who cries over his old girlfriends to someone in a bar. I apologize, and thank you for helping me out." He didn't want to get into a conversation now about Pam, and he was grateful that she didn't push.

Sandy handed him some Tylenol. "Here take a bunch. It looks like you're going to need more than a few to get going."

Chris popped two in his mouth and sucked down the rest of his water. They stood looking at each other in an awkward silence.

Sandy made the first move and gave him a pleasant smile while she put some dishes in the sink. "Listen, why don't you freshen up a bit? There's a clean towel in the bathroom, and there's plenty of tea if you don't want coffee. But I have to get going. I have another job. I'm going to trust you not to rob me blind, not that I have anything worth taking, but please pull the door behind you and make sure it's locked. There's no rush, take your time, or don't go at all if you need to rest," she hinted cautiously.

Chris stepped back and placed his empty bottle on the counter. "You've been very kind, Sandy, but I don't want to overstay my welcome. I'll just use your bathroom, if I may, and then I'll walk out with you, all right?"

Sandy tried to hide her disappointment but rationalized that this was a good option. "Sure, whatever you want, but don't take too long. I have a bus to catch."

"I'm on it; be out in two minutes, I promise."

On reaching the bathroom, Chris relieved himself and then

checked his look in the mirror. There was no getting around it—he looked like shit. After replaying the conversation with Sandy in the kitchen and the obvious interest she showed, he could not understand in his dilapidated state why. He unbuttoned his shirt to look at his shoulder, which was red, sore and swollen. His right eye was 90 percent open, which was a good sign meaning that by the end of the day it would be okay, save the blackness of the skin. His nose, except for the blood, was fine. It wasn't the first time he'd taken one to the schnoz, but it seemed intact, and that too would heal in a short time. There were a couple of scratches on his left cheek, and his beard was matted with dried blood. His brown hair was tussled and felt unwashed, and after running his fingers through it, he smelt the aftermath of flying beer and cigarette ash. He smiled and was happy to see that all his teeth were where they were supposed to be. *That must have been a good scrap last night.* He ruefully thought, *Wonder what the other two pricks look like.*

It took Chris two minutes and thirty seconds to exit the bathroom. "Sorry to keep you. You ready?"

Sandy picked up her backpack, which she threw over her shoulder, grabbed her keys, and made for the door. She handed him a note. "Here, take this. Call me when you get the chance, okay?"

"Absolutely, I will, and thank you, Sandy," he said sincerely while wondering if he really would call her.

As soon as they both traversed down two flights of stairs, they exited the apartment block and walked onto the city street. A wave of fresh air hit Chris like a ton of bricks, which made him feel nauseous. His first thought was that the hangover was out to get him, but on further reflection, he supposed that he could have a concussion from the fight. Nevertheless, he didn't want to show any weakness to his new "best" friend so staggered on, keeping up with her quick pace and engaging in conversation. "I hope I didn't cause too much damage last night."

"Not more than we are used to. It's not the most well-behaved bar in town."

"Second job, eh?"

"I'm trying to get into veterinary school, so I'm taking classes here and there, but I'm also getting some firsthand experience with a vet near the university. What about you, Chris? What do you do?"

"Oh shoot," Sandy said before he could answer, "there's my bus. I've got to run. Don't be a stranger, Chris. You know where to find me." As she scampered away, Chris shouted his thanks once again, but she was gone, and he wasn't sure if she had heard. *Oh well, it's not like I'm coming back this way again any time soon.*

As the bus pulled away, he turned around to walk off realizing suddenly he had no clue where he was. While he was doing a very slow 360, he tried to find a landmark, a point of reference, or something to latch on to, but nothing was triggering familiarity. He looked at his watch and managed to find some piece of mind with the fact that he did not have to work, thus leaving him almost twenty-four hours to get his shit sorted out. Without any general direction, he plodded onward for almost fifteen minutes until he found himself at the intersection of two streets named Barrow and Grand. Still disorientated, he took the right turn for no other reason than a truck was blocking his view to his left. While he was on Grand, he passed by a coffee shop that made him retch and rush to a nearby garbage can where he nearly departed with the previous night's fish and chips. Passersby looked at him scornfully, believing he was either a drunk or a heroin addict coming down off a binge, and gave him a wide berth. Chris was happy that nobody wanted to get into a conversation with him, as his hangover and throbbing wounds were worsening his disposition. He sensed that misery was on its way to ruin his day, and his mood began to spiral quickly downwards.

It wasn't the first time Chris had fallen into a pattern of self-pity and borderline depression on completion of a mission for the CIA. His current remedy was to get drunk, get in someone's face, start a fight, and wallow in regret and guilt the following day. He was lucky he had no office to work from, he had no immediate supervisor looking over his shoulder every day, and as such, nobody saw the suffering or coping methods he chose. Once he was on a mission, he was strong, decisive, brash, but controlled. Many of his peers wanted to work with him and relied on his expertise and skills, knowing he was dependable and resilient. He'd often been asked to take a management or training position to drive his career forward, but he declined and let it be known that he wanted to be a field operator with free rein with little or no umbrella to control him. But it was times like this, as he staggered down an unfamiliar street with plenty of downtime before his next mission, that he reached his angriest and loneliest depths. He still blamed his boss, Richard Nash, for the death of his girlfriend Pam in Berlin eighteen months prior. As a contract assassin for the CIA, she'd fallen out of a high-rise building when they were on opposing CIA missions. Nash claimed innocence regarding her death and blamed the mole at the CIA who betrayed Pam and the United States. Chris had dealt with the traitor as a means of appeasement, which at the onset of his current role sufficed to check his frustrations. Unbeknownst to Nash and others at the agency, Chris still bore resentment towards The Game and had serious doubts about continuing his employment with the spy agency.

The street names and places swept by a morose Chris Moorhouse, but as he trudged along, thoughts of Pam and his desire for a family with her clouded his mind. He had cried after her funeral, and sometimes when he was on a plane or alone eating a meal, something would trigger a memory, and he would shed a hidden tear. He was getting better at hiding his sadness, but sometimes his rage outweighed his sound judgement when he tried to relax; then beer became king. He knew he wasn't an alcoholic, but he was scared to find out how little it would take to push him over that edge. Each time he thought about the damage that drink did, he thought of his brother Terry incarcerated in an English prison for beating up a nurse and a doctor whom he blamed for not doing enough to save their mother from a massive stroke. Chris, who had been tracking and photographing Hezbollah terrorists in Beirut, could not be contacted and was only made aware of his mother's demise after she had been buried. On hearing the news, Chris once again hit out and hit the bottle hard. He naively blamed Nash for sending him into harm's way and was convinced that he had held back the news of his mother to save an operation.

"This fucking game," Chris muttered to himself as he moped along, head down, thumb up his arse, mind stuck in neutral. He was getting tired, the Tylenol was failing in the battle of the hangover, and he needed to sit down for a while. When he made it to a small park on a river, he searched for respite. *A chair, a chair, my kingdom for a chair*, he silently pleaded.

After a brief hunt, he happily spotted a welcoming bench near the water's edge and almost jogged to claim his spot before someone intruded on his prize. He sat down heavily. "Jesus, I need to stop doing this shit," he whispered as he leaned back on the bench and closed his eyes to the clear blue skies above him. His solace didn't last long as the morning sun drilled rays through his eyelids piercing the eyeballs and drilling out the other side of his skull. He leaned forward in pain and searched for some relief but once again felt nauseous as the bile in his throat crept slowly upwards. With his elbows now resting on his knees he took some deep long breaths, which almost made him retch, but he managed grimly to keep things under control, despite the protestations of his stomach. His head was spinning, and he opened his eyes to find a frame of reference, a solid mark, a building, a person, a duck, anything that would allow him to focus on his surroundings and not the beating mallet in his head. He needed to take his mind off his sorrowful state, but as he looked across the water to the opposite bank to some buildings beyond, he wondered what he was doing there with his mind flying off in multiple directions thinking about work, Pam, Nash, and how he ended up here, alone, miserable, and malcontent. While he stewed, a mixture of thoughts, feelings, and bodily functions all demanded his attention, though other than the loss of his fiancée, nothing else would be a priority. He knew it was futile to think of her return, so he willed himself to stop dwelling on the past and to reconnect with his current situation before he fell further into a blacker, deeper mood.

Pushing Pam away to another file in the back of his memory, Chris thought about his recent assignment as a means to cope with his physical and mental state. He rationalized that to get back to reality, the freshest positive memory would ignite some form of action, a thing to focus on, a movement that required some willpower to get off his arse forcing his body to comply and move on. Looking downward at the concrete path before him, he raised his left hand to his chin and began to rub and scratch his beard while reviewing his last operation.

He'd been tracking a Saudi diplomat for close to a year, but he reluctantly passed on surveillance to the FBI as soon as he arrived back in the United States. To say he was pissed off was an understatement, and he expressed his concerns that the subject in question was "dirty" and had some nefarious connections in the Middle East, connections that Chris could easily identify if they too were in the United States. As soon as the targeted Saudi's plane from Egypt arrived in the United States, Chris begged to continue with the operation, but he was slapped down and told under no circumstances was he to be involved. He was reminded that the law strongly forbade the CIA from conducting surveillance in the United States, and that wasn't going to change on the whim of a very junior CIA surveillance officer.

Chris's maudlin temperament continued as he searched the ground in front of him for answers. The lapping water on the bank provided a pleasant distraction, and the occasional plane flying high above made him ponder in a different direction *I wonder where they are all going . . . Casablanca, Honolulu, Rio?* He paused to think, his mind empty for a change, even for a few seconds as the plane became a distant vapor trail. *Lawyers, dentists, teachers, taxidermists, where the hell are they going? What the fuck am I doing? Why can't I be one of them?* he asked himself angrily. As he shifted his position, he sat upright and again thought of Pam. *Stop, stop, for fucks sake, stop!* He rubbed his eyes, rummaged through his hair, and then threw a troubling question into the mix, *Fuck, do I need a drink?* He took another long breath and tried to focus on something different, scared about the question he had just posed to himself. Chris stared across the water looking for an answer and then saw something that caught his eye. "Holy shit, he is low," he said to nobody. Chris kept looking at the plane that seemed to be descending even more, he stood up, and then froze in place. "Jesus fuck!" he screamed, as the plane hit a skyscraper in New York City.

CHAPTER TWO

Frederick, Maryland

CHRIS HAD JUST FINISHED HIS FISHMAC WHEN two FBI agents walked in through the door of the McDonald's on Maryland State Route 85 in Frederick. Wearing their standard blue windbreakers with the yellow letters FBI imprinted on the chest and back was enough to silence the normally busy evening crowd. Those standing in line took a step back to stare and then shifted awkwardly, not knowing what to do or say. While the two uniformed men began to scan the crowd, an older man who was wearing a black Vietnam veteran baseball cap stopped what he was eating and got up painfully and slowly from his chair and then hobbled towards the agents. The old man reached for his wallet and announced, "Whatever you want, it's on me, fellas. What'll it be?"

"Thank you, sir, but that's not necessary. We are only here for a minute," one of the agents replied. Feeling slightly rejected, the old man retreated back to his seat and stuffed his wallet back into his tired old jeans. "If you change your mind, you know where to find me," came the saddened reply. All he wanted to do was help just a smidgen on a day like today.

Chris, who had his back to the counter area heard and saw the exchange from the reflection in the glass window. He rose from his seat and made his way to the trash bin. The older of the two agents took a look at the stranger with the thick brown beard, bruised face, tan baseball cap, black jacket, blue jeans, and tan boots. Before the agent could utter a word, Chris sauntered up and nonchalantly said, "Ready when you are." Neither agent replied, but both turned to leave simultaneously.

As the trio marched out in single file, Chris reached into a pocket and pulled out a set of keys, which he dangled in mid-air. "I have a rental. Do you want me to drive?"

"I got it," responded the younger of the two agents and snapped the keys away from Chris.

"White Ford over there." He pointed in the general direction of the other cars in the parking lot. The older agent remained silent and punched the remote on a black Chevy Suburban, got in the driver's side, and immediately started the engine. By the time Chris opened the passenger door and sat down, the driver had already flipped the headlights on, selected reverse, and begun moving slowly away from the fast-food restaurant. The FBI driver made his way southbound onto Route 85 and was gathering speed quite quickly. Chris, still with a Sprite in his hands, struggled to get his seatbelt on while the Chevy swerved in and out of traffic. There was no need for this, he thought but kept his mouth in check. He looked at the FBI agent and could tell the man was stressed and wasn't going to be great company.

Chris didn't know how far they had to go or where they were even going. All he knew was that after finally contacting his supervisor, Gene Brooks, he was told to get to Frederick the fastest way possible. He knew from the brief phone conversation that a flight was out of the question, so he drove the 240 miles from New York in just over four hours. During the ride, it gave him a chance to listen to the radio and catch up on the day's events and the aftermath of the attacks on New York, the Pentagon, and the hijacked plane over Pennsylvania. He listened to the one hundred and one theories and assumptions from people who had no idea of the real situation or what was really going on. Reporters were speculating; experts, so-called experts, and retired experts were weighing in on what had happened, what could happen and what would happen; but the sad, helpless victims only wanted to know why. The only common thread Chris could identify from everything he was hearing was that most people felt a sense of insecurity, vulnerability, and the uncertainty of what was going to happen next. But it also seemed that the country was in denial as the Twin Towers smoldered, as the fires tempered in Washington, DC, and as the debris still fluttered silently in a field near the Stonycreek Township of Pennsylvania.

"Well, there's a name you don't see every day," Chris blurted as the Suburban took a right turn onto English Muffin Way. He wanted to play nice and just get in some kind of conversation, but the more he thought about it, the more he surmised that the events of the day might have affected the driver sitting next to him more than he could know. He decided it was best if he just shut up.

Within a few minutes, the Chevy slowed to a more casual speed. As it did, Chris's radar went into high alert. To his right, he spotted two police cruisers parked outside a commercial warehouse and, to his left, another parked on the grass accompanied by a military Humvee. Just beyond that, a parked Black Hawk helicopter. As they approached an intersection, the FBI agent switched on his blue, white, and red strobe lights and maneuvered the vehicle around a temporary barrier manned by an FBI agent, a police officer, and two armed soldiers. Passing the obstacle, the driver turned off his lights and took the first right turn into a warehouse complex whose gate was manned once again by soldiers and police officers. Without stopping, the Suburban drove straight into an open loading dock where the FBI agent doused his lights, parked, and killed the engine. Again, without a word, the FBI agent led the way up towards a set of stairs and then through a door to the warehouse. Upon entering the main building, they were greeted by a Marine who was sitting at a makeshift reception desk. The Marine was flanked by another who was carrying a shotgun in the port position standing guard at a door that led deeper into the warehouse itself. Chris was told by the desk Marine that he had to wait for someone to escort him before he was allowed passage; however, there were no chairs or coffee tables. This was not some doctor's waiting room with glossy magazines; it was bare, sterile, industrial. They all just stood there in silence, staring at each other as if in a Mexican standoff. Chris found a wall to lean on while the FBI agent parked himself on the corner of the table and folded his arms. It was plain to all that the agent wasn't a happy camper and he obviously wanted to be elsewhere.

Mercifully, it didn't take long for Gene to appear from behind a steel door. "Hey, partner, c'mon back."

While Gene held the door open, Chris passed by the agent and gave a quick nod and received a similar one in reply. *Hope his day gets better*, he thought.

Gene was four or five steps ahead of Chris and not waiting around for pleasantries. Chris wanted to know what was going on, but as they were traversing quickly through other doors and corridors, it became difficult to hold a conversation. When they finally made it into the expanse of the warehouse, Chris was taken aback by the sight before him. In the center of the hall, which by his estimation must have been fifty thousand square feet, was a raised aisle about thirty feet wide, and to the left and right were probably fifteen to twenty semi-trucks all backed up towards the center. Most of the trucks had one side or another raised, and inside were a host of people sitting at desks or consoles' monitoring screens or in conference. Cables and lights were strung out everywhere with technicians either laying new cable or relocating another piece of equipment to here, there, or anywhere things were needed. Gene continued his silence as they both marched down to the end of the aisle, often times dodging people rushing from one side of the space to the other. As they were walking towards the end of the concourse where it became slightly quieter, Gene threw Chris an over the shoulder question, "What happened to your face?"

"Beer, girl, boyfriend, you fill in the gaps."

Gene shook his head and led Chris to a trailer that had its side open and was fitted out for small meeting rooms. He led them into the first available room and motioned Chris to take a seat. "Welcome to the Mound," Gene offered as he too grabbed a chair.

"Um, okay, thanks, I think," he replied with a sense of trepidation.

"CTC mobile, if you will." Gene pulled his chair away from the table and made himself comfortable, loosening his tie. "As soon as the shit hit the fan today, we all scrambled to get the hell out of Dodge, and here we are. We have two other similar setups. One is always mobile; the other is either setting up or tearing down, and the third," Gene waved his hands around him, "is static. You may not be able to tell, but we are the hub right now, but that could change pretty quickly if the threat picture changes."

Chris was impressed. "Nice. I like what you've done with the place, Gene, but the waiting lounge could use some elevator music, flowers, and a sexy receptionist to brighten things up."

"You're such a dick sometimes, Chris, but you may want to watch out. I can appreciate your humor, but there're a lot of frustrated people around that might not take it so well."

Chris nodded in submission. Although Gene was his supervisor, they were on friendly terms and had been through a lot together over the years. The first time they met was in a holding cell at Washington National Airport when Chris was detained and accused of assassinating US ambassador to Germany Winston Heymann in an attack carried out by Turkish terrorists. Even then, the two prodded and jostled jokingly with each other, and their relationship had not changed since.

"So what the hell is going on here, Gene? From what I'm hearing on open source, it looks like we got hit pretty bad."

"It looks like the sky is falling in on us, and we really don't know what the hell is coming at us next," Gene responded gravely and then turned to look over his shoulder. "Over there, there's a bunch of generals and GI Joes sitting with a stack of launch codes in their pockets ready to take on the world. Then in another meeting room across the way, there's a bunch practicing group hugs and singing "We Shall Overcome." One part madness, the other part Johnny-on-the-spot, and I'm not sure which is which right now." He turned back towards his friend. "We find ourselves in a truly unprecedented situation, Chris, and there aren't many battle plans on the table that tell us what to do next. The only good thing so far is that we have degraded the air threat by grounding every plane in the US, including foreign carriers. You'll only see the military up in the skies right now, and I don't know how long that's going to last. Trouble is we aren't sure if there's going to be a ground base attack coming, so everyone who's anyone has taken off to the hills, hence the reason why we are here. The White House is empty, and all that is left in the Capitol is some intern with a hard hat and baseball bat trolling the halls wondering if he will survive the day."

"Casualties?"

"It's going to be in the thousands." Gene stroked his chin and stared off into the distance, as if he was trying to count the bodies himself. Chris was about to ask a question, but Gene carried on, "All the politicians in the world are pointing shitty sticks at us and are already asking why we didn't prevent this, or if we knew about this then why weren't they informed, and whom is to blame. They want answers now, blah, blah, blah, the usual bullshit. If you ask me, in situations like this, we can't afford to be throwing each other under the bus. There is work to do, and clear heads need to prevail to prevent the next catastrophe. But I'm glad it's above my pay grade to answer some of those questions because there are no easy answers, and I'm sure there's going to be a lot of pissed-off people with quick-fix solutions and calls for action."

Chris didn't have much to say. He was out of his depth, and in the scope of things, he was just another low-ranked soldier ready to follow orders. However, he was happy to be engaged and not sitting on a park bench feeling sorry for himself. He let Gene take a breath before he inquired as to the reason he was sitting in front of him. But Gene continued to look off into the distance. Chris could tell that the toll of the day was wearing on him.

"Why am I here, Gene? It's not like I can make any difference with my skill set."

Gene nodded but stared at Chris for a while before saying anything. He knew that Chris was right. Being a surveillance specialist for the CIA, Chris had skills honed for international settings, not domestic events. "Look, Chris, you're still not flavor of the month around these parts. The whole debacle in the UK with Pam has set us back a ways, and it still stings."

Chris didn't need reminding how his late girlfriend killed an MI5 officer based on a quarrel he had with the man over perceived CIA operations in the UK.

"I'm hoping this attack today puts some of our differences aside because we are going to need all the help from our allies moving forward if we want to catch the bastards that did this and prevent something similar happening in other parts of the world."

Chris was glad to hear that Gene didn't want to go down that road again. The last time they had met, Gene had informed Chris that he was *persona non grata* in HQ. Not that Chris had an office there or visited that often, but management wanted to kick the former British soldier to the curb. However, those that knew him protected him and kept him working overseas with the CIA's Viewpoint surveillance team. Out of sight, out of mind, Gene kept telling him.

"So where's Nash in all this?"

Gene squared himself in the seat; his focus was back. "That's why I brought you in, Chris. The succession tree was activated as soon as the first plane hit. If you weren't in arm's reach when this went down, then you were excluded from the immediate decision-making table. The trouble is because Nash wasn't around, some of these idiots behind me have written him off. He's the deputy director for Operations, and they think that as of this minute he is inconsequential to getting things back on track." Gene let his comment settle for as second and then leaned forward towards Chris and sternly added, "Sorry, but I don't buy that shit!"

Eager to hear what his friend had planned, Chris simply nodded and let him continue.

"Right now, all the managers, wannabe managers, and those that they think know shit are claiming all the assets that are not nailed down. Everyone has his own agenda, and I'm claiming my stake with you. Viewpoint is going to be re-tasked. We've been battling with the Office of Science and Technology for months now, as they want Viewpoint under their purview, not Operations'. It looks like after this they are going to get what they want because Ops is not going to be sleeping for a while; they're going to be busy. Our challenge is that there could be a thousand different targets out there that need eyes on, but nobody is agreeing to anything right now. We don't know if we need to go on the defensive or offensive to look for potential bad actors. It's just too early to say."

Chris wanted him to slow down and not give himself a heart attack, but Gene continued without pause. "I've sent out cables to all the station chiefs and department heads that Viewpoint is to cease all ongoing operations until we can form a cohesive plan. Nobody, and I mean nobody, can form a consensus yet, so basically, we have no direction. Political ass covering is now in effect, and we are waiting for the director to direct and tell us what the fuck to do. All that we can agree upon right now that this is a very bad day for the country, and people are heading towards panic mode. We as an agency need to allay those fears and instill confidence in our government to make the right decisions. . . . Don't worry, jerkoff, I can read your mind. I'm not going to hug you and start singing, but those of us who can walk and chew gum at the same time are going to be on point to get shit done. That means you and me, buddy."

Chris could tell that Gene was venting, perhaps a little too much, but Gene knew that Chris could be trusted to keep his mouth shut.

The older of the two men finally took a breath. He loosened his tie again, only to tighten it a second later, a sign of nervousness. "I know you're confused, but you are the only one in limbo right now and in arm's reach. I haven't forgotten you, but others have, which is a good thing, but that may not last too much longer."

Chris was starting to hope that Gene was getting to the point.

Once again, Gene read Chris. "Nash is MIA. I need you to go find him, and we need to do it now before the clown convention adds another ring to the circus."

"Say what?" Chris shot up straight in his seat. "Was he in New York, the Pentagon?"

Gene looked serious and gave Chris a one-word answer, "Afghanistan."

Chris leaned back in his chair and rubbed his face, "Jesus, Gene, what the fuck?"

"We think the Taliban have him. We're ramping up a team to go out there and dig deep, but that's taking time. I need you to go ahead of them and see what you can find out, perhaps give them a lead or two."

Chris opened his eyes as far as they could go and scratched the back of his head, still trying to process what he had just been told. He was feeling a wave of heat pour through him when a bead of sweat ran down the side of this temple. He told himself to maintain control. He was being thrown into a dangerous situation and needed to pay attention, needed to concentrate. *Eyes and ears, Chris, eyes and ears.*

"There's an air force plane leaving Dover Air Base with a Delta unit on board. They are loading right this minute, and there's a spare seat. They are going to wait for you but not too long." Gene got out of his chair. "Come on. I need you to meet someone."

They moved to an adjacent trailer, which had a few more meeting rooms, in one of which they came across an older man sitting at a table, alone, pouring over some documents. He did not look up as both men entered his meeting room. Gene and Chris sat down without invitation. Gene broke the ice. "Hey Rod, this is Chris Morehouse."

Rod remained in his seat and continued to look at his paperwork. After a few seconds, he looked up and then stretched out his hand. As he did, he stared directly into Chris's eyes. "Good to meet you, Chris."

Chris noted the steel grip and the death stare and surmised that this was not the type of man he needed to piss off.

"I'll make this short and sweet, Chris." His voice was southern, but the man wasn't a hillbilly or some good old boy from the swamps, more of a Carolinas man. "Nash is a friend, and we need to get him out of whatever shithole he's fallen into, but all new Afghanistan operations belong to me. I'm only letting you go because of Gene's recommendation and that Nash owes me. I don't know what you are going to find when you get there, but for the most part, you are on your own." Rod didn't take his eyes off Chris, who in return never flinched and looked back with intense curiosity.

"My team are still packing lunches and fighting over toilet paper, but when they are done putting their hot rollers in their bags, they will be on the next flight behind you. I'm expecting to have my guys' boots on the ground in the next seventy-two to eighty-six hours. Gene and I will figure out communications and such, but if you can't find him or haven't got anything solid by the time we arrive, you need to step back." Rod didn't pause for comment. "I like a man who looks me in the eye when I talk to him, but I'm not fucking around with you. To me and my team you are an unknown entity and, as such, a liability until proven otherwise. I'm not here to bust your balls, but we have a timetable and a plan. Don't piss my boys off, and we'll be fine, okay?"

Chris understood the seriousness of the message and recognized that the man had some serious pull if he was leading the charge into Afghanistan. He thought it pointless to dwell on the details with him. "Understood. I appreciate the help."

"Good. Now when you come across any of my team out there, code words "George Mitchell." Any spelling, any language variations, you are either George or Mitchell, or you're looking for George or whatever, and my team will help you as long as it does not interfere with their prime missions."

Chris figured that he would not get to know what the prime missions were, so he didn't ask. He stood up thinking that the meeting was over, "Chris," Rod added, "if he's dead or alive, you are leaving the country with him, and I don't really care if you are in the body bag next to him. Understood?"

Chris felt like he was back in the army and almost replied, "Yes, sir!" but refrained; he wanted to be on his best behavior with this man. He didn't know if he would meet him again, if he would be his saving grace one day or his gravedigger. He smartly nodded and headed for the door.

"Thanks, Rod. As soon as we get the commo package together, we will let you know," Gene chirped as he walked out with Chris, but it was too late. Rod was back to scouring his documents for where he had left off and never heard what was said.

The short walk back to their meeting room was done in silence. Chris was still mesmerized by the fluorescent digital arena and the sheer magnitude of the mobile CTC, and he wondered how much time and effort went into the planning and preparations for a day like today. He was still trying to take it all in when Gene closed the door to their room and both sat down again. He watched Chris and knew that he had a hundred questions to ask.

"Special Activities Division, SAD. They are the best of the best, Chris—ex Delta, Seals, Rangers, you name it. These are the guys we send into the night to do the most harm, so don't fuck with them because we will never find your body." Chris rocked back in his chair and gazed down into his hands contemplating his next words.

"So do we have an operations plan?" Chris asked quizzingly in a jovial tone.

Gene remained silent.

"Risk assessment?"

Still no reply.

"Support structure? Escape and evasion plans?"

His last question made Gene squirm in his seat.

Chris knew he was being sent into harm's way, but he felt as if he was in the *Monty Python and the Holy Grail* movie. The trouble was he didn't know if he was one of the knights without a horse or the guy galloping behind with the coconuts. "It seems like I have some great choices, Gene." He added sarcastically, "I go to Afghanistan where missing CIA officers obviously grow on trees and therefore I could be out of there in a jiffy. Or I could ask a friendly raghead if they have spotted a spy and then get my balls chopped off and fed to me by the Taliban. But on the other hand, if I piss off the guys who are supposed to help me, I'll end up in six different graves with a toenail sent back to you as a sentimental gesture."

"Chris, I—"

He held up his hand to stop Gene. "To top it off, you don't have any communications, no plans, no way to get me in or us out, other than hitching a ride with a flying container ship or, worse, walking home. Which leads me to believe that you are winging this whole fucking thing. Are you seriously that pissed off with me that you want to see me killed?"

"What are you trying to say, Chris? It is what it is. I didn't cause this to happen." He paused and then threw out the obvious question, "You don't want to go, is that it?"

"Don't' be a muppet. What's next?"

Gene shook his head and then rubbed his hands over his face. Exasperated, he let out a sigh. "This day has to get better."

Chris smiled at him. "The easiest day was yesterday, Gene."

Gene frowned and nodded slowly. He hoped he was making the right decision to send Chris and silently prayed he could get things in motion in time to give him what he needed to find Nash. "On the way out, we will have a bunch of documents for you to take with you. It's just maps and supporting country intelligence. All low-level stuff. The two Feds that brought you in will take you to Dover. It's about a two-and-a-half-hour drive, but I've told them not to stop to smell the roses and get you there ASAP, even if it means going blue light all the way. You don't need to swap war stories with these guys, Chris. Enjoy the countryside, take in the sights, relax a bit."

"It's the middle of the night, dipshit."

"You know what I mean." Gene grinned. "The gate guard at Dover is expecting you. and you'll be taken straight to the plane. Hopefully the ramp is still down when you get there. You'll disembark in Bahrain. Leave your documentation in a secure trash box on the plane. Delta will remain in Bahrain to do whatever they do, and you will go to Islamabad commercial and then on to Peshawar. When you get there, someone from the station will meet you, and by that time, they will have figured out how to get you across the border. With a bit of luck, by the time you get there, we may have more intel on the boss, and all this may be for naught. Don't forget, in all your communications to anyone when you are in country, use the zero-line terminology."

"Which means?"

"I thought you knew this . . . the Pakistan/Afghanistan border is the zero line. You will be either north, south, east, or west of the line. For example, Kabul is roughly 230 kilometers from the Khyber Pass, or as we would say, 230 kilometers from the zero line. Got it?"

Chris nodded and let Gene continue.

"I've really no idea how you are getting in or out. While you are in the air, crap may sort itself out, and Nash may walk into a bar in Karachi or Timbuktu. Who knows?"

"Any intel on what he was doing there in the first place?"

"Normally, I would say you don't need to know, but not today. He went with Guy Trimble, an MI6 officer. I don't think he is a counterpart to Nash, but he is senior enough. They had a small security detail with them, and they choppered into Northwestern Afghanistan from Tajikistan. He was supposed to meet with General Massoud, leader of the Northern Alliance in Afghanistan. Now, I don't know the reason behind the meeting or even if the meeting took place, but Massoud was assassinated forty-eight hours ago, and we haven't heard from Nash since."

"This just gets better and better. Taliban?"

"The Taliban have been harboring bin Laden for months, and our initial thoughts are that al-Qaeda was responsible for today's attacks. My guess, and you don't have to take this to the bank, Chris, is that bin Laden's a clever bastard and took out Massoud because he would have been a strong ally to the US if it came to going after al-Qaeda in Afghanistan. Bottom line, you would have to remove the Taliban before you could get to bin Laden. Massoud was capable of taking on the Taliban, and bin Laden knew that."

"Sounds messy. Do you think Nash was aware of the situation before today?"

"It's possible. The Brits have been heavily involved with this as well, and they have been providing some interesting material and theories, which Nash has been exposed to. The theory that I have is that Massoud knew what was going on with bin Laden and he was reaching out to us and the Brits. Nash may have been a day late in preventing all of this, but we don't know. I'm not sure if we will ever find out. Shit, what do I know? I just organize surveillance ops and manage sorry-assess like you. I've got theories, but that's about it."

"Why do you think the Taliban and not al-Qaeda has him?"

"I don't know, but bin Laden likes his propaganda. He hasn't claimed responsibility for today's attacks yet, but I think that if he had a senior officer from the CIA chained to a pole in a shitty sheep pen, he would advertise it. But the Taliban . . . my guess is they are a little more cautious. A whole world's worth of shit is coming their way if and when they find out that bin Laden is to blame for today's attacks. As such, the Taliban may need a bargaining chip or two to ease some of the pain, but like I said, what do I know?"

"Seems like an intelligence officer is waiting to come out of the closet, if you ask me."

Gene smiled at the compliment.

Chris thought Gene was wasted working the Viewpoint surveillance program. He should have been higher up in the Operations Directorate than he was. Chris shifted the discussion back to the reason he was in the United States in the first place. "What about the Saudi?"

"You've got to let that one go, Chris. You've got bigger fish to fry."

"Where is he?"

"After you handed him over to the FBI, they tracked him to Phoenix."

Chris was surprised at the news. "Really? Wonder what's so special about that."

"None of your concern now, but your old buddy Nick Seymour is on the case."

Chris was surprised again, "What? Why is he doing happy-snap ops?"

"Think about that one for a minute, Chris. . . . It's your fault."

Chris's head jerked back slightly, and his brain did a quick spin cycle; he didn't know what Gene was talking about.

"After the whole mess with Pam killing the MI5 officer in the UK, he got taken down a peg or two. He was demoted after it came out that he provided you with the intelligence on the guy. He's lucky to have a job at all."

Chris dropped his head in submission and slouched his shoulders. He didn't know what had happened to his FBI friend after the incident, and he had hoped he could shoulder the blame, but it seemed that Nick took the brunt of the fallout.

"Perhaps he can redeem himself and find something worthwhile," Gene added. "But it's not your concern, Chris. You did your job, you tagged him all the way from Asia to the Middle East, and now here, the FBI has taken over. It's not your concern anymore."

"I've got a bad feeling about him, Gene."

"I know, I know. You've been saying that for months. But I've come to find out it's very messy and very, very political."

"What the hell is that supposed to mean?" Chris was getting frustrated.

"He's connected. He's not just a Saudi intelligence officer; he's also a diplomat with strong ties to the Saudi royal family. Right now, he's down in Phoenix visiting a small enclave of royal family members, but we don't know what that means or if it is all just harmless stuff. It's the FBI's headache, so let it go. You need to get on the road. . . . Questions?"

"So, when I was in Malaysia in January tagging this guy, there just happened to be a meeting of al-Qaeda operators in the same area, and you don't think that's kind of fishy? Especially now that bin Laden probably had a hand in all of this today?"

"Chris, are you stalling?" Gene let the question hang for a second. "I've told you to move on—"

"I'm not stalling, Gene, but my gut is telling me—"

"Gut, nothing. You should be leaving, like ten minutes ago. . . . But now I'm getting the impression you don't want to do this. Tell me now, and I'll call you in a week or two when the dust has settled. I'll find something else for you. Go take a break somewhere, relax . . . really."

Chris could tell Gene was being serious but had nothing to say in return.

An awkward silence fell on the two friends.

Gene was trying to be patient and mindful of what was being asked of Chris, but he needed to get things moving, one way or the other. He pushed Chris for his help. "Look, everyone around here thinks that

Nash is dead. Personally, I don't think so, but we will never know if we can't get eyes on for confirmation. The SAD guys have some big missions ahead of them, and like I said, everyone is being tasked out and as such doesn't give a shit about one stray player out in the field. Some think that he shouldn't have gone off into bandit country in the first place, but you and I are the only ones who really care about him. Correct me if I'm wrong, Chris, but we owe him, even if it's finding his body in a ditch. I have this opportunity with limited assets to do something, and I may not be able to leverage too much after today. So, I have to make something happen and happen now!"

Chris bounced his head slightly. He didn't feel totally despondent, but he was masking his true fear of what he was going to be facing. He listened intently while Gene continued on.

"We've known him for a long time, Chris, and I'm sure that if the tables were turned, he would be doing the same for us."

"I'm not so sure he would . . . for me at least."

"Why do you say that?" Gene's voice was not soft. He was angered by the statement. "He's brought you a long way from being an embassy driver."

"Thanks for the reminder." *I don't want to go back to that shit again*, he thought. "But it wasn't that long ago that I wanted to cut his throat."

Gene remembered the incident and suddenly realized that Chris's grief of losing his girlfriend had pushed him to make irrational decisions, and it obviously still haunted him.

"I think we are way past that now, Chris, and I really don't think that he would have a problem having you kick in a door to pull him out of whatever hellhole he has fallen into. In fact, I think he would prefer to have a friendly face bring him home, but that's not your job; all you have to do is locate him, and we'll sort out the rescue party. You've got to tell me now, Chris. The decision is yours, go or no go?"

Karma is a bitch. Perhaps he's getting what he deserves. Anyways, what good can I do? These SAD guys seem like they are high speed. Leave it to them to sort their own shit out. They have all the toys to get things done, I don't even have a bucket and spade, he thought sullenly. *Do I need another flight, another rat shit hotel, another sleepless night, another night of sitting in a ditch shitting in a plastic bag waiting for something to happen? There has to be more to life than this. It's someone else's turn.* He took a long look into Gene's eyes, who was looking back at him with pleading puppy-dog eyes.

Gene doubted Chris's state of mind and was beginning to think that his scheme could be going nowhere before it began. *If he folds now . . .*

"There's a place and means for every man alive, Gene, but I'm not sure if it will be all's well that ends well on this one. You're asking a lot, and I don't have any tools at my disposal. In fact, you're throwing me into a snake pit. I've never been there; I have no concept of the conditions, no idea who will help or hinder me; there's no backup plan. HELL, what am I talking about? There is no plan period!"

Gene sat in silence and gazed questioningly at Chris. He had nothing to counter with.

"That being said," Chris continued, sprinkling hope in Gene's direction, "with as many differences I've had with him recently, I can't sit by and let him wallow in some medieval dungeon. If I can help out in the smallest of ways, let's do this. I may not get the results you are looking for, but after what we have faced today and what may come tomorrow, it's time to stand up and go the extra mile. We have to try something, but you need to get things sorted out by the time I get there. If not, I will expect you to come over so I can hand this shit sandwich back to you. . . . Don't leave me hanging, Gene. I sort of like my balls, and you don't need to see my toenails." Chris let his speech hang.

During the pause, a staffer turned up with Chris's reading material.

Gene handed it over to his friend; the time for talking was over. "Questions?" without giving Chris the chance to respond, Gene immediately said, "Good, didn't think so. Now go grab some donuts, read your material, and get some sleep on the plane. You're going to need it."

Paradise Valley, Arizona

The driver of the dark blue FBI Crown Victoria cringed as the vehicle struggled to pull away from a traffic light on East Lincoln Drive.

Special Agent Vincent Corelli had been stationed in Phoenix long enough to know that car batteries and air condition units never stood a chance against the constant oppressive heat in this part of Arizona. Although the vehicle was otherwise in good condition, Vincent knew the signs of a dying battery, and the last thing he wanted was to be sitting on the side of the road in one-hundred-plus-degree temperatures waiting embarrassingly for a tow truck to haul him back to the FBI field office.

Vincent had already explained to his passenger that they daren't crank the AC to the max with the headlights on, so both FBI agents squirmed and fidgeted and tried their best to remain as cool as possible. But every traffic light strained the car and the nerves and the sweat glands of the two uncomfortable, FBI agents.

Special Agent Nick Seymour closed his briefing folder. He was too uneasy to read, besides which he didn't want to use the passenger reading light for fear of burning precious milliamps. He felt as if he was on *Apollo 13* and on a mission from which he might not return. "So what do we know about PSI?"

Vincent concentrated on the road and the rev counter. They were approaching another light. "Prevention Strategies International, based out of Oakton, Virginia," he replied. "Another beltway bandit with ties to the government. They specialize in executive protection, but they have a good risk assessment and investigative division. They also have guard services, which incidentally are busy working malls up and down the East Coast." *C'mon, you bitch, just another hour or two, c'mon!* Vincent pleaded to himself as they sat at a long light. "But get this. They have a team called the Strike Mitigation Unit. These guys go into facilities where there's a strike taking place but work on the inside of the fence line. When the cops have their hands full at the main gate, SMU is on standby to deploy and bounce all over any fence jumpers. There're quite a few companies in the country that don't like having cops on their property so having a gang of thugs on standby to crack heads suits some people fine."

"Seriously?"

"Yeah, all legit. When you can afford these guys, you can afford a gang of lawyers too."

"How big are they?"

"The company as a whole is about two thousand strong, but they have a whole bunch of contractors on the books that can add another five hundred plus."

"How many here?"

"That number varies quite a bit. There are two shifts of permanent watchers at the villas we're heading to. The day shift number is lower than the night shift crew because the Arabs are night people, so they sleep through most of the day. The night shift team rounds up to twenty or so, but keep in mind that you have the close protection guys who are accompanying all the various Arab family members as well. All the PSI guys here are executive protection trained, so they are a bit savvier than the riot mob, and they are pretty well behaved too. They are mostly ex-military, but some are former Navy Seals, Delta Force, Marines; there are even a few ex-cops on the payroll."

Nick wanted to get the math right. "So we have static protection guys on shift protecting the villas and then, on call, protection agents assigned to family members. Right?"

"Yeah, it's a big program to run. The administration of all of this is a nightmare. There are some rumors of non-payment of services, late or missing payments to PSI and other contractors. It's an Arab thing that bean counters here in the US can't comprehend. But it all ends well when a bag man from Riyadh shows up with suitcases full of cash."

"Giving the IRS and Justice Departments headaches, no doubt."

"You got that right." The Crown Victoria gave an unusual mechanical chatter as they slowed down to navigate traffic. Both agents looked at each other nervously. Vincent shrugged his shoulders and then refocused on the traffic ahead and continued his narrative.

"At one point, there were over one hundred members of the royal family here. Prince this, Princess that; it was really tough to keep track of. Theoretically each member with a title required a single protection agent, but for most of the kids under eighteen, they bunched them in groups of four or five and assigned a couple of agents to babysit. When you have that many people here, the villas can't handle the occupancy, so they have a complete floor of the Phoenician Hotel Resort to themselves. PSI has a bunch of guys working around the clock there too. So, when you think about the logistics and cost of running this type of security detail, it's almost unfathomable."

Nick was trying to take all this in and wondered how this would affect his mission. "The Saudis also have non-royals here too, don't they?"

"Yes, there're about twenty Saudi military officers who are all trained in executive protection, but they don't do squat and leave everything to PSI. Then there's the servants, maids, cooks, admin staff, dishwashers, and what have you, so that's another twenty to thirty people depending on who's in town. Some of them are from the Philippines, Somalia, Bangladesh, or other Third World countries, and the Arabs treat them like shit. It's appalling the way they demean them; it's really sad actually."

Seymour was all business, not in a mood to talk civil rights. "US citizens on the payroll, besides PSI?"

"Private medical staff on site 24/7. These are locals from the area. There's one nurse camped in the bedroom next to the queen. She's not really a queen, by the way; there's no such thing in Saudi Arabia. But she is one of King Fahd's wives and is officially a princess. But the queen moniker is for western appetites. Since there are so many princesses in the family, it was felt that she wouldn't get the same respect and treatment as a queen would. So that is what everyone calls her."

Nick didn't get it, but then again, he didn't need to. "Well, how much convalescing does the queen of Saudi Arabia need? She's been here forever, hasn't she?"

"She's not a well person, Nick. Depends on who you ask, but she's eighty-three or eighty-four, and she's been close to passing a few times. The doctors from Barrow Neurological did wonders for her. As the second wife of the king, she still has some power and influence, so if she likes the Arizona sun, then here she will stay. She's also one of the family favorites, which you can tell from the number of visitors she gets. But some of them have to wait for days to get in to see her, and not everyone does. It doesn't matter if you are a prince or princess; there is a strict pecking order, which looks pretty screwed up to me, but I'm no expert on royal families."

"I know, Vincent, there are some in the bureau who understand some of it, and most of it is best left to the State Department. We don't need to get into the whole geo-political bullshit thing with the Saudis, and for the most part I really don't want to know. But with the Saudis controlling as much oil as they do and having so much wealth and spending in all corners of the world, it's up to schmucks like you and me to keep an eye on the little minnows from time to time. I'm not sure what our target's role is in coming here. He's not a royal, not a bagman. He's intelligence, so I guess that's something worth looking at."

Vincent turned the Crown Vic left from East Lincoln onto Inver Gordon Road. "It's possible we have eyes on us now." He motioned with his head to the right while keeping both hands on the steering wheel. "That short wall on the right forms the outer perimeter of the main house and annex. On the other side of the wall, there is a PSI guard, and he probably has night vision goggles lying nearby. But as you can see, the place is really well lit up." Vincent kept the car moving at a normal speed and found his way around the block to come to the first of the villas rented by the Saudis.

"We are just coming up on the queen's residence." He slowed his roll to a normal suburban-above-walking speed and pointed with his right index finger. "That guy coming out of the shadows at the main door is armed. A concealed Glock or Sig. This villa is known as Gold for obvious reasons." As they trundled past a small cul-de-sac, Nick spotted a Paradise Valley Police patrol car with another PSI guard standing close by. "Here we have the annex, and then directly in front of us is Silver. This is where some of the more senior family members stay so they can be close to the queen without being inside Gold. They have a swimming pool at the back that the princesses actually use, which is pretty unusual for Saudi women."

"The cop gave us the eyeball," Nick claimed.

"He's good people, Nick. Al Kline is our source. I gave him a call earlier today to let him know we'd be in the area. He'll run our plate, but it's just for show. He's keeping our relationship on a law enforcement basis. Neither PSI nor the Saudis are law enforcement, his words."

"Everyone armed?"

"Yup, pretty much, concealed permits, background checks, all above board."

Nick nodded while taking in the magnitude of the operation as they drove up to another villa.

"Bronze," Vincent announced. "There're some strange noises coming out of there. Rumors of drugs and wild parties. One morning a bunch of whores came out of there demanding money from the PSI guys. Al Kline got called in and dragged them off, but all in all, it was a bit of an embarrassment for everyone. The neighbors were pissed, to say the least. But there's also another story of videos and underage boys. Don't really know, but there's nothing concrete to substantiate the claim. Al and his buddies are trying to keep a close eye on that one."

Nick shook his head at the news and the expansiveness of the enclave that the Saudis had created for themselves. It was their little oasis away from their homeland, and it seemed that what the prying eyes of the Saudi establishment didn't see didn't concern them.

"This last house on the right is new. They are calling it Platinum. I'm not sure what this place is going to be used for—it's not occupied yet—probably overflow for guests and other visitors."

"Like our new friend perhaps?" Nick guessed aloud.

Vincent tried to pick up speed and urged the tired donkey on. They were past the last of the Saudi villas. It was time to call it a day. "What's his story anyway, Nick?"

"The CIA have been tracking him for a long time, not sure how long, but I'm guessing it's months if not years. Basically, Jawad Halabi is a Saudi intelligence officer with diplomatic status, meaning he's senior enough and has some kind of special skill set. Bit of a roving firefighter is what I read, though the CIA thinks otherwise. He's been showing up with some interesting company around the world, and he has possible ties to Hezbollah and other Islamic extremist groups, but none of that has been confirmed, or at least, that's what the CIA is saying."

"What do you think he is doing here?"

"No idea," Nick responded sharply, but he contemplated the question nonetheless.

Vincent didn't respond for a minute, but then he said, "Last time I checked, Nick, the FBI doesn't randomly follow Saudi diplomats or other allies. There has to be something more, don't you think?"

"I don't know, but it pisses me off when the CIA says jump and we don't get to ask how high or for how long."

"How long have you been on him?"

"Just before things in New York."

"Any news?"

Before Nick could answer the question, his cell phone rang. "Seymour."

Vincent tuned out the conversation and began an internal mantra, egging his car to stay the course to get them home to a well-deserved cold beer, *C'mon, you bitch, drive. C'mon, you bitch, drive. C'mon, you bitch, drive!* From time to time, he heard a yes, no, or uh-huh from Nick and then a more forceful "shit, really?" to which Vincent stopped his chants and waited for the conversation to end.

Nick placed his index finger on the button to end the call and then placed the phone on his lap. He stared out the window in front of him and did not say a word. Vincent could tell that he was in deep thought and waited for his colleague to open up. After a minute, Nick asked, "How many agents can we round up, Vincent?"

"I don't know. I can make some calls, three, four maybe?"

"Not enough, we need thirty to forty!"

"What? What the hell's going on, Nick?"

"We've just had the initial assessment on the hijackings. Sixteen of the nineteen hijackers were from Saudi Arabia."

Vincent's jaw dropped, but he couldn't find the words.

CHAPTER THREE

The Platinum House, Paradise Valley, Arizona

SALEH BAHAR CAUTIOUSLY poured tea for his guest and tried as best as he could not to show his nervousness. The intelligence officer watched and waited calmly for the glass to be filled, slowly stroking his beard, relaxed and sucked in by a large living room, leather couch.

"I trust you have rested from your long journey. You look well, given the duration."

"Thank you, Saleh. It has been arduous, and I am fortunate that I arrived before the events in New York. But there is much to do, and I have many more miles to travel before I can truly rest." Although the intelligence officer looked rested, he had not. Since the first plane had hit the Twin Towers, he was glued to the TV at his hotel while he waited for Saleh to arrive in Phoenix from Tucson.

"I must say, this environment seems to suit you. You look well. Arizona must agree with you, my friend."

"Peace be upon you, Jawad. It is good of you to say so, although this life I lead is not without its challenges."

Jawad pounced quickly at the first sign of dissention. "This work for our beloved family does not agree with you then?"

Saleh finished pouring the tea just in time. Any longer and he would have dropped the ornate teapot onto the coffee table. He sat down cautiously in an adjacent leather chair. "No, no, please do not misunderstand, but it is as if I am surrounded by a generation of deaf camels and mute goats. These Americans, they are so . . . so immature, uncouth sometimes. They have no sense of respect or understanding of our family, and although I am truly blessed to serve my king and my country, I sometimes have to work in strenuous conditions."

"Tell me, Saleh, tell me. I am eager to learn."

After twenty minutes of gossip, innuendoes of lies, cheats, and petty conspiracies, Saleh, while still feeling apprehensive towards his guest, wrung his hands between short sips of his tea. He saw that the intelligence officer was not taking any notes, but he knew that Jawad was taking everything in, each sentence, each inflection of tone, each raise of an eyebrow, each gesture or each non-verbal cue. The man before him, despite his lank youthful frame, was wise beyond his years, a master inquisitor who professed a wicked memory that recalled the slightest of details at the most appropriate or inappropriate of times. No matter Jawad's thin affectatious smile in his eyes and mouth, beyond the façade was a killer, conniver, puppet master, and conjurer of deceit. Saleh had to use his words carefully and chose his responses with guarded confidence, but he knew that what was being said, or not, would be used against him in some form or fashion, and it would not be at a time of his choosing. He told himself over and over to be careful, to think before he spoke, and to tread carefully.

Jawad listened half-heartedly to the Saudi bagman as he bemoaned his comfortable position as a royal banker to the House of Saud. He looked at the fat, balding older man with scorn and repugnance and secretly wanted to wring the man's neck for complaining about his trivialities and minor irritations. He continued to slowly drink his beverage and remained composed while watching the squirming oaf step on himself and blame everyone else around him for his imperfections. But time was running out. This tradition of small talk over tea and figs needed to cease; this wasn't the reason he was there, so he stopped Saleh mid-sentence and leaned forward out of the comfort of the couch. "What happened in Los Angles? Why didn't they board the plane?"

Saleh was happy to get to the crux of the visit at last. This was at least a way for him to steer the conversation away from his issues. He too leaned forward and looked squarely into the eyes of his visitor. This was time for a serious discussion. "One of the team got into a conversation with a guard as they were passing through security at the airport.

Apparently, he was an Egyptian who wanted to engage them in some pleasantries but became suspicious. The team leader ignored the chatting and went on to retrieve his belongings and then walked towards his gate, but after a short while he decided to abort the mission."

Jawad took it in. He had thoughts but let Saleh continue.

"They were just steps away from boarding, Jawad. They are not cowards."

Jawad didn't move an inch but silently questioned the last comment. *Not cowards? He has spoken with them at length, or perhaps he is too close. He must know them well. What has this imbecile been doing?* He acted cool in his response. "You have spoken with them. Where are they now?"

"Yes, I spoke with the leader myself. Two are in San Diego, one, the leader is in Palm Springs, and the others are in Carlsbad."

Jawad leaned back into the couch and closed his eyes. He kept his thoughts to himself for a moment. *Why, why, why did you speak to them? You stupid, stupid man. . . . This man will kill us all!* He opened his eyes and rubbed his forehead but stopped himself from giving away too many nervous or conflicting body signs. "Baggage?"

"As instructed, none. They left the airport in separate taxis."

"But they checked in for the flight?"

"Yes, but we don't know where the plane landed. The flight was destined for Washington, but the authorities grounded all planes, some in mid-flight, across the entire country so the situation is very confusing."

Jawad shook his head. He wanted to slap himself awake from what he was hearing. "So let me get this right, Saleh." His eyes stared directly at the banker, his voice firm and direct. "Five men, with only one who spoke passing English, got into taxis to addresses in various parts of California, addresses of locations that they either came from or were given before they departed for the airport. In addition to this, these men, who probably did not have enough money to get to San Diego or Palm Springs or Carlsbad, somehow are sitting on a beach or are enjoying the desert sun. Explain this to me."

"They were taken there, but they are safe. They are with friends," Saleh responded hastily trying to justify the actions.

"What are you talking about, you fool? What have you done? What friends?"

"I wanted to be sure that nothing could go wrong. I arranged—"

"WHAT?"

"I gave them my number if something went wrong. I told them to get into taxis and—"

Jawad was beside himself. He waved his hand to silence the man; he had heard enough. Closing his eyes again in an attempt to control his anger, he was surprised to feel as if his own heart was about to pound out of his body, and he felt the stickiness of sweat at his lower back and armpits. *There was supposed to be no contact. No contact! What didn't he understand about no contact?* Once more, he looked at the man, this time with utter contempt. "How did they get your number?"

"I gave it to them."

"How, Saleh, how?" Jawad almost shouted.

"I met them in Los Angeles."

Jawad sprang from his seat and slapped the banker across his face with all his force. The fat man was shocked, stunned, and quivered as he raised his hands to protect himself. Jawad stood over him with clenched fists. He wanted to pound the man into pulp but held back. He returned to the leather couch, sat, and then stewed in silence.

Saleh risked an opening of what seemed a forever stillness. "What do you want to do, Jawad?"

"Don't ask me what I want to do or what I am going to do!" he snapped. "I will tell you what I want you to do when I am ready!" Jawad's tirade continued after a short breath, "Don't ever question me. It is not your station to ask questions. You will do as I say when I say. No debates or discussion. Do we understand each other?"

"Yes, of course." Saleh babbled, "I was merely—"

"You were merely going to shut up! Now do that and let me think!" He was mad, furious, and enraged. Minutes ago, his icy cool façade was intact, and he was in control of his emotions and thoughts. But with one question, the fat useless banker triggered a reaction, and Jawad immaturely showed his temper. He got up from the couch and made his way to a set of French doors that led to a small balcony. He opened one of the doors, walked outside, and lit a cigarette while taking in the view of the street before him. As he did, he noticed a dark-colored Ford cruise the road below. He gave it a suspicious look, but his mind was elsewhere.

After his third cigarette, Jawad walked back into the room. Saleh was still there waiting on a command or, worse, another reprimand. He gazed at Jawad with sad droopy eyes, hoping for the former.

Jawad had regained his composure and sat down on the coffee table, inches away from the banker. "Saleh, how many of our family are here in Phoenix?"

"I don't know exactly. Our numbers fluctuate quite often. There are no precise records."

Jawad took a deep breath to control himself once more. "You don't know?" He calmly suggested, "Really . . . somebody must know," but only received a blank stare in return. "I need to know where everyone is, and I need to have them all remain in place until I say otherwise. Nobody travels, understand?"

Saleh nodded so quick his bottom lip bounced.

But Jawad had not finished. "I need an update on Her Highness's health, and get me the name of the most senior prince and arrange a meeting. I need to see him at once. I also need to see the senior military officer—I don't care what he is doing; I need him here. . . . And Saleh, I need a car; arrange it."

Saleh nodded at the commands and made a move towards the door.

"Sit down. I am not finished with you yet." Jawad barked like a soldier, "You will explain everything to me that has happened in the last few weeks. I want every single detail, every call, every meeting you had, where and when and what was said. But understand this, Saleh." Jawad leaned forward and grabbed the man by both wrists and brought his face close enough that they could smell each other's breath. Jawad's voice was full of doom and foreboding, but he spoke in a whisper. "If there is something that you omit, something I find out later that you have done or said, whether it is relevant or not . . . I will cut out one of your balls and feed it to you. Once I have done that, I will have your son brought to me, and I will feed him the other." He released Saleh's wrists. "Tell me, Saleh, tell me now."

The civilian-clothed Saudi major stood apprehensively in front of the man that was deeply engrossed in a whispered conversation on his cell phone. At first, the soldier thought the man was unaware of his presence and continued to stand waiting for a gap in the conversation so he could introduce himself. Even after brief eye contact, the major with his hands clasped firmly behind him began to pace slowly trying to garner some form of recognition or at least a polite excuse for the phone call.

Jawad drew out the phone call as long as he could. It was a game he played on more than one occasion, betting himself how long a subordinate would become frustrated or impatient and begin pacing. He thought it was the measure of a man who sat down without bidding, stood and waited patiently, paced without purpose, or simply walked out of a room in frustration. There was no winning solution to his game, but as he watched the soldier pace with his head down, hands firmly grasped behind him, Jawad's instinct told him he was dealing with a nervous man. The question wasn't just why he was nervous but also why he had not walked out or sat down or done something else. Jawad ended his call.

"Major, please sit down. Sorry to keep you waiting," he lied.

"Thank you, sir."

The steam rose from Jawad's tea. A teapot and an empty glass lay in front of the visitor, another one of Jawad's games. *Will he pour for himself, or will he ask for permission to fill mine?*

"How may I be of service, sir?"

Good, straight to the point, not so nervous after all. A bold man under the circumstances. "Major, my name is Jawad Halabi, and as you may or may not know from our mutual banking friend, I work for the General Intelligence Department. I have the equivalent military rank of a general, and you now report to me on all matters of security regarding the family and this enclave. I also have a wider authority over other Saudi nationals in this country; however, that is not your concern."

His palms pressed onto his knees, the major leaned forward in anticipation, almost sitting at attention, eager to learn.

"My objective here is to return Her Highness to the kingdom at the earliest opportunity. Your new mission is to assist me and follow my orders without question." Jawad was expecting a form of protest as he was circumventing the military's chain of command, and indeed, there was a slight frown on the major's forehead; he could tell a comment was coming.

"And General Amari?"

"He is no longer able to assist. He is not in the country at this moment, and he will not be returning any time soon. Now . . . please take some tea." Jawad motioned politely and then continued, "There are a lot of things to consider, logistics, manpower, timing, and all that. As you know all the parties here, I am going to allow you to take command of all of these matters. You will consult your decisions with me and me alone. Saleh will assist you in every way possible, and please keep in mind that money is not an obstacle. I cannot emphasize that more. If you need money, do not *ask* Saleh; *tell* him you need it. Be firm with him. If there are any problems along that front, you will inform me, understood?"

"Yes, sir," was the obedient reply.

Jawad smiled and continued his brief. "Now as soon as the American FAA has lifted the no-fly ban, we will land a 757 from the kingdom at the Deer Valley Airport to await the family's departure. There are discussions taking place with the American State Department to expedite this arrangement and His Excellency the ambassador in Washington, DC, is negotiating on our behalf. I will keep you apprised on the relevant details as they transpire. I am sure I don't have to tell you to be discreet about what I have just told you. However, it leads me to another more precarious subject. The news reports that are circulating have indicated that a number of the hijackers were Saudi nationals."

The major had heard the same reports. He was about to utter a response but Jawad pre-empted him. "If that is true, then our presence here and the safety of Her Highness is in jeopardy. I do not know what your men are doing right at this minute or what their duties are right now, but I want you to assign twenty-four-hour armed watch over her." Jawad paused and then bore daggers into the major's eyes. "Do I need to tell you how important this task is, Major? Do you have any idea of what would happen to you, to your men, or to your families if Her Highness even breaks a fingernail while she is in your charge?"

A small bead of sweat ran down the side of the soldier's right temple. He knew all too well that his soul would be dammed for eternity if something went wrong. Images of mass beheadings flashed before him. "I will give my life for—"

"Yes, yes, I understand that, Major, and your loyalty I'm sure exceeds no bounds, but it is not your life that I want to forfeit. I need you to be in charge of the men who will lay down their lives for Her Highness, and you, sir, need to guide them. Nothing, *nothing* must come to harm her while we are orchestrating this transition, so focus on making that happen as smoothly as humanly possible. Your task is to create a plan and an emergency plan and subsequent alternate plans to absolute precision for moving Her Highness to the plane as soon as it arrives. I have been assured that the best medical team from the kingdom will be on the flight, so that may alleviate some of your concerns, but security is paramount. It is quite likely that the American State Department will soon become involved at our level here in the enclave. We must be cognizant of the fact that they will come for our safety, but rest assured they well breathe easier as soon as we are all on board that flight."

Jawad could see that the soldier had a ton of questions to ask, but he did not want to get bogged down with the details. This was a high-level briefing, and he wanted the man to take over the minutiae and day-to-day issues. Jawad had other more important things to take care of.

"We also need to be mindful of the press, Major. It is quite possible that the local media have an idea of what this community is, and it may not take long for some hillbilly to take matters into his own hands and pay us a visit because of some twisted story a reporter has spun. When the State Department comes, I hope it will protect us from prying eyes and wandering shotguns. However, my other concern is a threat from the inside. This company PSI may be a risk to us. We have no idea of who these men are or if they are connected in any way to the events in New York. We may be the victims of our own catastrophe. A threat from within is very real, Major, so you will need to consider that in your planning, and since we have no idea of how soon the plane will arrive, you need a defense-in-depth strategy for a medium to long-term stay. But from now on, no American citizen will be near Her Highness, except for medical staff. I am arranging for a female security officer to join us here shortly, but until then, you or one of your men will be in very close proximity to Her Highness at all times.

"I understand, sir."

"Good. Now I must leave soon, but I will return in twenty-four to forty-eight hours. I have other duties to address, which will include your planning for five extra seats on board that plane. It is not your concern who these individuals are, but they are to return to the kingdom with us, and you are to make arrangements for them to reside here while we wait." Jawad handed the soldier two notes of paper. "In the meantime, I need you to check a license plate for me. I noticed the car earlier in the street . . . and the other note is my number; I already have yours. I want to hear only from you, not one of your subordinates, because if I do it would mean that you have failed."

Pearl Continental Hotel, Peshawar, Pakistan

Chris smirked at the sign in the hotel lobby that read, "Hotel Guests are asked that their bodyguards kindly deposit all firearms at the front desk." Although he smiled, he realized that the message had a profound meaning. He was now entering another world where guns were as prevalent as cell phones and the patrons of the establishment were well-to-do and had a genuine need for bodyguards. Likewise, if you were a guest there, you'd better have a gun for when you do leave. *Well, at least the bad guys know where to shop if they need to restock,* he thought morosely.

After checking in, Chris made it to his room on the third floor and placed his backpack on the bed. He scanned around the room and found a curious green arrow stamped on a desk. He sat on the bed and tried to make sense of it and then rattled his brain to see if there was a mention in the intelligence package that Gene had given him for the plane ride over. After a minute, he got off the bed, went to the large floor-to-ceiling window, and opened the curtains, which revealed the expanse of the bustling Peshawar city. In the distance, he saw the minaret of a mosque. He looked back at the green arrow and mentally lined up the landmark behind him and realized that the arrow pointed towards the Islamic tower and hence westwards and onwards towards Mecca.

Thankfully, he had found his bearings and was now one degree more comfortable than when he had first landed in the city. But there was one more duty to take care of before he would be able to reach the next level of adjustment. He took off his jacket and made his way to the bathroom and found the welcome sight of white porcelain.

Ten minutes later, feeling totally relieved, he scrubbed his gums with the bottled water he found in the room. He contemplated taking a shower but stopped himself from doing so. The last thing he wanted was to smell like lavender and rose-petal soap when he could be upwind of unwashed Taliban. When he exited the bathroom, he was surprised to see a note that had been shoved under the door. If someone had knocked while he was on the throne, he had not heard it, but he was expecting some kind of contact from the local CIA station so perhaps this was it.

"Top floor of Hotel, the GUL Bar, 6pm, Bill."

Enough said, he thought and checked the clock next to the bed. *Three hours, time for a nap, then hopefully some grub, I reckon.*

Chris's internal clock worked to a charm; he woke fifteen minutes before his meeting, which was enough time for him to get dressed, grab his bag, and make his way up the two floors to the hotel bar. When he walked in, he was astounded to find that the large room lacked both customers and any type of hotel bar paraphernalia. It was a miserable place with only a small bar and a few white cabinets that displayed a mediocre selection of beer and spirits, nothing on tap. The bartender, dressed smartly with a red waistcoat, white shirt, and white towel over his arm, stood from his stool and beamed a pearly white grin, eagerly waiting for a much-needed request of something to do. Before either party could utter a word, the barman produced a set of documents from under the bar and placed them in front of his customer. Chris, perplexed by the paperwork, took a seat on one of the three bar stools and studied what was laid before him.

Form PR-IV (See Rule-13-1), APPLICATION FOR GRANT OF PERMIT FOR THE POSSESSION AND CONSUMPTION OF FOR-EIGN LIQUOR BY NON-MUSLIM FOREIGNERS

What the hell is this? You can't be serious, he said to himself, grinning back at the barman.

"Don't bother. We're not staying," came the American voice from behind.

Chris spun around to see who made the announcement and got off his stool. "Shall we?" the voice commanded. Chris, still with the permit slip in his hands returned the document to the dejected barman, shrugged his shoulders, and whispered, "May be later, pal."

As Chris joined the American, he was greeted with a warm smile, firm handshake, "Bill Pike, Islamabad COS. Gene sends his regards."

"Nice to meet you, Bill. How are things shaping up?"

"Let's get out of here. We have a dinner appointment. We can chat a little on the way."

"Sounds good. I could eat a horse right about now."

"Well, horses could be on the menu of where you're going, but I may be able to rustle up a steak at the American Club. I have someone there you need to meet."

Chris didn't relish the thought of eating anything too exotic on this trip. Plus, he was always a picky eater with a delicate stomach that he would never admit to.

"I have some other things to give you later, but take this for now." Bill passed Chris a brown, padded envelope.

Chris patted it quickly and glanced over at Bill as they waited for the elevator.

"Makarov 9mm, four magazines," Bill said quietly.

"Thanks. Do I need it here?"

"I'm the station chief, Chris. If I'm carrying, then everyone around me should. This is Pakistan. You're not going to find a horde full of liberals and tree huggers around here. This is a frontier town, and that means bush justice. You saw the sign at the lobby?"

Chris nodded. "Yeah, that was reassuring."

"Fact of life, I'm afraid."

Chris ripped open the package in the elevator and loaded a magazine into the weapon. He jammed the gun in his waistband and stuffed the remaining magazines into his pockets just in time before other hotel guests joined them in the lift.

As they approached Bill's car, Chris immediately jumped in the front passenger seat, startling the driver. Bill was also taken aback for a second and watched as Chris opened the passenger door window and adjusted the mirror to suit his rear view. When he was satisfied, he gave the driver a once over and then leaned back to speak to Bill. "Sorry, I just like to take in the sights as we go. Hope you don't mind."

"No not at all. Your boss said you had your ways, but each to his own, I guess."

"How long of a drive?"

"Fifteen to twenty on a good day, an hour at worst."

Following operational security guidelines in the presence of an untrusted third party, the two CIA officers conversed about nothing in particular. As trained, they did not talk about their local environment or politics, religion or local scandal; instead, they focused on sports, namely the English Premier League. It was plain to see that the driver had an interest in the conversation, and although the chauffeur was disciplined enough to remain quiet, he did let out an involuntary snort or giggle every time that Chris chastised a player or team. When the discussion switched to American football, the driver's demeanor changed dramatically as he began to slouch in his seat more and leaned on his car horn longer than usual as he navigated the busy Pakistani streets.

Although Chris was facilitating the chat, he was simultaneously surveying his surroundings and taking in as many details as his brain could handle. He surmised that in the backseat Bill was doing the same, as on a few occasions, the conversation from the rear was sometimes intermittent and distant. Both officers were on high alert while maintaining a façade of nonchalance. Both were looking for threats or potential avenues of escape if things were to escalate into a confrontation. At first, despite his words of acceptance, Bill took issue and was slightly miffed at the position Chris had taken in the car. However, after remembering that Chris was a former bodyguard, was a surveillance expert, and had extensive anti-terror training, Bill was glad he was with someone who was switched on and aware of his surroundings, though he didn't envy Chris's mission and journey into Afghanistan.

As they finally sauntered into the American Club, Chris couldn't help but notice an oil painting on a wall and paused to take in the image in front of him.

"*The Messenger of Death*," Bill announced. As Chris continued to stare, the older CIA officer continued, "The piece is formally known as *Remnants of an Army* by Butler. It depicts Dr. William Brydon who slumps wounded on his exhausted horse, the only survivor of the retreating British army in Afghanistan in 1842. It's not entirely true that he was the lone survivor, but it does invoke thoughts about how a primitive society of brigands, tribal militias, and farmers in the nineteenth century overcame one of the greatest armies of the time. And to think they did the same to the Soviets in the 1980s."

"Not to be underestimated, then?" Chris asked.

"Most definitely not, Chris. Listen, you probably didn't read this in your intel package, but you have to understand that this whole Taliban mess is a soup sandwich we have not been able to wrap our heads around for years."

Chris didn't need a lecture on the politics of Afghanistan, but any background information couldn't hurt.

Bill looked over and around Chris as he spoke in a hushed tone, "I think Nash was meeting Massoud to patch things up with the agency. The State Department was all over Massoud and wanted him to be their go-to guy in the north with the hope that there could be a cessation of hostilities one day, and if there were to be peace, then he would be a leading figure in whatever coalition government that could be formed. Trouble is he wasn't our flavor of the month, so we backed other Afghan leaders near the Pakistan border, which he wasn't too happy with, tribal jealously and all that. I'm not going to go into the reasons why State went that way and we went this way, or we'll be here all night. It's mostly Washington politics and big money. Suffice to say we knew that the Taliban were going to be a long-term problem for us and the US needed Massoud to get back on board with the agency and form a decent strategy for stabilizing Afghanistan."

Chris nodded and took everything in. He was beginning to understand the enormity of the task in front of him. "So is Massoud's Northern Alliance going to be an asset for me when I get there?"

"That's a million-dollar question, Chris. We have nobody there in place to give us a read on how they view us now. But here's something you have to understand about how much Massoud was revered in the north. In 1984, his men gave him a gift. It was a Soviet made Volga sedan. It was captured on the Selang Highway and was intended as a gift from the Soviets to the Afghan defense minister in Kabul. When

Massoud's men captured it, they didn't put it on the back of a tow truck; there wasn't one. They took it to pieces and carried every nut, bolt, and washer on their backs across hundreds of miles of rough terrain through the mountains. My point is this: these guys will move heaven and earth to find his killers. Each and every one of them would have laid down their lives for him at the drop of a hat, and they often did. If we can leverage that type of commitment, that deep sense of loyalty and reverence, to fight the Taliban, it will get us one step closer to bin Laden. Don't get me wrong, Chris. This is not something I'm asking of you. Nash had the ties. He'd been in and out of Afghanistan for years trying to foment a relationship, and so had a number of other intelligence agencies. But I don't know if Nash had met Massoud before he was killed or even if the Alliance thinks we killed him. The best thing for us right now is for bin Laden to come out and say he did it. That may get us off the hook and then get things rolling in our direction."

Chris quickly realized that Bill was echoing Gene's thoughts. The statement was probably the new thinking at the agency and more than likely accurate.

"Look, Chris," Bill could tell the young man was apprehensive, "our SAD team will be in the north pretty soon. I think they are less than forty-eight hours behind you. They are the ones that are going to assess and establish contacts with the Alliance or others in the region. I'm here in Peshawar to get our southern Afghan allies around a table to organize and support our upcoming efforts. Your job is to get in there first and meet some assets that are already in place, identify if Nash is in fact alive and if so, where he's being held, and report back to us so we can formulate a plan. If you want to back out, I don't have a problem with your decision; nobody would."

Chris continued to look at the oil painting, two superpowers, portrayed by a solitary man on a tired horse, defeated by goat herders. *Is he alive? Is this a waste of time? Am I out of my depth again? Am I going to ride out of there as a dead body on a donkey? Am I going to get out alive?* Waves of self-doubt coursed through his mind again and again. *What the hell am I doing here?* He needed to stop himself before he went too far with his worries.

"Who are we supposed to be meeting, Bill?"

"Buck."

"As in Buck Rodgers?"

"Not quite." Bill chuckled. "He has a few names but it depends whom you ask. Sometimes he is Raj; sometimes he is Panditha or Abey. His actual name is Rajakaruna Abeykoon Panditha Wasalamudiyanse. Do not ask me to repeat that or spell it. We just call him Buck, and he's okay with that. He's a retired Pakistani Air Force colonel, a helicopter pilot, and he is going to get you across the border."

Just as they turned to head for the dining room of the club, a very short man with salt-and-pepper hair and a giant handlebar mustache, which would have suited any Hells Angels rider, appeared around a corner. Immediately, AC/DC's song "Highway to Hell" popped in Chris's mind. *Can this day get any better?*

"Gentlemen, gentlemen, the time for art appreciation is over."

Buck strode quickly over to Bill and took both his hands to shake them vigorously. "So good to see you again, my friend, so good." Chris was hastily presented and warm handshakes were shared.

"Come, come, let's sit," Buck urged.

As the party sat down and situated themselves in a quiet corner of the dining room, Chris couldn't help but notice that the jovial, likeable colonel repeated words in almost every sentence. He was sure this was an act for, as soon as waiters were out of earshot, Buck's easy-going bearing changed to one that was softer, serious, and to the point. Once the meals were ordered, the everyday conversation turned to the task at hand.

Buck turned to Chris, and in a casual voice, he laid out his plans. "Tomorrow evening at 1910 hours precisely, you will be picked up at the Peshawar railway station. It is less than a mile from your hotel. Please bring everything with you for your journey as you will not be returning—sorry, sorry, poor choice of words—you won't be staying at the hotel any longer. But there is no need to check out. Your driver's name is Rizwan, who will bring you to me. He will be driving a small, white van with two Pepsi stickers in the back window. The *SI* on the lower sticker will be missing. He may ask you to hide in the back of the vehicle, but please don't be alarmed. This is all just a precaution, as I don't foresee any problems. But this is Peshawar. Do try to understand that things have a habit of changing frequently in the city, but this is not your concern, my friend."

Chris didn't understand that last comment but concentrated on Buck's words and noticed that Bill was reserved and silently sipped on a glass of water. It seemed that this was a practiced exercise, and he had fleeting thoughts about how many others were smuggled into Afghanistan this way. He had questions for Bill, but he let the colonel continue.

"Rizwan will bring you to the hangar where you will find me and my flight engineer. At the moment, the weather forecast is good for a night flight, but we will be checking things throughout the day and also before we leave. I will not bore you with the details of the flight plan, only to say that we will cross over the border north of the Khyber Pass. Once we have crossed the zero line, we will head north-northwest on to our final destination."

Chris's word radar picked up on the mention of the zero line. *Okay, this guy's either agency or a contract pilot. Good, he's trusted.*

Buck continued, "The flight time is approximately three hours from the zero line; however, that may change if we are challenged by ground or air forces."

Chris shot a look at Bill. "WTF?" must have been written on his face.

Bill recognized the concern and then held up a reassuring hand. "The Taliban do have air defense assets and some fixed wing, but it's nothing to worry about. This route is well-known to us, and we are not expecting any opposition."

Assurances to the contrary, Chris only heard, "Don't worry about this rat poison in your dinner. Be happy. It's all good."

Buck wanted to get back to his briefing. "I will remind you of this before we take off, but when we land, I will be facing east. You will exit to my left side. Please close the door behind you after you have exited. I will not wait long for you to clear the aircraft, so give me an all clear sign, and then I will leave. I suggest that you wait but a few minutes to leave the area and, when you do, you should head due north."

Buck turned to Bill. "I assume you have clothes for him?" Bill nodded in reply, and Buck continued, "Tomorrow evening when you get to the hangar, I will give you a set of night vision goggles, a compass, a map, some basic survival items, and a satellite phone. Once you have your feet on the ground, you will head northwards for 2.5 miles where you will come across a road. It is more of a track than road, but as soon as you reach it, head northeast. I am not sure how far you may have to go as our contact on the ground has not given me precise details. I believe he does this for his own safety. Nevertheless, he will have a motorbike, and he will take you on to your next destination."

A tray of food arrived before Chris could field his first question.

"Ah lamb, lamb, succulent, fresh, minty, delectable." Buck made a theatre with his hands by waving the aroma into his thick handlebars. He turned to the waiter, "Thank you, thank you, kind sir, for this beautiful presentation, and please pass on my thanks to your esteemed chef for this gracious feast. Thank you."

The conversation during the meal reverted back to the everyday. Waiters were circling, and other patrons were enjoying their meals nearby. Chris still had questions he hoped he could field with Bill before his joyride across the border. At least he wasn't fast roping in. The last time he did that from a Puma weighed down with a heavy Bergen, platoon radio, and long rifle, he fell the last eight feet causing a permanent bone chip to gnaw at his right knee tendon ever since. Back then, he was picked up and dusted off by his platoon mates. This time, he would not have that luxury. He was going in, and he was going in alone.

CHAPTER FOUR

Phoenix, Arizona

THE FBI AGENTS SCRAMBLED TO GET as many vehicles on the road as quickly as they could when the call came from Vincent Corelli that the target was on the move. With all hands to the pumps at the Phoenix Field Office, it became a tough task for Nick Seymour to round up enough manpower and vehicles to mount a semblance of a surveillance operation. It was not enough time to get all his team to Paradise Valley to familiarize themselves with the Saudi enclave and the special circumstances of a royal family in its midst.

"Westbound 101center lane, white Honda Accord, intersection with State Route 51, remaining westbound."

"Roger that, Vince. Break off, change vehicle, and catch us, Nick ordered.

"Ten-four."

Nick gunned the Toyota pickup and merged onto the westbound lanes of 101 from East Beardsley Road, searching for the white Honda as he swerved and accelerated around multiple cars and other road users to find his quarry. A motorcycle, a Ford explorer, an old Chevy Camaro, and a Dodge Caravan all followed in his wake. He sent the motorcycle forward to scout ahead.

Within a few minutes, Red 2 reported back. "Red 2, westbound, 101 center lane, intersection I-17, sixty-three miles per hour. I'm in front."

"Roger, Red 3. Identify, Red 2. Remain right lane westbound 101."

Red 3 acknowledged the command, and the Ford Explorer powered ahead to take up its position. Minutes were ticking by before Nick in Red 1 could see Red 3. Red 5 and Red 6 were trailing behind, cruising and waiting for orders.

"Red 2, southbound 101, right lane."

"Ten-four," Nick responded. "Red 5, take over Red 3. Red 3, trail behind us.

The mobile surveillance unit was changing up and down swapping positions speeding up, taking exits, rejoining later and trying to blend into the environment with Nick quarterbacking each move from Red 1.

"Red 4, westbound Interstate-10, right lane sixty-five miles per hour."

"Ten-four," Nick replied but was gravely concerned. *Shit! Where the hell is he going now? Phoenix is out. Tucson is the other way.* He continued to manage his team while trying to fathom the route and destination of the Saudi intelligence officer. *It will be make or break soon*, he thought solemnly, and then the call come through from Vincent in Red 6.

"Red 6, westbound I-10, right lane sixty-seven miles per hour, passing State Route 85."

"Goddammit, LA!" Nick shouted to nobody in his vehicle, but he knew every other agent would be thinking the same. It was now 4:35 p.m., and the sun was going down. The team was on the long freeway to Los Angeles, and there was no way they could maintain roving surveillance for a five-hour drive without being spotted. Air assets were non-existent, and getting support from the Los Angeles Field Office would be impossible to arrange this late in the day. His options were getting limited by every mile, the radios were silent, and he was left alone to make his decisions. He thought he could get pretty close to the LA suburbs with his team, and although the vehicles had a mixture of Arizona and California license plates, it would be an exercise in futility to follow someone on the LA freeways.

Nick decided to keep the rolling surveillance going for a while longer. He determined that his turnaround point for the team would be State Route 95. If the Saudi headed south for Yuma, then there was a good possibility that he was heading for San Diego or the Mexican border. If not, then he was likely heading to LA.

State Route 95 came and went, and the train trundled along I-10 without deviation. Nick called the inevitable mission end to the team and instructed them to meet at the Valero gas station on the north side of the little town of Mesa Verde.

"Thanks, guys. I think we all know that he's heading to LA. Correct me if I am wrong, but I'm sure there is no way we could have gotten him to his final destination. Even if we had air assets, it still would have been a challenge." The group surrounding him nodded and someone grumbled in agreement.

Vincent was the only optimist out of the bunch. "We'll grab him on the way back, Nick. We've got a good house to work from near the enclave. If he comes back, we'll have him."

"*If* he comes back, that is," Nick replied pessimistically. "I'm pushing on to LA. I'll hook up with the office there, and perhaps they have some Middle Easterners under their watch, and he may turn up out of the blue for a kebab or whatever. It's worth a shot, and it's better than what we have now, which is squat."

Nick handed over his radio and bid farewell to his makeshift team. After gassing up, he hit the road westbound towards the City of Angels, depressed over his failure and unsure how to find a single man in a city of over three and a half million. *The CIA can follow him halfway around the world, and I can't even mange three hundred miles. How am I going to explain that one?*

⸺⸺∞⸺⸺

Jawad Halabi took a long hard look in his rear-view mirror and then smiled. *I'm disappointed and almost offended. Only six and they give up so easy. I suppose the FBI is not so resourceful after all . . . amateurs!*

Northsight Park, Scottsdale, Arizona

FBI Agent Leroy Lewis meandered through the south parking lot of the small park with a cool beverage in his hand, looking for his confidential informant. Although late in the evening, there were still groups of people playing basketball and tennis under the fluorescent lights, despite the mid-eighties temperature. The six-foot-two Chicago native usually enjoyed a game of basketball, but he would have to wait until midnight or at least until the temperature dropped ten or fifteen degrees before he would entertain the thought of shooting some hoops.

Still prowling the park, he made his way past the volleyball players and onward to the north parking lot. There he spotted the car that he was looking for, the engine running, a single male driver behind the wheel. He got in the open passenger side. "Hey, how ya doin'?"

The CI, never comfortable with this type of question, simply answered, "I am well, thank you for asking."

"Dude, lighten up. You don't have to answer. I don't really care how you are. It's just a saying, okay? Chill out a bit, relax."

"Is it common for Americans to be so frivolous?" the informant asked resentfully, "In my country, we are more formal in our meetings and show respect for each other, so when you ask me how I am, I believe the question to be heartfelt and genuine. So please do not disrespect me with your carefree attitude and your fake concern."

"Get off your high-horse, asshole! I don't need a lesson in morals and ethics from you." The agent wanted to get straight to the point. Usually his confidential informants were lowlife scum, junkies and thieves. This guy was different, but Lewis still considered him with disdain. The CI had committed a crime, so he was Lewis's to work with and was there to answer his questions, not the other way around. "What do you have for me?"

"What about the charges against me?"

"That's not of your concern right now. We've discussed this enough. As soon as I think that we have a mutual understanding, and that means you giving me information that I can use, then we can discuss your case. Until then, give me something I can work with, and don't waste my time!"

Major Karim Basrawi reluctantly outlined the discussion that he had with a Saudi intelligence officer about plans to move the Saudi royal family out of the United States. After ten to fifteen minutes of questions and answers, Lewis realized quickly there was something worth pursuing from the conversation. He was not part of the investigation into the New York and DC attacks, but he knew it would be a matter of time before he would be knee-deep in it. This new information was something worthwhile kicking up the totem pole. He decided to smooth out the remainder of the meeting and spoke softly to stroke his informant. He needed to placate him and keep him close.

"This is good information, Karim." Leroy placed his hand over his chest in a show of gratitude. "I am really grateful for this, and I am sure that you think your reputation will be tarnished with the charges against you, but I know you were just following orders with finding the women and drugs. I'm sorry but I can't do anything about that right now. These things have to run their course. Our justice system is very complex, which I am sure you understand. However, I am still interested in maintaining our relationship, and if the information can continue to flow, perhaps we can look at lesser charges."

"Lesser? That is not good enough Agent Lewis. I need the charges dismissed!"

"Let's chat about that at a later date. I don't think under the circumstances that we want another international incident on our hands, now do we?" Lewis let the comment sit a second longer. "I think you know what I am talking about with the actions of some of your countrymen."

Basrawi nodded solemnly. "That's an aberration. Our countrymen are not all—"

"Okay, okay, I get it." Keen to get things back on track, Leroy pushed for more. "Is there anything else I need to know, anything that you have forgot to mention?"

Basrawi stared out the window in silence. Lewis could tell there was something else. The information about a pending vacating of the Saudi enclave, while valuable to the FBI, would not ring any major alarm bells, but it would at least give the agency a heads-up on the movements of Saudi nationals. "If you forget to tell me something now, Karim, it will go against you. You understand, that right?"

Karim nodded. "Yes, quite."

"Well?"

"I am not sure what this means, but Jawad told me to reserve five seats for the plane. All he said was that there is someone that needs to return to the kingdom and who they are is not of my concern."

"Are they here in Phoenix?"

"I don't know."

"Where is he?"

"I don't know. I'm sorry. He will communicate with me when he needs me. He did not tell me where he is going or when he will come back. I don't know him well, or his methods. I don't know where he is."

The two FBI cars almost collided as one exited the parking spot and the other negotiated his way around the tight Phoenix FBI headquarters parking garage. The driver of the first car opened his driver's side window and called out to his colleague who stopped nearby.

"Yo, Leroy, when you taking your driving test?"

"Screw you, Vinnie. You heading to deliver pizza or what, ya dumb wop?"

"Yeah, I'm heading to your mamma's house."

"Ohhhhhh, that's low, man, that's low. Can you hang on a second while I park?" Leroy found an empty slot, exited his car and made his way over to Vinnie's. "What's this, man, part-time today?"

"Busted surveillance. You?"

"CI, prostitution, drugs."

"It's been a long day, buddy. I'm heading home. I'm hoping tomorrow will be easier."

"I hear ya. Listen, I want to run something by you in the morning," Leroy said. "You get going. I don't want those pizzas getting cold on ya. Don't want you to lose your tip."

"Your mamma tip good then?"

"Asshole, see ya in the morning, bruther."

"Be safe, man."

***

It was close to midnight when Leroy Lewis finally was able to shut down his computer. He could have easily written up his notes at home and attacked his formal report in the morning, but he wanted to make sure that everything he heard and was still fresh in his mind was documented and stored electronically. Three times he had to reboot the old computer that he had received a month earlier as a pass-me-down from another department. On the third and final time as he waited for the antique to shut down, he repeated the words that were floating around the office when it came to the FBI's computer technology, "yesterday's technology, tomorrow."

After turning out his desk light, he made his way over to the kitchen to see if there were any remnants of coffee still left in a pot. Normally, a brew was always percolating but not tonight; he was out of luck. He reluctantly trudged through the almost-empty office and headed back towards his car. He was tired, in need of a shower, and a bite of food would not be amiss, but all he wanted at that moment was to get on the freeway and get home in twenty minutes or less to his air-conditioned apartment and a soft bed.

Traffic was pretty light as he expected while he traveled north-bound on I-17. His eyes were drooping slightly, so he cranked up the AC and late-night jazz on KSLX 100.7 FM, which soon boosted his energy and got his fingers tapping on the steering wheel. In the black of the night, off to the west, he caught a glimpse of a blue-and-red light speeding away in pursuit or off to a burglary in progress or to some other nefarious criminal activity that broadly peppered the sprawling Phoenix city. It was one of the reasons he was there, why the FBI were there—crime.

Lewis paid no attention to the distant lights as he took his exit to-wards West Pinnacle Peak Road but slowed his car down the freeway off-ramp towards the intersection where the light welcomed green.

Behind him, another blue-and-red light followed him down the ramp. He concentrated on the flashing lights behind him and took the gamble of entering the intersection to clear a path for the emergency vehicle. His car was dead center of the junction when a stolen pickup truck being pursued by a police car from the west slammed broadside into him. The impact flipped his car on its side, on its roof, and then on its side again. The vehicle spun twice a full 360 degrees, spilling fuel from the ruptured fuel tank. The impact with the guardrail on the side of the road and the traffic light caused enough of a spark to ignite the discharged gasoline, and Leroy Lewis was consumed by a fireball that lit the night sky.

Peshawar Airport, Pakistan

Bill Pike opened the sliding door of the Pepsi van. "Okay, Chris, you can get out." Chris dutifully complied and pulled himself off the floor. He wasn't totally surprised to the see the CIA officer there, but he was a little confused as to why he had to ride with someone else and play the smoke and mirrors routine. *Not my circus, not my clowns, I guess.*

Chris found himself in a large aircraft hangar, which was currently occupied by a white Beechcraft B-300 and the meanest looking Puma helicopter he had ever seen. Having served as an infantryman in the British Royal Green Jackets, he'd ridden in his fair share of Pumas while stationed in Germany and two operational tours of Northern Ireland. Those "shake and bake" choppers were pretty average with no frills and more holes where screws should have been than holes filled with something that resembled the right size screw.

As Chris took in his surroundings, Bill caught his bewilderment. "This is our hangar, Chris. We've kinda been here a while. There was a time in the sixties when we ran U2 flights out of here, but we've held onto it ever since. It's helped us get a firm foothold across the border, and guys like Buck have been helping us get us over and back as long as I can remember. He's good people, Chris. You're in the best hands. He wants to give you a preflight brief, by the way, dos and don'ts, flight path, and all that good stuff. I would recommend listening."

Chris nodded to the suggestion. "But isn't he retired?"

"Yes, but as soon as things kicked off in New York, he gave me a call. I can't waste his talents and of course the use of this beast." He nodded towards the black chopper.

"There's something off about the color, and I don't know what that pod is underneath."

Bill was surprised in Chris's above-average comment. "That's forward-looking infrared with GPS. The paint job is still classified, but let's just say it helps with defeating radar signals. Those other bug eyes are pink-lights that can survey the terrain all around the aircraft. They help see where you are putting down in the mountains. You don't need some big rock up your ass that you weren't expecting."

Chris was impressed. "Um, and the weapons pods?"

"Yes, they are loaded. Soviet AT-5 and AT-6 rockets, a 23 mm Gatling gun, and a nice 12.7 machine gun for backup. But we had the two AA-8 anti-aircraft missiles removed, a little overkill, I suppose."

"Overkill, what were you hunting for, dinosaurs?"

Bill chuckled. "There is a weight and maneuverability factor with everything we do, so we opted to remove them."

"But these are all Soviet weapons. Aren't they obsolete?"

"Well now that you mention it . . ."

Oh Jesus, here it comes.

"This platform has been in mothballs for some time. We weren't going to reactivate the bird, and it was slated to be disassembled and shipped back to the US. We were just waiting on funding to decommission and take it apart."

"How long has it been in service?"

"Since we first started shooting the Sovs down. How else do you think we got the weapons systems?"

Chris marveled for a few seconds longer but then heard something not so impressive. "Is that a ratchet?"

"Small leak, nothing to worry about."

He turned to face Bill and tried to hide his apprehension but wasn't doing a great job. It wouldn't have helped to complain about the situation, so he fell back on his humor to cope. "I just realized I didn't have time to write a will before I left."

"Guy like you can write it in the palm of your hand, anyway," Bill bounced back.

"I think I'll take a shit. You'll be able to see what I own then."

"Seriously, Chris, I'll reiterate what I said last night. You can back out now. Nobody would think less of you."

"I know. Thanks for offering. But the thought of the boss hanging out there by himself haunts me. I know what happens to CIA officers when they are caught. I don't want him to end up like William Buckley."

"Nobody wants that either, Chris. Beirut was a different animal, but then again, the Taliban have an atrocious human rights record, and their value for life is somewhat different from ours."

"As Gene said, I was in arm's reach. I can only try."

"We both know your brief, Chris; dead or alive you two are coming out at the same time. Don't go kicking in any doors or slap the natives around. Leave that to the SAD gang. Special Forces are also en route to the region, so the best thing you can do for us is to identify his location. Leave the heavy stuff to the guys with the big guns and things that go bang. Okay?"

"And if I get lucky and I see him standing on a street corner before the cavalry comes?"

"We'll get Buck to come for you."

"But I have to get there first. Is this thing going to make it?"

The black CIA Puma helicopter was airborne and headed towards the Khyber Pass at 2230 hours. Chris was strapped into the canvas bench seat with no creature comforts to speak of or others to share his fate. He was now at the mercy of the man with the longest name in the world, his co-pilot, and the leaky aircraft.

At first, the flight was pretty standard and what he had been used to with other similar jaunts. However, things changed pretty quick when he heard Buck announce over his headset, "Zero line." Chris looked forward to the cockpit to see the pearly, white teeth of Buck. Chris gave him a thumbs up but thought, *You want to keep your eyes on the road, bud?* A few seconds later, the straight flight line altered as the aircraft dropped down to just above tree height. The roller coaster began as promised over the Pashtun tribal lands of the Jalalabad desert.

The constant shaking and the lack of visual cues to give him an outside reference point shook Chris's brain to where his stomach was and put his guts up to his throat and where his arse was trying to get to. The incessant pitch and yaw changes of the helicopter increased his disorientation, and he wasn't sure if Buck was putting on a show, trying to piss him off, or actually taking their covert insertion into Afghanistan seriously. Buck told him he was confident the Taliban air defense and detection capabilities were lacking and there was no need for concern, but on the other hand, he didn't intend to become target practice for an obsolete rocket system for some gung-ho Talib.

Chris shut his eyes, not because he was scared but because he was feeling nauseous. The smell and the sounds of the helicopter didn't help with the bile that was attempting to exit his gullet along with his last meal, so he held on a little firmer and closed his eyes just a tad tighter. The only thing he could relate the turbulent ride to was sitting backwards on a roller coaster.

He had lost track of time, but true relief came only when he noticed the tone of the chopper's engines had changed. It seemed as if it was under strain, signaling the flight's northeast turn for the long climb up into the Hindu Kush mountain range. The hedge trimming ride was over for the meantime.

With a straight-line trajectory, the frequency of competing noises around him settled into a more mechanical normalcy, and all systems were behaving as designed. Still, Chris worried as they approached the eastern slopes of the Mir Samir mountain and the hefty altitude of nineteen thousand feet. Pressure started building behind his eyes, and his sinuses were building up to the same pressures of the Hoover Dam.

Sitting in an unpressurized cabin, he sucked up the pain but silently feared the ill-fitting nuts, bolts, and screws that were taking aim at his head, his eyes, and his nuts, as he sat alone with only bad thoughts and visceral feelings to keep him company. He opened his eyes and looked around at the interior mechanics of the machine, trying in vain to decipher if things were in or out of place. He felt it to be his job to inform Buck if he suddenly spotted a hole in the roof and starlight was creeping in. He gave up the exercise for feeling childish but then felt a little less confident as he spotted multiple rolls of duct tape stored in a bin. He pessimistically questioned if the tape was deemed for an undisciplined device inside the aircraft that would attempt to leave its home while shuddering under the extreme pressures, which at these lofty heights would doom the aircraft to die unseen on the slopes of the Hindu Kush.

As the change in altitude rose, the temperature inside and outside the helicopter dropped, matching the downward march of the snow-capped mountains. He was glad they were making this journey now, as it would be only a few more weeks before the valleys and peaks would become impassible for man, beast, or machine, compounding the prospect of a successful extraction by helicopter over the same conspicuous route.

Chris knew deep down that trying to play a what-if game with the interior workings of a helicopter was an exercise in futility as everything was out of his control and would be so until he got his boots back down on terra firma. Thinking about his situation was equally chaotic. After witnessing the gruesome attacks in New York, he was full of piss and vinegar and eager to try to make a mark somehow and get on board to find and kill those responsible. Now his inner macho voice had called his bluff, and he was living his altruistic dream from the front bench. There was no one before him on the ground, ready with Hawaiian leis or high school bands blaring out tinny versions of the "Star-Spangled Banner." He was on his first unsupported covert mission into a hostile environment. It was everything the CIA had prepared him for and everything the CIA said not to do. Looking around the interior of the helicopter, Chris morosely pondered if he was the only expendable item in the cabin.

His inner voice challenged his rationale, but his will to do something outweighed his fear, doubt, and apprehension. His adopted country was attacked, thousands of people were dead, America was at war, and at heart, he was still a soldier who could march into battle. He didn't know if what he was doing was an act of true bravery or sheer stupidity, but he swore an oath of loyalty, which to him was a promise, a duty to fulfill, no matter what. At one time in his life, he had wanted to kill the man he was trying to rescue, and one miniscule portion of him said, "Let him fry," but Richard Nash was the man that put him here in this helicopter, on this mission, in the Central Intelligence Agency. Even in Chris's warped mind, he knew that he owed Nash, but more importantly, he had found true purpose and Gene had given him the chance that he had been waiting for.

Staring off out into the darkness through the window on the door, he thought about Pam but was jolted by a brief notice over his headphones, "Two minutes, Chris." Chris replied the same, and held both thumbs up. He didn't know if his automatic response was fear of the inevitable touch down or if he was signaling to let Buck know he got his message and was ready to go. He undid his seat belt and reached for his backpack. By the time it was fastened over his shoulders, he felt the Puma flare for its landing. As it was maneuvering for position, Chris removed his headset, donned his night vision goggles, and kneeled at the sliding door with one hand on the lever. He looked to the cockpit for the signal to exit.

<hr>

The helicopter hadn't been on the ground for more than fifteen seconds. As briefed, Chris walked purposely to the left of the chopper, took a knee, and faced Buck who was staring out of the cockpit window. Chris waved his hand then quickly turned his back to the chopper and without receiving a response from Buck, the Puma took off leaving

Chris in a storm of dust, debris, and small rocks.

Without following the path of the helicopter Chris searched in vain for cover and began to jog over bare terrain. Within a few minutes, the lay of the land changed as it dropped downward and away from him. Before he took another step, he kneeled and retrieved his compass to get a bearing. Although the night was cool, he realized he was sweating. He put the perspiration down to nerves as his senses caught up with the moment that he was in. The distant hum of the helicopter finally dissipated over the next valley, and then he felt very alone. A wave of dread attempted to break his confidence, but he managed to stay composed and let his body tune in to the new surroundings. Silence enveloped Chris, which he welcomed as now he was in control of his actions. From here on out, it would be his decisions that would either find Nash alive and well or get himself captured, killed, lost, or returning to Peshawar forlorn and riding a donkey. He took long, deep breaths until he thought his singing lungs could be heard for miles around. Composed and self-assured, he realized that his senses were so attuned that if a mouse farted or a snake shed its skin half a mile away, he would be aware of it. He was ready.

Taking a knee and employing his compass, he found north and then looked up to find a landmark to keep his heading. Even with the aid of night vision googles, finding a true object to march towards was a real challenge, so he made sure his way points were to be short and his compass checks were frequent. Once Chris found his bearings, he did a slow 360-degree check on his surroundings. Satisfied that he wasn't facing a horde of terrorist goats or the barrel of a gun, he got up and marched north, as ordered.

At first, his trek was difficult as the undulating terrain threw him off his beat, and more often than not, he found himself trekking east or west for a number of steps and then finding his true bearings again on the northern track. As the elevation dropped, the increase in identifiable landmarks bolstered his mood. Chris was quite pleased with himself when he found a well-worn path that, after a short walk, turned into what could pass as a road. Previously, his steps were measured and slow for fear of tripping or falling down a gully, or ragged slope. Now he strode with more purpose, although reservedly with a pinch of trepidation of walking into the unknown.

Chris had been on the dusty road for roughly an hour, making his way cautiously from ditch to ditch, tree cover to tree, never walking straight down the track and more than once stopping and checking his rear for unwanted visitors. He brought all his stealthy skills to the fore and relived his British army days of stalking IRA terrorists in County Armagh and County Down during his tours of Northern Ireland. As much as he was in his element, he had to remind himself that he was alone and he still had to be cautious.

He stopped and knelt once more to check the compass and his watch. When he looked back up at the track, he noticed a small brick wall with a motorcycle leaning up against it. His heart tried to escape his rib cage, but he willed it to stay down. He remained in place and slowly scanned the area around. As he did, he saw a lone figure appear from the opposite side of the road carrying a machine gun of some type and wearing night vision goggles. He stared directly at Chris for thirty seconds and then slung his weapon strap over his shoulder so the gun was covering his chest. The man got onto the motorbike and started it up. He didn't look back or say a word, but Chris didn't hesitate. He jumped up from his crouched position and walked briskly towards the bike and got on. *In for a penny, in for a pound, I guess.*

The man smelt like a dried-up mophead that had been baking in the sun for too long. He never said a word to Chris and only concentrated on the road ahead, dodging potholes and rocks along the way. Chris didn't know if he was an Afghan, an American, or from Botswana as the man was obviously not interested in socializing or sharing quaint stories of life in the Hindu Kush. They rode for almost an hour before the landscape changed from the barren rocky foothills of the mountains to more arable lands with farms, villages, and gushing streams. On more than one occasion, they were harassed by bands of dogs disturbed by the lateness of the hour and the mechanical monster that dared wake them from their slumber. At one point, Chris thought how easy the mission could end on these roads before things actually got under way. The image of charging rabid dogs gnashing at his heels didn't sit well with him, but his rider plowed on as if without a care in the world.

Chris lost track of time and the number of dogs that received a size nine boot in its face as they sped through the flat farmlands northeast of Kabul. He wasn't sure if the dogs had names, but after passing through numerous farms and villages, there were at least five more "fuck-offs" and three "motherfuckers" left in his wake. His usual auto-function of taking snapshots of his surroundings was gone as everything looked the same under the green light of his goggles. But his senses became piqued as the bike slowed down to take a sharp turn up a slight hill, which led them to a number of buildings that looked from his limited vision like a compound of sorts. The bike came to a halt as it faced a large iron gate sandwiched between high mud walls. The rider turned off the bike, held up both hands in the air, and then took off his goggles. Without words being said, the gate opened, and Chris got off to help push the warm bike into the compound. With a light clunk, the gate shut behind them, and they pushed the bike towards what looked like the main dwelling. As they leaned the bike up against the wall of the house, shapes from different corners appeared in silence and looked at the two visitors. Chris looked around him in the darkness to see the glint of rifles and machine guns. Fortunately, none was pointed at him.

Chris followed the biker into the house, which was dimly lit and very quiet. For a second, he thought they were alone, but when they walked into a large dark living room, it seemed as if they had disturbed large animals burrowed in bundles of rags in each corner. It stank like a gorilla's pen in a zoo. A light bulb hanging by a thin wire was turned on in the room, which couldn't have had more than 10 watts of power, as it was hard for Chris to make out what the creatures were. The biker left the room, and Chris was left to interpret the images. Slowly he began to see pairs of human eyes staring back at him. He didn't know what to do so, he removed his headscarf and backpack and extracted his water bottle. Before he could drink, there was a disturbance directly in front of him on the floor as one of his hosts shed his camouflage.

Chris squinted his eyes to get a better look at the man.

"When they said that someone from the Central Incompetence Agency was coming, I didn't know how accurate that was going to be."

Chris's brain broke a spring, he almost dropped his water bottle, *what the fuck?*

CHAPTER FIVE

Parvan Province, Afghanistan

THE SHAPE GOT OFF THE FLOOR, shrugged his rags off behind him, holstered the pistol that he held at his side in his right hand, and looked directly at the visitor. There was a pregnant pause before anything else was said, but to Chris the flippant voice had a strange air of familiarity. He racked his brain to find a connection, but the man moved towards him and added casually, "Chris Moreshit, as I live and breathe. Who would have thought it?"

Nobody had called him that in years. Chris was shocked to hear it now. "Spud?" He grabbed the outstretched hand as a warm smile appeared on Spud's face. "Mark Pacito, you old twat, what the hell is all this then? Did you get lost on your way home from the pub or what?"

"I could ask the same, mate. CIA? What's that bollocks about? The last time I heard, you were dancing the pole in a gay bar in Hamburg."

"What do you mean 'heard'? The last time I *saw*, you were trying to find your cock with one hand and throwing money on to the stage with the other, fucking pervert!"

The banter drew a few chuckles from the other mounds of rags in the room. Chris heard the unmistakable sounds of weapons being de-cocked. A huge wave of relief washed over him when he realized he was in good company. He quickly put two and two together—SAS. He looked around as his vision improved in the dim light.

Spud could see Chris had a bunch of questions. "Welcome to Stonehenge, temporary lodgings of Mobility Troop, A Squadron, 22 SAS."

Chris liked the name, as he remembered from his briefing material that one CIA officer called Afghanistan a country of rubble farms. After all the civil and military strife that destroyed so much, Stonehenge was quite apt. "Shit, Spud, you've come up in the world only working Saturdays and Sundays. Not bad for a complete wanker like you."

"And you've done no better, I see, CIA. What the hell?"

"Long story, mate, long story. We'll have to get the sandbags out for that one. So you getting a brew on or what? Could murder a cuppa right about now."

"I can manage a warm cup of piss if you like. Take a pew. I'll see what I can do." Before Spud could leave, mophead the biker walked back into the room.

"Ah, I see that you've made friends then."

Chris was taken aback by the aristocratic intonation of the voice. It didn't suit the tall bearded scruff of a man.

"Major Kieran McFadden, SAS," he said and offered his hand. "Pleasure to meet you. Sorry about the ride, short notice, and we've been a little preoccupied. I've been told that you've come for one of your officers."

Chris switched automatically to military mode. Despite his joking with his friend, he had the utmost respect for the SAS and even more for its officers. "Yes, sir. I wasn't told who'd be supporting me, but I'll take all the help I can get as long as Spud's not involved."

McFadden looked confused.

Chris could sense the curiosity. "Sorry. Corporal Chris Morehouse, ex Royal Green Jackets. Spud and I were in Northern Ireland together."

"But you are CIA?"

"Yes, it's a pretty long story, but I work for the CIA's Counterterrorism Center. I'm here to find my boss, Richard Nash."

"Let's take a seat in the briefing room. I've let your people know you have made it, despite the hounds on our heels." He turned to walk out but called out over his shoulder, "Spud, get some tea on. There's a good chap."

As Chris followed McFadden, he turned back to look at Spud who made a hand gesture and mouthed the word "wanker." Chris smiled and carried on walking. He hadn't seen Spud in almost ten years and realized that he missed his old friend but was impressed that he'd made into Britain's most elite fighting force. If their shared experiences from Northern Ireland were to go by, then the Taliban needed to be worried.

The briefing room was directly across the way from the dining room where McFadden sat at a large table, removing his Afghan Chitral hat and neck scarf while motioning Chris to sit on an old wooden chair. In one corner, there was a cot and sleeping bag, which Chris assumed belonged to McFadden as was the AK-47 the biker was carrying when Chris was picked up. Otherwise there was a well-worn couch, some boxes of ammunition, and ten or so boxes of American MREs. Another dim bulb hung from the ceiling, almost pleading for extra juice to shed some decent light into the space. Chris was tempted to head for the couch, but he joined McFadden at the table.

"So, Chris, why don't you start? You show me yours, and I'll show you mine."

Chris knew what he meant and didn't for one second think this was a sexual invitation. "On the ninth of September, Ahmad Shah Massoud, leader of the Northern Alliance, was assassinated by what the CIA believe to be two members of al-Qaeda. Prior to the attack, the deputy director of Operations for the CIA, Richard Nash, had flown in by helicopter from Tajikistan to meet with Massoud, but we don't know if he met him as he has been missing ever since. There are some at CIA who believe he is either dead or is being held by the Taliban or al-Qaeda. As of this minute, I am the only person who has been sent to find out if Nash is dead or alive, and if he is still living to get him out of the country."

McFadden sat in silence and alternately rubbed his thick black beard and the hair on his head. He stopped once when he found something crawling around his left ear, which he scratched away. Then he nodded and let Chris go on.

"Major, I'll be upfront with you, but . . . I'm not the pointy tip of the spear here. My job is to find out where he is and let somebody else drag him out dead or alive. Although I have a personal relationship with Nash, I was the guy within arm's reach who could drop everything without baggage and get on the first plane. I didn't even know that I would be meeting you," he waved his hands in the air, "and all this when I got off the chopper. I have no idea where to go from here, but my guess is that someone back in Langley has this magical crystal ball that put you and me here, and they know something I don't, or at least things have happened since I've been in transit."

"You're right, Chris, things have changed. I'm not going to go into details for obvious reasons, but we have been in Afghanistan for a very long time, way before what happened in New York. Let's just say we have a good idea of the Taliban's military makeup."

Spud walked in with three cups of steaming hot tea. He didn't say a word and passed around the beverages and let McFadden continue.

"Mobility Troop has been reassigned to conduct a search and rescue mission of one of our own, Guy Trimble, an MI6 officer. We've located him, and he is with the Taliban about eight miles from here. We have a forward OP pretty close to the target, and we have an unidentified westerner with him, which I can now assume is your guy. Spud, what's the latest on the planning for the extraction?"

"We are ready to go, boss. We will have a final briefing in the morning at 0900 hours, but for all intents and purposes, we are leaving here tomorrow evening by convoy to a lie-up position where we will park and continue on foot. We will go in and find the hostages, neutralize any threats, and once we have Trimble and Chris's guy, we will extract by vehicle and RV with a Hercules and head home. That's the gist of it. I will be giving you a more detailed brief in the morning."

"Good. Now, Chris, you are welcome to come along for the ride. I need you to identify your man, anyway. The last thing I want is to find someone we don't know like a missionary or Red Cross worker pretending to be someone he isn't. During our briefing in the morning, we will discuss exactly where you are to be. I don't think I need to express myself too much when I say this, but you are not part of the extraction team, you will remain with the vehicles, and you will follow orders."

Chris felt somewhat relieved that someone was giving instructions. Although he wanted to be part of the decision-making progress, he knew he would be in the way as hostage extraction was the meat and potatoes of what the SAS did. McFadden's terse commands did hit home, though he felt a pang of jealousy wanting to be first through a door to rescue Nash. He would have to be content with holding onto the horses while the tough guys fought the Indians.

"Understood. Thanks for allowing me to come along."

"As a bonus, Spud can hold your hand," McFadden added with a grin.

The last statement stung. As cordial as the meeting was going, it was plain to Chris that he wasn't trusted. He nodded in submission and rubbed his eyes. The pressure from the helicopter ride hadn't dissipated yet.

Spud, standing directly behind him, didn't say a word or object to babysitting duties.

"When was the last time you had some sleep, Chris?" McFadden asked.

"It's not the sleep I need. I have a headache that could crack a walnut in two, kind of dizzy as well."

McFadden reached for a bag under his cot and retrieved a bottle of Tylenol. "Get your head down for a while. I need you fresh for tomorrow's op. If you need me later, I will be either here or in the radio room down the corridor. Spud will get you sorted with some bedding and will show you around when you're ready."

"Thanks, I'll take a nap, but I'm not getting undressed in front of him." Chris pointed his thumb over his shoulder.

"Arsehole!" Spud retorted.

Immigration and Naturalization Service, Los Angeles

Louisa Chavez sat patiently in her boss's office and watched as the clock on the wall ticked passed 10:40 a.m. and still no words were spoken between employer and employee. The meeting was scheduled for 10:30, but Louisa, who showed up three minutes before the meeting start time, was simply shown a seat to sit in while her manager, Janet Wyman, finished some paperwork and typed a few keystrokes on a keyboard. Not once did Janet make eye contact or offer a word in apology or explanation as to the delay. Finally, at 10:48, Janet opened up the conversation. Without looking up from a folder in front of her, she sternly addressed her employee.

"Louisa, I'll get straight to the point. I've been reviewing your annual performance report, and I have to say that it does not make encouraging reading."

Shocked by the announcement, Louisa sat up straight and blinked her eyes more than a few times, as if she could deflect the comment she just heard. "I'm sorry, Janet, but I don't understand. I've been a good worker. I have never had a bad review, not once in all my years here."

Janet finally looked up at Louisa and saw that she was getting uncomfortable. "Well, things have changed, and the Immigration Service is having to refocus its efforts to the demands made on us with new policy changes and guidelines. As you well know, these changes have been around for some time, and you have yet to show any competency in the new systems and processes that were implemented to address the new rules."

"But Janet!" Louisa pleaded.

"Don't interrupt me when I'm speaking!" Janet bawled. "It's that sort of attitude that puts us in this position. I have something to say, and I will be heard. Now, when it's your turn, I will let you know. Do we understand each other, Louisa?"

Louisa was infuriated and shocked. Regardless of the changes Janet mentioned, Louisa's work performance had never been a concern in the twenty-eight years on the job. What, she wondered, was really behind this blowup?

"Under normal circumstances, I would consider putting you on a personal improvement plan, but these are not normal times. It's my job to bring the level of education and understanding in this department up to the highest possible standards. That means not only on the job skills but also in higher education, something I've noticed in your file that you also lack. How you've skated by all these years without a degree is beyond me."

Louisa desperately wanted to interject that in all her time she had never been subject to a PIP, nor was her education ever called into question. She was a popular person, favored by many, disliked by few.

She recalled the first time she met Janet, who was hired on as a clerk at the center reception desk almost fourteen years prior. The young, bubbly blonde attracted a lot of attention, and the gossip amongst the other females there was that she was gaining a reputation for not being able to keep her legs closed. Sure enough, she climbed the ladder quickly and overtook others who had tenure in the organization. After two sons by two different fathers and two divorces, she had turned into a bitter bitch of a woman.

"Further, I need to protect the image of this department, and the recent arrest of your son may cast a dark shadow on the service, and I for one do not want that to happen."

"I have not seen my son in almost six years—"

"I don't care . . . he's a criminal and has gang associations. How do you think it would look on me if I allowed a relative of one of my workers to cause trouble by coming here for whatever reason? I will not let this department fall into disrepute because one mother could not control her son!"

The insult forced tears to stream down Louisa's face. She didn't care what was said about her, her work, her attitude, but to say she had failed as a mother was the straw that broke her back. She began to sob uncontrollably.

Janet passed a box of Kleenex across the desk. "Get a grip on yourself, woman. Stop crying. I'll give you the rest of the day to clear out your desk."

"You're firing me because of my son, now with all that is happening around us?" she gasped.

"No, I am firing you for your incompetence."

Louisa started to control her sobbing, and in-between wiping her face clean, she managed to gain some composure. "You are firing me for one bad review? You have been my manager for eight months, and you think you know me! Maybe it's you that needs a review. How many internal transfers have you seen this month, Janet? How many people have resigned? Perhaps I should ask your boss how your review is going?"

"Get out of my office! Get out now before I call security!" she spat back.

Louisa rose from her chair and threw the Kleenex box back onto Janet's desk almost knocking over a coffee cup. As she reached the door Janet's cell phone rang.

"Mandy! How are you?"

Louisa looked back at Janet one last time. Less than ten seconds ago, her face was a shade of thunder, a scowl, a lightning strike. Now Janet was all primroses, daisies, and broad smiles. It was obvious a friend was on the phone. She hesitated and listened to the conversation before she left Janet's office.

"Tell me about the new man. I saw the picture. He looks delectable. Let me look again . . . oh yeah, he's got yummy written all over him."

Louisa was astounded. *Oh my God. What is wrong with her? One minute she's about to get me thrown out the building. Now it's as if nothing happened at all. It's as if I'm not even here!* As she finally exited the door and could hear the laughter coming from behind her, she grabbed the door handle, and with all the strength she could muster, she slammed the door so hard that Janet's framed university diploma fell off the wall. She could not smile, she could not cry, she just could not believe.

———— ∞ ————

Louisa was a very conscientious worker. As soon as she got back to her desk, she stared at her computer monitor for only a few minutes before she started to shut down, ending her career. Within the hour, word had spread to her work colleagues, and the wave of sympathy began. By lunchtime, there was a tear fest in the break room with some of her closest allies. Hollow promises were made, innuendos floated, and revengeful plots semi-jokingly hatched, all which would come to no avail.

When Janet got wind of a smattering of a mutiny in the break room, she thundered in demanding that everyone get back to work and that Louisa had to clear out her desk within the hour. Louisa was the first to leave the room to diffuse Janet's wrath and promptly began loading her knick-knacks into a cardboard box. She strung out her packing as long as she could, and when a delegated co-worker showed up to take over her work load, she dragged out the process even longer. She contemplated leaving some damage behind by deleting files or misplacing documents, but she conceded that she would not be harming Janet; she would be hurting those she had sworn to help, needy immigrants.

It was an unfortunate sight then when a security guard showed up to nudge her departure on. The guard, a friend whom she had helped get his job, also shed a tear and told her to take her time. Selfless as she was, Louisa packed up the remainder of her things within a few minutes and left her desk behind for good.

At five foot five, Louisa looked timid next to the giant, soft-spoken guard who, with another close co-worker, helped her carry her things as they traversed the corridors towards the exit. She said her tearful goodbyes along the death march, and before she left, a crowd of clapping, loyal, but sad-looking workers lined the corridors. Tears streamed down her face once more, and she hung her head in shame. She had no more words.

By the time Louisa finally made it home, she was out of tears and devoid of anger. All that remained now were countermeasures, which she mulled over as she drove. She had texted her son from the INS parking lot, who pulled up in the driveway not more than a few minutes after her arrival. He asked about the boxes she was unloading, and she told him about losing her job and these were the remnants of her twenty-eight years of working at the Immigration Service.

Once secured inside, Louisa was all business. "Come, we have things to take care of." She scurried to the basement with a bemused son in tow.

"I thought you didn't want me here."

"It doesn't matter now. It's all over," she despondently said in a flat tone. "There are things you need to do."

At the foot of the stairs, Louisa cleared away a laundry basket full of soiled clothes and moved towards a disused, oval-shaped heating oil tank. She reached behind, and with a slight click, she released a compartment that dropped down below the belly of the vessel. She retrieved three packages from the spring-loaded, hidden shelf and handed the items to her son.

She took a long breath before she spoke next. Inside she was trembling, but she could not show any sign of weakness towards her son, especially now with what she was about to ask. "Alejandro, you must do something for me. I need you to take your cousin with you to your uncle in Denver. Take this money." She handed him a plastic-wrapped brick brimming with cash. "It is enough to keep you going for a while. When it is safe, I will come for you."

The young man was startled. He accepted the cash but could not fathom her actions. "But why? Why do I have to leave?"

"You are going to kill that blond bitch for me, Alejandro. Come sit. This is what I want you to do." The request came across as confident. It wasn't the first time she had ordered him to kill someone, but he could tell there was some apprehension in her voice, her manner, her dismal eyes.

They both pulled two outdoor lawn chairs together in the center of the basement, and mother and son stared directly at one another.

"Take this bag."

Alejandro peeked inside. It was full of passport-size photos of Latinos, men, women, and children. "Hide it somewhere in her house. Somewhere not obvious but hidden away, in some luggage or one of her purses, I don't know. Put some cash in there as well, maybe ten thousand dollars or a little more. Separate things out in different places."

Alejandro looked on in silence and contemplated what was going on.

"Here are some passports," she continued. "Take one blank one and put it underneath her body. Put the others in her car or in the garage. Be imaginative, son. Kill her in her house, but keep it quiet. No guns, Alejandro, and do not do it when there are children in the house, you understand?"

"But why are we doing this? What we have been doing is all going to stop?"

"Yes, it's over. I can't go back. What we have been doing, helping all of those people find better lives, it's over." She leaned forward and grasped his hands. Hers were warm and clammy; his were icy cold. "You can't go back to jail. You have to do this so we can get away. You need to buy us some time. You understand, don't you?"

Though in denial, he nodded in subjective submission. She carried on with little pause, "I've been able to cover my tracks for years, but it won't take them long to realize things have been going missing. We need to focus the attention on someone else; otherwise they will come looking for us."

"They will come looking for you, you mean. We agreed that I stay away; I am not in any danger." The exasperation in his voice was telling, but Louisa forgave him for being hostile. He was her only son. In her eyes, although he was a criminal, he could do no wrong, particularly when it was at her behest.

"Don't be an idiot, Alejandro Miguel. It may take a long time, but if they do an investigation, they will trace all the passports back to those people we have helped. The government will probably not prosecute them. They want people like us and the people who you have used to distribute, and they will turn on you. I have a passport for you and your cousin with new names, new identities. I've been preparing this for a long time. I knew this day would come."

Alejandro was trying to take it all in and said nothing in reply.

A momentary break in the discussion gave Louisa time to think a little more. "There's something else you can take." Louisa got out of her chair and took down a large container of photographs from a nearby shelving unit. She dug into the middle of a box and extracted a folder containing blank citizenship certificates. "Here, take these as well. You may get some more money for them on the streets, but leave some at that bitch's house. . . . Wait, there's something else I just thought of, something else we can do to that miserable cow." She looked at him with a wry smile. "Steal a car, a good one, a Mercedes or Porsche. Leave it outside her house, and anything you find in the car, documents or whatever, leave them in her house." She straightened her back when she talked. The crease lines around her eyes were shifting upwards. She was pleased with her cunningness, but it didn't last long.

"And you need to cut your ties with your friends Alejandro," she added sternly. "You need to leave without anyone knowing."

Alejandro sat silently seething. He was earning a lot of money providing passports to illegals. His underworld reputation was growing, along with the size of his crew. He wasn't totally prepared to let it all go. "When do you want it done?" he asked with an air of resignation.

"I will let you know, but soon, two days from now, perhaps."

He nodded. The wad of cash was tantalizing, and the new identity would prove to be a priceless tool that could keep him out of the eye of the authorities for some time. If he left now, with his standing complete, he would have the respect of his peers that he longingly desired. He changed his focus. "What about you? What will you do?" His question was sincere, his tone shifted to genuine concern.

"Don't worry about me. I have made my arrangements, I have a new identity. I may leave the country for a while, a vacation, somewhere warm, a beach perhaps." As much as she loved her son, she was not about to give away her plans. She knew that he was not stupid, a little naïve, yes, but under pressure from a good interrogator, he could slip.

"I will leave in a few days, but let's focus on you. You will leave, Alejandro. You must. We can continue this in Denver with my brother.

We can start over. It's not the end. Tell me you understand."

The conversation with her son went on for another hour from which another of Louisa's sly plots emerged that gave Alejandro a sense of pride and a tint of jealousy towards his mother. He knew she was smart, but to be so devious was impressive. He knew then, no matter what his personal ambitions were, he needed to remain under her wing, to learn from her, and to retain her protection so that he too could succeed. Alejandro finally departed with a shopping list of items to take care of.

Once he left, Louisa got on with packing up and destroying whatever could connect her to her part of the criminal enterprise. She attacked her task half-heartedly as thoughts of doubt plagued her motivation in ensuring a clearing of the decks. She was loath to do it, but she had no choice. She estimated that she had at the most a month before somebody would discover the discrepancies in her casework and the bias in approving almost all citizenship and green card applications from Latino countries.

On finding her certificates from a local community college, the ones that she failed to divulge to her employer, she reminisced how much time and effort it took her to learn as much as possible about computers, servers, and networks. She was proud of the fact that she was able to fool those around her at her place of work to think she was inept, stubborn to learn anything new, and computer illiterate. Her hidden skills however, allowed her to navigate the murky IT world virtually unseen, creating hidden accounts that allowed her to access the very innards of the antiquated INS systems.

Removing blank passports, proof of citizenship certificates, green cards, and even rubber stamps from the INS was easy. Everyone trusted her, and there was never an ounce of suspicion. The hard part was to cover her tracks electronically. At first, it was a struggle, but once she found open servers with little or no security controls, she exploited the systems to the max. It didn't take long to market and sell her ill-gotten gains on the streets of Los Angeles, making her a tidy profit that she could bank and live from if the day like today came and she had to make her escape.

On her second visit to the basement, Louisa removed a panel in the air conditioning duct and retrieved two packages and a set of New Mexico license plates, which were wrapped in plastic. Opening the package, she fished out a new passport from Costa Rica with her new name, a New Mexico driver's license, and a Social Security card. The bounty, however, was the final package that she promised to deliver personally to a customer.

She then found a fully charged power drill amongst some tools and set to work on the drywall next to the oil tank. She removed all the screws, and the wall came away gently to reveal packs of money wedged between the studs. Her mood buoyed, and she almost began to salivate at the sight of the money and laughed a little when she realized she had lost count of the number of hundred-dollar bills she had stashed there over the years. Being the queen of frugality, she never spent a dime of the money she earned peddling her wares, save for the expenses of taking care of nuisance customers from time to time. Although only drizzling at the moment, her rainy-day fund was going to compensate for more than she bargained for, and it would be much needed before the thunderstorm came.

Looking at the pile she had created on the floor, Louisa guessed close to a million dollars was sitting there, and with one more final customer to administer, another $150,000 was coming her way. She smiled, and her feelings of revulsion and hate subsided with each passing hour. Realizing she was rich, Louisa beamed from ear to ear. She felt no remorse in her surreptitious lifestyle and then giggled at the sight before her. *Fuck you, Janet. Fuck you!*

Parvan Province, Afghanistan

Chris woke up with another blinding headache. He cracked his eyes slightly open to avoid letting too much light in at once. Daylight had arrived at Stonehenge, and he hoped he hadn't slept past the 0900 briefing. He checked his watch, which read 11:33, and then closed his eyes again. *Shit. Why didn't they wake me?* He lay there for another minute before he rubbed his hairy chin and then his heavy eyes.

"Wanna brew, Chris?"

"Thanks, Spud, two sugars please, mate."

He opened his eyes fully to look at the ceiling and scratched his head and then his balls. *I must be getting soft. I think I need a shower.* He got up in to the sitting position and swung his legs onto the floor from the cot. Chris was still fully clothed from the night before, and he knew that this was just the beginning. If he wasn't going to get a hot shower anytime soon, then the chances of getting his clothes clean were virtually nil. By the time he got out of Afghanistan, his clothes would be able to walk out by themselves.

Chris began to look around the room that he was in and saw that Mobility Troop was up and about packing gear, cleaning weapons, and generally getting squared away. He looked on in silence; everything he saw evoked long-past memories when he had served in the British army. As he watched the soldiers go through their activities, he couldn't help but wonder what would have happened to him if he had passed SAS selection. Would he be the one sitting in this room, cleaning a weapon, staring down the visitor knowing that he wasn't one of them, that he didn't belong, that he couldn't be trusted? His mind wandered with futile what-if scenarios of days gone by.

He reassessed his current circumstance and beat himself up again for missing the meeting. The one great takeaway Chris gained while he was in the army, which he found out when he attended the first day's instruction at Sterling Lines, Hereford, home of the SAS, was that he was there by invite. If he didn't want to be there, then he didn't need to show up for an event. The SAS will give you a time to be somewhere. He learned if you don't show up or are late, then it means you are really not interested in being part of the SAS. He felt like that now; he had missed his briefing, and he felt gutted.

Spud read the body language of his friend when he returned with two cups of tea. He remembered Chris well enough to tell when something was up. He sat on an old couch in front of him and passed him a cup.

"The boss told us to leave you in peace. It's all right, mate. You needed the kip."

Chris appreciated the concern, but he felt he had failed. Now he would have to ask questions, and typical of Special Forces, they would probably give direct yes or no answers without expanding. He hoped his relationship with Spud would ease his troubled mind. "I should have been there."

"It was more tactical than anything, who goes in what doors, who kicks what, who gets the blonde with the big tits. You know, the usual."

"Where do I fit in to all of this?"

"We leave at 1800. It will be plenty dark by then. We will convoy out of here to meet up with the other half of Mobility Troop down the road a ways."

Chris took his first sip of tea and grimaced. "Jesus, Spud, cats' piss tasted better."

"CIA train you to taste cats' piss then?"

"I'm a trained killer, Spud. Watch your mouth."

Spud chuckled. "You haven't changed one bit, Chris. You still think you're the dog's bollocks."

"You haven't changed either. You're still an ugly twat."

They both smiled at each other.

Spud took a long drink from his cup. "Delish, if I don't mind saying so myself."

"Say something worthwhile already. So we're heading down the road and . . ."

"We meet up with the boys at Lie-Up 1 where we split up and the attacking force goes on foot. You and I are going to be with the vehicles. We will provide the quick reaction force if things go pear-shaped. If all goes well, McFadden's team, sixteen in all, will extract to us with the goodies, and we will all depart as if on summer holiday, hopefully with a bunch less Taliban stealing oxygen from good people."

"That's a fair size gang, Spud. Opposition?"

"We have a couple of good lads with a .50 cal long gun on a ridge right now, been there a while. They estimate ten to twelve tangos. You can never be too sure, and some don't like to come out in the sun that often. I guess they like their hovels."

"Are you sure that they are Taliban and not al-Qaeda?"

"Yeah, we thought about that. The local help are convinced they are, and our boys have eyeballed them long enough to gauge their discipline. They look like typical guards who don't give a shit, except for keeping their prisoners alive. Although they are pretty close to the front line between them and the Northern Alliance, since the war is at a stalemate, they don't feel threatened. We got close and personal the other night. One of the lads heard one of the Taliban snoring and found two more crouched up all snug like keeping each other warm. Not really high caliber, Chris," Spud stated almost nonchalantly.

"Hostages?"

"They were seen yesterday. I haven't heard the latest sitrep, but they have been up and about, taking a piss outdoors, and whatever. They're in an old Soviet army base at the foot of the Topdara Hills overlooking the Dawlatsah plains about eight and a half miles west of Bagram Air Base, which is roughly two miles south of the Takhar Front, the front line of the war for the uneducated amongst us."

Chris shook his head. Spud never gave up on throwing out a jab or two when he was on a roll. He smiled and let him continue.

"There's a road that runs north to south, which leads directly into Kabul. Our target is a half mile west from that road. We've cleared a path down a road parallel to the Kabul road, which we have close eyes on, as that will be our way in and out. Best advice of the day, mate, don't wander off the road. It won't be dry cow shit you're stepping on."

Chris frowned and looked solemn for a minute. He didn't need a reminder about anti-personnel mines but still was grateful Spud brought it up, "Understood, mate. Thanks."

"I don't understand why they are at this base. The Taliban are dug in well at outposts on the front that are made up of bunkers and small villages, which are reasonably comfortable and easier to defend in comparison to the base we're going to hit. There's not much there in way of defenses, and it looks like a soft spot to me, which rubs my nuts the wrong way."

Chris nodded silently for a minute and understood Spud's concern. The Takhar Front cut Afghanistan into an uneven 90/10 split with the Northern Alliance playing the role of trapped mouse in a corner surrounded by two large cats. *Why there?* Chris thought strategically. *Why, unless they don't know whom they have.* He took another sip of tea and then threw in another packet of sugar that Spud had given him earlier. He tried to ignore his taste for civilian spoils. He was in a war zone and needed to get over it.

"I don't know why this place bugs me so much, Chris. I know that both sides in this war are trying to dig in before winter arrives, but to place the hostages so close to the front lines is weird. It's like them saying, 'Don't come this way unless you want your buddies killed.'"

Chris tried to deflect the philosophical conspiracy theories and reverted to an earlier comment that Spud had made. "Standing on two pins is not a bad thing, Spud; means they can walk, at a push, run."

"Exactly. As soon as we have them on board, we are heading to a place called Gol Bahar. It's further north, about twenty-five miles, so we have to get the lead out to get there. It's an old airfield used by the British Air Force in in the third Afghan War, 1919, the year you were born."

"Jerk."

"Oh, aren't I the offended one? Fucking Yank!"

"Get on with it, you old sod, before I die of your bad breath and boredom."

"Before I was rudely interrupted . . . three Hercules will land at intervals and pick us up. The boss says that we are headed to a friendly country, but don't ask me where that is around here. We haven't exactly been sending Christmas cards to the Pakistanis or the other Stans to the north, so your guess is as good as mine once when we're airborne."

"An airfield good enough for C130s, last used in 1919? This is getting good."

"Don't be such an ungrateful prick. We're doing you a favor, remember? The other half of Mobility has checked it out; fit for purpose, they say. The Third Battalion Parachute Regiment landed last night to secure the field, and they have some Northern Alliance soldiers keeping them company. Only trouble is that it is in range of the Taliban artillery. So, if you were wondering why we are playing at night, there's your answer."

"What if they come running after us?"

"If they do, they will be half-assed about it. The Taliban military is not conventionally structured like a traditional army. They are very reactive and have no formal lines of command and control, unless there's a large concerted push for strategic value. If they react, then it's small time and disorganized. The nearest al-Qaeda muppets are based in a former Afghan army base in Rishikor, south of Kabul, which is way out of earshot for our party. Those guys are more organized, fanatical, better trained . . . known as Brigade 55."

"Well, my, my, my, look at you. The potato head has gone all Rupert on us," Chris jabbed, throwing in the derogatory name for a British Army officer. "When did you go to Sandhurst?"

Spud could have countered with more joviality but remained solemn. "After all this time doing this shit, Chris, you get to listen to what the fuck is going on in the world. People like the SAS are going to get dragged into more and more of this type of warfare, not that I mind, but I've got thirty days before my time is up. I think it pays for me to know whom I'm up against. No raghead is going to punch my clock."

"What, before you rotate out?"

"No, before I'm done, out of the army."

Chris smiled. He was happy for his friend. "I hear they are looking for security guards at Tesco. I could put a good word in for you if you want."

"You do know that you have to wear a Day-Glo orange vest tonight, right?"

CHAPTER SIX

Parvan Province, Afghanistan

CHRIS HAD BEEN SUMMONED to the Stonehenge radio room where he found McFadden standing behind two radio operators from 264 SAS Signal Squadron who were frantically decoding messages and handing them back to their superior. In between messages, he turned to face Chris and handed him a decoded report. "It seems that some Americans have landed in the Panjshir Valley."

Chris gave a surprised and cheerful look. "I'm guessing that's going to be our Special Activities Division. How far from here are they?"

McFadden gave Chris a perplexed look. "The Panjshir is quite large. The highway that goes right down the middle is about sixty-five to seventy miles long, so it depends where they landed. Are they halfway up, near the top end, or down at the southern mouth of the valley?"

"Good questions. I'm assuming they gave you no particulars."

McFadden didn't reply but cocked his head sarcastically as if to say, "Stupid question. I would give you the information if I had it, idiot." Instead, he said, "All I can tell you is that the valley is northeast to where we need to be tonight for our ride out of here."

Chris spoke with conviction; it was a time for a decision. "I don't think it changes anything, Major. I don't want to jeopardize the mission by having you take us up there. My job is to get Nash out of Afghanistan. Your plan is the best way to achieve that."

"Good man. London is saying the same thing." McFadden turned back to his operators, becoming engrossed in other radio traffic, a sign for Chris to leave.

Chris walked outside and found Spud loading his pack onto the back of a Land Rover Desert Patrol Vehicle (DPV). He could tell Spud was taking his time; there was still much of it left before they would mount up. Chris filled him in on the latest non-development.

"Can't wait to get back?" Spud asked.

"I dunno. Even as smelly as you are, I kind of like being around. If I'm not here, I'd be in some other shit hole, so what's the difference?"

"What do you do anyway, Chris?"

"As little as possible, but generally pissing people off is my forte."

"So nothing's changed then?"

Chris motioned with his head. "Let's go and find somewhere to sit . . ."

It was the first time Chris had been outside the main building since he had arrived at the SAS base, so he followed Spud's lead. As they walked, Chris saw they were in a small compound that had been used at some time as a farm that had thick stone walls, which, from a military standpoint, was excellent for defense as they were very hard to destroy. The walls were at least three feet thick and eight feet tall with an iron gate allowing the only access to the facility. Apart from the main building where McFadden had his HQ, there were two other buildings that might have housed livestock or been used as a residence for guests or rooms for storage.

On finding an empty corner of the complex, Spud took off his web gear, planted himself on the floor, and leaned against the wall. Chris squatted next to him. Spud took out his water bottle and took a long drink and then passed the bottle to Chris, who did the same.

"It's been a long time since we slotted those Provos in County Tyrone, Chris."

"Jesus, now that was a day." He vented and relived the mayhem in his mind for a second.

"We lost some good people, but I wouldn't be here right now if it wasn't for you. I haven't forgotten, Chris."

"It's all right, mate. It's what we do right . . . just a job. It doesn't mean I like you or anything."

"Well, I'd go to war with you any day of the week, mate. I'm glad you're here."

Praise from an SAS soldier was rare. Although they were old friends, Chris felt Spud's sentiments were genuine and heartfelt. Chris's morale was on a high, and the longer he spent around the SAS, the more comfortable he became. "You wouldn't believe how relieved I was walking in here. I about shit a brick when you opened your mouth."

"You were the last person I expected to see. I thought some cowboy was going to show up wearing Ray-Bans at night when they told us an American was coming. Some of the boys weren't too happy, mind you. McFadden wanted to leave you here tonight, by the way."

He shot a quizzical look at his friend. "You changed his mind?"

"Yeah, told him we could send you out front to do some mine-clearing for us. He was good with that."

"Thanks, arsehole."

"You're welcome, arse-wipe. So you want to tell me about the CIA? What the hell possessed you to get involved with that mob?"

Chris began the long story about when he left the army and had no job, then being a driver at the US embassy in Bonn and saving the life of the US ambassador in a terrorist attack. He talked at length about the anti-terrorist training he received in the United States and other parts of Europe.

Spud interjected from time to time with stories of derring-do with the SAS and his travels around the world. Chris was jealous and disappointed with his efforts in trying to get into the SAS. He knew those who succeed in being selected never regret it, but those who fail regret it for the rest of their lives. Chris fell into this latter category.

Chris's stories continued with his getting an education, meeting Pam, and becoming a contractor for the CIA. He talked more about his training at the CIA's farm in Virginia, which turned out to be more of folklore than reality. He told Spud that although there were a lot of smart people at the CIA, there were very few who, contrary to belief, were gung-ho and happy triggered, and it was shameful the way Hollywood portrayed them. He further explained that Nash was one of those who knew his shit, but Chris left out the part where he wanted to kill the man for hiding facts about his girlfriend and for her demise. After her death, he said he wanted to leave Nash and The Game behind but was persuaded otherwise and became a full-fledged CIA officer working in counterterrorism, which up until he saw a plane crash into the World Trade Center wasn't doing it for him.

Spud asked him what was in store for him after this mission, to which Chris could not give him a straight answer. He assumed the world of counterterrorism was going to change moving forward, and it would only be a matter of time before the United States would start getting serious and dealing with the likes of bin Laden head on. If so, then he could be busy. It would be something worthwhile to get involved with, but he was still unsure what his role would be. Chris speculated that if he was able to pull Nash out of Afghanistan, then his reputation and standing with the higher echelons of the CIA would look on him favorably and thus utilize him in the greater scheme of things. He mentioned to his friend that he was under no illusions of grandeur. He was still an outsider, to some a minion who came up through the ranks without attending an Ivy League college and therefore not worthy of consideration.

Spud was sympathetic. He, like all British non-commissioned soldiers, understood the army caste system of officer breeding. It was, Spud claimed, the real reason he joined the SAS, to get away from the Eaton and Harrow snobs and work with real professional officers in Special Forces. Educated, street smart, no bullshit, no agendas, and tough as nails.

Spud's last comments struck a chord with Chris. He missed interacting with people like Spud and the other SAS soldiers. They were a different breed. He felt at home with them, which drudged up thoughts of confliction. He was at heart British, but he had dual citizenship, and as an American, he was given a massive opportunity by working for the most famous intelligence agency in the world, for which he was grateful. But today, happily sitting in the dirt with his friend, he really didn't know what he wanted out of life. He was still *persona non grata* in the UK for the murder of an MI5 officer by his girlfriend, so his options were limited. But being with the SAS in the middle of a war zone gave him a different sense of purpose, and he was enjoying being at the sharp end.

∞∞∞

The eight SAS DPVs, bristling with multiple 7.62 GPMGs, MK19 40mm grenade launchers, and a MILAN wire-guided missile launcher on one, formed a steel circle of defense at the center of a dry riverbed known as Lie-Up Position 1 (LUP1). Strung out amongst the vehicles were 84mm LAW anti-tank rockets, Stinger missiles, 81mm mortars, and large slabs of explosives known as bar mines, which were capable of flipping a tank. In addition to the heavy arsenal on the vehicles, each soldier carried a myriad of personal weapons that included grenades, explosives, ammunition, flash bangs, pistols, knives, shotguns, and automatic or semi-automatic machine guns. Chris, armed with just a Makarov pistol, felt out of place, but Spud, who contravened orders, placed his friend on a vehicle to man a GPMG, not so much to appease him but to put his eyeballs and trigger finger to use. It had been over an hour since the two eight-man teams and McFadden had left the vehicles for the stealthy approach to the Taliban base. The intent was to go in silent, but they were prepared to go loud at the drop of a pin. Chris, stationed comfortably on a DPV, sat behind a GPMG and scanned his arc of control steadily with his machine gun. His sector of control faced east and overlapped with the DPVs to his left and right. Spud, normally static behind a GPMG, was slowly patrolling between vehicles and taking a knee from time to time to observe the territory before him. It was silent in the riverbed, and coming out of its dark phase, the moon provided enough ambient light to make the most of the night vision equipment. Chris was in a disciplined mood; the time for joking and farting around was over. He was prepared to take orders from the SAS without question or concern. It was not as if he was out of his depth, but he reminded himself that he was a guest and they were in charge of the tactical situation.

Although anxious at the prospect of a firefight, Chris felt, for the first time in an age, an air of contentment. He knew that in a second the shit could hit the fan, but he didn't mind. His mood reminded him of his days of patrols in Northern Ireland and the real threat of the IRA. He had lost count of how many nights he lay in wait for terrorists to attack a base or plant a bomb or attack a British patrol on the streets of Belfast, Newry, or Londonderry. There were times in Northern Ireland that he was scared, times when he didn't care what was going on, and times when he should have been scared but was not. The faint smell of gun oil, diesel engine fuel, camouflage paint, camouflage netting, smelly uniforms, putrid war rations, and really bad body odor made him nostalgic, and at one point, he questioned the reason he left the army and why he didn't try once more to get into the SAS. Scanning the open dead ground expanse before him, he knew his thinking was just a method to stay awake, remain focused, and switched on to possible attack scenarios. Spud passed silently behind his position, taking notes of bushes that moved with the light wind in the near, mid, and long distance. Chris did the same. His brain was trying to compute the scene—were the bushes there before, did they just grow six feet tall, are there midgets in the Taliban that look like bushes? A ton of questions wracked his brain; he felt as if a major adrenalin rush was on its way.

Chris's ears pricked up when he heard the unmistakable sound of explosives followed by bursts of small arms fire. He gripped the stock of the machine gun tighter, keeping his right index finger firmly on the trigger guard, ready. The rescue team had gone loud.

He blinked a few times to stave off straining his eyes from using his NVG too long. When he did this, he realized sweat balls were running down his forehead and into his eyes, causing a mere irritation. The small arms fire was continuing from the base with some pauses, which he surmised was from the teams clearing building to building. A feeling of dread caught up with him as he thought that meant the teams had not found their quarry and were still searching, potentially a bad sign.

Spud walked up on Chris's right side, tapped his shoulder, and held a thumb up, his signal to let Chris, the only person in the force not to have a personal radio, know that things were progressing well. Spud refocused to his front. "CONTACT! CONTACT!" he screamed.

Chris saw the movement Spud had seen and opened up with the full force of the GPMG. Spud was still by Chris's side and began using his AR-15 to shoot at the black faceless targets that had appeared.

Cool and collected, Spud ordered, "Advance to contact, advance to contact."

Two SAS soldiers appeared to his right and another to his left. The two men to his right began to move.

"Suppressing fire," Spud ordered, which caused other GPMGs in the group to open up on the targets to the front. In his NVG, Chris could see bodies running and falling before him. Tracer fire was pouring fire down range in the form of a shower of hot molten lead. Chris, not used to controlling his rate of fire, shouted, "Reloading." But as he did, metal shards of popcorn started exploding around him, making him dive for cover. More rounds hit the base of the DPV, causing dust and debris to fly all around him. The incoming fire stopped for a second, and he got up to mount the vehicle again when he saw the prone, unmoving Spud lying before him.

"Spud, what the fuck!"

Spud didn't move or say a word. Chris looked at his friend but didn't hesitate for long. He picked up the AR-15 and Spud's gun belt and advanced into battle. He joined the SAS soldier to his left, who was coordinating the covering fire, and awaited his commands.

To his right, two SAS soldiers went firm and fired at the enemy, allowing Chris's team to move forward and then go firm, enabling the other team to move forward. The leap-frog-like maneuver, known as pepper-potting, was extremely effective in engaging the enemy at close range. Pushing forward, Chris came across the first of the Taliban who in his infinite wisdom decided to pop his head up at the worst possible time and ultimately lost the top of it. Chris moved past the dead body, searching for cover to go firm. When he did, he heard the whoosh of the MILAN off to his right. Trying his best not to follow the glow of its trajectory, he took a knee and saw the night sky light up when the rocket hit a Taliban pickup truck.

Still advancing forward with the team, he came across more bodies, which he had to ignore. There was no time to search or look for signs of life; they had to clear the area of the immediate threat. After a few more minutes of pepper-potting, the team reached the main Kabul road, where they found no new target but searched for cover and ceased fire. Each of the soldiers reloaded and took up defensive positions.

Fire from the DPVs had ceased, and so had the action from the old Soviet base. An envelope of silence fell upon them, and Chris, waiting for instructions, took a long breath but didn't relax. Expecting another attack, his head was on a swivel, his senses were working overtime, and his head was pounding. The headache that hadn't gone away since he had arrived in the country now turned into a sledgehammer smashing an iron girder. His adrenaline was on a super high, if he cut a major artery now, an express train would shoot out of his veins. He tried his best to control his breathing, but it sounded if he was sucking in an ocean only to exhale the crash of waves on a rocky shore. Chris willed his heart to calm down so he could hear what was happening around him. Void of a radio, he had the advantage of hearing every blade of grass move, which normally would have made him paranoid, but these were not ordinary times. Everything was a potential threat; he had to be aware.

It didn't take long for his nearest teammate to signal a withdrawal. Without needing to shoot their way back, the team used the pepper-potting tactic in reverse, each pair covering the other as they moved back to the LUP. Just when Chris thought they had made it back to the safety of the group, a wave of energy, light, and extreme heat knocked him off his feet. His ears ringing and head spinning, he was totally disorientated.

One of the SAS men showed up and dusted him off. Chris couldn't hear a thing, but he was okay, although missing his night vision goggles and his weapon. He got to his knees and then searched the ground in front of him, finding his weapon and a boot with a man's foot still inside. He finally found his goggles, and as he did, shots rang out again. The Taliban realized someone had stepped on a mine and opened up in the general direction of the sounds. The team was pinned down. Chris found the SAS soldier who was missing his right foot and tried to cover him with his body. He began to shoot his weapon in the general direction of the enemy, unsure if he found a target, but the shooting continued from both sides.

The two uninjured SAS soldiers crouched nearby and began taking aimed shots into areas where the fire was coming from. At the same time, a mortar from the LUP began lobbing shells over their heads to suppress any forward movement by the Taliban. Chris, who had regained his composure and his hearing, got to a crouching position and then lifted the injured soldier into a fireman's lift over his shoulders. Before he made a move to the LUP, he kicked one of the shooting SAS men to let them know he was on the move. For some reason, he thought to bring Spud's rifle with him, and with the injured soldier on his shoulders, he bent down to pick it up. The action saved both their lives as tracer fire from the Taliban streamed overhead, which turned into more bad news for the Taliban as sustained GMPG fire finally silenced the racket.

Chris began a slow jog with the injured man on his back. Without pause, his steady slog and will to save the man pushed him back to the LUP. As he was retreating, more SAS soldiers were advancing to assist the two still left in the field.

When he arrived back in the LUP, he staggered into the center where he saw a group of men and McFadden administering to a soldier on the ground. Chris made it to the group and gently laid down the man he was carrying on his shoulders. As he removed his goggles and tried to help the injured man, Chris saw Spud lying there, his eyes open.

"Taking a break, mate?" Chris asked with a smile, happy to see some life in his friend.

"Took a bullet for you, boyo." He pointed to his left foot, which was missing a chunk where his toes used to be. "Smacked my head when I fell over, lights out."

The squad medic was ripping a hole in Spud's jacket while holding a morphine auto injector in his mouth. Chris knew Spud was putting on a brave face and must have been in pain. McFadden began to wrap a field dressing around Spud's foot.

The combat medic jabbed Spud in the shoulder and then drew his attention to the soldier Chris had brought in. The medic didn't waste any time. He saw the foot had been completely lost and immediately pulled out a tourniquet from a pouch on his belt and placed it halfway up the man's calf muscle to stop any bleeding. While he was doing this, McFadden ripped open the injured man's jacket at his shoulder, pulled out another morphine auto-injector from the medic's pack, and applied it to the man. Once the tourniquet was secure, the medic ripped open a QuikClot packet, sprinkled the coagulant powder over the injury, and then dressed the wound with a trauma pack. Satisfied with the first aid, the medic checked the injured man's vitals and gave a quick thumbs up to McFadden. Then pointing at his watch, he shouted, "Stable," over the din of the firefight. McFadden nodded, picked up his weapon, and ran to the nearest DPV to assess the ongoing skirmish.

Chris stayed with Spud, rifle in hand, and waited for orders. His excitement was dying down, his breathing was back to normal, and his headache had somehow disappeared.

After tending to the seriously injured soldier, the combat medic turned to Chris. "Do you want me to take a look at that?"

Chris gave himself a once over. "What?"

"Your elbow, it's bleeding."

Chris looked at his left arm on the inside and out but found nothing. He checked his right arm and saw a big patch of blood on the inside of his right elbow.

"It's not mine," he asserted.

The medic reached over and grabbed his elbow gently.

"Shit!" Chris remonstrated.

"Let me have a look."

Chris removed his jacket, and to his disbelief, he saw a hole in his elbow with a trail of blood leading to his hand. He thought he must have picked up the wound when the landmine exploded.

The medic went to work and surmised Chris had picked up some shrapnel but the wound wasn't serious enough to worry about, at least for the moment. He used a cleaning fluid and dressed the wound with a bandage. "Don't go through any airport scanners until you get that sorted, mate."

"Thanks. I don't feel it."

"You will later. Come and see me if the pain gets too much. But you need an X-ray and a doctor to sort you out."

Chris nodded in disbelief. He felt fine and wanted to get back to the action and continue to play his part, officially or not. He looked at Spud who was holding his head and thought he couldn't help him or the other wounded SAS soldier anymore. He was about to get up to run to one of the DPVs.

Over the rattle of small arms fire and mortar rounds a question came out of the dark. "Chris?"

Chris looked around for the source and spotted two men taking cover behind a DPV. "Mr. Nash?"

The SAS convoy patiently waited for the C130s to land at the old airstrip at Gol Bahar in an all-round defensive position at LUP 2. Safely behind Northern Alliance lines, the combatants allowed themselves a small reprieve, which gave them a chance to evaluate their combat readiness in case they came under attack or the evacuation by the Royal Air Force had to be aborted.

Although the Third Battalion Parachute Regiment had secured the field, the SAS team remained outside the secure cordon but within a mile of the landing zone. McFadden erred on the side of caution by placing his men outside the airstrip inside a tall brick-walled structure, surrounding an old storage yard, which still held old tractors and other antiquated agricultural machines. With three escape routes out of the area, there was also a road that ran straight and true to the western end of the runway, which was designated as the pickup point for the SAS team. Both the Special Forces team and the Paras were in constant contact with one another, and for now, the situation remained calm.

After performing an inventory of men, fuel, food, water, and ammunition and satisfied they were able to redeploy into the field if necessary, McFadden ordered his men to stand down and post pickets around the DPVs. Those who were not on guard didn't need to be told to sleep, and most crashed in or around their vehicles. McFadden checked on his wounded soldiers and then made his way to the two signalers, who were busy doing what communicators did best—wait for the radios to tell them something. The welcome silence of the moment gave everyone a chance to reflect; however, the tranquility was dashed as rain began to fall. One of the SAS soldiers hastily erected a lean-to next to one of the DPVs to shelter his wounded comrades from the onslaught of rain and the heavy gusts of winds that now rushed down from the surrounding foothills. Earlier, the night vision googles were working optimally, as designed, from enough ambient light. Now with clouds covering the moon and stars, depth perception was skewed slightly and sometimes off-putting.

Chris took the down time as an opportunity to seek out Nash. During the hurried extraction from LUP 1, there was time only to say a brief hello. He found him standing next to McFadden and Guy Trimble, the rescued MI6 officer, at the signalers' Land Rover, patiently waiting for a message to be decoded.

After a minute, McFadden read the traffic and turned to the small gathering, keeping the news succinct. "RAF has called it off. Bad weather forced them back. There's going to be a three-hour delay. That's going to be 0600 local."

"Where are they coming in from?" Nash asked.

"Tashkent, Uzbekistan."

"Are we far enough from the Taliban artillery?"

McFadden could have easily lied but thought the CIA officer already knew the answer. "No. Come daylight, things could get interesting around here. Although there is no real reason for the Taliban to know we are out here, as soon as they see something trying to land, they might just drop a few rounds in for the hell of it to see what goes bang."

Nash went quiet. He wasn't afraid of being shelled, but he was confused. He turned his attention to Chris. "Why are you here, Chris?"

"I came to get you out, boss."

"I'm very flattered that you came, but what the hell is going on? Why you? Why aren't you on your . . . shouldn't you be somewhere else?" Trying to be vague, Nash didn't want others around to know what Chris did for the CIA.

McFadden put two and two together. He looked at Nash and then Trimble. "I think we all need to sit down and chat. A lot has happened since you've been in captivity."

Another lean-to was constructed up against a DPV, and mercifully, hot tea was passed around for everyone. Trimble asked for some food, which the SAS supplied in cans of warmed-up chicken stew, and he tore into it.

As everyone settled in for story time, McFadden opened up the proceedings by doing a formal introduction and then said to Nash and Trimble, "Frankly, we were very surprised to find you so close to the front lines with the Northern Alliance. If anything, it was a stroke of luck that we were in the vicinity. Otherwise, we might not have found you, as we were about to head north towards Kunduz."

"That was my idea," Trimble said between gulps of stew. "Back in August, missionaries from a group called Shelter Now were captured by the Taliban and thrown into a Kabul jail. They were going to be put on trial for attempting to convert Muslim Afghans to Christianity. No comments necessary there. When we were captured, we convinced them, with the help of some Christian literature I was carrying, that we were part of a Northern regional outreach program. The idiots believed us, so they were trying to ship us to Kabul, but the truck we were in broke down, and we have been waiting ever since." He looked gratefully at McFadden and said, "Thank you, by the way. I think our chances of pulling that off any longer were getting slimmer by the day. The truth would have come out in Kabul."

McFadden nodded as if to say, "Don't thank us. It's all in a day's work," but casually replied, "It's all right. The beers are on you when you get back."

Nash, getting a little perturbed by the warm chat, wanted to know what was really going on. "So, Chris, you want to fill me in?"

"I don't know if you are aware of this Mr. Nash, but Ahmed Shah Massoud was assassinated by what CTC thinks was bin Laden."

Both Nash and Trimble physically rocked back on the news.

"It must have happened while we were at his base," Nash said. "Jesus Christ, what the hell is that going to do for this country now?"

"I don't think we can think that locally anymore," Chris said. "Things have gotten more serious than Massoud."

"What are you talking about, Chris?"

"On September 11, al-Qaeda crashed two airliners into the World Trade Center in New York. Another hit the Pentagon, and a fourth crashed into a field in Pennsylvania. Last I heard, there are thousands of casualties. The US is on a war footing, Mr. Nash."

Nash jumped up in shock and hit the makeshift canopy, causing it to collapse and letting a deluge of water onto the party below. It took a few minutes to reorganize with Nash apologizing profusely for getting everyone wet, but everyone settled back in to discuss the news with Chris leading with the latest information once the shelter was reconstructed.

The details Chris was providing silenced Nash. Trimble was speculating what the British response would be, and McFadden concentrated on the tactical situation, rather than the long-term strategic possibilities. As the MI6 officer and the SAS major continued their suppositions, Chris gazed over at Nash and could tell he was in deep thought.

"So, Richard, what do you think the American response is going to be?" Trimble asked.

"We're going to bomb the shit out of the Taliban until they give us bin Laden."

"He needs to be found first." The comment came across as valid and not flippant.

Nash looked up from his morose mood. "We'll get some of our people on the ground here and start kicking some doors in. We'll find him, and we'll fucking decapitate him and his organization."

"Boss, we have people here. SAD are in the Panjshir Valley."

Nash perked up. "Do we know where?"

McFadden jumped in with a variant of line he had given Chris. "The valley is pretty long. It's a lot of territory to cover. They could be anywhere, and I'm sure they will need time to get set up."

"Are you in communication with them?" Nash asked the SAS man.

"Nope, not our bailiwick. That's a London slash Washington call."

Nash looked over at Chris as if expecting something.

"My SAT phone bit the dust back at the Taliban attack," Chris added despairingly.

Nash, silent again, looked down on the ground. Nobody said anything for a while as both intelligence officers mulled over the tragic news from the United States. Then Nash broke the silence. "Didn't someone say earlier that there were some Northern Alliance soldiers around here?"

McFadden replied, "Yes, they have been our local liaison. They are up at the Third Para command post." Nash gave him a blank stare, McFadden got the message. "Okay. Give me a minute, I'll see if I can get them down here." then sauntered back to the signalers and made the call.

Chris gave Nash a look of bewilderment. *What the hell is he going to do now?*

CHAPTER SEVEN

Parvan Province, Afghanistan

EVERY SAS SOLDIER TOOK THE TIME to shake Chris's hand and thanked him for standing up when the time mattered and for being a part of the team that freed the MI6 and CIA officer. Each one made a promise to copious amounts of free beer if he were back in the UK with an open invitation to the home of the SAS in Hereford. Chris relished the compliments he was receiving and felt a great sense of achievement and pride that he had not let himself or anyone else down on the battlefield. During the brief conversations he was having with the soldiers, he realized he was never expected to rush into the fight. He was not asked; it was just an instinct he felt, and training and duty took over. Chris was glad he got engaged, happy he was still alive, and thrilled the SAS praised his efforts. He was on an emotional high, but he knew it wouldn't last long.

"Sorry to see you go, mate," Spud called from a DPV.

"Spud, I feel pretty bad for you, mate, all that time you put in, just to cop it right at the end. It's horseshit."

"Yeah, I know, but in the big picture, I got off lightly. It could have been a lot worse. You did good, Chris, really good."

Chris gave Spud a lame smile but began to feel like crap. Although Chris finally found his true calling, fighting with Special Forces, it came to him indirectly and was not of his choosing. And now it was over. He tried to find some positives with the situation, and the only thing that he could encourage himself with was that Nash did not want to leave with the SAS; they were going to remain in Afghanistan.

"I guess you're going to have to give up your dream of becoming a drag queen when you get back to the UK."

"I'll leave that one to you, ya muppet!"

"Then again, you can always dance with them. Nobody is going to step on your toes."

"Fuck off!"

"If you ladies have finished swapping spit, I have this for you, Chris." McFadden showed up with an AR-15 and backpack that broke the jousting.

Chris, grateful for the bounty, warmly accepted the gesture. He had a quick peek inside the pack, which revealed multiple rounds of ammunition, medical supplies, water, and some basic rations.

"I have no idea what your boss is up to," McFadden added, "but my guess is Afghanistan is not going to be the same ever again, and you may be in right at the start of things. I envy you a little bit, Chris, and I hope our paths cross again." He reached out to shake his hand and grabbed it firmly.

"It's been an honor, sir; the feeling is mutual. Just hope we don't meet in a trench somewhere." The drone of an aircraft interrupted the conversation, a sign for Chris to join Nash and the two Northern Alliance soldiers in the waiting Toyota pickup.

"Keep your head down, mate," Spud chirped.

"You keep yours up." They shook hands, and then Chris turned, jogged over to the vehicle, and hopped onto the rear of the pickup, which pulled away slowly, unsure if he would see his friend or the SAS ever again.

As the Toyota pickup reached the northern outskirts of Gol Bahar, the Taliban artillery began shelling the airstrip that was being used by the SAS. Chris ordered the vehicle to stop. As it did, he retrieved a set of binoculars from his pack, another gem of a gift from the SAS, and focused his view on the airlift. He quickly found what he was looking for and saw the three Hercules transporters spewing huge amounts of prop wash towards the rear of the planes being boarded by the SAS

DPVs.

Fortunately, the barrage was sporadic and haphazard, leading Chris to believe the Taliban were taking potshots and had no real target information to concentrate all their fire. Still, the rounds were hitting the very edges of the runway, giving him a smidgen of concern. He decided then, even with Nash sitting right next to him, Chris would be off and sprinting to help if things went pear-shaped.

The hapless Taliban artillery barrage continued in vain as the first C130 aircraft reached for the skies with its cargo onboard, climbing at an incredibly steep angle while discharging a rain of flares from its underbelly. When the plane reached a comfortable height, it banked away sharply northeastwards and up into the relative safety of the Hindu Kush mountains, turning its shower of flares to raindrops, still wary of being locked onto by surface-to-air missile systems.

The second aircraft swiftly took to the air in the same trajectory and with the same defensive tactics, fueling Chris's confidence that all would get out safely. To his dismay, he spotted the last C130 with all propellers spinning, still stationary on the ground. He focused his binoculars once more to get a better view and saw that one of the SAS DPVs was static. He didn't know if the vehicle had been hit or had had a breakdown of some sorts. Whatever the delay, it only increased the frequency of the Taliban attack. Chris could tell the artillery had found its target range and was walking fire towards the waiting aircraft.

"Jesus, fuck, move, move," Chris demanded to an audience way too far away to hear.

"What's going on, Chris?" Nash begged.

Chris explained briefly but was concentrating on the rush of men trying to fix the problem DPV. Then he noticed two men carrying another in a chair lift. "Spud!" Chris pressed the binoculars harder and harder into his eyes, willing the men to hurry. More soldiers came rushing out of the plane to the stranded DPV and began to offload equipment and rush it back into the aircraft. Chris's view was momentarily obscured by rounds of green smoke from Taliban shells in an attempt to get other artillery batteries to join the fight.

When the brief barrage of smoke rounds cleared, Chris saw a distance growing between the now abandoned DPV and the C130. He watched as the aircraft taxied to line up on the runway, and out of his peripheral vision, he saw the DPV explode in a ball of flames. At first, he thought the Taliban had found its mark and the aircraft had only seconds to live, but on reflection, he reasoned the SAS had exploded it to deny the enemy use of their stranded vehicle. Relief came when the Hercules shot for the skies, leaving a huge starlight waterfall of flares behind it. But as it reached its steep climb, a shoulder-fired missile raked the sky and flew at supersonic speed upwards towards the aircraft.

Following the northeastwards flight path, the last Hercules pilot pumped out starburst flares as if they were going out of fashion, but the lumbering aircraft seemed too slow to outrun the missile. Chris, no longer using his binoculars, stared upwards in amazement. Nash and the two Afghans watched eagerly in anticipation as the clunky transport plane attempted to thwart the sleek, poisoned supersonic dart. More and more white flares were deployed from the aircraft as the pilot banked hard to avoid contact. Chris hoped all on board were strapped in; otherwise, someone would be picking pieces of flesh and bone off the ceiling. He saw a glint of sunlight flash off the missile, but then he saw something unexpected—pieces of silver garbage flying from the plane. It looked like they were dropping a ton of propaganda leaflets instead of more flares.

"Chaff!" Nash declared in pre-triumph.

The small group stood in awe, mouths agape, waiting for the inevitable collision of warhead and target, but it never came. The chaff had done its job by diverting the missile away from the plane and sending it downwards to earth, ultimately exploding as it hit the ground. The two Afghans cheered and slapped each other on the back, Nash bore a grin from ear to ear, and Chris still following the plane giggled to himself. "That plane is going to stink of puke and shit by the time they land. Glad to be on the ground for a change."

"Can we go now, Chris?" The smile from Nash had disappeared.

He was back to all business.

Chris shot him an agitated look. It was a small tactical victory to Nash but a huge one to Chris that his friends made it out alive. He didn't like the change in attitude from his boss, but he figured he had other things on his mind. "Yes, Mr. Nash," Chris conceded. "Thanks for indulging me for a minute. We should go."

Chris motioned to the two Afghans that they needed to get on the road. As they did, both he and Nash made themselves as comfortable as possible in the back of the truck. Chris had a strange feeling and looked carefully at his boss, who was rubbing his left shoulder and arm.

"You okay?"

"Yes, I'm fine," came the dismissive reply.

This is not the place to cop an attitude; it's just a question, he thought. Chris could tell there was something wrong and decided to push a little. "Is there something you want to tell me, Mr. Nash?"

"No, let's just focus on getting where we need to, okay? No need for chit-chat." The reply was blunt, orderly, almost militaristic, and out of character for the normally open and inviting Richard Nash.

Chris nodded in submission, suppressed his response, and then looked the other way. *What's he hiding?*

Culver City, California

The black Chevy Suburban mercifully escaped the slow crawling traffic on southbound 405 and finally reached the Sawtelle Boulevard exit with a sigh of relief from both of its FBI occupants. With only eight blocks to go, they were both confident they would meet the 11:30 a.m. deadline to meet an informant who stated she overheard two Middle Eastern men in the A&S Market on Venice Boulevard talking about 9/11 and that someone should bomb Hollywood. The woman, who did not give her name over the phone, also stated that one of the men who worked at the market knew of someone who could build a bomb.

"Thanks for allowing me to tag along, Rhonda."

"You're welcome, Nick. It's good to have backup. Everyone is pretty strapped right now. Not enough bodies to go around. Anonymous calls like this one are usually a dead end, but we've got to follow up on everything. My guess is this is nothing. The call came in last night, and the duty officer stated the woman was either scared or holding something back, but he didn't have a good feeling."

"So why couldn't we get some local cops on it?"

"I'm just following orders, Nick. Management says anything Middle Eastern needs to be handled with kids gloves and we've got to be careful. Trouble is every concerned citizen out there is calling in all sorts of crap. Family feuds, neighborly disputes, rednecks wanting some action taken on Muslims, all sorts of innocuous shit, but you don't know what's real until you've hit the streets. I've been on the road since seven thirty this a.m. checking out two other stories like this one. By the time I get back to my desk, there're going to be at least another five to look at, then overnight, another dozen or so. It's killing us, mentally and physically, but they've got to be checked out."

"I don't envy you, but thanks for the ride along. I've been pacing the corridors looking for a lead on my guy, and I'm clutching at straws here, but the Saudi consulate isn't far from here, and if my hunch is right, then he could be in the vicinity."

"Every good investigator needs only one good lead, right?"

Before Nick could reply, Rhonda leaned on the horn a little too long. "It ain't going to get any greener, lady. Move your ass!" Nudged onward by the FBI Chevy, the lady gave Rhonda the finger, which first made Nick smile and then alarmingly think, *Don't respond, Rhonda, don't respond.*

"Another day in LA traffic. Got to love it, or you'd end up shooting yourself or someone else," she quipped.

Nick could tell she was stressed. Normally FBI agents, although human, were conditioned not to draw attention to themselves or their mission, and honking of horns was an escalation of opinions and bad actions in this part of LA. It was bad enough cruising around in a look-at-me vehicle that might as well have had big, white stenciled FEDS emblazoned on its side, but to advertise law enforcement presence was not what he wanted in his current operation. He wasn't happy with her outburst but let things go. It wasn't his place to admonish anyone, but as she explained earlier, she was on a short fuse. Along with a number of other FBI LA field agents, she had been working fourteen to sixteen hours straight since the hijackings, and a lot of the leads they were following were total dead ends. He understood her frustrations; he too was tired of getting nowhere.

As Rhonda turned off Venice Boulevard and onto Midvale Avenue, the clock struck 11:29, and all she needed to do was find a parking space. The street was tight, and the only parking option—actually two spots—had just been taken by a blond-haired woman, who had a cell-phone glued to her head, behind the A&S Market with a flashy-looking white BMW. She obviously wasn't paying attention to her surroundings or cared who she pissed off.

"Seriously?" Rhonda complained. She gunned the Chevy and sped down the street where she found a spot to parallel park into.

The two Middle Eastern men paced casually along Venice Boulevard as they headed towards the A&S Market. Given the circumstances, being Muslim in America gave them concern as they thought everyone was watching them and everyone was out to target them or at least confront them in some accusatory, demeaning, callous way. The older of the two sensed the young man's apprehension and softly placed his hand on his friend's upper wrist in a re-assuring manner, and without turning to face him, he simply said, "Relax, Omar. It is God's will."

Omar nodded.

The older man wanted to get him focused on the task at hand. "You received the package last night, and everything is in order?" Jawad asked.

"Yes, they are exceptional. They are real, and they will stand up to any scrutiny."

"The driver's licenses, Omar, what about them?"

"They are arriving from Tucson tonight."

"Then why are we here? We have everything that we need. We have paid, yes?"

"Of course, Jawad. My contact called last night. She said there was a bonus package for us, and someone will be waiting for us here. I told you we were coming to this place. Is there a problem?"

Jawad stopped mid-stride and turned to Omar. "Who is this some-one? What if we are walking into a trap? What type of bonus are you talking about? We have everything we need. Why are we deviating from our plans now?" It was his turn to show a measure of trepidation.

"There is no need to worry. These people I have been dealing with have been paid well. I trust them, and we have some followers here." He nodded towards the market. "They will not betray us. They know me; they will tell me if there is a problem." Omar spoke with a slight air of confidence but saw Jawad was still concerned. "My source is a woman from the immigration service. Her name is Louisa Chavez, and her son, Alejandro, will be waiting for us. She is a stupid woman, Jawad. She thinks she is a criminal mastermind, but she is uneducated, and her son is a gangster, a gang-banger, as they call themselves, who only wants to spend money and impress women. They are worthless people."

Jawad nodded but wasn't happy. Omar was one of the people that he had to work with, and his position as cultural attaché at the consulate of Saudi Arabia in Los Angeles offered him a unique perspective, not to mention freedom, to conduct missions on behalf of the organization. Omar was allowed extensive discretion. While Phase I of The Big Wedding, the operational attack on the United States, was complete, Phase II was underway but still in a pre-deployment stage, and with Omar's impressive West Coast network of Muslim brothers and followers, he was a priceless asset.

"This woman does not know us, Jawad. She only looks at the mon-ey. She is an infidel and has no morals. There is no need to worry. I know all about her, and after today, we have no use for her, and she will be dealt with along with her silly boy."

They reached the outside of the A&S Market, but their attention was drawn away by someone shouting "fucking sand-niggers!" It was enough for them to turn their backs to the entrance of the market, thus masking from them any who entered or exited the establishment behind them.

Omar made a move to drag Jawad away, but Jawad remained stolid. He wanted to know who hurled the insults, and he got his answer as two Hells Angels motorcyclists cruised by, both with their middle fingers raised on their left hands. "Go bomb your own country, camel fucker!" one shouted. Both Arabs stood in silence with nothing to say. He thought the bikers were going to stop, but the presence of a black-and-white police patrol car, to his relief, had them gunning their engines and hastily speeding off along the boulevard.

The blond-haired lady bustled into the cramped, overstocked A&S Market, stuffing her phone and her sunglasses into her purse as she entered. Oblivious to the altercation outside, she paid even less mind to who was in front or behind her.

The Egyptian market owner looked up from his newspaper and stared at the bimbo who had entered his store. He was used to westerners patronizing his establishment, but it was usually the student crowd or ex-pats from the Middle East who frequented the market. A woman such as this was an exception. He tried not to stare, but his rage began to build as he looked at her, the short skirt, the tight blouse, the affluence of high-end jewelry, the makeup, and the high-heeled shoes that made her look like a western whore who showed too much skin; she had no shame. Did she not know how offensive she looked? He eventually looked away in disgust and silently hoped that his younger westernized cousin would return from the storeroom so he could deal with her. He averted his eyes and stared out towards the traffic on Venice Boulevard, hoping beyond hope that he would be rescued.

The blonde scoured the isles of the market for the young man who had called her the previous afternoon, but the place was empty. It was a mysterious call from the man as he was hesitant to give any details over the phone, but the information he gave about immigration fraud was tantalizing enough for her to secure her investigation, especially when he mentioned that a female Latino was involved.

Finding only frustration, she headed to the front of the store where she almost bumped into two other patrons who just entered. She stood there for a moment looking at the pair but decided they were not here to meet her. Turning to her left, she spotted some open tables and chairs and made for a seat at the market's window, facing the door. She impatiently threw her purse on the table, knocking over a small table menu and decorative flower. The Egyptian gave her an annoyed look, but she paid no attention to him. Mad at a potential waste of her time, she didn't even attempt to reconstruct the table décor. She settled into her chair, ruffled her hair, and then generally adjusted her look, pulling at her skirt and adjusting her blouse.

The Egyptian continued his internal pleading for his cousin to show up, but it was to no avail. Two new customers had entered, and he glanced in their direction, hoping for a welcome distraction.

The blonde paid no attention to what was going on around her in the market and, instead, looked out the window and hoped she wouldn't have to wait too long. She vowed that she would give it another ten more minutes before she left. Ideally, she wouldn't have come at all, but she actually felt duty-bound to hear the caller out, and she needed some good press after the fallout of Louisa Chavez's departure from the INS. To keep her mind occupied, Janet Wyman thought about her actions with the firing of her subordinate. As much as she had tried to justify her decision to her superiors, she realized she had left a bad taste in the mouths of many and, as a result, was getting a reputation amongst her other employees of a person who could not be trusted.

She continued to watch the vehicle and foot traffic when she saw with dismay two Arab-looking men walk into the market, appearing quite relaxed until she heard the words, "FBI." Her head spun to her right and then saw the black female who had entered with a white male holding up credentials to the man behind the store's counter. Her partner, who at first was also looking at the man behind the counter, stiffened as he heard the market's door open, and then he stared intensely at the two men who had just entered.

Jawad entered the market first and spotted the blonde sitting at a table who was looking desperately at two other people—a tall black lady and a white male—in the store. He couldn't hear the conversation they were having with the man behind the market counter; all he could see was the lady putting something away in her inside jacket pocket and then the man staring directly at him.

Omar followed close behind Jawad, eager to get into the safety of the market and away from the offensive streets. His thoughts meandered to strong tea and a relaxing place to smoke a hookah. Lunch was still over an hour away, but he was hungry and sure the market owner would provide a small appetizer in appreciation of his patronage. Confused by Jawad's stiff posture, he moved around his friend to take a seat in the corner of the market just in time to avoid another visitor to the store, a large burly bear of a man. He was a youthful blond-haired, blue-eyed man dressed in a business suit who wore a permanent frown that drew his eyes unnaturally close together.

Jawad felt the man's close presence and could almost smell his breath. The Arab considered leaving the establishment, but the exit was barred by the giant, and the stares that he was getting from the man next to the black woman gave him pause. If his instincts were right, then he was staring directly at law enforcement.

Jawad felt trapped but knew that if he left now, he would be followed. He had worked hard to ensure that he left Phoenix cleanly and did not relish the thought of regressing to a covert mode based on a hunch. He wanted to play things cool all the while planning an exit strategy. He realized the front was barred but spotted an open door behind the counter and then a long corridor that led to a third door behind the man, who was still staring at him, which he assumed led to the rear parking lot. His last option was the large window facing the street and the chairs that abutted the glass. Realizing it was plate, he rationalized it was worth the risk.

As he walked to the table to join Omar, Jawad noticed out of the window a brown UPS truck stop at the intersection. His mind changed up a gear again as he thought the worst. *A SWAT team?* The heavy-set man still stood near the doorway looking around as if someone was going to say something to answer his yet undeclared questions. He looked over at the blond lady who was staring at him. He saw that she had some form of badge ID around her neck. He was about to walk past her when he was bumped to one side by a UPS courier, who upon seeing an unusual crowd in the Arab market obnoxiously announced, "Package for Wyman, package for Wyman. Anyone . . . anyone?"

Stunned, Janet raised her hand gingerly as if admitting an offense in a high school classroom, all the while trying to fathom why a package was being delivered to her.

As if on cue, the big man moved towards the counter as he too had a hunch law enforcement were in the establishment. He reached into his inside suit jacket pocket and produced his ID and showed it to Nick and Rhonda. "Chad Peters, INS Investigations. You are . . .?"

Janet paused in writing her signature on the courier's electronic pad when she heard the INS investigator announce himself. She shifted nervously in her seat and then concentrated on the package in front of her.

"Special Agents Nick Seymour, Rhonda Webster, FBI," Nick announced.

Both Jawad and Omar heard the discussion taking place. Omar made to move for the door, but Jawad held him back. "We stay," he quietly but simply said.

"Holy shit!" Janet shrieked in excitement as the contents of the ripped-open package fell to the table. Peters shot a look over to her and saw the thousand-dollar bills lying on the table and, more interestingly, Janet's INS picture ID around her neck.

Peters, without excusing himself from the FBI, walked briskly over to Janet and identified himself.

Jawad and Omar were sitting directly behind Janet and up against the wall. Jawad was trying to comprehend the situation he was in and decided to let things play out. The tall black lady was still talking to the market owner, the INS man was becoming engaged in the conversation with the blonde, and the other FBI man sauntered over to the table in front of him and continued to look suspiciously at him. Although cornered physically, he did not feel threatened. Omar on the other hand was starting to quiver. Jawad shot him a look of authority, willing him to remain controlled, calm, and collected. They had done nothing wrong, at least not here; the authorities, he reasoned, were here for something else, not them.

The INS investigator identified himself and read Janet's badge. "It seems like it's your lucky day, Mrs. Wyman."

"Um, I . . . I don't know what to say, but this is not mine."

"Well who does it belong to? The courier was looking for you when he came in. You signed for it."

Janet looked up from the loot on the table sheepishly at the investigator. She felt she was in deep trouble.

"Well, why do you have, let me see," he counted the notes on the table without touching the bills, "ten thousand dollars in your possession, Mrs. Wyman?"

"Wait a minute." Janet composed herself. "I don't like your tone. What's it to you, anyway?"

"I really don't care if you like my tone or not. I am investigating crimes of possible immigration fraud originating from this location. Now please imagine my surprise when I'm told that someone will be delivering a package to this location today in regards to my investigation, and low and behold, an immigration official is sitting here with ten thousand dollars in her possession."

Janet was speechless, Jawad ruminated the possibilities, Omar was confused, and Nick became more curious by the minute.

"Well, is there something you want to tell me now, or shall we conduct a more formal interview at my office?" Peters persisted.

"This is not mine!" she screamed. "I was told to come here to meet someone about the same thing . . . someone told me he had information about a Latino woman who was doing something illegal."

"Yet here you are with a big wad of money in your possession. So where is this person you are supposed to meet?"

"I don't know. It was supposed to be a young man . . . someone I helped in the past."

"Oh! So you've done this thing before?"

Nick stood behind Peters, listening to the woman digging herself a deeper hole.

"No, no, this is not mine," she protested. "What part of that don't you understand? Are you some fucking idiot?" she blasted.

Nick intervened before Peters could go off on her. He looked over at the two Arabs in front of him. "Excuse me, gentlemen, Nick Seymour, FBI. Could you show me some ID?" he gently asked.

Jawad produced his passport, and Omar did the same and stated without committing anything, "We are diplomats. We have diplomatic immunity, and we are not obliged to say anything to you."

Peters, calmed at first by Nick's presence, squinted over to the two Saudi diplomatic passports, went on the offensive again.

"So you guys part of this little package deal?"

"We have nothing to say," Omar restated.

"I'll take that as a yes," he replied.

Janet was gathering up her things in a move to vacate her table.

"You can sit right there, Mrs. Wyman. I am far from finished with you."

"I have to be somewhere. I don't need to be involved with this. It's got nothing to do with me!"

"You will let me be the judge of that. Right now I suggest you be quiet." He turned his attention back to the Saudis. "So what are you two doing here, anyway?"

"I hate to sound like a broken record, Mr. Peters, but we have nothing to say to you." Jawad let Omar, who had regained some of his nerve, do the talking, but the intelligence officer was concerned that the FBI agent still stood there looking on while his female partner continued to talk with the store owner.

"How about we all go down to my office in a more comfortable setting and we hash this thing out?" the INS investigator fished.

"Mr. Peters, in all due respect," Omar recited an often-used statement when challenged by authorities, "we have nothing to say to you. Now if you wish to formalize a discussion with us, you will have to file an application with the State Department, which will in turn request permission from our government in Saudi Arabia. We of course will comply with our government's wishes. However, those sorts of processes take quite some time to resolve. I would think there are more pressing matters that need to be addressed by your government. Therefore, I have to reiterate, we have nothing to say to you. Now, I think you have wasted our time enough for one day, and as such, I must invoke our right to diplomatic immunity and bid you good day."

Omar stood to leave. Jawad got up a little slower, expecting a reaction from the FBI agent. He knew the INS man was not the threat. Although on the surface the problem with this blond lady was important to the investigator, it was trivial in the larger scope of the problem beforehand. Jawad surmised that both he and the blonde had been set up. If his assumptions were correct, then he would have to quiz the Egyptian market owner to evaluate the line of questioning that he was subjected to. However, what was more important, he thought Omar had been played; it was a serious turn of events.

Nick stepped back to allow the two Arabs room to leave the market. He got into a staring contest with Jawad for a brief second and then averted his eyes. He had found his target, but he never intended to get this close to the subject. His cover, if he ever had one, was now gone. Each player knew of each other, and Nick wasn't sure how to proceed. Omar from the Saudi Consulate of LA was going to be his start point.

After the pair left, Peters pulled up a chair and sat opposite Janet Wyman. Rhonda, who had finished with her line of questioning, joined everyone at the table. Peters stared menacingly at Janet. "So now that little circus has ended, let's get better acquainted, shall we?"

"I don't have to talk to you. I've done nothing wrong." Adamant in her response, Janet pushed back from the table and folded her arms.

Peters leaned forward with his massive girth pushing up onto the table, his giant hands slapped face down on top, the little table almost crushing under his weight. "You need to understand something here. Those two camel jockeys, I can't touch, at least not now. But you . . . now that's a different story. You had better start talking to me, or I will have you locked up for suspicion of immigration fraud. Now let's not forget what's still in front of you on the table. I saw the courier giving you the envelope; I saw you open it, which means to me that you have been paid for something." He let the statement hang for a second and watched her face blush. First it was narrow and focused into a permanent state of stubbornness, but after a second or two, Peters could see there was armor to defeat in her body language.

"The other thing is that I have two FBI agents right here. They are not involved in my investigation yet, and honestly I don't think you want them to be. But what worries me are the two Saudi diplomats who have just walked out the door. Are these two men going to commit the next terrorist attack in this country, Janet?"

She jolted at the last statement. "What? What are you talking about, terrorists?" Her demeanor changed, her arms dropped to her side, and her facial façade began to weaken.

Peters saw the change and, with it, toned down his attack. He spoke softer, "Janet, you do know that it was the Saudis who carried out the attacks in New York, right?"

"Yes, yes, of course, but I haven't done anything wrong. I don't know who they are. I don't know anything about any terrorist attack."

He wiped his face down with his right hand, as if changing a mask. "Okay, let's start from the beginning. Why did you come here today?"

Nick walked away after a few minutes of interrogation. He actually began to believe Janet, and he could tell that, although she was a difficult person, deep down she believed she had not committed a crime. He pulled Rhonda away to get her up to speed on the INS issue and the Saudis. He then asked about her discussions with the Egyptian.

"There's nothing here, at least on the surface. He has no idea about making bombs or threats, and he doesn't put up with anyone else gossiping about politics or religion. Do I believe him on that? Ah . . . probably not, but I think I will have the local PD swing by here more and see whose coming and going."

Nick nodded. "Anything on the two Saudis?" he asked her.

"Yeah, the younger of the two has been in here quite a bit. The Egyptian knows he works for the Saudi government and likes having him around, adds a little class to the place, he said."

"Nothing on the older one?"

"No, never seen him before. I watched you staring at him. Is he your guy?"

"Yep, and that's—"

"A problem," Rhonda answered for him. "Now that he's come face to face with you, he may go underground."

"Yep," Nick answered despondently and then added, "we need to focus on his buddy, Omar Abboud. He's going to be the new target, and if either of them is involved in this immigration investigation, then we have another twist to the case. Did you ask the Egyptian about blondie?"

"I asked him if he had seen her in here before. He had not. He was actually offended that she came in, and I believe him. He had some distasteful words about her."

"That's a puzzle that I don't get. She seems contrite right now and professes innocence, but how many of that type have we come across on our journeys, right?"

Rhonda nodded and looked over at Janet to see how she was doing. There was a change in her posture, and she was actually leaning forward on the table as if she was giving details to the investigator.

"Here's something that bigfoot of the INS mentioned a minute ago that grips my shit."

Rhonda turned back to face Nick.

His face was stone, and he was staring down at the floor, arms folded across his chest. He then added skeptically, "He asked Janet if those two men were going to commit the next terrorist attack in this country."

Panjshir Valley, Afghanistan

Chris braced himself for the bounce as he saw the driver of the pickup spring up in his seat and bang his head on the roof from the giant pothole in the road. The man gave a yelp, but his co-pilot raised himself off the well-worn seat and pressed his hands into the roof, braced for impact. It was a tough situation for Chris to handle as his spidey sense was put to one side as he concentrated on physically preparing his body for the cratered roads instead of focusing on his situational awareness. Every time they found a relatively quiet part of the road, he managed to analyze the surrounding hills, valleys, and rivers, but a minute wouldn't pass without the obligatory pothole attack.

Nash, who was sitting opposite him in the rear of the Toyota pickup, was starting to look the worse for wear. He had his head down looking at the flatbed, rather than preparing for or being able to anticipate the next jolt or shudder that had the potential to cause physical harm. Now and again, Chris would lose control and let out an expletive, directed not at anyone in particular but to his general discomfort. He often thought how comfortable it would be to sit in the back of an RAF Hercules transport plane on the way out of the country.

After passing through the latest hole in the road Nash looked up, "You're running out of original curses, Chris. You're starting to repeat yourself."

Chris was happy Nash was still engaged. For a while, he had thought that his boss was slipping into a downward spiral, almost into a depression of sorts. "I learned to swear from the best drill instructors in the British army. But don't worry; I'm sure there's no shortage of potholes to bitch about, so I'll be switching to German soon. Sounds just as good."

"Things haven't changed much around here; the state of these roads is enough for a priest to start cursing."

Chris chuckled but could not help notice the eye baggage on Nash. The hostage drama had taken something out of him, as he looked tired, haggard, and genuinely fed up. "You've been up here before?"

Due to the incessant bouncing around, if Nash nodded in the affirmative, Chris couldn't tell, but his boss's words did. "When the Soviets were looking for the Mujahideen, this is where they would come. For the longest time, they had a measure of control over the valley, but when the CIA got involved, that kinda changed."

"The Stinger program?"

"At the beginning, no; that came later. We first gave them anti-tank and anti-personnel mines, then small arms. You and I are now witness to the destruction that the US government funded, with help from the Saudis, Israelis, and Pakistanis. When we eventually introduced the Stingers, this valley became a little less traveled by the Soviets, but I guess repairing the damage wasn't on anybody's list of priorities."

"Well, having a civil war will do that to a country. Bullets over tarmac, I get it, but shit!" Chris almost fell out of the vehicle when they swerved to avoid boulders that cascaded down the hillside. "If you wanted to mobilize a force, wouldn't you want to have good roads to get them there on time?"

"That's not the Afghan way, Chris. These guys know how and when to fight. If they truly want to be somewhere, they will find an unconventional way to get there, pretty much like the Viet Cong; they will carry everything into a battle if they have to."

"Are they ready to take it to the Taliban . . . now that Massoud is out of the picture?"

"That's a million-dollar question, Chris. That was part of my mission, to find out what they had and what they needed. We were hoping they had enough resources to take the fight to them, but we don't know what the psyche of leadership is now and if they are willing to push before winter."

Chris nodded but still could not comprehend the fact that this sometimes scenic but menacing topography could put armies into stalemate until the thawing of spring. He had a lot to learn about Afghanistan. "How much time is there . . . before winter, I mean?" he asked.

"It's a matter of weeks, probably early October in the Panjshir, and that's going to make both air and road travel nigh on impossible."

Chris looked up and around him. From time to time, he could see glimpses of the high peaks of the Hindu Kush with their snow-capped peaks—beauty mixed with foreboding danger and a dash of adventure for the wild hearted. He wondered why they were headed up the valley into the clutches of a chilly brief autumn, not knowing where their next meal was coming from or their next shelter would be, instead of remaining in the relative safety of Gul Bahar. He looked at Nash, who seemed resigned to staring at the flatbed of the Toyota. He was back out of his brief talkative mood and into a mode of silence. Chris, in need of a stretch, lifted himself up and gripped the rooftop cab of the Toyota. He needed to see where he was going.

After thirty minutes of using his knees as Toyota springs, Chris regretted putting his arms up on the cab. The injury to his elbow the night before was beginning to bleed through his jacket. He sat back down just in time to be thrown up in the air and land flat down onto the bed to rest at Nash's feet. Are we having fun yet?" Chris mockingly asked.

"Yes, and there's plenty more where this came from soldier."

They both smiled at each other.

"Then sign me up, sir."

Fortunately, the vehicle slowed down as Nash helped Chris back to his sitting position. When they straightened themselves up, they saw they had entered a village with a hundred pairs of eyes interrogating the newcomers. After a few minutes of crawling through the place, the driver stopped to talk to a village elder. The conversation was brief, but the gesturing was easy for Chris to interpret as a request for directions. Nash also realized the intent of the interaction and buried his head out of sight of the onlookers. Chris quickly did the same.

When the vehicle got going again, Chris peeked through his scarf to take in the new sights, witnessing a typical Afghan village nestled neatly along a river and plying its wares for travelers and locals alike. Now and again, there were vendors peddling fruits and vegetables or tiny mechanic shops with young tool men battering pieces of metal into shapes or objects of unknown use. The driver had to use his horn from time to time to clear the way from sheep, goats, or even children who ran alongside or in front of the Toyota, not to impede their progress but just to have something to do. Although the road followed the river to the right of the valley, the pickup veered to the left into a furrowed and bare field.

To Chris's surprise, they came upon a Northern Alliance outpost, which was surrounded by a high fence topped with barbed wire. Inside the fence was an assortment of wooden and mud-walled structures that resembled a military post with barracks, administrative buildings, outhouses, and an ammunition dump. When they pulled up to the gate, they were challenged by two guards who seemed adamant not to let them pass. Nash jumped up to see if he could add to the progress, but an argument was brewing as the Afghan in the passenger seat tried to get out but was pushed back into his vehicle.

Chris became concerned as the voices of reason were turning more vociferous and was worried that things would escalate to something far from diplomatic. He knew not to get involved, but he was pissed off, tired, and hungry, which was not a good formula for him. He heard the driver and passenger repeat "American" several times, but the two gate goons were having nothing of it. Chris had had enough.

"Mitchell, George Mitchell," he shouted as he beat his chest.

Clueless, Nash looked at him with astonishment.

Chris repeated himself to no avail and then jumped off the pickup. He pulled his scarf down from his face to reveal his western features and then got in the face of one of the guards. He pointed at his chest once more and repeated, "George Mitchell, me, George Mitchell." He waved his hands in the direction of the compound. "Go! Go! George Mitchell here, Go!"

Nash was astounded. "What are you doing?"

Chris didn't take his eyes of the guards. "If SAD is here, they will know George Mitchell." There was a brief interaction between the two soldiers, and then one ran off to find someone who could make sense of the crazy westerner who had just showed up.

CHAPTER EIGHT

Panjshir Valley, Afghanistan

WHEN THE HEAD OF THE CIA SAD TEAM heard the name "George Mitchell," he sloppily placed his cup of tea on his desk, spilling most of its contents over the map he was reviewing, and rushed outside. By the time translations were made, Ed Guild had given the gate guard permission for George and his fellow traveler to enter the compound. While the guard rushed back to his post, Ed rounded up some of his team members, who joined him at the top of a stone staircase that led down to the courtyard below. Not knowing what was going on, they cautiously brought their side arms and a shotgun to the affair.

When the Toyota pulled up at the base of the stairs, Ed took two steps forward staring intently at the passengers in the rear. Chris jumped straight down with a weapon and a backpack. Nash moved laboriously towards the end of the pickup, waiting for someone to drop the tailgate. The driver of the Toyota obliged and helped him down from the bed of the truck, and Chris, now with the gun strapped over his shoulder, also stepped in to help. Still unknown to Ed, Nash removed his headdress and scarf from around his face and revealed his identity.

"It's Nash!" Ed claimed to his partners and then made a hasty move down the steps.

"Hello, Ed, good to see you," came the strained response.

By the time Ed got to the bottom of the steps, he could see Nash was more than a little worse for wear. He was disheveled, dirty, and generally unkempt and could probably do with a good meal and a decent bed for the night. Ed struck out his hand and was surprised by the weak return.

"Are you okay? Do you need anything?"

"A gin and tonic wouldn't go amiss, but I'll settle for coffee if you have one please, Ed."

"Let's get you sorted out." He looked over at the man called George. "You must be Chris."

Chris was feeling gloomy. He wasn't sure if the mission to find Nash was over and they would be heading back to the United States. He kind of liked playing in the dirt. All eyes were on him. "Yes," he simply replied.

Ed marched over to him and stuck out his hand. "Good to meet you, Chris. Come on in. Let's get you boys settled."

Chris spotted fuel drums as they entered the compound. "Um, Ed, I'd like to get the Toyota fueled up and send these guys on their way, if possible. They really helped us out."

"Sure, sure, absolutely, I'll get someone to take care of them. Don't you worry."

Chris nodded and was about to say something else, but it was too late. Nash was already at the top of the stairs with Ed bounding excitedly after him. Chris turned to the two Afghans who had helped them. Placing his hand on his chest, he thanked them each and wished them luck, not really knowing if they understood him. He hung around for another minute before another Afghan came down the stairs and took care of the refueling request.

When Chris hit the top stair, there was nobody around to guide him where to go next. He sauntered into the front door of a large, whitewashed stone house that appeared to have housed in the recent past a wealthy family but had lost its appeal and opulence due to conflict.

Once inside, Chris could see the cracks, flaking paint, and corners or edges where plaster had fallen off after too much abuse or shifting people. The ceiling was crumbling, but it seemed sound, and from the exterior, he noticed that at least the roof was whole, which meant it was dry inside. Standing in the foyer, Chris saw a corridor that ran in front of him for about twenty feet with doors on the left and right. He meandered slowly looking for Nash, not knowing if he would receive another warm welcome. He got his answer when he looked into a room on his right that could have passed for a sitting room or parlor, as three sets of western eyes stared back at him each noncommittal and slightly threatening, all of them silent.

He said nothing and then shuffled on by to the next room to his left, which was occupied by another westerner. But this one was too focused on operating a large radio set to notice Chris's presence. Slightly disappointed, he turned back towards the front door, contemplating finding his own accommodations outside with the Afghans. Taking another look down the corridor, he saw Nash stick his head out of a room.

"Chris, there you are. Come on in. We are in here."

Chris complied with the request and hopped towards the door to find a rather large, windowless study where Ed sat in an overstuffed leather chair behind a desk with Nash seated comfortably on a matching sofa, each piece looking as if it had been conquered by a herd of goats once upon a time.

Ed threw Chris a bottle of water and pointed to another leather chair. "Make yourself at home, Chris."

Chris dropped off his backpack, sat down heavily, and laid his rifle on his lap. He opened the water bottle and guzzled down three quarters of the liquid before he came up for air. With the remainder, he let his scarf get wet and then wiped his face with it.

"I bet you both could do with a shower," remarked Ed. "We don't have hot running water yet—some of the guys are working on that right now—but plenty of the cold stuff, if you're keen."

Chris didn't say anything, but Nash wanted to get up to speed.

"So what's going on Ed, what brings the SAD way out here?"

Ed shot a look at Chris and then back to Nash, who allayed his fear.

Chris, sensing yet another "should this guy be here" conversation, broke the spell. "I'll go get tidied up," he said and began to get out of his chair before Nash interrupted.

"Take a seat Chris. This involves you. Ed . . ."

"We got in yesterday. You may or may not have seen it, but you passed our helicopter landing site about five miles down the road. You know of the Mi-18 we had up in Tashkent. Well, we shuttled that down to Dushanbe, flew in over the Anjuman Pass, which was a little hairy to say the least, and here we are. This little piece of paradise is known as Barak and is our HQ, at least for the meantime."

"How many of you are here, Ed?"

"Eight total, officially named JAWBREAKER."

"Orders?"

"Primarily to interface with the Northern Alliance command, and that's General Fahim now that Massoud is out of the picture. I assume you are aware of that mess."

Nash nodded and looked down on the ground.

"You care to share anything about that, Richard?"

"Carry on with your orders, Ed. I'll fill you in later."

Ed was leaning forward, intent on getting his superior up on events and the situation on the ground. Nash was leaning back on the couch sipping a bottle of water, closing his eyes from time to time but listening intently to every word.

"Well, I'm going reach out to their intelligence chief and foreign minister, Dr. Abdullah, in an effort to let them know the US is committed and deadly serious about coming in here and making a difference," Ed began. "I will express to them that the gloves are off and we are coming at this at full bore. It's my job to convince them we want them to cooperate with the CIA and the US military to hunt down bin Laden and al-Qaeda. In addition, my team will evaluate the Northern Alliance's capabilities, strengths, and weaknesses to see how ready they really are to take on the Taliban. We are also going to get a read on the front lines using GPS. Right now, it's a bit foggy as to where the Northern Alliance control of territory begins and ends, so my team will look carefully at that in preparation for an air campaign."

Nash rubbed his weary eyes. He had heard most of it before and grudgingly wondered how committed the White House really was this time. "How's the State Department taking all this?" Nash asked solemnly.

"So far, they are playing ball, but it's really early. I know you have had issues with them over Afghanistan in the past, Richard, but the president really wants bin Laden, and it looks like everyone's pulling it all out to get what he wants done."

"You know what gets things done in this country, Ed. You've been in and out of here as much as I have."

"Chris, lift up my sleeping bag, would you," Ed ordered.

Chris got out of his comfy battered chair and walked over to a corner of the room where he saw a black sleeping bag perched about three feet off the ground. He pulled the bag off to reveal a black canvas tarpaulin, which he also removed. Below that was a stack of boxes. Chris stepped back with a curious look.

"Three million dollars, Richard, the only thing that lubricates Afghanistan."

"It's a good start," Nash added with a thin smile.

Chris tried not to look surprised or blurt out an expletive but replaced the tarp and sleeping bag to its initial state.

"What are our other challenges, Ed? It's not going to be that simple."

"The Pentagon," Ed replied while shaking his head. "We all thought they would be hot to trot to get out on the ground with us, but they are way behind the curve. It's a pretty sad situation."

Chris decided to join the conversation, asked or not. "I flew in to Bahrain with a Delta team and went on to Islamabad, but as far as I know, they were moaning about being held outside the theater. I don't know where they are now, but last time I heard they were staying in Bahrain."

Ed nodded at the information and then added, "It's stuff like that, Richard. We don't know who is actually going to be deployed to support us. If it's Delta, Seals, Green Berets, or whomever, the Pentagon has gone silent on us. You would think that with all their war games, this was a scenario that was played out at some stage and they would already be here."

"It was played, Ed; it was. But it doesn't mean the politicians like the plans or volunteering troops on the ground. I can understand their concerns, but I oppose their hesitation too. Once we have a firmer picture of the ground and the backing of the Northern Alliance, we will have to badger Langley for action. What else, Ed?"

"A few other things. The other problem the military has is they are reluctant to drop any boots on the ground as there is no search-and-rescue capability in the immediate region."

Nash shook his head again. It was a historical issue—every time the CIA deployed into a country, most times without military backing, it went in alone and relied on local support to achieve its missions. The paradox is that the Special Forces community thrived on working behind enemy lines but was hamstrung by overextending men who were in harm's way with no direct access to rescue if things went awry. Nash simmered on the last piece of information for a second. "I get it, Ed, I get it. Any idea where they may set up shop?"

"Kazakhstan or Uzbekistan would suit us fine. Pakistan, well, we both know that's not going to happen."

"What else?"

"General Dostum . . ."

Nash rolled his eyes at the mention of his name.

Ed carried on, "My initial read is that he is going to be a problem. He's fully entrenched up in Mazar-e Sharif, but word is that any anti-Taliban effort should start there with him. He needs resources and money. We have no direct contact with him right now, but I think we will have to deal with him sooner or later."

"I think you will have your hands full down here, Ed," Nash replied. "Fahim is a good commander, and Dr. Abdullah will be a great ally for us. This operation needs to take a political and military approach, and Dostum, while strong militarily, is a bully. Let's chew on that for a while longer. We may need to send a second SAD team up there to coordinate."

Ed thought that was a sound suggestion. "The last item I have is getting you back Stateside. With the weather not cooperating right now, we have to get things lined up with our supply runs, which I am hoping to run every other day, which I know is optimistic, but I have a logistics team setting up at an airbase just over the border in Uzbekistan—"

Nash waved his hand for Ed to stop. "We're not going anywhere, Ed."

"What?"

Chris stared across at Nash. *What the fuck?*

"We are staying right here with you."

"I don't think that's a good idea, Richard. The director—"

"Let me worry about that. How are communications?"

"We've got a good grip on it already. I've already sent a cable letting Langley know you're here. They'll want you back pretty quick, Richard."

"Chris and I have another task. I am not going to get in your way, but we have another mission to complete."

Chris looked bewildered.

Concerned, Ed said, "Chris, would you excuse us for a second?"

"Ed, stop asking him to leave," Nash objected. "He is part of this conversation now and moving forward. Get over it."

"Okay, but I want to go on record to say that I don't agree with your staying or that Chris be party to these conversations."

"Duly noted, Ed. Write it up if you have to. I am not here to usurp your authority; I am here to address a common task, and that is to find bin Laden. Now, you will carry on with direction from Langley, while I will go about my business. I will need some limited support to get us going, but I will not impede you in anyway."

Ed was furious. He had been told before he left that if Nash turned up on his doorstep he needed to be on the very next flight out of the country, no matter what. Ed's mission was secondary until Nash was wheels up out of Afghanistan and boots down in a friendly country.

Nash was now countermanding that order, which left him in an uncomfortable position. If Nash was captured again by the Taliban, it was Ed's fault. For a fleeting second, he considered disobeying Nash, drugging him, and throwing him onto a helicopter, but his sense of mission changed his mind. "Langley is going to have to hear about this."

"I know, Ed. This is not your fault. I will draft a cable, and we can take a look at it together, but Chris and I are staying."

Ed didn't want to give up and hoped Langley would be more forceful. Until then, he decided to play along. If he could stretch things out, perhaps that Nash would change his mind. Looking at the man, Ed thought, *He needs some serious rest. He looks like a zombie. Get him some food, change of clothes, and a hot shower and take it from there.* Ed gave a long sigh. He wanted to appease Nash but not give away the farm. "What do you have in mind, Richard?"

"Remember TRODPINT?"

"Seriously? The Afghan bounty hunters?"

"Not quite bounty hunters, Ed. They came pretty close in killing bin Laden in ninety-eight at Tarnak Farms. We just lacked the will to have civilians pull the trigger at our behest and the potential collateral damage of bin Laden's extended family being in the way."

"Not to mention that the Afghans were amateur special forces."

"Granted. I'll give you that, but the plan came close enough, and these guys are still out there, on our payroll, and if I'm right, they'll be willing to help us find bin Laden. Don't get me wrong. It's not my intent to use these guys to take him down. I'm going to need you and the military to do that."

"That's all warm and fuzzy, Richard, but I'm not wrapping my arms around it just yet. These guys were old and cranky back in ninety-eight, and they've been milking the CIA for years. I don't think they are reliable. Besides, we don't even know where they are."

"Kabul. You get the Northern Alliance to move on Kabul or get close enough with US support, and the Taliban will fall. They are not interested in the capital, anyway. Kandahar is home for them and will be a tougher nut to crack. As soon as I can get with the TRODPINT guys, I can get the search for bin Laden underway, and then we will decapitate him."

Flabbergasted, Chris's eyes grew to the size of dinner plates. He knew Nash had something up his sleeve, but going after bin Laden directly was not on Chris's list of things he needed to do. Plus, it would have been nice to have been consulted on the issue and not ambushed in this forum.

Nash looked over at Chris, expecting a response, but instead got a shrug of shoulders as his young protégé took another long drink from his bottle of water.

"Now, how about that coffee, Ed?"

Montecito Park, California

It was easy for Alejandro Chavez to access Janet Wyman's house. Sitting at the end of a cul-de-sac on Sierra Glen Road, the house and its immediate neighbors gave a false sense of security, leading most people in the neighborhood to believe they were somewhat impregnable, and thus an air of complacency overruled common sense. Having a busy LA freeway nearby also did wonders for the criminal intent to do harm and enter a property virtually unheard. But Alejandro, who did not need his bag of tools to enter, simply slid open the unlocked back door and entered the premises unchallenged. His most strenuous exercise to this point was his solitary trek from the parking lot of the Verdugo Hills Hospital, along the walking trail, under the freeway, through some untamed brush, and into the rear of the property. Masked by darkness and the remnants of rush-hour traffic, he was disappointed that it was such an anti-climax.

Scouring her deserted house, Alejandro looked for appropriate locations to deposit the incriminating evidence that his mother provided in the form of cash, passports, and blank citizenship certificates. He found what he was looking for in a bedroom converted into an office, replete with file folders, half-full boxes of documents, and a shredder. He took out the bag of Latino passport photos and spread a few on her desk, then opened a file, and placed a handful of certificates inside. On the desk, he created three piles of cash, each with five hundred dollars, and then placed a Latino photo on top. He then moved to the closet where he found a number of coats and jackets and stashed more cash. On the floor of the closet, he found some luggage where he placed five thousand dollars in one and two thousand dollars in another.

Moving to the main bedroom, he raised her mattress and placed under it the remainder of the certificates along with a handful of blank Social Security cards from his private stash. He treaded carefully in the dimness, mindful of obstacles that could hinder his progress, and rifled through some drawers and shoeboxes that contained underwear, stockings, and to his surprise, a large bag of weed. Alejandro laughed and was tempted to take the find for himself, but discipline got the best of him, along with the distraction of his phone silently lighting up. He saw that a message was waiting for him and opened it up to read that his cousin was ready. Alejandro replied that it was clear for him to enter and then walked quickly to the front door and unlatched it.

He dropped the bag of marijuana on the kitchen counter, and to rub salt into the wound, he removed a small baggie of crack cocaine from his jeans pocket and dumped the contents onto the marble. Under the kitchen sink, he found an empty jar and stuffed passports and cash inside. As he reared his head, he caught the sight of headlights in the street and watched as a shiny black Mercedes navigated the circular dead end and parked directly outside Janet's house. His cousin didn't waste any time, didn't lock the car, and didn't look around. He walked directly up to the house with two bags in his hands, tapped on the door with his foot, and then let himself in.

Few words were spoken between the two. Alejandro continued his exercise in finding hiding places, and his cousin began the same task with the contents he had found in the Mercedes. He left most of his booty on the dining room table and then smiled at the bag of weed he could see on the kitchen counter. He went over to it and held it up for a second, but his cousin shook his head and pointed at his watch. Disappointed, he carried on pulling items out of one of the two bags and placed the vehicle registration and some unpaid bills from the owner of the car on the table. He then dropped a leather jacket over the couch and left a pair of men's shoes on the floor.

Once both men had completed their hide and seek game, they met in the living room where Alejandro began to remove the contents of the second bag. Both were already wearing gloves, but he pulled out two pairs of plastic booties, two full body painter's suits, two sets of goggles, two lower facemasks, duct tape, pepper spray, an Uzi, a Glock handgun, a hammer, a machete, handcuffs, a video recorder, and an assortment of knives.

Before they got dressed, Alejandro closed the curtains and locked the front door. He then went to the garage where he found the electrical panel and turned off everything except for the garage. The house was now in complete darkness. On his return, he saw that his cousin was dressed and standing quietly next to a sofa, playing with his googles in one hand and holding a pack of condoms in the other.

Alejandro raised his eyebrows at the suggestion and mulled over the thought with various facial smirks, but he did not relent. He didn't need a complication; he wanted to get away clean. "No DNA!" he mouthed.

Slightly despondent, his cousin dropped his 220-pound frame heavily onto the couch. Bummed that this wasn't going to be one of his regular parties, he thought it wise not to mention the Vodka in the kitchen he had found, now with a third of the contents missing. They waited for over an hour before another set of headlights lit up the dead-end street and shone briefly through a small gap in the curtains. Both men jumped out of their seats, donned their hoods and goggles, and placed the masks over their faces. Then purposefully but calmly, they walked over to the corridor that led from the garage. Alejandro carried pepper spray, and his cousin a clear plastic bag. The Uzi was left on the kitchen counter as a last resort.

Both men stood with their backs to the walls, one on either side of the hallway waiting patiently for their prey to enter. The facemask, hood, and goggles that Alejandro was wearing dulled his senses as all he could hear was the beating of his heart and his heavy breathing, which he was sure the whole neighborhood could hear. Although in position for only a minute or so, beads of sweat from the heat of the body suit and his pent-up adrenalin ran down his spine and down the side of his temple. He looked over to his cousin who he thought was experiencing the same sensations, as he frivolously attempted to wipe his brow. They each took long deep breaths as they heard the automatic garage door open and then close.

There was a pause, but the female target had still not entered. Alejandro strained his hearing to its maximum ability to identify what could be going on. He got his answer when he heard the car door open and a female voice virtually shouting into a cell phone. He cringed at the vision and instantly thought of another attack scenario. If she was carrying a phone when she entered, it could compromise their stealthy kill. He had to think quickly and somehow communicate his new plan to his silent cousin.

Fortune smiled on the killers, as Janet finally hung up the phone. She entered the interior corridor and cussed, "Sonofabitch . . . these fucking lights. What the hell is wrong now?"

Alejandro could hear Janet's footsteps getting closer. He sprang out of his covert position and punched her so hard in the face that she immediately fell to the floor on to her ass. A second later, a clear plastic bag was placed over her head.

Yucca Valley, California

It was a logistical nightmare that Omar successfully unraveled to get all five Saudi men in one spot. Jawad recommended that, due to their close encounter with the FBI, he should remain at the consulate and on the phones to delegate and cajole their supporters in getting the men to a place where he could debrief and brief them for their next mission.

He spotted the white Ford transit van pull into Fred's Tire Shop on the Yucca Trail from his vantage point on the side of the road next to a heating and cooling company. As soon as the van parked outside the closed store, Jawad rolled his car forward and away from the cooling company and began his counter-surveillance of the surrounding area. Fortunately, the streets were deserted, not a single soul in sight, with the exception of a coyote that scampered along the desert roads as the clock ticked past 03:30, aiding in his job of ensuring good operational security. He had been in the area for three hours surveying the meeting place and the streets and byways to gauge what type of traffic was in the area, memorizing which cars and people belonged and which didn't. His aim was to allow the transit van to enter the parking lot, let things calm down, and observe what activities followed.

Satisfied that the transit van had not picked up an FBI surveillance team, Jawad made his move after another hour of observations and parked his Ford Windstar next to the van. He nodded at the passenger and driver who in return moved into action. Within a few seconds, the passenger of the vehicle exited the van and opened the sliding door to reveal four other men sitting on the floor of the vehicle. The passenger then moved quickly over to Jawad's Ford Windstar, opened the sliding door, and got in the front passenger seat. By the time the passenger had secured his seat belt, all four men from the transit van had taken up positions in the Windstar, and with the sliding doors closed on both vehicles, Jawad urged the engine gently forward and entered Route 62, the Twentynine Palms Highway.

Tense silence occupied the passengers of the Windstar. Keeping just above the posted 55 mph speed limit, Jawad was concentrating on the road and the rear-view mirror, not only to watch for the purported omnipresent FBI but also to analyze his young passengers squirming silently in their seats, devoid of information as to where they were going or whom they were with.

As they reached the eastern edge of the small city of Joshua Tree, Jawad killed the silence but surprised the men, as some of them began to believe the driver was just another courier who was tasked with transport duties.

"Peace be upon you, my brothers."

Muffled, ill-confident responses of a similar nature were returned, but Jawad, keen to establish authority and a sense of assurance, engaged the five-man team in conversation. At first the men were guarded in their answers, and some would only give simple yes or no replies, which Jawad could understand, given the circumstances and their operational failure at LAX. He surmised that with all the sacrifices, training, and preparation these men had given to the Big Wedding, being sociable to a complete stranger in the middle of the night somewhere in the California desert was not so appealing.

Jawad pulled the vehicle over at an Indian Market. He kept the engine running but turned around to the four passengers in the rear, "My brothers, peace upon you."

Three of the men spoke in chorus, "And upon you, peace."

He smiled warmly in return. "I understand your hesitancy to speak with me, but let me assure you all," his voice was stern, authoritative, devilish, "I am not here to engage in small talk with you. I am not here to take you from one city to another like a taxi driver. I understand your mission, I understand the sacrifices you have made, I understand that mistakes were made. I know why you did not get on that plane." All eyes were on him; he had their undivided attention. "I admire your dedication to your duty, and we, we martyrs who have a higher calling who have been blessed by the sheikh himself to carry out God's will, must succeed. Our mission is not over; it will begin again." He saw they were attentive and paused to let things set in. "It is we, my brothers, who must carry on with our jihad against the United States. It is you and I who make jihad, and as explained in the good words of the sheikh, as God's word is the one exalted to the heights, we must drive the Americans away from all Muslim countries. We must prevail; we cannot fail."

There were silent but safe nods from the five men he was addressing. They had heard the same words from bin Laden on numerous occasions, and now coming from this man, they realized they found someone whom they could trust.

"Now, we must keep moving, my brothers. Our mission continues, but you must tell me everything that has happened to you since you arrived in this forsaken land of infidels and whores. You!" he nodded to the man in the passenger seat, "you are the leader of this group. Tell me your duties and everything about this mission. Leave nothing out."

"I must ask you your name, brother," he sheepishly replied.

"That is of no consequence. Is it not enough that I am a martyr and brother? Continue before I leave you at the side of the road."

Jawad selected a gear, checked his rear-view mirrors, and joined the highway as the leader of the terrorist cell began his detailed report.

By the time Jawad had reached Palo Verde, he had all the answers he needed from the group who had opened up to him wholeheartedly. As they continued their journey southward, he briefed them on the next steps of their new mission, which was to be in Mexico. He enthusiastically explained that details, while scant, were advanced enough for this team to deploy to Mexico City to meet brothers who would then provide the information and logistics for an attack on a US facility.

The mood in the Windstar was upbeat as the men, exonerated for their failed mission by this man, who obviously had close ties with the sheikh, was indeed attentive to their personal jihads. Morale was climbing, and Jawad, for the first time, saw white teeth greet him in the mirror. He had succeeded in gaining their confidence, and he had retrieved enough intelligence from them that he was happy to pass the group along in the next stage of their journey.

After crossing the train tracks at Glamis, an off-road adventure encampment, Jawad slowed the vehicle down but then did a quick 180 degree turn in a wide-open, dusty parking lot. Dawn had broken, and the first dune-killer enthusiasts were congregating around the local store, smoking and sipping on hot coffees when the vehicle arrived. As the off-roaders looked on, they at first were curious as to why a Ford Windstar would be in this area at this time of day. Their inquisitiveness turned to anger as a wave of gray-brown dust and loose dirt chips flew in the air, which lightly peppered some of the quads, dune buggies, and motorbikes. One hothead, with his brew totally ruined by the air attack, ran to his bike and contemplated giving chase but instead threw his helmet and coffee at the now disappearing Ford. His friends howled at the futile gesture and subsequently turned their ire to poking fun at the helmetless rider. They promised it wouldn't be a story they would soon forget.

Jawad chuckled to himself at the sight of the rider in the mirror. Satisfied he had completed a needed task, he got on with the business of finding his contact. Now retracing some of Route 78, he took a right fork off the main highway just past the regional landfill and on to Vista Mine Road. Roughly two miles down the way, he spotted the backside of a black Chevy pickup truck with two dirt bikes mounted on the rear. Although the Chevy was parked on the side and almost in a ditch, Jawad parked squarely in the road and tuned off the engine. He said nothing as he exited the vehicle and approached the Chevy on its driver's side.

The five men sat in silence as they all stared forward, waiting to see what would happen next, but their solace was destroyed when the rear window of the Windstar was blown inwards by a blast from a shotgun. Each one of them ducked for cover as glass splinters filled the vehicle as more shotgun rounds pumped into the car. Groping for cover, the five men did not see Jawad return with an AK-47 but only heard the sounds of bullets riddling the front end and blasting in the windshield. None of the occupants thought to lock the doors or at least grab a handle in defense, but Jawad, who saw the men cowering, slid open the sliding door and let off a full automatic burst of fire into the cab. After his magazine was expended, he drew a pistol from the small of his back and shot each man, dead or dying, in the head two times.

His contact appeared from the rear of the vehicle. Jawad, surrounded by a thin veil of blue acrid gun smoke, ordered the man to pick up the pocket litter from the dead men. While his man carried out his instructions, Jawad retreated to the Chevy and took out a set of binoculars from the cab, then jumped onto the rear, and began a scan of the immediate area. Satisfied they had not attracted any untoward attention, he remained in place until his contact returned with five passports and five US driver's licenses. *At least they followed orders not to bring anything else*, he thought.

"Clean the driver's side thoroughly. I did not touch anything but the controls."

The contact nodded and then bumbled off to get the cleaning supplies in the Chevy while Jawad kept an open eye from the rear of the
bed. He stuffed the driver's licenses in his shirt pocket and, in between
using his binoculars, watched the man vigorously clean the Windstar.

When the man returned from his duty, Jawad could not help to see
that the man looked scared. "Fear not, my brother, fear not. I have
other uses for you." He threw him one of the passports and said, "Place
that under one of the bodies. Then we will be on our way." He smiled
broadly and almost laughed, "This will give the Americans something
to worry about."

CHAPTER NINE

FBI Field Office, Los Angles

NICK SEYMOUR HAD HIS HEAD buried in a thick file, desperately trying to figure out if the information before him would help his cause. As Rhonda had told him, reports were coming in thick and fast about sundry items—Arab-looking men acting suspiciously at the mall, Muslim terrorists plotting the next attack in mosques in Sacramento, Arabs being targeted in San Diego, mosques attacked by skinheads, graffiti plastered over Middle Eastern businesses, Muslim kids at schools being beaten and chased down the street. The list went on and on, and the information was out of date by the time Nick had reached the bottom of the page. Hundreds of incidents across the country were popping up by the hour, and it became a serious drain on manpower within both the FBI and local law enforcement communities.

He was slightly relieved when an agent stopped by and dropped another folder on his desk. "Don't know if this will interest you, but it's the latest hot one. Doesn't look good for the bureau!"

Nick's brow furrowed. Mystified, he opened up the file, which originated from the Phoenix Field Office. He glanced over the obligatory distribution lists, circulation acronyms, and other internal jargon to find the meat and bones of the memo written by Special Agent Kenneth Williams. In the outline, he read that this memorandum was written on July 10, 2001, sent to FBI headquarters recommending a worldwide listing of civil aviation schools. His recommendations were based on his investigation of students who had attended these schools and potential links to terrorism.

Nick, who had been sitting up dead straight in his chair, now stood up, document in his shaking hands. He couldn't contain himself. "Holy shit!" he blurted and then read on. "'Advise the Bureau and New York of the possibility of a coordinated effort by Osama bin Laden to send students to attend civil aviation universities and colleges. Phoenix has observed an inordinate number of individuals of investigative interest who are attending or have attended—'"

"Nick, call for you on line two," Rhonda shouted across the office cubes, breaking his astonishment and his train of thought.

He fought to control himself as he picked up the phone and answered, "Hello, this is Nick." Still shaking, he sat back down in his chair.

"Hi, Nick. Chad Peters, INS. How ya doing?"

He rubbed both eyes hard with his thumb and forefinger and tried to cringe away a lingering headache. "Jesus, Chad, I've had better days. What can I do for you?"

"I just thought you would like to know that there's been quite the development with my investigation. Janet Wyman was found dead this morning."

Nick was trying to multitask by reading the document in front of him but stopped himself when he heard the news. His instinct kicked in. "What the hell happened? Homicide?"

"Oh yeah, pretty nasty one too. You don't need the details, but I will leave it up to your imagination, one limb here, another there etc., etc. The woman was a bitch on wheels, but she didn't deserve that."

"I hear you, Chad. Thanks for following up. Any suspects?"

"Yes and no. It's too early to say, but one name does come up. This has nothing to do with what you're chasing, but Janet mentioned a former employee, Louisa Chavez. She got fired recently, and there was some bad blood."

"You saying this was a revenge thing?"

"We don't know yet. We've had our eye on Louisa for a while, and we were just going through the process of creating a task force to see what she was really up to. It's too bad she was fired; we could have kept a closer eye on her if she was still in the office. But there's been some discrepancies with passport issuance, missing forms, you know the usual bureaucratic bullshit, and it looks like she had some unusual clearances on some of our servers. Anyway, don't mean to bore you with this, but I need a favor."

"Shoot, anything I can do to help. Just keep in mind that we are up to our asses in quicksand over here. What do you need?"

"During my interview, Janet informed me that Louisa has a son, Alejandro Miguel Chavez. I can only dig so deep Nick . . ."

"Already on it. Stand by."

Within a few seconds, Alejandro's rap sheet popped up on the computer screen. Nick began to scour the contents; then he scrolled and scrolled and scrolled through the pages. "Found a choirboy if that's who you are looking for, Chad."

"How many pages?"

"On page four, some good mugshots, lots of ink. He's done time in San Quentin."

"Can you—"

"Sure, I have your email address. I'll get it across to you. Just watch the distribution. Okay? Keep it internal."

"Homicide is not my thing, Nick. I'll just pass his name to the local cops and let them handle it."

"Anything else, Chad?"

"Not really, but if my gut feeling is right, you and I will be having another conversation pretty soon."

"How come?"

"Let me find Louisa Chavez first."

No sooner had Nick replaced the phone onto its cradle than Rhonda showed up with a notepad in hand.

"When it rains, it pours. You ready for this one?" she asked.

"No, but that's not going to stop you, is it?"

"California Highway Patrol got a call from some off-roaders in a place called Glamis, which is about 120 miles southeast of Palm Springs. Seems they found five stiffs in a minivan out in the desert."

"Okay. What's that got to do with us?"

"Well, two things. They want us to get involved with the investigation since they were all shot to death, and not just a little bit."

"Interesting, and the other . . ."

"A Saudi passport was found in the car matching one of the deceased."

Nick stared at Rhonda for a long time. He was trying to digest the information, but his head was too full of data. Rhonda could almost hear the gears churning in Nick's head. Although he was staring at her, she could tell he was having a hard time processing the information.

"We got to get out there," he said eagerly. "Do we know the passport holder?"

"No. That's where I thought you would help. Perhaps it's your guy."

"That's not wishful thinking, Rhonda. I'd like to find out what the guy is doing here, and that's pretty difficult to find out if a bullet is affecting his speech abilities."

Another agent called across the room, "Rhonda, can you pick up? Call from Phoenix for you."

She waved in acknowledgement and headed back to her desk, leaving Nick leaning back in his chair to survey the ceiling with his hands behind his head. He closed his eyes and began to toss around large and tiny pieces of information in his head, searching for answers. But he deemed it useless; it was as if he was looking for the winning number in a tombola as it spun endlessly around.

Within five minutes, Rhonda had returned to Nick who was back to reading the files spread out before him on his desk.

"You want to go for a ride into the desert?" he asked excitedly.

"The SAC wants us in a meeting, like right now. I can see a bit of a congregation heading towards the large conference room. Let's go."

Nick grabbed his notebook and pen and followed Rhonda's lead. They found a couple of empty chairs in the quickly filling conference room. A few people were chatting, but each looked at each other for answers.

As soon as Special Agent in Charge Ron Hilts walked in, the room went quiet. He was followed by a staffer who placed a CD into a player underneath a large TV screen.

"Thanks everyone. Let's save the chit-chat," Ron started. "We have a priority situation here. New information has become available to us from the security department at LAX from 9/11." He stood back from the TV and then nodded to his assistant who set the CD in motion.

When the screen came alive, an image of a busy security checkpoint came into view with a number of passengers being screened through metal detectors and security guards going about their business. Everything seemed quite normal, but as it continued to play the SAC said, "That was scene 1. Here comes scene 2." The next image showed a traveler talking to a security guard, which to the unaware seemed harmless enough. The agents in the room still didn't know what the issue was but held onto their patience when the next scene revealed a central corridor where passengers traversed from the security check-point to the actual airport concourse. It showed the man who was previously talking to the security guard being chastised by another man.

Some of the agents in the room leaned forward to get a better look at the images, but before they could surmise what was going on, the tape rolled on to show three more men approach the other two and then all standing in limbo as if waiting for orders or for someone to make a move. The group suddenly split up and were picked up on a concourse camera with the two antagonists still talking to one another. A different camera from an oblique angle spotted the other three stragglers of the group, meandering their way slowly down the busy walkway. But one of the three was checking over his shoulder to see what the other two were doing. The man stopped to look at his watch and then turned around quickly.

The edited video images showed the two arguing men walk back towards the security checkpoint with the other three men following a short distance behind. The camera system followed the twosome and threesome as they walked past security, back out to the departures area, and then on to the outside envelope of the airport building. The video ended abruptly to some quick exclamations and hushed words.

"Do I need to spell this out?" There wasn't a vacant stare from anyone in the room. Each person was internalizing myriads of likelihoods.

"This, ladies and gentlemen, is a terrorist cell that did not get on the plane on which they were booked from LA to DC." He let the information sink in. Although he already had everyone's attention, he wanted to convey the gravity of the situation, but Rhonda beat him to the punch.

"Ron, sorry to interject here, but I got some information this morning about five John Does killed outside of Palm Springs. A Saudi passport was found in the vehicle. I hate to suppose, but I know you are going to ask us to find these guys. Is this the start point?"

"Yes, good call, Rhonda. Get yourself a partner." He looked quickly over to Nick and pointed, "Not you. Five deceased is a lot for the locals to process. If it's not our guys, then they will still need some support from us. If it is our guys, then it's going to be all hands to the pumps." Ron loosened his tie and then stood with his hands on his hips.

"Tom, Kim, Wayne, Donnie, I need you to get to LAX and start working that end. I need witness statements, I need more camera time, I need airport layouts, I need the works. Get up and go NOW!" The four agents didn't hesitate. They knew what was needed.

As they were leaving, Rhonda got up and grabbed a junior agent. "You don't need me here any longer either, right?"

"You got it. Vamoose!" The herd in the room was thinning. "Now, the rest of you . . . by the time you get back to your desks, you will have this video feed in your inboxes. You need to analyze the shit out of it. I need composites, descriptions, blown-up images. I need body language synopsis, behavior analysis." Ron was animated and talking faster than a horse race commentator. "I don't need to spell this out, but you all need to work with the LAX team that just walked out the door. I need results. I need to have some information to process and kick back to DC before we go home tonight, or if necessary, we are ordering pizza and then donuts for breakfast."

There were solemn and serious faces around the room. They didn't need a pep talk to do a good job. They were already doing more than what was asked, giving their all, and nobody complained. They just got on with it.

"Nick, what's your game? What do you have? What do you need?" Ron queried.

"Status quo, I'm afraid. I still need permanent eyes on the Saudi consulate and Omar. It seems my person of interest has gone underground, as I expected. My gut feeling is Omar is going to be the one to give us something worthwhile."

"Okay, keep in contact with Rhonda. Who knows, one of the desert five could be your man. I'm going to keep our surveillance team on the consulate. But now that we have this latest development, I may need to pull the manpower. Do what you can with what you have; otherwise, you will be on your own. No offense, buddy."

"Understood, Ron, no hard feelings."

"Okay, mush-mush people," he waved both arms towards the door like a flight attendant giving an emergency demonstration. "Get out of here; go find me something. Nick, stick to your seat. Got one more thing."

When the last person left the room, Ron walked over to Nick and sat down next to him. "I got to get on a call with the director in five minutes, but I want to ask you something first."

Nick didn't have anything to say but waited patiently for Ron.

"I got a buddy in the office in Cairo who called me earlier about a feeler sent from headquarters to all overseas liaison officers asking if anyone knew about FURLONG." Ron was waiting for a reaction but didn't get an eyebrow twitch from Nick.

"What's that, Ron?"

"I was hoping you could tell me. It seems the Brits have a FURLONG. We don't know what it is—an operation, an agent, a system, a task force, maybe military hardware. We just don't know. I thought that since you were in the UK for a while you may have heard or seen—"

"No, never heard of it, but wouldn't that be a question for the CIA?"

"You would think. I guess it's above my paygrade to figure their crap out. Just thought I would ask. Forget about it."

"Dumped already, Ron. Listen, thanks for humoring me here. I know you've got manpower issues, but thanks, really. If I can be of use if my operation goes nowhere, I'd be happy to help out."

Ron stood to make a move for his call. He liked Nick but knew he was tainted goods. His career with the FBI would be closing in on him soon. It would be better if he distanced himself from Nick before he roped him in to help with the latest tasks. Ron shook his hand and smiled but did not commit to any undying friendship, "Thanks, Nick. Got to run."

Nick looked at the back of Ron's head as he was leaving and then looked around the room. He was the only one that was not given orders. Suddenly, he felt very alone.

Panjshir Valley, Afghanistan

Chris had had enough. He had been at the JAWBREAKER compound for twenty-four hours, and not much was happening, save for the forfeiture of his dwindling patience. The upside was that he had managed a lukewarm shower and a good, solid vacating of his bowels, which pleased him to no end as others around him struggled to regulate. He earlier heard Ed comment that when you were in Afghanistan, as the clock slows down, your bowels speed up. Chris wondered if he too would be affected by butt rot and swap his rifle for a shovel and a roll of toilet paper. But so far, so good.

The downside that counterbalanced his bodily functions, however, was that he'd been sitting in philosophical and strategic discussions with Nash and Ed Guild for hours on end on the probable outcomes of the Afghan theater of war. At the beginning, it was attractive, intriguing, thought-provoking, but he was at a loss. These men were higher thinkers, experienced in the art of covert war, geo-political warfare, counterinsurgency, regime building, demoralization of governments, theater politics, and all sorts of tightly woven plots and counterplots. He excused himself from the conversations grudgingly as he had hoped that he could garner some kind of game plan, exit strategy, or way forward, but to him, it seemed everyone was stuck with glue on his boots waiting for something or someone to come up with the solution.

Walking slowly out of the villa into the bright sunlight, Chris squinted his eyes and shielded himself from the shiny yellow orb in the sky. With his right hand over his forehead, he looked around for a quiet spot to relax and perhaps take a nap. The compound was peaceful, as it seemed the Northern Alliance was also in a holding pattern scratching their butts waiting for orders. Chris noticed a group of three Afghans in the shade of a low wall cleaning weapons. Falling back into his own military doctrine of downtime activities—sleep, eat, and clean—and before being volunteered for something he didn't want to do, he swiftly marched away from the JAWBREAKER house and set out for the cleaning party.

Upon arriving at the group, he faced the wall, removed the magazine from his AR-15, cocked the rifle to release the 5.56mm round in the chamber, which he caught, held the breech open, checked inside, and then released the action and the trigger. The three Afghans, who were sitting on a canvas tarp, looked up at him and, without any words being said, made room for him to sit and join the party.

Sitting cross-legged with his AR-15 over his knees, Chris skillfully went through the motions of stripping and cleaning the weapon with the tools and lubricants offered by his hosts. It was unfortunate that he couldn't converse with the men, though he did find some solace by not having to listen to Nash and Guild hypothesize over angles and projections. However, his morale was boosted as the combined task of cleaning weapons was enough to make a connection with the men who thankfully accepted his presence and made him feel welcome.

By the time he had reassembled his rifle, a young boy of around fourteen or fifteen showed up with a batch of AK-47s slung over both shoulders. Chris was about to start cleaning his Makarov but held off as the guns were distributed amongst the cleaning crew. Without needing a prompt, Chris took one of the AKs and set to work.

The cycle of weapon cleaning continued throughout the day, and by the time the light started to fade, Chris became aware that his pile was becoming larger than his newfound friends' and that he was being taken advantage of. He smiled each time a weapon was put in front of him but didn't complain. However, when the young boy returned in a large truck with a driver towing a Soviet-era artillery gun, he stopped what he was doing and looked on with interest. An older member of the group motioned to Chris and then pointed at the gun, saying, "You, you."

Chris looked at the man, whose face was as serious as a parade sergeant major, then looked at the huge gun, and then looked back at the man. *Get the fuck out of here. You can't be serious*, he thought. There was a moment of tense silence as the three Afghans and the young boy looked at Chris with an air of demonstrative apprehension. He pointed to his chest and then the big gun. "Me? You want me to clean that?" The lack of other words told Chris these men weren't messing around. He rose from his sitting position and looked at the beast again. Then he turned to the group and pointed backwards at the piece, saying, "You're having a laugh if you think I am going to clean that mother-fucker."

They didn't understand a word he was saying, but the look on Chris's face was enough to crack the first smile, which turned into a giggle, and then become outward laughter and hand slapping. He'd been had.

The laughter was loud and contagious. Chris joined in but added and pointed at each one after another in jest, "You fucking muppets, I thought you were serious for a minute . . . you bastards." They didn't understand a word he said, but they got the gist and just kept on smiling and laughing.

Chris was still chuckling when he sat back down on the cleaning tarp and was about to get back to work when one of the Afghans snatched the AK he was working on and passed it to the young boy. From the body language, Chris understood that the work was done for the day as another young Afghan showed up with a host of food containers. He was tempted to take his leave, but before any words or motions could be interpreted, the first empty plate was offered to the guest. The foreigner, honored by the gesture, accepted the plate with his right hand as was customary and then waited patiently as a washbasin was presented to him to cleanse his hands. Glad that he had retained some of the intel package he had read on the plane, Chris checked himself as he almost reached for a fork that he kept in his inside jacket pocket, realizing that utensils weren't used in this type of setting and the shared meal would be consumed by hand.

By the time each of the group had finished cleaning his hands, plates of fresh naan bread, rice, and seasoned lamb were placed directly before Chris, which was another honorable gesture that was not lost on him. He realized then that he was being treated as a special guest, even though they had never met him, knew of him, or owed him anything. Even as the group failed to verbally communicate with each other, the common practice of soldiers cleaning guns as if in preparation for a battle cemented a bond that would be hard to break. It was in that moment that Chris felt at ease, and for the first time in a very long time, he also felt quite content.

The next morning, Chris awoke to the sound of rain beating the tired roof of the JAWBREAKER villa. As he lay in his cot, he wondered how much longer the sun-baked tiles would hold. His thoughts were answered as a bead of water traversed its way down the wall, forcing a trail of cockroaches from their home. He jumped out of his bed, scooted his cot away from the infestation, and then shook his boots before donning them to exit the room. Picking up his weapon, he made his way out to the entry of the villa where he spotted Ed Guild looking over the Afghan compound while drinking a cup of coffee. Chris, tempted to find another activity, was caught before he changed direction when Ed turned around.

"Morning, Chris."

Chris walked to Ed's side and kept his response curt, without trying to be brash, "Morning."

There was an awkward silence between the two, and Chris, still feeling out of place, remained solemn. Ed too seemed deep in thought, so the pair stood in the shelter of the villa and watched as the rain punished the dry earth to form a myriad of rivulets that crisscrossed the Northern Alliance military complex.

Ed broke the peace after a few minutes. "Another day in paradise."

"Doesn't get better than this."

"How was dinner last night, Chris?"

"Fine, no complaints here."

"Not yet. You may want to stay near a bathroom today."

Chris wasn't sure if Ed was warning him of pending bowel doom or being offensive towards Afghan cuisine and hospitality but assumed the former in his response. "When you've eaten British army rations for most of your young adult life, you develop an iron stomach to most things Ed. Granted, dinner wasn't in the most hygienic of settings, but my body has been adapting to eating all sorts of unusual things since I've traveled the world for this job."

"It will catch up with you one day, believe me. I've been keeping a large Coke bottle at the side of my bed since I've been here."

Chris raised his eyebrows and turned slightly to the taller man.

"You don't need the details. It's pretty disgusting," Ed offered. "But I don't think I am getting away from here anytime soon."

The rain continued to pour, and another interlude of verbal silence encased the two westerners as they let their thoughts wander.

"Where's the boss?" Chris asked after a while.

"He's still sleeping. He was up for most of the night conferring with Langley."

"He looked pretty haggard the last time I saw him."

"Yeah, he's really taking this hard. He has a long history in this part of the world."

Chris waited expectantly for Ed to elaborate as he sipped more coffee.

"He was here during the Soviet occupation, and when he worked as the station chief at the US embassy in Islamabad, he left his third floor office light on every night until the war ended and the Sovs retreated; he was that committed. He knew of bin Laden's activities in the country, hell, we all did, he cautioned us but nobody paid too much attention. The focus was on beating the shit out of the Sovs and anyone was welcome to try. The thing was bin Laden and his followers were more of a hindrance to the Mujahideen than a help, and people like Massoud asked us to contain the Arabs somehow. Nash said yes, we'll give it a go, but the White House didn't care so they let him be."

The conversation was interrupted as a radio operator handed Ed a cable. He read through it quickly and nodded to the man who went back to his duties.

"This whole thing with TRODPINT was Nash's operation," Ed continued as if the note he received wasn't important. "He was still considered the regional expert and had the passion and in-country contacts to see something that bold through. Trouble was a new administration in the White House put an iron clamp on seeing good opportunities and ignored intelligence and actionable operations. Nash was here in ninety-eight as well, getting in harm's way with the TRODPINT team. He was just waiting for permission to pull the trigger, but instead, the rug got pulled out from under him. Since then, he's had a chip on his shoulder, and now he's trying to justify his past warnings and put things to bed."

Ed turned to Chris and touched his arm gently, and they faced each other. He spoke softly, "He's got it in his head that he is to blame for the attacks in New York. He basically poured it out last night. He's pretty cut up that the agency is partly at fault. I agree to some extent, but what people don't see, what people don't get to hear about are the successes that people like Nash have accomplished. They just want heads to roll when things go wrong. No doubt, bin Laden is a stain on the agency, which should never have happened. History will tell us if it was a colossal mistake not to have contained him back in the eighties or nineties. Perhaps it already has, but the boss wants to make it right, and he doesn't want to leave until it's done."

"He shouldn't be here, Ed. He needs to be on a plane and back at his desk where he belongs. This shit sandwich is not of his making, and whatever he thinks, he cannot be the one digging in ditches looking for bin Laden."

"It's not my remit either, Chris . . ."

"I know Ed. I'm not implying that it is, but I think we both know it isn't his either. When can we get him out of here?"

"Not any time soon." Ed held up the cable that he was given. "It seems that a lead has opened up. Three miles up the road, there is a prison camp full of Taliban religious leaders. We ran the names through our database, and one popped out, one who had ties to TRODPINT."

"Does Nash know?"

"Not yet, but it was his idea to fish. Soon as he finds out, he will want to get up there and start talking."

"Talking to whom?" came a voice from behind them.

Ed and Chris turned to see an untidy Nash ruffling his hair and straitening his clothes. He looked as if he had just fallen out of a clothes dryer.

Ed offered Nash the cable to read.

"Good," Nash said. "How soon can we leave?"

"Richard, I think you need some more rest before we go on an expedition."

"I'll be the judge of that, thank you, Ed."

Chris joined in with the concern. "Mr. Nash, how much sleep have you had?"

"What the hell is this?" His face was flushed, and his voice was raised with a tinge of anger. "I'll sleep when the victims' families sleep, and that is when bin Laden is strung up. How we achieve that is my business, and you need not concern yourself with my well-being. We have a duty to perform and, as I see it, a new mission in hand. Ed, make some arrangements . . . get me a vehicle and a translator. I am heading up to that prison this morning. Chris, pack your gear. You have a choice—get on board with me, or wait for the next chopper to take you home."

Ed was about to protest, but Nash was holding his ground and not moving an inch. Chris read Nash's body language and didn't like what he was seeing. Nash was red faced and shaking his left hand vigorously as if it had a piece of sticky tape attached. His actions were slow, and he looked beyond weary; he looked exhausted.

"I'm going to find some coffee, Ed. Let's get this ball rolling, if you please." He turned and walked back into the villa.

Ed was about to march off to carry out his orders, but Chris held him back. "He's in no shape to do this. Is there any way you can contact Langley and overrule him?"

"I tried last night, Chris. Seems the director thinks it's worth pursuing. My mission is too far along to get involved with this sideshow. I can support him somewhat, but I can't hold his hand."

"When does the bombing campaign get underway?"

"Honest answer?" Ed's shoulders sagged in submission. "I don't know. The first ODA is supposed to be here already."

"ODA?"

"Operational Detachment Alpha, US Special Forces. Their mission is to conduct laser targeting of Taliban defenses. As soon as boots are on the ground, the sooner lead hits heads."

"Great, just fucking great. So he wants to go talk to some mullah, who may or may not help us find TRODPINT, who are more than likely in or around Kabul, which, if I'm not mistaken, is still in Taliban hands. My guess is that this mullah will say anything to get out of jail and then lead us off into the wild or back across to Taliban lines. If we do end up going across, there's a good chance we will get hit by friendly forces if they show up or we'll get whacked by the Taliban."

"There's no way Langley is going to allow him to do that, Chris, especially unsupported."

"He's not himself, Ed. I've seen a change in him. Ever since I picked him up with the SAS, he's been off his game. We need to slow him down before he completely goes off kilter."

"He gave you the choice to leave, Chris. Is that what you want?"

"Wait a minute!" Chris became pissed at the mere suggestion of his retreat. There was no way he was going to leave Nash hanging. He would stick by his side, no matter what, even if the possibilities of Nash going rogue and countermanding his agency's orders were high. "I'm in this for the long haul. If there's an angle to find bin Laden and pull his liver out with a rusty bayonet, then sign me up. But I don't think Nash is the one to lead this charge. There has to be another way."

"Let him go talk to the guy. Perhaps this is not such a bad idea. My team's focus is on weakening the resolve of the Taliban, so I can't look at anything else right now. I have neither the resources nor the authority to run down empty leads. What I do have are presidential orders to take the gloves off and fuck these guys back to the Stone Age. I can do that only with the military's help, so my hands are tied while I wait for them to get here. If Nash has the energy and gumption to track bin Laden, then I say good, chase it down. It can't hurt."

Chris was lost in thought for a second. He was happy to have some makings of a plan, a direction of sorts, but he wasn't comfortable with the premise.

Ed saw the concern. "Look, Chris, it's not as if Nash shows up there and he automatically springs this guy. The mullah may not want to help, or the Northern Alliance might not let him go. Either way, it buys us time, time that we can use to convince Langley to corral Nash and get him home."

"You forget one thing, Ed, and you've said it yourself: you can't buy Afghan loyalty, but you can rent it."

"Meaning?"

"You're sitting on how many millions in your office?"

Ed didn't answer.

"Nash is going to pinch your money to get where he needs to go, with or without you. I think it's in your best interest not to let that happen and for you to start screaming at Langley that Nash is putting your mission at jeopardy and he is about to take your funds to go fight his own war."

CHAPTER TEN

Panjshir Valley, Afghanistan

NASH'S EXPEDITIOUS INTENT of getting out of the JAWBREAKER compound by mid-morning floundered when the vehicle that was to transport the small team refused to start. While Nash paced around the vehicle, Chris, along with the Afghan driver had their hands deep inside the Toyota's engine compartment troubleshooting various power and fuel remedies, none of which to Nash's chagrin were quick fixes.

After an hour of knuckle scraping and yoga contortion under the vehicle, Chris surfaced with a fuel line that was blocked with copious amounts of dust and debris. He presented it to the driver who sprinted off in the direction of another like vehicle. However, an argument ensued between other Afghans who protested at an attempted cannibalization of a perfectly functioning pickup truck. While the ruckus continued, Chris snuck behind the group and slid under the vehicle unnoticed and got to work. Nash finally calmed down and looked on as Chris went about his task. Fearing that Chris would be spotted, Nash rushed to join the fray as the arguing Afghans took to pushing and shoving each other. Chris worked his tools as fast as he could and, hearing Nash's voice amid the chaos, hoped he was engaging with the ruse and thus distracting the group from his mini-mission while silently willing clenched fists to stay out of Nash's way.

No sooner had he extracted the fuel line from the pickup than he heard the thud of a body hitting the ground. As he feared, the vociferous altercation escalated past the monkey dance to full-on bone-to-flesh mashup as the voices disappeared. He contorted his head as best as he could from under the vehicle to see who the victim was and saw Nash lying on his back with his arms above his head, protecting himself from the melee above him. Chris extricated himself from under the carriage, stuffed the fuel line in his jacket, and then scrambled over to Nash. He grabbed both his arms and dragged him out of danger and watched as other Afghans arrived to break up the confrontation.

With the arrival of cooler temperaments, the antagonists broke off contact, straightened their clothing, and dusted themselves off. Chris by this time was kneeling over Nash who looked the worse for wear. Alex, a SAD team member and innocent bystander, saw what had happened and rushed over to their side with a bottle of water.

Chris took the water and doused Nash's face. "Mr. Nash, are you okay?"

"Did you get it?"

Chris smiled. "Yes, it's peeing fuel down the inside of my jacket."

Nash returned the smile with a grin of his own. "I'm not too old for a scrum."

"No, just too stupid. Are you hurt?"

"I'm fine. Help me up, would you?"

Chris and Alex pulled him up to the sitting position and then slowly up to stand. He wavered, and his legs buckled slightly, but his protégé caught him before he leaned too far in one direction.

"Let's get you back to the villa. I think you need to lie down for a while."

"I'm fine. Let's get out of here, Chris."

"Mr. Nash, it will take me another hour to put this thing together," he lied. "There's no point in you standing around to watch me. I'll come and get you when we're ready."

"Are you sure you got what you needed?"

"Yes, don't worry. I'll get us on the road as soon as I can."

"I could do with an aspirin actually; my head is starting to throb."

"I can help you with that," Alex offered. "Let's get you inside."

———※———

By the time Chris had made the necessary repairs to the Toyota, Ed made an appearance and said with protest that Alex would be joining the expedition to the Taliban prison. Chris was nonplussed by the news at first but on reflection was slightly relieved to have a capable backup if things went awry or another brawl were to break out. While the altercation had ended peaceably this time around, by Afghan stand- ards, he was not so sure they would escape with just a few bruised egos again.

Nash appeared at the top of the staircase carrying a large black bag that Chris assumed was more than a fistful of dollars. Alex strode past him with a tricked-out AR-15 strapped over his shoulder and a six-pack of water bottles in his right hand. His face was a grimace, and his taut body communicated to Chris that he had been volunteered for the assignment and would be an unenthusiastic player for the game ahead. Chris confirmed his supposition as Alex threw the water into the back of the truck and mounted without saying a word.

Don't get your knickers in a twist, ya big girl's blouse, Chris reflected.

Nash followed behind and then passed over the black bag to Chris. "If you need parts, here's some petty cash."

"That's some big tip money, Mr. Nash."

"That's our 'get out of jail money' . . . literally. Keep it in arm's reach if you would."

"I need to drive."

"What? Don't be stupid. It's not your job anymore, Chris; we have a driver. This is not our town. You're just going to piss off the locals if you carry on. Mount up. Let's get out of here while we still can."

Chris continued to remonstrate, "Mr. Nash—"

"I don't want to hear it. Let's go," he replied, fed up with delays.

Chris jumped into the bed of the pickup where he came face to face with Alex. *Don't get your panties in a bunch, little girl*, he thought as he watched the frustrated Brit make himself comfortable. Chris stared back at Alex, trying to gain some inkling of his mood, and could tell he was angry but was getting a dead man's stare in return. Alex looked Chris in the eye and received the same.

When the pickup finally lurched forward, the two passengers in the rear focused their attention on the gate and the road ahead. As soon as they left the compound, Chris positioned himself with his back to the cab and laid his AR-15 across his lap, signaling to Alex that he would provide rear watch. The SAD officer got the non-verbal communiqué and concentrated on the road to the front and sides.

Aside from the ridiculous road conditions, the journey to the Taliban prison was uneventful and quiet. Neither Alex nor Chris engaged in any conversation in the rear, copying the silence between Nash and the English-speaking driver in the cab. It seemed the start of the day put a damper on everyone's mood, and each hoped the earlier mechanical issues would be the worst of the problems they would encounter, as nobody really knew if this small mission would be met with success or downright failure.

The Toyota pickup came to a halt at a large, double wooden gate, which was set firmly in a high-walled structure. Chris propped himself up into a sitting position and began a scan of the area. The first thing that struck him was that the building was more of an ancient sandstone fort than a typical prison. He noted a few beady eyes looking down on the party below from the ramparts, tense body language and fingers dangerously close to triggers.

"Five," he said quietly to Alex.

"I have two fixed anti-aircraft guns trained on us from the hill to the east and west," he replied.

The driver and Nash got out of the cab, but Alex and Chris remained in their positions trying their best to look relaxed and not overly concerned.

"They are expecting us, right?" Chris asked in a whisper.

"Yeah, but it doesn't mean they trust us. Would you?"

Chris for some reason liked Alex's response and nodded. "Make that six pairs of eyes," he added, noting another lookie-loo that had shown up.

"I have a vehicle coming in behind us. We've parked too close to the gate; we may get boxed in."

"Should've let me drive," Chris stated.

Nash and the Afghan driver were challenged by a guard who came out of a door within the double gate. After a few minutes of discussion, the guard disappeared inside, closing and bolting the door behind him, leaving the four of them to wait. Alex's warning of the vehicle proved true as they parked within ten feet of the Toyota and thus blocked any speedy exit. Chris sped through mounting bad scenarios and worst-case options. He looked over at Alex who had a serious but in-control look and assumed he was doing the same mental exercise, which put Chris's mind at ease and once again made him feel grateful for the backup.

Chris made a closer assessment of his new partner. The tall, thin-waisted, broad-shouldered man espoused a military bearing and quiet attitude that probably took a lot of getting used to. He seemed all business and no frills, which suited Chris well. He didn't know anything about the man's background, skills, or mission with JAWBREAKER, but he knew such a man wouldn't be on the team just because he was standing around the office doing nothing but shooting the shit over coffee and donuts.

Alex Faber looked over at Chris from time to time to see if he could gauge his new business associate. So far, he had no complaints. When Ed Guild told him he would be going along on Nash's trip, he took the orders as such, but inside he was seething. The former Delta Tier 1 operator hadn't volunteered to the JAWBREAKER team to play security for a senior CIA officer; he had joined because his country was attacked and he had the skills, aptitude, and wherewithal to actually make a difference. Alex was no armchair quarterback, no corporate politician or desk jockey. For the fifteen years of military service he gave to his country, twelve of which were in Special Forces, he was trained to take life, save life, and protect life. A single man with no firm ties to family, he was therefore the perfect candidate for the CIA Special Activities Division. When the planes crashed into the World Trade Center, he was in the midst of a training exercise in Virginia with the

FBI's counterintelligence team and stopped what he was doing immediately. As the horde of evacuating CIA employees looked to the skies for the next hijacked plane while they sat gridlocked trying to get out of the parking lot of the Langley headquarters, he was one of the few who went in to work and waited at his desk for orders.

Watching Chris now, Alex couldn't help but notice the professional attitude the young Brit was taking. He enjoyed the spectacle and initiative Chris showed by fixing a transport issue but also admired his lack of panic. An obstacle was presented. He didn't wait for orders; he came up with a solution, and now they were together in the thick of things measuring up the Afghan prison guards, hoping none had a grudge against westerners. Alex saw that Chris was alert but not overly sensitive, which he liked, although there was a long way to go. He was intrigued to see what else the Brit could do.

"I reckon that if we're invited in, one of us needs to stay with the vehicle," Chris said out of the blue.

"Agreed, we don't need to start another fight to get more engine parts."

"I want to leave the cash out here. What do you think?"

"You're damn straight. It's my ass on the line with this as well. Frickin' accountant pukes want a strict balance sheet on any kind of payment, bribes included."

"So you volunteering to stay out here?"

"Guess so."

"Even if they don't take my weapons off me, I'm leaving them here with you. The last thing I want is the shit to hit the fan in there because I am the only one tooled up. Besides, I'm guessing there won't be enough room to swing a dead cat, let alone use the long gun."

"Roger."

"And if you hear me shouting Armageddon, it isn't because there's a hamster stuck up my arse."

The comment drew a faint smile from Alex. "I get the picture, Chris." They were still talking in hushed tones. "Don't leave me hanging here either. We need to be out of here before it gets dark. That road isn't fit for nighttime driving, especially if it rains."

Chris nodded. He felt the sooner this show got on the road, the sooner he would be able to relax.

After forty-five minutes of Nash's pacing, Chris's Afghan prison guard eyeball counting, and Alex's trigger-finger watching, the main gate opened up, and three unarmed Afghans exited with a table and two chairs. Alex and Chris swapped looks, both surprised by the small party. The men planted the items away from the main gate but well within eyeshot of both the guards on the ramparts and the covering pickup truck. Once the men had set up, they scurried back inside the fort, only to be passed by two armed Afghans escorting another man heading straight towards Nash.

"Well that makes sense," Chris whispered to Alex. "They don't want us causing an attraction inside the jail, which limits our exposure, and they don't want his buddies inside knowing what's going on out here."

"Smart."

Chris watched in anticipation as the "guest" took his seat and the Afghan guards stood back to let the conversation begin. Quickly measuring up the Afghan cleric, Chris first thought was that he looked fat, which piqued his interest and led him to study him closer. The religious man wore a clean white turban, black waistcoat over a slightly crumpled white salwar kameez, a traditional suit worn by many men and women in the country. He also sported a well-kept beard and stylish glasses that gave him an air of academia and authority. The cleric sat back in his chair with both hands placed on his knees, away from the table, neither leaning forward to show interest nor adversely lying back as though not engaged.

Finishing his snapshot of the man, Chris returned to scanning the area around him for potential threats and challenges. As he looked at the men around the gathering, he realized the cleric was the fattest person there. Most of the Afghans looked gaunt, malnourished, even sick in comparison, but this fat cat who was well dressed, clean, and healthy did not look like a prisoner under duress. Chris and Alex were out of earshot of the discussion but knew of the parameters that Nash would be working under. The first would be for the captive to tell him where the TRODPINT team was, and second would be for him to take them to TRODPINT.

"Water?" Alex offered, taking Chris's mind off things.

"Sure, thanks." He took the offered beverage. "Hurry up and wait I guess."

"They'll be done soon enough if it rains."

Chris looked to the skies, which were filling with a gang of low, graying cumulus clouds. The winds hadn't picked up yet, but he knew the signs. "Hour, two at the most."

"We're going to get wet, if not here, then on the road."

"And that's why I wanted to drive," Chris almost sang.

Alex was perplexed. *What is it with this guy and driving?* Then he continued his security duties and watched as some of the Afghans in the guard pickup were about to fall asleep.

Arlington, Texas

Abdo Ihab had been sitting in the parking lot overlooking the baseball diamond at the Mike Lewis Park for almost twenty minutes when a large, dark pickup truck with tinted windows pulled up beside him. Unsure of the vehicle, Abdo strained to keep his eyes looking forward, but beads of sweat ran down the side of his temple as he willed himself to keep calm. Trying to use his peripheral vision, his face contorted making his unease worse and his outward appearance suspect. Without moving his head, he looked up into the mirror with Ping-Pong eyes, then straight ahead, and then down at the gear shift. The coded crumpled note in his hand instructing him to be at this specific spot was getting damp from the warmth of his nervous hands. With the engine still running, he was just a few seconds from selecting reverse and hitting the gas.

Jawad exited the passenger side of pickup truck and opened the door to Abdo's car. "Slide over," he ordered.

Abdo's stomach had dropped three floors as his door was opened, but then he regained its equilibrium as he recognized the face. Still astonished to see the man, he obeyed the command but struggled to get into the passenger seat. Jawad gave him a moment to settle, turned off the engine, and then leaned over to give the man a hug.

"Abdo, it's been a long time. Peace be upon you, my friend."

"And upon you, Jawad. You have surprised me, but it is truly good to see you."

The embrace was warm, and the words were sincere as both men who had been friends before colleagues looked each other in the eyes and reminisced for a few seconds.

Jawad broke the silence with a smile. "You look well. You are healthy, I see."

"I am, I am. I have had a few minor things over the years, but it is God's will. Praise be his name that I am so fortunate. And you, my friend, you are well, I trust?"

"Of course, Abdo, of course. I have also been blessed."

The pleasant conversation continued for a few minutes more, but Jawad wanted to get down to business. While they were talking about Abdo's immediate family, Jawad abruptly changed the subject.

"Abdo, my friend, you have become lazy. Your security is in jeopardy."

Shocked at the intervening of social protocol, he replied with genuine astonishment, "What? Wait . . . what are you talking about, Jawad?"

"The FBI is monitoring the mosque. They are closing in. It is just a matter of time before they have cause to search and investigate activities there." Jawad looked deep into his friend's eyes. His voice was direct and disapproving; his look was hostile. "Abdo, you were told to leave before the Big Wedding. Now here we are, and I am disappointed. Do you know that I have been watching you?" He let the accusation hang for a second but didn't give Abdo a chance to respond. "Of course not. You have become sluggish, careless, stupid. That is not what I expected from you!"

"Jawad, they are not looking at us. We have been very careful."

"Not careful enough, I fear." Jawad's voice was raised in borderline anger, but he managed to hold his rage, lest push his friend too far on the defensive. He needed to gain confidence and compliance. Jawad dropped his accusatory manner slightly. "This company you have created, Abdo, Docu Points, it is too close to Imam al-Hallak and his fundraising actions. I have come to warn you, to get you to leave, because the imam will be the focus of the authority's attention, and he cannot be the one to bring you and the organization down."

"Then you must warn him too, Jawad," he pleaded out of concern for the religious leader.

"No!" Jawad barked. "He has brought this on himself. He is not my concern, but my question is how much does he truly know?"

"He knows of the Global Relief Foundation."

"This is the organization that sends you money from overseas?" Jawad hypothesized.

"Yes, from our brothers in France, Belgium, Bosnia, Serbia, Albania. All that money comes to my company."

"Which you pass on to the imam?"

"Yes, some, but not all funds. We have to show earnings and pay taxes, which we do in compliance with the local authorities. The rest goes back to the organization."

Jawad paused and looked out of the window. He was aware of the basics of the shell company, but he needed to cover each base. Looking at his friend again, he said, "You must show me all this information, Abdo, and you must do it now, for tomorrow you will leave this place and leave America."

Exasperated, Abdo reeled at the mere suggestion. He shifted uncomfortably in his seat. "Leave, but where? What of my family?"

"You and your family will be safe. First, we will get you back to the kingdom, and then on to Yemen, where you will rest. You may settle there with your family, and we will have other opportunities for you to continue the jihad."

Agitated, Abdo reverted his eyes from Jawad and towards the baseball field. His fate was being taken out of his hands. He felt deflated as he was losing control of his part of the operation. "But how will I get there? The FBI, you said they will be watching."

Jawad reached over and touched Abdo's wrist gently, which made him turn back to look at his commander. "This is what you will do," he said calmly. "Do not tell your family they are leaving until an hour before. You will leave everything behind. Pack only what is necessary and do not tell them where you are going. You will drive to Phoenix. I will give you an address, and you will wait there until instructed to board a plane."

"But how—"

"Do not worry about the details, my friend. A plane from the kingdom is being sent for our queen. I have space reserved for you and your family. Now, we have business to attend to. Believe me, my friend, I take no pleasure in doing this, but we must go over every detail. I want to ensure that enough security measures are taken so you and your family are safe and our organization is protected. Do you understand?"

"Of course, Jawad, of course."

"Now tell me of our new guests. How soon will they leave Europe?"

A confused, Abdo replied, "They have left, Jawad. They left a few days ago. You didn't know?"

It was Jawad's turn to look surprised and taken aback. "What are you talking about? That is not the plan. They are too far ahead of schedule. What . . . how did this happen?"

"Omar."

"What about him?"

"He sent the passports through the diplomatic pouch to each of the embassies. They were collected, and now they are on the way. I thought you knew. I thought you ordered it so."

"I have been travelling for a few days. Something must have caused him to act, perhaps the FBI. We have had more than one encounter with them recently." Jawad was lost in silent thought for a few seconds. Abdo shifted nervously in his seat again, but the intelligence officer seemed relaxed and contemplative. "That is precisely why we need to conclude our business here, Abdo. This is surely another sign they are closing in."

"What of Omar? Will he be safe?"

"Of course, of course, he has diplomatic immunity. He will always be protected from the authorities."

"What of the passports? Will they stand up?"

"Yes, yes, that is not our concern now. If they are stopped at the borders, there is nothing we can do. They have been trained well enough not to talk. What we need to do is ensure that all of your contacts are accounted for and the equipment that our guests need is in place. I fear that tonight will be a long night. We have much work to do. Come, let us begin. Give me your office address. My driver will go ahead and secure the area. And, Abdo, pray for us. Pray to Allah, praise be his name, that the FBI is not there waiting for us."

"Who are these people on this list, Abdo?" Jawad was reviewing a document before stacking it in a pile for Abdo to shred.

Abdo sauntered over to his friend while holding a sheaf of papers and glanced at the list of ten names. "They are close supporters of the imam."

"Support how? Are they devout followers? Are they active participants? What, Abdo?"

"It's mainly finance. They each have extensive contacts throughout America at many other mosques. They are close to the imam, but I do meet them on occasion. They have been very generous and supportive of our cause."

"How much do they know about our current operation?"

"Nothing."

Jawad was pensive. The unconcerned body language and the quick response of his friend put him off. "Abdo, you cannot lie to me. Both our lives are at stake. How much do they know?"

An edgy silence captured both men. Jawad bore steel daggers into Abdo's eyes but waited for him to speak.

"Jawad, I did not have enough resources . . ." he blabbered, almost stumbling over his words, knowing he was in the wrong.

"Tell me!" Jawad shouted.

"They asked to assist. I have used them for our logistics for our guests, nothing more."

"And we know nothing of these men . . ."

"But they have sworn an allegiance to our leader. They are good Muslims, Jawad. They can be trusted."

Jawad sprang past the shredder and grabbed Abdo by the throat, forcing him backward. Then Jawad wrapped the backside of his right ankle around Abdo's left, making him stumble and fall heavily to the floor. "What have you done!" he screamed into his face.

Abdo panicked as air was squeezed out of his body. He clawed at the strong hands around his throat and thrashed with his legs, begging in his mind for the violence to stop.

Jawad released his grip slightly to stop the flailing arms and legs of his victim. He placed his knees on Abdo's chest but still held onto his throat. "What have you done to us, Abdo? These men are not part of our organization. This was not sanctioned. Don't you see, you fool?" The last words were said in pity, in remembrance of the time the men had been very close friends—playing soccer growing up in the back streets of Riyadh, both joining the police academy, serving as attendants at the other's wedding.

Abdo yanked Jawad's hands away and then managed to get the weight off his chest and roll away from his attacker. He gasped for breath while still holding his throat. "I have done nothing wrong," he spluttered. "It is you that is the problem. You were never here. Where have you been?"

Jawad looked hard at him. "What?" he asked in disbelief.

"I was given command of this operation while you . . . you were fraternizing with our enemies. It is the organization that does not know who *you* are colluding with. It is *you* we should be wary of. What have *you* been doing?"

"Abdo, Omar was supposed to be running this operation, not you, my friend. You are too valuable. He has his position and consular protection. That is why I am here. This operation needs to move forward, but Abdo, I cannot emphasize any more than I already have: we need to shut this down and get you out of here. You are not safe."

"You are not answering me," Abdo pushed, realizing he was being placated. "Where have you been? It's been years since I have seen you? What have you been doing?"

"Abdo, my friend," Jawad said in resigned compassion as they both sat across from each other on the floor, Abdo with his back to a wall still nursing his neck, Jawad kneeling as if in prayer, "I do not know where your suspicion is coming from, but it is unfounded. I need not explain myself to you as you may have forgotten that my mandate is strategic and yours is purely operational. Whom I fraternize with is not your business, be they friend or foe. I do not answer to you or Omar. On the contrary, it is operational management who need to follow my lead and my orders. Once again, I reiterate I am here to help, and we still have business to conclude. Now if you don't mind taking your eyes off that pair of scissors, we should get this mess cleaned up."

Abdo remained silent and contemplated what he had just heard but was prompted by Jawad, who was eager to get things in motion. "I will investigate these other men in good time. If I feel they are a danger to the organization, I will deal with them personally." He looked down at his Cartier watch. "But we are running out of time. You need to give me everything. You need to go home soon." Jawad waved his hands around him. "This jumble of paper, I will take it all. You also need to give me anything that is electronically saved, Abdo. We cannot risk the authorities searching you when you board the plane. Find me some garbage sacks. I will get my driver to help."

"What if I don't want to leave, Jawad? What if I want to stay here in America?" Abdo replied casually.

"Don't be such a fucking imbecile!" Jawad shouted at the top of his voice, his temper overcoming his sympathetic feelings towards his friend.

"I . . . I just . . ."

"I just nothing, Abdo. What is wrong with you?" Jawad continued to rant, "You are not this stupid. You are not this naïve. How could you possibly think that is remotely possible? What has gotten into your mind?"

"I can make it work. I have papers, Jawad. I can stay and remain in place. I can continue the fight from here. I will leave Texas if the authorities are closing. I have new identities for my family. I can go anywhere," he pleaded.

Jawad looked at Abdo in disbelief and shook his head. His back warm from sweat, he was feeling tired, and his head was aching. Exasperated, he let out a long sigh. "That is not going to work, and you know it."

"I had nothing to do with the Big Wedding, Jawad. There is nothing for the Americans to tie me to that."

"Quite true, the Big Wedding has caught them off guard, but this new operation, it will bring America to its knees. It will force the Americans to recoil and take stock. But their wrath will be immense. It will be like nothing we have witnessed before. Believe me, Abdo, none of us will be safe in this country, no matter who we say we are."

Abdo stared back at Jawad, not sure of what was true or what was a lie. There was a knock on the door, and Jawad rose to let his driver enter. Abdo, feeling dejected had nothing to say, had no will to help in the clean-up, and sat as if in squalor, depressed at his own state.

Jawad stood above his friend. "Your mission has ended, Abdo. You have your new orders. Give me the files that I need and go home. You will get a phone call, and you will get on a plane. Do you understand?"

Abdo succumbed to the inevitable and nodded his head.

Jawad knelt beside him and put his hand on his shoulder. "Abdo, you have done well. God willing, Operation Najd will succeed, America will suffer, you will be hailed a hero, and our beloved sheik will call on you again. He has other missions for you. Come." He helped Abdo off the floor and said, "Give me five minutes more of your time and then go home."

FBI Field Office, Los Angles

Nick Seymour's snoring was enough for his FBI colleagues to initially find funny, but after thirty minutes of rising and falling volumes, they were becoming annoyed and agitated. More than one considered waking him from his slumber, but everyone at the field office understood and was feeling the same tiredness and the same level of exhaustion, so they turned a sympathetic, deaf ear.

Suddenly, Nick woke with a start. Raising his head from his desk, he wiped a trail of drool from his lower lip. He rubbed his face, ran a hand through his hair, and then felt disappointed that his nap had not erased his blinding headache. Nick got up from his chair and stretched his arms above his head to hear a distant jeer.

"It's awake. Yay, now we can all get a bit of peace and quiet."

Nick tried to identify the voice, but another jibe came across the cubes, "I'm going to hog-tie you and slam you in my trunk if you do that again." There were a few more comments and giggles that Nick paid no attention to. His head was pounding, so he headed for the break room for a stretch and to find some Tylenol. As he began his search, a female agent poked her head through the door.

"Rhonda, line 3."

"Thanks," he said, but it was too late; she was gone. Nick grabbed the phone from its cradle on the break room wall and tapped the lit line 3.

"Hi, Rhonda, how's it going?"

"I'm hot, hungry, and dirty. Need I say more?"

"Same shit, different day then?"

"You got that right. Listen, I got the name from that passport. Thought you could run that down for me."

"Yeah, hang on a second. Let me get something to write." Nick pulled a pen from his shirt pocket and scribbled the name on a notepad hanging on the wall.

"Mean anything to you?"

"Nope. As soon as I get back to my desk, I'll run it through the mill to see what I can find out. What did the scene look like?"

Rhonda went on to describe the mess that she found and the particulars of who found what, where, and when. After a few minutes, she threw something new at Nick. "We have another spin on the ball, Nick. You probably didn't hear, but an agent was killed in a car accident in Phoenix recently. Someone's been going through his files, and something interesting popped up."

"I heard about the accident. We may have crossed paths while I was there, but what was he working on?"

"The Scottsdale Police Department arrested a major from the Saudi military a few weeks back on drug charges. Apparently, he was also hiring hookers for whatever reason."

"I heard this while I was there. Go on."

"Anyway, the Arab was acting as a CI for us, Leroy Lewis, the agent who died, was about to drop him to focus on the trade center attacks but got an interesting nugget that sparked my interest."

"Shoot"

"Your man, Jawad, told the CI that there is a plan to get the Saudi royal family out of the States by plane."

"Hmm, that's understandable, Rhonda. I'm sure our government won't have a problem with that and would want to put some distance between us and the Saudis, given the number of terrorists they spawned."

"I agree, Nick, but the CI's name is Major Karim Basrawi. He's with the Saudi army, and this guy says he was told to reserve five seats on the plane. Now according to Leroy, he stated that Basrawi asked who needed the seats but was told it was not his concern, leading me to believe that Basrawi knows exactly who needs to be on the plane besides the occupants of five seats."

"So, let me follow your line here. Are you trying to say that your five John Does are the five that were being shipped out?"

"I'm guessing so, Nick. And the other thing, if we get positive IDs from LAX that match my five, then we have a serious problem."

Nick stared at the white wall in the break room but six inches from his face and filled the momentary void in conversation, "That someone facilitated a plane ride for them out of the country and then somebody stopped them."

"Precisely."

"Shit, Rhonda, this opens up more than a can of worms. How the hell did it get to this point? How come this CI intel never made it to us?"

"C'mon, Nick, you know as well as I do. With the lack of decent computers, we couldn't handle all the intel even before the 9/11 attacks. Have you been to my desk? Did you see the 386? It was built in 1994," she complained. "I've been hearing stories that guys in the office were working from their home computers so they could solve crimes with local law enforcement. So it's no surprise to me that stuff doesn't get to us. Leroy's intel had to be pulled from one system, copied on another, then printed and faxed to our office; then someone called me and gave it to me over the phone. It's no wonder things get lost."

"I know. It's not much better overseas. It's actually an embarrassment dealing with our foreign counterparts. But look, we're getting off track." Nick's head was still throbbing. The wall in front of him was about to invade his personal space, so he turned his attention to the ceiling, then the floor, and then the kitchen countertop just so he could regain his focus. He hadn't eaten for a while either. "The prevailing thought around here right now is that the five LAX guys were a cell that aborted its planned attack, which is great, but it means someone gave them an escape plan. To me it looks as if that exit strategy went sideways and they met their Maker in the desert, which in my opinion is fitting. But anyway, if these five are not getting on a plane, does that mean there is now space for five others?"

"Good question, Nick. I think we need to get a passenger manifest."

"Now that's going to be tricky. How the hell are we going to get that? We're going to have to bring State into this."

"Unless we can lean on the CI," Rhonda proposed.

"Unless we can lean on the CI," he repeated, bouncing the prospect around in his already busy brain.

"Nick, I can't. Ron Hilts has me all over this one; I'm going to be here for days."

"I know, I get it. I'll go see him and ask for some more manpower, which I don't think I am going to get. All my guys who were working on Omar have been re-tasked. I'm on my own for now."

"Let me talk to him, Nick. We were tight once; he still owes me."

"Thanks, Rhonda. It's a stretch, I know, but I need to take one more look at Omar before I can head to Phoenix. I have a gut feeling about the guy, and there's more I need to know before I get too comfortable leaving. I'll call the Phoenix office as well and see if we can get some eyeballs on this Basrawi guy. But we need to figure out more about this flight. I can at least make some calls back to DC on that one."

"What about your man, Jawad?"

"Jawad told Basrawi to hold some seats on a plane, which leads me to believe he knew of the LAX five, meaning he is deep into this as far as it goes. Here's the scary part. If he is legit, the Saudi government knew of the 9/11 attacks and is covering its ass by getting as many out as possible. If he is dirty, then he is a major player, and he is trying to clean up the mess."

"What if there is more?" she asked.

"What do you mean?"

"What if there are more cells out there or more attacks on the way?"

CHAPTER ELEVEN

FBI Field Office, Los Angles

AN HOUR AFTER NICK SEYMOUR hung up the phone with Rhonda, he stared at his notes not seeing what was before him. He'd been racking his brain without sufficient breaks to find a link between Jawad, Omar, and the five passengers in the shot-up minivan. There was something missing, but the more he bounced ideas around, the less information he was getting in return. He ended up drawing the two names on a piece of paper and a circle around them. Then he wrote five passengers in the middle of the circle and willed an answer to spring from the pad, but nothing was coming. He looked at the wall, then the paper, then the wall, then back to the paper, and read and reread what he'd written, which basically amounted to nothing, so he began to whisper the writings to himself, "Omar, Jawad, passengers, Omar . . . Jawad . . . passengers." Nick paused to start his Ping-Pong game of wall and paper again and then whispered, "Passengers, Jawad, Omar . . . wait, wait, wait!"

"Passengers!" he said out loud to no one. "The five dead were passengers, so the driver was the killer." He continued to himself and then mulled that thought further. *The driver . . . the driver. What the hell was it that Chris told me one time? Need intel, go talk to the drivers. They go everywhere, they see everybody, and they all talk amongst themselves.*

Nick grabbed the phone, dialed the receptionist, and asked for the name of the local counterintelligence agent. The girl transferred the call. As she did, he heard a phone ringing across the cube farm. A tired voice came on the line, and Nick stood up to see if he could identify the agent he was trying to reach.

"This is Stan."

"Hey, Stan, this is Nick Seymour. Can you do me a favor and stand up? I think we're in the same area."

On command, a tall, balding man wearing a blue shirt and loosened red tie stood up on the other side of the room while holding a phone.

"Can we meet in the middle? I'd like to pick your brains about something."

"What's your name again?"

"Yeah, uh, Nick Seymour."

Stan dropped back down to his seat. "Look, Nick, I'm really swamped right now. I've got four layers of crap on my desk. I've got to get to that before I can rescue the pizza that's been there since last night."

"I need just a few seconds. I'll bring the coffee, and I'll take that pizza off your hands."

"What's this about anyways?"

"The LA Saudi consulate."

Stan's interest was piqued. "Come on over."

Nick made himself comfortable in the spare chair in Stan's cube.

"So what are you working on?" Stan asked his visitor.

"Well, like everyone else around here, running down leads for the attacks, but I'm working on something with Rhonda right now."

"The John Does in the desert?"

"Yep. I've also been chasing a Saudi intelligence officer for a while now who has ties to the Saudi consulate."

"You've got my attention, but give me a story; I need some context."

Nick liked Stan's approach. He was quiet but direct and possibly a sympathetic ear to Nick's quest for answers.

After a few minutes of background story from Nick, Stan rescued a note pad from under the debris of his cluttered desk. "So what do you need from me?"

"I'm assuming the consulate has a number of diplomatic cars. Can you tell me how many?"

"Stand by." Stan swiveled in his chair to his desk and pulled a file from a drawer. He opened it up and skimmed through while Nick watched in shock and awe.

"This is not on a computer?"

"Sure, if you have twenty minutes to wait while the sucker reboots." Stan found the relative page. "Here you go. Old school, nothing better than the human touch, if you ask me. I make thirteen."

"I'm guessing that at least one or two are for the consulate general himself and the rest are fleet vehicles."

"Good guess, but I think some are probably assigned to various diplomats for official use, and I suppose there's a pool to choose from."

"Am I right in thinking the consulate general would have his own driver? If so, any idea of how many other drivers there are?"

Stan replaced the file and then retrieved another. He went through the same motions.

Nick shook his head in disbelief. *So much for automation*, he thought.

"Here we are . . . there's a top dog driver then five others, none of which is a Saudi national, which is no surprise. The last entry here, which is almost three years old, states that there were four Egyptians, one Yemeni, and one Tunisian, but all naturalized citizens."

"Shit," Nick conceded. "The chances of getting one of them as a CI is virtually nil. Any dirt in the file, traffic violations, naughty habits, etc.?"

"You're grasping at straws, Nick. These Middle Easterners are tight. Even after the attacks, these guys won't want to rock the boat, especially with the Saudis having deep pockets to pay their wages."

"I've got to find a way of tracking Omar, Stan."

"Well, if Omar is hiding behind a diplomatic cloak, then you can bet your house he is driving a diplomatic vehicle right now, and yes, before you ask, I have the plates, and no, you cannot take the list."

Stan fished another file out and passed it over to Nick, who repressed the fruitless request for a printout and scribbled each license plate number as quickly as he could. "Is this address at the top of the page the consulate?"

"Sure is. That's where all the cars are registered."

"But what about this other address?"

"That's probably the motor pool, where the drivers hang out, garage the cars overnight, that type of thing."

Nick gave a wan smile. He was definitely throwing a pebble in the ocean trying to hit a fish, any fish. "So by process of elimination, I can actually figure out which vehicle is being used by Omar."

"Jesus, Nick, you want a bungee cord to stretch that further? What's the deal with him anyway? You got a personal vendetta?"

"Stan, I lost Jawad twice, and five people are dead. Omar is in arm's reach. I just need to pin him down. I need to figure out how or if the Saudi government is involved and how deep it goes. I have to start somewhere."

Stan looked at Nick for a second longer. He could tell the man was struggling—he looked bedraggled, frustrated, and worn. The guy needed a break. "Well, now thinking about it, I did see something the other day, let me . . ." Stan dove into his pile of papers on his desk and retrieved a report. "Here's something that may interest you."

Nick sat up a little straighter in his chair. A flash of hope danced in his eyes, and his face lit up, even if faint.

"I've got this from an LAPD contact of mine. It's a bit of a story, so bear with me." Stan rattled off the usual time and place headers, reporting agencies, and reporting officers and then got down to the meat and potatoes. "There's a Filipino guy that goes by the name of Romeo Washington. Mr. Washington works for the Saudi consulate as a maintenance/custodial worker who mainly works at their offices, but now and again he worked at various residences of the diplomats. It turns out that poor Mr. Washington had a fire at his home some time ago, which destroyed most of his property. Now the Saudis are known to be quite benevolent from time to time and decided to help the guy out, and even some of the diplomats' families decided to pitch in."

Nick was engaged but couldn't understand where this was going. He was still leaning forward, waiting for the punch line.

"Mr. Washington," Stan continued paraphrasing the report, "was asked by one of the diplomats what he needed to get himself back on his feet, as the man had a family to care for and no viable domicile. So the Saudi consulate found him some decent temporary lodging, and then Washington provided a list of things that he would need to get set up, beds, couches, TV, etc. Here's where it gets interesting, Nick. One of the more astute diplomats questioned the long list of items he was asking for, like who needs ten mattresses, six TVs, dozens of blankets and pillows, that sort of thing. Then someone from the police department also heard about the charity and was about to chip in but held off as a fire marshal deemed the fire questionable and under investigation. Long story short, Mr. Washington was using his home as an illegal immigration mill. It turns out that he was a link in a chain that stemmed from Central and South America for illegals who were transiting from the border to LA and onwards to other parts of the US. At one point, he had space for about twenty illegals in his basement before his house caught on fire. The theory is that one of his illegals started the blaze, don't know why, but the fire started in the basement."

The news sparked Nick's interest at last. "Wow, Stan, that sounds like a little embarrassing for the Saudis. Where is he now?"

"Locked up pending trial, but get this, Nick. He's been trying to sing. This all went down a few days before the New York and Pentagon attacks, so the case took a back seat. None of us here had time to follow up as it should be an INS issue, but he was trying to tell investigators that he had something he wanted to share."

"Let me guess, another perp with a story for a deal."

"I guess so, but this is where you might come in. He says he has something on the Saudis."

Panjshir Valley, Afghanistan

Richard Nash was sitting in the front seat of the white Toyota Land Cruiser with another bag of money lying on his lap, tolerating the boredom while waiting for the Taliban cleric to be released from the Northern Alliance prison. It had been almost twenty-four hours since Nash and his compatriots had been sitting in the same position.

However, yesterday they came away $50,000 lighter, and the prison warden walked home $50,000 richer. The heavy cash bag contained $200,000 as an initial down payment for the cleric's cooperation in getting Nash's team across Taliban lines and into a safe environment to begin the investigation of locating the CIA TRODPINT team. Nash, aware of Afghan negotiating contracts, was fully expecting to dole out more money to get where he needed to go and to financially tempt the TRODPINT team to once again put their trust in the CIA and hunt down bin Laden. As such, the remaining $750,000 in the bag would be used to bribe, cajole, entice, and woo potential allies or turn skeptics to the American side, even if only on a temporary basis.

In addition to the extra cash, the expedition to find the TROD-PINT team required extra resources and manpower. Hence, a second vehicle was added to the mission, along with two Northern Alliance soldiers and a driver. Nash, who learned from the previous day's melee at the Afghan compound over spare Toyota parts, exercised his authority over Ed Guild and demanded more reliable forms of transportation. Although not new, two white Land Cruisers, which were probably the most sought-after vehicles in all of Afghanistan, were provided by the Northern Alliance, along with a promissory note of replacement, eagerly signed by Nash guaranteeing three new Land Cruisers would be delivered in exchange for the two used vehicles. It was a lousy deal, but Nash, relegated to being a beggar rather than a chooser, wanted very much to get away from JAWBREAKER so he could get his mission underway before the director of the CIA changed his mind and had him forcibly extracted from Afghanistan.

As it was, Nash was given seventy-two hours to locate TROD-PINT, and if successful, he would coordinate the efforts of landing a Special Forces team into the area with the remit of pinpointing bin Laden's location. However, Nash was told unequivocally by the director that his mission would end as soon as the first American soldier's boots hit the ground. Nash, grateful for the chance to redeem his past decisions, agreed but in secret held onto the hope that he would be the one to deliver the Arab's head to the president of the United

States.

"Do you ever regret hitching your horse to my wagon?"

Chris looked over in amazement at the question. Nash was in the passenger seat of the first Land Cruiser. Chris, five feet away from the vehicle, providing security didn't reply but looked at Nash with an air of curiosity.

"You could have stayed at the embassy," Nash continued. "I've put you through a lot, and there is a good chance things are going to get worse before they get better."

"Mr. Nash—"

"Why do you keep calling me that?" he interrupted, agitated. "You know my name."

"I call you that out of respect, Mr. Nash. You know that. Back at the embassy, that is how I was introduced to you, and that suited me fine. As far as I am concerned, I still work for you; only the job title has changed."

"But you've come a long way since being just a driver, Chris. Do you have any regrets?"

Chris contemplated the question for a few seconds before answering. He pretended to survey his area of security responsibility, glancing over at Alex from time to time. His foremost thought was of his late girlfriend, who had covertly worked for Nash without Chris's knowledge. He thought of his actions at Nash's house when he had interrogated him with a Taser, demanding answers as to why he had put her in danger. He thought of the words he had said to him after the affair at a beach bar in the Honduras and how much he had wanted to slash his throat open in his anger and frustration.

Chris looked over at Nash again. It was hard seeing the tired man in front of him who slouched in the passenger seat. But Nash was right. He had come a long way from British soldier, to US embassy driver, to saving an ambassador's life, to falling in love, to rescuing a man he once wanted to kill. Chris didn't know where this line of questioning was going, but he focused on a key word that Nash mentioned.

"Regrets . . .," Chris chimed, "I have a few . . . but then again too few to mention."

Nash smiled for the first time in a long time and then shook his head.

"I did what I had to do," the Brit continued to sing. "And saw it through without exemption."

Nash put up his hands in surrender. "Okay, okay, Chris, spare me the Sinatra songs. As much as I love them, not right now, please," he jested.

"Mr. Nash, it's been a long time since you've smiled. It's good to see some color back in your cheeks. I . . . I worry about you," Chris stated sincerely.

Thank you, Chris, but I am fine, really. There's no need to worry about me. This altitude, this dust, it gets the better of us older folk. But that's not the topic of discussion, is it? You've deflected."

"Do I have regrets?"

Nash nodded, anxious for a response.

"Regret is not the right word. Would things have been easy for me if I never would have met you? Probably. Would I have been comfortable working as a driver at the embassy for the rest of my life? No." Chris wondered how much he should share, how much longer they had before the cleric emerged from the prison. He averted his eyes away from Nash again, but walked backwards and closer to the vehicle while continuing his vigilant security duties.

"My ambitions were always pretty simple, Mr. Nash," he said over his shoulder. "I always wanted to be a soldier, and I knew I had to get an education, which I have, and I always wanted to travel the world, which I've done. I never knew the CIA would be the vehicle to get me to achieve those goals. But in all honesty, all this stuff, here and now, I wouldn't swap it for anything."

Nash knew he was being forthright and confident in his answers. He knew Chris had very few ideological reasons for what he was doing, but since they had been in Afghanistan, he felt that his protégé had changed. He could tell Chris was more at home—totally in his element—with a rifle in his hands, happy with dirt under his finger nails, content with meager rations and few amenities. Nash was hoping to groom him into being a deep-cover case officer for the agency. But what Chris had done without hesitation with the SAS, how he had dispatched a CIA mole, how he had killed terrorists in Bonn and Northern Ireland, made Nash pause and reconsider what he really wanted to do with Christopher Morehouse. "What do you want to do when you get back to the States, Chris?"

"I'll have a shit, shower, shave, and then pack a bag, ready for the next job, Mr. Nash. If you want me, that is."

Nash grinned, the exact answer he expected. "No ladies in waiting?"

Chris turned around to face Nash. "Like you don't know the answer to that one."

"I've been kind of out of the picture for a while, Chris. You know that," he smirked.

"And you know everything about me, Mr. Nash," he insisted. "You know I'm single, my brother is in jail, and both my parents are gone. You are well aware of my last girlfriend's demise, and you know full well I don't commit to anyone, so there's no need to be sly with me."

They both looked at each other, each with a mutual understanding and respect for one another. Nash had hoped Chris had gotten over the loss of his girlfriend and wished he would find someone someday but not now, not when he needed him most. Nash wanted to get back on track, wanted to address the current situation with him, needing his full attention.

"This situation that we are in, and I don't mean us, I mean . . . the United States is at war, Chris."

Chris gazed once more at Nash, who looked serious and back to his grump demeanor.

"It's going to be a war that will go on for a very long time. In fact, it's going to take years before anything is resolved in this country. That's why we need to find bin Laden. If we don't, then we will need to eradicate the Taliban, and we—you, I, and JAWBREAKER—are the pointy tip of a spear that hasn't even been invented yet." Nash paused for a second to collect his thoughts. "I don't think even the Pentagon has come up with a viable strategy to get such a campaign fully functional and effective and is probably scrambling to pull its shit together. It's easy for us to say get some troops in here pronto, but the amount of crap they have to think of to make that happen is unfathomable."

"Meaning what, Mr. Nash?"

"We are going to be on our own for a while."

"If I recall, the director gave us seventy-two hours. When will the bombing campaign start?"

"That, my young friend, is one of our dilemmas. We don't know, and the Pentagon is not saying. We are going to cross enemy lines, and we need to establish a safe area where we can operate from. The Special Forces teams will coordinate with JAWBREAKER, and that is why we have Alex on board. He will be the one that will keep us alive if the bombing starts while we are still out there looking for TRODPINT."

Chris remembered and envisioned the black-and-white grainy images of pinpoint airstrikes from the Gulf War. "And he will call in a strike if we find bin Laden, right?"

"No . . . I want you to go in and kill him, Chris."

Chris turned away from Nash. He had no words, no smart comebacks, no song lyrics to lighten the mood. He walked a few feet away from the Land Cruiser and dove deep into a soul-searching mood. *Jesus Christ, what the hell have I gotten into now? Has he lost the plot or what?* Chris stared down at the ground for a moment and kicked the dirt in front of him. He began to change positions with his rifle, first pointing downwards to his right thigh and then nervously slinging the rifle on his back. He bent down to the ground, picked up a rock, and threw it a few feet in front of him. Trying in vain to keep his mind on his job, Chris looked around for threats, but Nash's statement didn't sit well with him.

Who the hell does he think I am? Bin Laden? Really, bin Laden? So I'm an assassin now. Is that it? Like I've got the tools for that shit. Chris stood and kicked around some rocks, taking away his concentration of what was going on around him. He nervously scratched the back of his head and then removed his sunglasses to rub his eyes. Taking a deep breath, he looked over to Alex who gave him a nod as a pointer to look in a certain direction. Chris replaced his glasses and saw Alex's concern as an old man and a young boy were pushing a cart full of fruit and other supplies up the rocky road towards the fort.

Chris, pulled his rifle off his back and held the pistol grip firmly with his right hand, trigger finger resting on the trigger guard. He placed his left palm under the rifle stock but kept the barrel pointed down. Then he began his scan of the man, first checking the hands, then the eyes, and then the feet. Chris took his level of awareness down a notch as he recognized the man from the day before, but he scrutinized the cart the same way a jeweler would eyeball a diamond. Glancing over at Alex, he could see that he too was running the same mental exercise, silently evaluating the potential target, readying himself for an unseen danger.

The fruit vendor waved at the Northern Alliance soldiers, and a few friendly comments were exchanged, so Chris slung his rifle back over his shoulder and frowned slightly as the man and boy labored slowly up the hill with their wares gingerly perched on the decrepit cart that had seen better days.

The young boy, startled by Chris's stare, slipped on the dusty track and let go of the cart. The old man, struggling between helping the youngster and balancing his transport, was now in danger of toppling his load. Chris strode forward quickly and grasped the cart with two firm hands. The old man, scared at first, soon understood he was being helped, picked up the young lad, and berated him for not holding on. Chris never let go; rather he began to push the cart with the old man towards the old gate of the fort, which opened slowly with a long, rusty creak.

The old man began blabbering, which Chris assumed was thanks, but before the fruit vendor disappeared into the prison, Chris, grabbed some apples off the cart and gestured, "Okay, okay?"

The vendor smiled a toothless grin and blabbered something more in reply, which Chris took as an affirmative response. With his bounty in hand, he returned to the Land Cruisers and tossed one over to Alex and then gave one to Nash.

"You're too kind sometimes, Chris," Nash complimented.

"Make your bloody mind up. A second ago, you wanted me to kill bin Laden!" he snapped.

It took another thirty minutes before the creaking gate of the fort opened again. Chris walked over to the Land Cruiser and gave it a tap with his knuckle to wake a dozing Nash in the front seat. As Nash blinked his eyes to clear his vision, he saw before him the Taliban cleric walking casually out of the prison. In tow was a young man carrying a backpack on his shoulders and another bag pressed firmly between his arms and his chest.

"Mr. Nash, what's this bollocks? Did you know he had a sidekick?"

Nash stumbled over his words, and blinked his eyes open. "No, no . . . I have no idea."

As the two men approached, Nash exited the Toyota and made his way to meet the pair. Nash regained his composure and extended his hand. "Imam Alim, welcome, welcome. But who is this? We weren't expecting another."

"Richard, my friend, you have no need to worry," he said as he shook Nash's hand with excitement and energy. "This boy is my servant Azzami. He attends to my needs."

Chris rolled his eyes and gave his new friends the once-over. He wanted to search the contents of the bag but thought better of it. The imam was as before, well dressed in a clean white turban and black waistcoat over a crumpled white salwar kameez. Chris guessed him to be in his late fifties or early sixties, and when he smiled, he showed a perfect set of straight, white teeth. His hands and nails were clean, and Chris guessed at a pinch, he moisturized on a daily basis. His beard was dark with a spackling of gray, and below his turban, salt-and-pepper hair was neatly trimmed. Chris gauged him to be a shade under six foot, but he did not carry his weight well as a large belly gave the imam a permanent crook to his back, an obvious sign of good living and overindulgence. What surprised Chris, however, was the imam's command of English. At first, he couldn't place the dialect, but there was a distinct Britishness to it that told him to be wary. If this imam was educated in the UK, which wasn't outside the realm of possibility, then Chris needed to be on his guard and avoid long conversations about his own background.

More, his instinct told him something was off, false, deceptive about the man. Chris felt the imam was pretending to be something he wasn't and was giving off vibes that he had things to hide. Chris didn't know if he was being overprotective of his boss or his gut was sending him warning signals, but he didn't like the air and attitude surrounding a man who obviously wanted to be the center of attention with cheesy smiles and quick words.

Chris shifted his attention to Azzami. The boy was exactly that, a teenager replete with acne and poor hygiene. He was tall, dark, and skinny, and his eyes looked sad. He held onto the bag at his chest as if it were a baby about to be wrenched from a mother. Chris didn't quite understand the cultural nuance of this arrangement but gave the young lad a reassuring smile. Before Chris got a closer look at the baggage, the imam interrupted his scan, grabbing Azzami and shoving him in the direction of the rear of the first Land Cruiser.

"You have no need to concern yourself with Azzami," the cleric repeated to everyone. "He is of no consequence to our arrangements; he is here to serve. Please, please let us depart this place. Let us not give the warden any reason to delay our mission, shall we?"

Nash nodded at Chris, who in turn nodded to Alex.

Nash got into the rear of the Land Cruiser with the imam, and Azzami got into the rear cargo space. Chris got into a reluctant shotgun position, and the Afghan driver got in behind the wheel. Chris glared over at the driver and cursed to himself for taking his coveted driver's spot.

In the second Land Cruiser, Alex took his post in the front passenger seat, while an Afghan driver took the wheel and the two Northern Alliance soldiers became passengers in the rear. The mission to find the

TRODPINT team was finally underway.

It took some time for Imam Alim to settle down. He was both jovial and talkative, and it seemed to Chris that he was happy just for being finally free from the prison. He had no idea how long the man had been incarcerated, but from his appearance, the cleric looked as if he hadn't been suffering under close lock and chain, and to come out with a servant carrying his wares gave the impression the prison was a low threat affair or the cleric had some influence in his treatment.

Close to an hour from the old fort, the driver and the imam began a conversation in Pashto, sounding like double Dutch mixed with a dash of Mandarin to Chris. Needless to say, Chris had no idea what was being said but surmised that the discussion was one of navigation as Nash broke out a map and thus beginning a conversation of mixed English and Pashto, which perturbed Chris to no end. As usual, he was pissed off that he couldn't drive, and to rub salt on an open wound, he had no navigational control of the direction they were taking. During the ride, he felt like a spare prick at a wedding; he had nothing to do, and his input was not required. Fuming, he continued to look out the window hoping that Alex in the rear vehicle was monitoring their progress with his GPS system.

Silence finally prevailed in the vehicle, which was music to Chris's ears. He got into a silent rhythm of looking to his front, looking at the rear-view passenger mirror, then out the passenger side window, and then over to the driver side window. As the monotonous journey carried on, mile after mile, hour after boring hour, to keep his mind busy, Chris fell back on an old surveillance detection method of identifying everything that he saw as they drove. During his training, he was instructed to vocally call out every single object that he saw while he was driving a vehicle. This method of narrative driving allowed his instructors to hear what Chris was actually looking at. The exercise ended when the instructors told him what he missed or, equally, when he caught what they had missed. After a week of open mic driving, he no longer needed a debrief as he was catching everything that was laid out in front of him—each vehicle, each person, each movement, each traffic signal, each turn signal, each wave of a hand, each person waiting at a bus stop, and the list went on and on. It was a skill that he prided himself in maintaining when he was alone as he drove, but when he was working as a driver for Nash in Germany, he used it in real time, knowing that what he saw could have been the difference between life and death.

Now, thousands of miles from Germany, away from urban sprawls, Chris practiced his silent narrative as he watched each boulder, each rock formation, each farmer in a field, each donkey pulling a cart . . . each and every item that he could focus his eyes on to maintain a high level of concentration. As the miles passed by, the level of effort to remain attentive was becoming more and more of a challenge as sometimes the desert landscape had nothing to offer in the way of mile marker or prominent feature.

"You are the strong silent type, I see."

Chris blinked and looked briefly behind him and saw the imam staring at him with an eager expression anticipating a reply. Chris didn't answer. He wasn't trying to be rude; he just didn't have anything to say.

"Chillingly silent, I see. You have nothing to worry about with me, my young friend. We are simply two travelers on the same road. I merely wish to engage in some polite conversation."

Nash opened his eyes. He had dozed off again, and content not having to chat with the imam, he was happy to pass the mantle over to Chris.

Chris was conflicted. It wasn't as if he didn't trust the man; he just didn't know enough about him to have a conversation. On the other hand, he wouldn't know anything about him if he didn't at least appear to be cordial. "There's really nothing to say. I'm not from around here if that helps."

The imam smiled at the flippant response but was unable to mask his surprise. It was the first time he had heard Chris speak a full sentence. "British, well that is a pleasant surprise. Where are you from? I spent many years there."

"Here, there, everywhere," Chris replied, noncommittal.

The imam was disappointed and told Chris as much. "That is very vague and a little sad if that is all you have to offer. I think if we are to get along, we should at least be a little polite to one another, don't you think?"

Chris relented, realizing the man was on board to help in the mission and appeared compassionate. If Nash put his faith in him, then he must have some value. "I'm sorry, Imam, you're right. Where were you when you were in the UK?"

"I spent most of my time in Finsbury Park, London. You?"

"Oh." Chris knew the reputation of Finsbury Park. It was a hotbed of dissident and militant activities. He told himself to continue his wariness and decided to stash that little piece of information away for another day. "Did you spend time at the mosque there?" Chris asked, deflecting the imam's previous question.

"Yes, yes, I have many memories of London. It's a wonderful city full of culture and history. However, I cannot recommend the food. It baffled me how such a prosperous place can exist on fried fish, tripe, and offal."

Chris smiled, Nash snickered.

"You have a point there, Imam; you have a point," Chris said.

"So tell me, my British friend, where are you from?" the imam pressed.

"I consider myself a citizen of the world. I have no fixed abode. I prefer the life of a nomad."

Nash perked up but remained silent. He wasn't sure where Chris was going with this, but it was strange.

"But you must have been born somewhere. You must have memories, family, friends."

"I have no parents, no siblings. Where I rest my head tonight will be my home," Chris replied almost Zen like.

What a crock of shit! Nash thought. *What game is he playing now?*

The imam could tell when he was being patronized. He recognized Chris for the man he was, a soldier, a CIA killer. He needed to be very careful around him. "You are very philosophical, my friend. I think you and I will have much to discuss in the coming days. I believe you are a man that should not be underestimated, of that I am sure."

And I'm going to take the piss out of you every time you start a conversation with me, you nosey old prick! Chris thought contemptuously. "I'll take that as a compliment from such an educated man as yourself, Imam. Thank you."

The Afghan driver broke the weird conversation and shouted something in Pashto as they navigated around a bend. Chris saw it too, a roadblock. He grabbed his 9mm Makarov, which was wedged under his left thigh. He held it in place not needing to draw the weapon . . . yet.

"Snap roadblock!" Chris called over his two-way radio to Alex. But no sooner had he released the microphone switch than he had to lean over to the driver to prevent him from exiting the vehicle. "Stay! Stay!" he snapped.

"Chris, what's going on?" Nash inquired.

"Snap roadblock, Mr. Nash. We need to sit tight and let them make the next move."

Chris scanned the area in front of him and then quickly took in the rest of his surroundings. *Okay, three targets to my front. Two are hiding behind two oil drums, and there's an old piece of timber lying on top of the drums. Left and right are small boulders and rocks preventing a drive around. We can get through this if the damn driver stays behind the wheel.* "Alex, I have three tangos to my front with a makeshift barrier. We can blast through this. Stand by."

"Roger. We are clear back here."

Chris glanced quickly in the passenger side mirror. He could see Alex with one foot out of his Land Cruiser looking to his right and front. He couldn't see his hands, which meant they were on his rifle. One Afghan soldier had exited the vehicle, walking a short way back up the trail they had just come down, looking for new threats. Chris imagined the other Afghan soldier was monitoring the left side of the vehicle, and the driver remained behind the wheel.

He refocused his view on the roadblock and the tangoes. *Shit, these are kids . . . one's carrying a Lee Enfield bolt-action rifle that will knock him on his arse if he fires it. I see one AK-47 with no magazine, and the slide is being held open, and one kid has a slingshot. Out of all the weapons that's probably the most lethal right now.*

"Alex, three tangos with small arms but appear to be no serious threat."

"Roger."

"Chris," Nash whispered, "it's probably a local gang trying to extort travelers on the road. It's not uncommon in this country,"

Chris nodded his head. He drew his Makarov from under his thigh to rest on his lap, waiting to see what would happen next. He had no doubt in his mind which one he would shoot first. *They may be kids*, he thought, *but there may be other unseen's that could escalate the situation.* He wanted to be prepared.

The oldest of the three who was carrying the AK marched over to the driver's side window. Chris opened his door and placed his right foot on the ground. He had still not shown his weapon but kept his eyes on the approaching kid who could only have been twelve or thirteen.

The driver opened the window.

"Not a word, Mr. Nash," Chris whispered, his right knuckles turning white around the pistol grip.

The young boy stuck the AK in the face of the Afghan driver, who hadn't yet realized the gun was not loaded, which made him recoil towards Chris. The young boy assaulted the driver with a barrage of words that, even if Chris could speak Pashto, were too quick and garbled to make any sense.

This kid is nervous, which makes him dangerous. He may not have the tools to make good on his threats, but we don't need an incident this early in the game, and who knows where his big brothers are . . . go the fuck away, you little shit!

The verbal assault continued for a minute longer and ceased only when the barrel of a live AK-47 was pointed at the young boy's head and the shouts of a more mature man taking control of the situation. Not to be out-intimidated, the boy with the slingshot let a pebble loose, almost hitting the head of the Afghan soldier with the gun. More shouting ensued with the young boys becoming louder and the Afghan soldier and driver getting more animated by the second.

"You good down there, Chris?"

Chris did not reply to the radio request. He changed his grip on his pistol from right to left and then stuck a right thumb out to his side indicating to Alex that he was cool.

"Not a word," Chris whispered once again to Nash, who didn't need to be told a second time.

Chris's head was rotating like a spinning sprinkler watering a lawn, taking every movement in, waiting for a new unusual event to push him to the next level. What he didn't expect was the imam getting out of the vehicle and coming between the Afghan soldier and the boy with the AK. His thoughts went straight to the practical. *I don't give a fuck if he goes down or decides to play hopscotch with these kids. We will leave his ass if we need to bail, and Michael Schumacher here can walk with him. I'm driving us out of here.*

"Chris?"

He stuck his hand out once again, but this time he gave Alex a 50-50 wave with his right hand. Alex took the signal as an escalation indicator and moved away from his vehicle to find a vantage point.

Chris looked over to the imam, who seemed to be getting things under control, as the shouting match was dwindling, the Afghan soldier retreated back to his vehicle, and the boys who held the slingshot and rifle lowered their weapons.

"It would be nice if he could work some magic," Nash remarked in a hushed tone.

"Yup. Although these kids aren't much of a threat, it would become a problem if they aren't home for supper."

They both looked on in anticipation as the imam gathered the three boys around him. From his body language and those of the highway bandits, Chris could tell the threat was waning.

"We're getting somewhere, Alex. If this thing still goes south, I'm leaving his sorry ass behind."

"Roger that, Chris. I concur."

"You are not leaving him, Chris. We still have a mission to complete."

"Mr. Nash, mission or not, I am responsible for your safety, and honestly, I don't give a shit about your opinion right now . . . in all due respect, that is."

Nash was about to reprimand his subordinate but was pre-empted by the imam's return. He went to the rear of the vehicle and spoke briefly to Azzami who began to dig into his baggage. Within a few seconds, the servant produced a roll of Afghani currency and handed it over to the imam who peeled off a number of bills and handed the remainder back to be stored away. He began to walk away but called out to Nash and Chris, "We shall soon be on our way, gentlemen. Nothing to worry about here."

Nash and Chris watched the imam walk back to the group who had already removed the old piece of timber barrier away from the road. They were too far away to hear any of the conversation, not that it mattered, but from the smiles of the boys and the stack of cash wadded in the cleric's hands, it looked like things were moving along nicely.

Chris, still waiting for an escalation indicator, was zooming in and out with his eyes at each of the boys . . . hands, eyes, feet; hands, eyes, feet; hands, eyes, feet. His gut was telling him things were winding down, but his training told him it wouldn't be done until they were way behind in the rear-view mirror, waiting for their next prey or lying dead by the side of the road.

The imam doled out the last of the cash and did something that surprised Chris. He brushed the hair of the older boy with his right hand in fondness and then kissed him on both cheeks. Azzami in the back of the Land Cruiser shifted and gave an involuntary gasp. The imam did the same to the other two boys and gave the smallest of the three a long affectionate hug.

What the fuck? Chris questioned.

"They are the sons of the Taliban," Azzami hissed.

Chris continued to concentrate on his front, but Nash, shocked by the imam's servant, turned around briefly to look at him and asked, "Does that mean we are in Taliban-controlled territory, Azzami?"

"Yes."

CHAPTER TWELVE

Kapisa Province, Afghanistan

BY CHRIS'S RUDIMENTARY calculations of time, speed, and distance, he estimated the small convoy had left the improvised roadblock roughly three miles ago. He searched his mind for a reference point from the map he had studied before departing JAWBREAKER, and with the sun waning to his left, rear side, he reckoned they were heading southeast but was unsure where exactly they were.

With the headlights now leading the way, Chris's eyes were getting weary, and his head was beginning to ache. They had been on the road for the best part of the day, and it seemed that only the imam knew exactly how far they had gone and how far they still had to go. But now with the mission hours fading and the ambient light diminishing, Chris found himself in an uncomfortable position. Not only did his arse ache from sitting so long, but also the pressure of securing Nash was weighing on him with every passing mile. The deeper they trekked into Taliban country, the more nervous he became. It wasn't lost on him that the only one not putting his life on the line for this mission was the imam, and now to Chris's annoyance, he was taking over the job as if it was his own.

A thousand attack permutations ran through his head, causing him to shake himself mentally in denial or disbelief that they would happen. The more he dug, the more negativity he found, compounding his throbbing head. More than once, he rubbed his eyes and swigged quickly on his bottle of water, un-camouflaging his stolid look. He shifted in his seat, leaning over to look at Nash, who seemed off in his own world, oblivious of Chris's dilemma and carefree of his surroundings. The imam flashed a white smile in the dim light, making Chris think that he knew more than he did, which was probably true, adding to his list of worries. When he got comfortable in his seat again, he braced himself.

"Slow down for fuck's sake!" he shouted at the driver, as they plunged nose down into a crater in the road. "We'll lose a fucking axle if we keep this shit up!" He continued to bellow hoping that the driver understood and would comply.

The driver cursed back at Chris in Pashto and waved his right hand in the air indicating that he knew what he was doing.

Chris was still pissed off but wasn't the only one.

"Jesus, Chris, did we just land on the moon?" Alex squawked over the radio.

Chris didn't reply. There was no need to but, calming his voice, he fielded an obvious question. "Imam, how much further?"

"Not long now, my friend, this road, ah . . . the Northern Alliance, well . . .," he paused as the Land Cruiser hit another massive hole in the road, "they shelled this area constantly in the past. I fear we will all have shaken bones by the time we arrive. But please, don't concern yourself. We have maybe an hour or less. It will all be over soon enough."

This shit is beginning to stink. It's almost pitch black. We are in the middle of butt-fuck nowhere, and he thinks it's just another hour. Did this guy do a sermon in one of those holes once upon a time, or how the hell does he know where we are? Chris asked himself, not happy with the glib reply from the imam. He braced himself again as another tank-killing crater ate the road in front of them. This time the driver slowed to a crawl.

As if by clockwork, the first dwellings the team had seen since the roadblock appeared within the imam's promised hour. Chris sat up straight at the same time as the imam leaned forward in between the rear and front passenger area. The cleric began issuing orders to the driver to navigate his way through the streets. Chris was relieved to find they were small in number, matching the few structures of the tiny village. They finally slowed to a halt outside a squat structure that had but one entry portal that would allow passage for a small cart and donkey but not enough room to fit a mechanical vehicle other than a motorcycle. The imam was the first to make a move out of the vehicle. Chris opened his door and placed one foot outside, drew his Makarov, and held it out of sight with his right hand behind his passenger door. He quickly glanced back at Alex, who had already exited from his Land Cruiser and was placing his night vision goggles over his head. Chris reached into the glove compartment and retrieved a flashlight that he had put there earlier and placed it in his left leg cargo pocket. He'd already instructed the driver to keep the engine running, and he assumed Alex had made the same command to his driver.

The village was quiet, save for the running engines and tapping of the wooden door to the abode by the imam. Chris stared at the door, praying that it wouldn't suddenly pop open with a one hundred mad Taliban storming out to rain terror on the small party. He knew his first action would be to let off as many rounds as possible and get the driver to move off the X if the shit hit the fan. His second option for escape would be made on the fly. It was not a plan he was proud of, but given the circumstances, that was all he had.

The imam tapped the door with more vigor when it wasn't answered the first time, and he turned to Chris with a reassuring smile as if to say everything was under control but received only a dark scowl from the Brit in return. Chris's didn't hear it, but a faint whisper spoke from behind the door, piquing the interest of the imam who began identifying himself. After a brief silence, the door opened slowly at first, presenting a set of untrusting, watchful eyes, but the imam, in a reassuring, calm, collected voice assured the proprietor of his identity and requested entry into the house.

As the imam entered, Chris turned to Nash, "Stay here." He depressed the switch on the radio and said, "Alex, I'm going in."

Alex understood that he was securing the property and replied with a brief, "Roger." Then he moved to take up station next to Nash.

Chris walked into the small house with his right hand and Makarov hidden out of view behind his back. He once again had no qualms about killing the imam to ensure his escape, thus damning the mission, nor would he hesitate to leave him behind if they were walking into a trap. Passing through the main entry door, Chris walked down a short corridor that opened up to a large family-type room. A single dim light hung from the low ceiling, illuminating the faces of a feeble man who cowered before the imam, while his two young children clung to their mother and looked on in abject fear. They were obviously caught pre-dinner, as a pot of water brewed on the corner stove, while a table setting for four, void of food, indicated they were not expecting visitors this late in the evening. Chris smiled at one of the children but did not let down his guard. He craned his neck to the left first to see a half-open door that he assumed was a bedroom. Then he looked down another short corridor, which led to two more doors, and anticipated the worst. While the imam and the feeble man talked, Chris ambled around slowly, not giving away his purpose to secure the area or subjecting the family to any undue nervousness. Satisfied that if there was a trap it would have already been sprung, he took care to place his gun in his holster while the children were distracted. He felt no threat or tension from the small gathering and let down his guard a tad but wondered if this was going to be a safe place for the night.

With a quick tour of the home, the imam confirmed to Chris that this was indeed going to be a resting place, but they would be back out on the road at the first opportunity after sunrise.

Chris retraced his steps and met up with Nash and Alex at the first Land Cruiser. "This is it. We're crashing here tonight. Not much to speak of, man, wife, and two kids. They seem friendly enough. Haven't looked under the beds, but no boogie man to speak of."

"Security?" Alex asked.

"We'll check that out in a few. The imam told me to get the vehi-cles off the road and around the back. There's a separate entrance we can use."

Alex nodded and headed off to get the drivers in motion.

"Mr. Nash, you want to hop out? I'll bring you in this way. Azzami, you too."

Too tired to offer any comment, Nash obliged and followed Chris into the residence. He held onto to his money bag as tightly as possible but put his complete trust in Chris. As soon as they entered the family area, the imam stood from the kitchen table and introduced the visitors in a manner that surprised Chris. Although he couldn't tell what was being said to the family, the imam's presence and kind tone put the family at ease. No sooner had the imam finished talking than the man of the house pulled out a chair for Nash and then ordered his wife to fetch some tea. Nash sat down and nodded his thanks.

Taking the motion as a sign to find Alex and perform a quick security survey of the property, Chris quietly extracted himself from the pleasantries. He found Alex assisting one of the drivers backing up a Land Cruiser under an awning. "You want to walk?" Chris asked, almost in a ghost whisper.

Alex nodded. There was no need for a discussion. They had no idea who could be listening or intrigued by two English speakers. In silence, they both strode around the property and then made their own mental calculations of where threats could come from and potential escape routes should an intrusion take place. After a short time, they circled back to the Land Cruisers. Chris pulled out a notebook and began sketching a map. Alex added a few items to the simple drawing, and once they both agreed on their plan, they called the Afghan team over for a briefing. Satisfied each of the team had his assignments of sleep and or guard duty, Alex and Chris moved back towards the rear of one of the vehicles.

"Is Nash okay?" Alex asked.

"He's tired and in need of rest. We'll be out of here in the morning. But we need to figure out where the hell we are. Your batteries still good on your GPS?"

"Yeah, I've been trying to follow along, but we need to stay stable for a few minutes so we can triangulate, get a good fix."

"You want to try now?"

Alex reached into his pack and extracted his Thuraya satellite phone and Garmin GPS.

Chris took his map and tried to orientate as best as he could while holding his flashlight in one hand with two fingers masking the bright light.

"As far as I could tell, we were on the Sarobi Road for quite some time, and if we carried on before turning off we would have been in Jalalabad by now."

"Don't need that shit," Chris replied. "But on the other hand, that's about fifty to fifty-five miles from the zero line. That's a good direction to take if we need to bug out of here."

Alex bounced his head up and down a few times. He liked Chris's train of thought—escape and evade, find a friendly border. The GPS unit beeped twice and offered a digital readout of longitude and latitude. "Let me plot this sucker." Then he pulled the map gently away from Chris who held the shadowed flashlight for Alex. "Here we go . . . well, on this map, this place doesn't have a name. Nothing new there; that's just Afghanistan for you." He took the nib of his pen and indicated a point in the desert. "According to the GPS, we are right here."

"But I don't see the McDonald's. What the fuck?"

Alex looked up at Chris and smiled and then continued with the navigation. "We are roughly twelve miles south of the main road. Any idea of where we are heading tomorrow?"

"No, but I'll tell you something for nothing, Alex. I'm content dumping the happy imam and heading for the border. With your GPS, we can skirt around Jalalabad. We'll take Nash and the money and make our own way. The Afghans can take the other truck and make do."

"What about the mission?"

"You know as well as I do we are not equipped to go after bin Laden. There's a shit ton of other things to happen before we even get close."

"TRODPINT?"

"Yeah, I've got a bunch of questions about all that, like how the hell does the imam know how to go about finding them? We are already in bandit country, so whose side are the TRODPINT team on? If we are in Taliban country, then so are they."

"Nash seems to put faith in them. That's got to be worth something."

"If these guys are still allies to the US, then they have to be dormant to stay below the radar, so how the hell does the imam know where they are?"

"Is that why you want to bail?"

Chris shook his head. "Don't get me wrong. If bin Laden sticks his head over that wall right now, I'd be happy to put ten rounds in his head and then run over it with the Land Cruiser to be sure. But I have reservations. One, I don't think the imam can produce the goods. Two, Nash is not himself. I'm really surprised the director has let him loose on this excursion. Three, Nash assumes that TRODPINT can or will help. And four, a bombing campaign is imminent, and the Taliban front lines are going to get hammered."

Alex let the thoughts hang, simmered on the points Chris brought up for a few seconds, and then gave his point of view. "I'm with Nash on this one, Chris. If there's a chance we can get within a rifle shot distance, then we go find that spot. Fuck the deadline for the bombing runs. I can take care of that."

Chris was surprised. In his heart, he didn't want to give up so easily, but he was being pragmatic; he saw the risks, the tools at hand, and the disadvantages that were presented. The one thing he forgot was the resolve of a former Delta Force soldier. He didn't think Alex was being an idealist, but he was trained to take risks and operate behind enemy lines. If there was a sliver of hope of identifying the location of bin Laden, even if it cost a life, then to a man like Alex that risk was worth taking.

"So far we've done squat," Alex insisted. "You're right. We've got pretty lousy odds, and the easy option would be to haul ass out of here right now and make for the border. But I like you, Chris, and although you analyze the shit out of everything, sometimes you have to take risks and deal with the cards in your hands."

The two men were staring at each other in almost complete darkness under the awning while the Afghan guards were making themselves comfortable or patrolling the small encampment.

"I can't tell you what to do, Chris. Nobody would fault you if you decided to get out of the country, but I won't be leaving any time soon. Even if the TRODPINT mission is a bust, I still have my JAW-BREAKER duties to complete. If I'm behind enemy lines to achieve that . . . then all is well in my world. I don't think I've underestimated you, but you and Nash have a certain bond. Even if you have doubts, I don't think you want to let him down."

"I don't think he's making rational choices, Alex. I don't know what's wrong, but he hasn't been the same since his kidnapping."

Alex realized Nash was becoming less of an asset and more of a liability. He was beginning to think Chris's idea to escaping or get away from danger was to protect Nash and not to save his own life. "We can't forget, Chris, Nash is still the one to issue the orders. Both you and I work for him. If he says go, we go. You're ex-army; you know how to take orders."

"Back in the days when I wore green, we didn't question orders. But now I have a disease called a conscience, and like a dumb ass, I went off and got an education, making me question everything. I wouldn't want to wish that affliction on my worst enemy; education is overrated."

"You're also a smart-ass who can handle himself, rare talent."

"You don't give a shit, do you?"

"I do, Chris, but I channel my thoughts and actions differently. I'm not happy being out of uniform, so this is the next best thing. The CIA has allowed me to play judge, jury, and executioner on more than one occasion, and I am comfortable with that. I have been given a mission, and I intend to carry it out to the best of my ability, but to do that, I need your help."

Seattle, Washington

"A serious incident is blocking four lanes of northbound I-5 just past the Spokane Street entry to the expressway in Seattle. State troopers are advising motorists to avoid the area if at all possible and use alternate routes until the area is cleared. State police have informed us that the incident occurred when a semi-trailer was apparently cut off by a sedan causing the semi to roll over and pin the car directly in the center lane.

"Troopers stated that the drivers of both vehicles had to be extracted by the Seattle Fire Department, which took quite some time, and both drivers are in critical condition and have been transported to Harborview for treatment. This initial crash also caused a chain reaction involving a number of other cars. Two other drivers were also transported to Harborview with minor injuries.

"As you can see behind me, it's quite a chaotic scene as all four lanes are blocked and are unlikely to be opened for some time. Seattle PD and state troopers are turning traffic around and redirecting traffic onto I-90. So, if you are about to head north towards Seattle, you need to consider other routes, or if you are expecting someone home soon, you many need to contact them to let them know of this long delay. Once again, state troopers are advising all drivers to reroute to I-90 and then north onto 405, or alternatively SR-99.

"Reporting live in downtown Seattle, Essex Porter, KIRO 7 News."

FBI Field Office, Los Angles

Nick Seymour sat in the fourth row of the large auditorium with almost two hundred other FBI agents anticipating another briefing from Special Agent in Charge, Ron Hilts. The cacophony of raised voices belied the actual number of people in the room, as every person had equally important discussions and large lists of wants and needs. It was refreshing to Nick that everyone was communicating, albeit on a shouting-match scale; however, it seemed that things were being agreed upon and no fists were flying. As he had nobody to speak to, he picked up on multiple conversations as everyone waited for the all-hands-on-deck meeting. Unfortunately, his radar failed to pick up any mention of

Omar, Jawad, or the Saudi consulate, so he sat doodling on his notepad listening for clues until Hilts arrived.

It took another ten minutes for the SAC to climb onto the stage and place himself behind a lectern. Tapping the microphone a few times, "Is this thing on, is this working?" he asked nobody in particular.

"Yeah, we got ya, Ron," came a distant reply.

"Okay, okay, everybody, settle down, take your seats." He stared at the crowd and waited until all were situated and he had everyone's attention. "As you can tell, ladies and gentlemen, this is an all-hands meeting, meaning we have some new developments. I wanted to pass this on to you as I have just received the information from the director who held a conference call for all the field office SACs in the country. He is now placing another call as I speak with the same briefing to all overseas embassies, consulates, and external FBI offices worldwide." Hilts paused to clear his throat. "The director informed us that a meeting took place earlier this morning in DC that included the heads of the CIA, NSA, Defense, Justice, and a number of ranking members of the House and Senate."

Nick felt the tension in the room spring forward. It wasn't unusual for the director of the FBI to engage with so many senior level politicians and heads of government agencies; however, given the current state of affairs, something new was coming down the pipeline. Ron Hilts definitely had everyone's attention.

"The director informed us that some new intelligence has come forward indicating there is a strong possibility the US is about to be hit again by foreign aggressors."

Nick took note of the words "foreign aggressors." It was typical jurisprudence jargon that the director sometimes bandied around when sound definitions of more appropriate words were hard to come by. To Nick, the language meant the definition of "terrorism" had been debated once again, but drawing a blank or lack of consensus with other agencies, the director fell back on a lame but neutral, politically correct term.

"What does this actually mean?" Ron asked hypothetically. "The

FBI does not have any intelligence at this time to indicate there is a definitive plan or set of bad actors in play. However, the information has come from overseas to the CIA and down to us that has warranted this release of information. The CIA and NSA have been monitoring various means of electronic intelligence gathering, but they have also been working with other countries to share information. I'm happy to say that the Brits have once again stood by us, and this latest batch of information has come from one of their sources."

Nick thought back to his discussion with Ron a few days ago when he inquired about FURLONG. Perhaps this was the crux of the new source.

"In the next few hours, I will be meeting with the mayor of Los Angeles and a number of other city mayors in the region, as well as law enforcement, FEMA, and other aid agencies to brief them on this new information, however vague that may be." Hilts looked up from his notes and saw a few agents rolling their eyes. "Vague" was law enforcement's worst choice of words. Unperturbed, Hilts continued, "Other SACs or delegates will be conducting their own meetings throughout the country, so word will spread quickly, and we all know what that means." He searched the crowd for a familiar face or two. "Where's media liaison?" he challenged before anyone could interrupt.

A hand shot up in the rear of the room, another close by.

"Good, meet me in my office as soon as we are done here. We'll be drafting a press release, but we will get some direction from headquarters before we do. That being said, we cannot be spreading this information until the president or the director has issued a statement. I can't reiterate this enough, people: if any of you leaks a word or even a hint that there is second wave or a new cell active in this country or an attack is imminent, then think now about starting a new career as a school bus driver or chief bottle washer because you will not be welcome in my FBI."

Hilts never gave his audience an opportunity to raise questions. He'd made his point, picked up his notes, and started to walk away but turned back to the microphone. "Dismissed."

The Platinum House, Paradise Valley, Arizona

Jawad Halabi watched in disgust as Major Karim Basrawi exited a taxi in front of the Platinum House. Jawad had been back in the Saudi enclave only a few hours when two police officers in an unmarked police vehicle arrested the major as he walked between the Gold and Platinum Houses. Jawad saw the incident from the balcony as he was conversing with Saleh Bahar, the Saudi banker who immediately panicked, convinced that he would be the next one to be picked up.

Perplexed by the arrest, Jawad questioned the blabbering banker to establish the real reason for the apprehension and not finding a just cause was forced to wait with pensive uncertainty for the major's return.

The major paid his fare and walked away towards the house, but for some instinctual reason, he looked upwards towards the boring eyes of Jawad as he waited for the major on the balcony. The major immediately averted his gaze, pulled his jacket tighter around him, stuffed his hands deep into his pockets, and walked head down reluctantly towards the villa.

Jawad had retreated to the upper floor sitting room where they had first met. He lit a cigarette, poured himself a tea, and then sat behind a desk collecting his thoughts while the major traipsed slowly into the house and up the stairs to meet his superior.

Surprised and disheartened that Jawad was back in Paradise Valley, the major too tried to gather his wits. He ascended the stairs feeling like a man climbing towards the gallows. When he reached the sitting room, he tapped gently on the door, hoping beyond hope that Jawad did not want to see him and that he could win a brief reprieve, but it wasn't to be.

"Come."

Basrawi opened the door, shut it behind him, and then stood with his hands behind his back as if in parade rest, waiting for a command, the mark of a military man.

"Major Basrawi, please relax. Join me for tea. Sit, sit," Jawad implored, throwing the soldier off balance.

Basrawi had expected a hostile reaction, not one of friendliness. He told himself to be aware. Behind the dark eyes of the intelligence officer were murky thoughts and cunning schemes. Welcoming a beverage to quench his dry mouth, he poured himself some hot, steaming tea. Sipping his drink, Basrawi sat in a comfortable chair opposite Jawad, once again avoiding eye contact.

"Please tell me of our progress, Major. How are our plans to move Her Majesty coming along?"

Basrawi saw another curve ball coming his way. *This is strange. Perhaps he doesn't know about my arrest. Be careful, Karim Basrawi, be careful.* He cleared his throat and looked over at Jawad, who was leaning back in his desk chair, relaxed, holding a cigarette in his right hand and nursing a glass of tea in his other.

"Things have been going well; however, as we have no definitive date for departure, it has been a little difficult to pin down each detail."

"I quite understand, Major. But a man with your skill and expertise should find that as a challenge, no?"

"A challenge that I have been blessed by the Prophet, praise his name, to undertake and fulfill."

The religious reference was not lost on Jawad. He could tell from the moment the soldier had stepped out of the car that he was troubled. Now his nervous disposition confirmed Basrawi was going to ask for an understanding. "So please share. What are these details? Perhaps I can help."

"Sir, I do not have my documentation with me. Perhaps I can—"

"Yes, indeed." Jawad cut him off and pointed at the phone, heading off a request to leave. "Please call one of your lieutenants."

Basrawi leaned forward to reach Jawad's desk and clumsily placed the tea next to the phone. He picked it up and dialed a number.

Jawad looked on almost salivating and enjoyed watching the man squirm. He took a long drag of the cigarette and let the exhaled smoke conceal his devilish intent. He watched Basrawi stare his eyeballs into the desk, ordering one of his men to drop everything immediately and join him at Platinum, cursing the man loudly for questioning his orders.

Jawad smiled, it seemed out of character for the major to be so boisterous and so direct. Even though he didn't know the man that well, Jawad judged the major was acting out because he was scared. The major finished his call and sat back down. Jawad raised his left hand to his face and then toyed with his lips. *A scared rabbit will freeze and then run. Basrawi has nowhere to run. He knows it, but he cannot clam up on me, not yet.*

Jawad got up to leave, prompting Basrawi to spring out of his chair. "You will excuse me for a minute, Major. I have another matter to attend to."

Basrawi saw an opening for escape and made a move for the door.

"No, no, please wait for me here. Make yourself comfortable I shan't be long. Relax, Major. I shall return shortly. We shall review your plans quite soon."

There was foreboding in Jawad's words. As much as he didn't want to, Barsawi placed himself back down on the edge of the chair and watched Jawad leave. He saw the door close, then stood, and looked around the room searching in vain for answers to a myriad of conflicting questions. Karim Basrawi wracked his brain trying to figure out how much Jawad knew, how much power the intelligence officer wielded, how much pain his tormentor could inflict, and most importantly, how he was going to get out of this mess and get away from Jawad. He paced around quickly.

Unbeknownst to him, Jawad stood at the other side of the door, smiling to himself as he heard the quick footsteps race around the sitting room. *The little rabbit is trying to run.* Although he enjoyed meting out physiological pain, time was wasting away. Jawad made his way down to the kitchen where he found his driver and ordered him to watch the door of the upstairs sitting room. He then made his way to the garage where he found an old wooden chair. He stared at it for a minute and then went to work.

———✼———

Although the major was told to relax, Jawad saw the opposite of someone who was calm and collected. When he entered the sitting room with the lieutenant that was ordered there earlier, Basrawi did not stand at attention or on alert; he simply stood there with a limp posture, arms hanging loosely at his sides and distant vacant eyes.

"Let us begin, Major. I am eager to hear of your plans. I assume the lieutenant here has all the necessary documents for your briefing?"

Basrawi took the notes from his subordinate, perused through them quickly, and then nodded. "Yes, sir, I have what I need."

"Good day, Lieutenant," Jawad ordered.

Basrawi's eyes popped open wide for an instant, a flash of hope. He didn't want his young ally to depart. "Sir, I may have more items that need clarification. He may be able to help."

"Very well. You may wait in the kitchen," he said to the young soldier. "Have some tea. I will summon you if required."

The young man bowed his head and exited as quickly as he could. It was no concern of his to question the man, but he was worried that his normally stalwart commander seemed so anxious and meek around the visitor that he had never seen before. Something was amiss; however, he was there only to follow orders. He made for the kitchen and ordered a pot of tea from the maid.

Jawad took a seat behind his desk and let Basrawi begin explaining his plan. The major laid his documentation on the desk before him but began to sweat when Jawad, after a few minutes, joined him on his side of the desk. He was surprised at Jawad's interest, which seemed genuine. The questions he asked were well-thought-out, precise, and not condescending. Jawad brought up a few points that Basrawi needed to add to the overall design, but in principle, the plan was sound. All that was needed was a start time and date to get all moving parts in place for the queen's departure.

It took almost an hour to get through the plan, and it was reassuring for Jawad to see that the major had regained a level of composure. It was an obvious reaction from someone who knew what he was doing when it came to military planning and the timely execution of an operation.

"You have done well, Major. I am impressed with the level of detail. You have, I see, reserved the five seats that I requested."

"Yes, sir," he replied with confidence. "I just need to know when they will arrive. They will, of course, be accommodated here while they wait."

"Yes, I will give you the full details when the time is right. But tell me, who else is aware of these plans?"

"My staff have assisted me in gathering all the necessary details. But Saleh Bahar has been instrumental in coordinating our efforts. It has truly been a team effort."

"Good, good. I expected nothing less. I will be speaking to my colleagues at the Ministry of Defense on my return. I don't want to get ahead of myself, Major, but if this plan of yours succeeds, you will have the gratitude of the royal family and my personal recommendation. We both know there is still a lot of work to do, but please thank your men for me. This is a great effort so far. If the Prophet, praise be his name, desires it so, the queen shall be home and with her family very soon."

Basrawi felt a small sense of relief. He knew his plan was good, and before this recent encounter with Jawad, he was extremely confident it would work. It seemed quite perfunctory to transport a person to an airport, but it was vastly different when that person was a member of a royal family, was an invalid, and had a huge entourage. The eyes of the entire Kingdom of Saudi Arabia would be upon him. Succeed or fail, his name would be whispered in the halls of the great palaces, and his fate would be out of his hands if things were to go wrong. He nodded and gave a thin smile to the complimentary words from Jawad. He had no response, and none was expected. The meeting was over.

"I am famished. It's time to eat. You will join me," Jawad proposed, "won't you, or do you have other duties?"

"Yes, sir, I must attend to some other things." Another glimmer of freedom flashed in the air in front of him.

"Nonsense, I do not like to eat alone. Come, come, let us see what the cook has for us."

His hopes dashed, Basrawi acquiesced and gathered his papers.

"Leave them; we can pick them up later," he ordered as he headed for the door.

The major followed the command and then fell in step behind Jawad. The weight on his shoulders forced his head down. All he could see were the heels of Jawad's shoes and the blurry tiles beneath him. He thought he was willingly following his executioner.

When they reached the bottom of the stair, instead of heading for the dining room, Jawad walked towards the garage. Basrawi followed his master like a dog, neither questioning nor hesitating in his step.

Jawad entered the garage from the hallway and turned on the light. "There are a few more questions I have for you, Karim," Jawad offered with a sly inquisitiveness.

Basrawi was felled by the use of his first name. It was out of protocol to be so informal and spelled his impending doom. He dutifully entered the garage and saw the chair in the center that he knew that was meant for him. The major didn't need an invitation but sat down with a slump. He dropped his head and looked at the floor as his head spun. He didn't even look up when he heard another set of footsteps behind him and then another.

"Saleh, so good of you to join us. Please take a seat." Jawad was polite but pointed over at a seat in the corner. The fat banker began to waffle, but Jawad cut him off and rushed up to his face. He screamed at him, "You will remain silent!"

Saleh back-pedaled as quickly as he could, but Jawad continued to advance towards him. He fell backwards in the chair, raised his hands to protect his face, winced, and closed his eyes, feeling only the breath of Jawad on his face. He trembled not knowing what he had done wrong.

"Shut up and stay there," Jawad spat at him.

Basrawi continued to study the floor. He knew not to look over at the banker and his plight; it would only enrage the inquisitor. But out of the corner of his eye, he could see a set of feet, a man, silent in waiting.

"Look at me, Karim!" Jawad bellowed at him.

Basrawi raised his head without defiance, only submission.

"I have a problem that you will help me out with." The statement hung in the air. Nobody said anything more; nobody moved, but Basrawi swallowed hard. Jawad stood in front of him with his arms crossed and a stare that could have stopped a charging rhino.

"Help me understand this . . . I saw you getting arrested this morning by the Paradise Valley Police Department. I saw them put cuffs on you and put you in the back of a car. Now, after my astonishment, I sent Saleh here to find a lawyer to assist you for whatever reason you were picked up. On arrival at the police department, they stated to Saleh and the lawyer that you were not in their custody but were being held by the FBI. What have you to say to that?"

Basrawi did not reply, but Jawad pounced forward and slapped him in the face, hard with his right hand. Saleh gasped but after a stern look from Jawad, he held his thought.

"Do not make me restrain you, Karim. I want you to talk to me. I want your answers. I am not a torturer."

Saleh shifted in his seat. The chair that he was sitting in was off-kilter and leaning to the right at the front. Jawad saw the movement and was happy that his tactic of cutting a quarter of an inch off one leg ensured the fat slob Saleh did not get comfortable, physically or mentally, during the questioning.

"Explain, Major," Jawad demanded.

"It was not my fault," he said in almost a whisper.

Jawad nodded a little. *Typical of a suspect in denial or guilty, ready to come clean . . . rabbit is on the menu.* He pulled up another chair, sat, leaned forward, elbows on his knees, and glared at the soldier. "I'm listening."

"It began when I procured," he didn't know how else to put it, "extra services for the family." He looked at Jawad with pleading eyes who was quiet and listening intently. "I was arrested for arranging parties and inviting . . . special guests who brought with them certain substances."

Jawad rocked back into his chair. It was a sign of momentary compassion. He knew of the reputation of some of the princes and their vices. It wasn't the first time a subservient was caught by authorities trying to appease a certain royal taste.

"I was passed on to the FBI by the police who promised me a reduction of charges in exchange for information."

"Information about what, Karim?" Jawad's voice was unswerving.

"About the family, about you . . ."

Jawad's face frowned for a second. "How do they know about me?"

"Only that when you arrived you asked me to plan the queen's departure. I gave them your name."

Jawad looked at the man before him. He understood his dilemma, trying to appease a family he swore to protect only to fall afoul of the authorities. The major was definitely in a bind as a military officer with no diplomatic status to protect him. Jawad stood and walked around behind his captive. He needed a time to think. "What of the five reservations that I asked you to make? Does the FBI know of that?"

"I'm sorry, Jawad, but I was trying to-t-to-to," he stammered, fear getting the better of him. He began to sweat. Because he could not see Jawad but felt his presence somewhere close behind, it made him even more anxious. He tried to focus on the garage door in front of him. Strangely enough, the smell of the garage invaded his senses, he could smell a mixture of oil and gasoline, a moldiness that could only come from empty boxes or old insulation. Tears began to well up in his eyes. He remembered his home, his family.

"So you have betrayed me, Karim. Is that what you are telling me?"

Basrawi nodded in submission, not knowing what to say or do next. Jawad stopped pacing and rested his back on a washing machine. He folded his arms again and crossed his lower legs. He stared at the back of the major, considering his next move. He heard Saleh's feeble attempt at getting comfortable.

He hasn't done anything that a man in his position wouldn't do. Would I have done the same? he asked himself. *It's sad choice he had to make, to kowtow to the family at all costs. The problem isn't the FBI knowing of the plans for Her Highness to leave. It is Abdo . . . Abdo and his family. They must be on that plane. The FBI doesn't know his name yet. Perhaps it still can be done, but does this man need to be sacrificed to save Abdo?*

He looked over at Saleh, writing in his own hell, wishing he was elsewhere. *And this slob, this excuse of a man, too decadent to care about anyone than himself, his fat belly, and fat wallet. He would eagerly throw Karim to the wolves to save his own skin. His time will come, but not today. His profile is too high. He will be missed by the family if he was not here tomorrow. Give me five hundred Karim's for one gluttonous banker.* He resisted the urge to spit. *But the soldier, should he die . . .?*

CHAPTER THIRTEEN

The Platinum House, Paradise Valley, Arizona

JAWAD CONTINUED TO STARE at the back of Major Basrawi. He needed more time to decide the man's fate but realized he needed to move on as his attention needed to be elsewhere. He moved away from the washing machine he was leaning on and exited the garage quickly.

Saleh's eyes followed Jawad out the door, but before he could make a similar exit, the silent man in the garage walked in front of him, arms crossed with narrow focused eyes and delivered an unspoken message: the way out was barred. The banker averted his eyes from Jawad's henchman and tried once again to get into a comfortable position and figure out a reason for why he was there at all. *Is he going to make an example of this soldier? Is he going to kill him in front of me to warn me of the same fate if I talked?* The logic of Jawad's reasoning escaped him and his fear outweighed his judgement. He had never been in this type of situation, and he hoped he would never have to be again. There were times in his life when he had been frightened, but this feeling surpassed that in bounds. For the first time in his life, Saleh was truly scared.

Karim Basrawi remained hunched in his chair in the center of the garage, not looking around him, not moving an inch save for his psyche dragging his soul down deeper into despair. His mind was becoming a void; his thoughts of his family and home disappeared; his reason for being was vanishing fast. He knew he had only a short time left in this world, but he resolved not to beg for mercy. He would take his death like a soldier and stand to meet his executioner when the time came. Unconsciously, however, he began to rock back and forth, lips trembling, eyes closed tight.

Jawad's guard saw the change in the soldier's bearing and slight movements. He had seen it before, a man who has already surrendered to death, unable to control physical motions. He only hoped the man wouldn't try something stupid and force a violent reaction from him, not that he couldn't handle it, but cleaning up a bloody mess was not on his list of things to do that day. There were easier, quieter, and cleaner ways to kill a man, without struggle or strife.

It took Jawad fifteen minutes to return to the garage holding a single sheet of paper. Saleh, get out. Go to my sitting room and wait for me. Go now."

Saleh did not want to wait for a second invitation and slithered off his wonky chair and made for the door. He slouched over as he walked, not only because he was scared of being attacked as he made his way out but also since his obese shape required extra effort after sitting for so long and so uncomfortably.

Jawad watched Saleh scrape painfully out, noticing the trail of sweat running down the man's fat back. He snorted in disgust and then turned his attention to Basrawi. He stood in front of him waiting for the door to close and then held the piece of paper two inches from the major's nose. "I have this, Karim."

Basrawi opened his eyes but struggled to focus. He had to blink a few times to get an idea of what was on the paper in front of him. It looked like photographs. Raising his right arm and wiping away the sweat from his face with the back of his wrist, he blinked again and was then able to see what Jawad was holding. He gasped, "No, no, please, Jawad, please." His eyes bulged as he contradicted his earlier thoughts of not begging.

Jawad took a step back and looked down impassively at the man's tears as they began to fall. He took the sheet of paper and laid it on his own right hand. "I have this in my open palm Karim . . . and I can easily close my fist."

"Not my daughters, please, Jawad. My life for my daughters, please, I beg of you, Jawad."

"You understand there is no witness protection from the Americans for you or your daughters, Karim. You are here; they are in the kingdom. It will be of my choosing if you die or they die."

"Please, Jawad, please, they are innocent in all this. My life is forfeit. Please, take me if it is Allah's will but save my daughters," he pleaded, leaning forward in his chair, sweat and tears running down his face, eyes swollen, spittle forming on his lips.

"Enough. Do not beg anymore. It is beneath you. You are a soldier; behave like one," Jawad commanded.

Basrawi tried to compose himself and nodded, but between long breaths, he sobbed and rocked on his chair. He pressed his knees hard together almost constricting the blood flow but said no more as he stared at the paper in Jawad's hand.

"Fetch me the lieutenant," he ordered his accomplice.

"Straighten yourself up, man. You are an officer. Behave like one before your subordinate comes in, quickly now," Jawad directed Basrawi who did the best he could to wipe away the sweat and tears before the young officer entered the garage.

"Lieutenant, the major is under house arrest—"

"Major Basrawi, sir?" the young confused soldier interjected.

"You will follow orders, Lieutenant. Do not interrupt the general," Basrawi shouted almost at the top of his voice.

Jawad smiled and crossed his arms. Then he paused for effect. He wanted total control of the stage. "Shall we continue, Lieutenant?"

"Of course, sir, I was merely confused . . ."

"Understandable. I appreciate your loyalty to the major; however, he is now under house arrest and is now your responsibility. He is to be guarded inside this house twenty-four hours a day by a Saudi officer, not an American. They are not to be made aware of this order. Do you understand?"

"Yes, sir."

"Good, now go to his residence, pack all his things, and bring them here, including personal items and any documentation that you can find. He will continue to work with plans for the departure of Her Majesty from this location, but he will not leave unless he is accompanied by me or my friend here."

The young soldier looked over at the muscle-bound chaperon with tiny eyes and no neck and quickly identified the risk. He nodded his understanding of the situation and waited for further commands.

"Go, go now. I don't have much time, and Lieutenant, this will not come to the attention of the family. If it does, I know whom I can turn to for the reason." Jawad waved his hand in dismissal and then waited a few seconds after the door was closed.

"Karim, I think you have a good grasp of the situation. I am protecting you from the FBI, but one step out of line, my friend, and it is not you that will die." He held up the picture of Basrawi's daughters.

Harborview Medical Center, Seattle

Chad Peters was getting a little tired of the runaround. He called the FBI LA Field Office trying to get hold of Nick Seymour, but all he got was transferred and stuck in the 'please hold' cycle of death. Just a second before he was about to hang up, Nick came on the line.

"Seymour."

"Nick, Chad Peters. How are ya?"

"I'm good, Chad. What's up? What can I do for you?"

"Just wanted to give you a heads-up. I am in Seattle. Our friend Louisa Chavez has surfaced."

Nick sat up in his seat. He was still twiddling his thumbs trying to get a good fix on Omar but was coming up empty again. He didn't really know where this contact with the INS was going, but he was intrigued nonetheless.

"Is she in custody?"

"She's in a hospital unconscious. She got banged up pretty good in a fight with a semi on the freeway in downtown Seattle."

"How'd you get involved?"

"An astute state trooper ran the plate on the car she was driving. Turned out to be a stolen plate from New Mexico. He then ran the VIN and the car came back as being registered to her son, Alejandro. Since our favorite choirboy is being sought in connection to Janet Wyman's death, there's a nationwide BOLO for him raising everyone's interest. In the end, Washington State Patrol called California Highway Patrol, who then contacted me, so here I am with an umbrella in one hand, a coffee in the other, waiting for her to wake up."

"You know it's a myth about it always raining in Seattle, Chad."

"You wouldn't say that if you stood where I'm standing right now, Nick. The rainy season around here starts on January the first and ends on the thirty-first of December. Anyway, listen, I'm going to be here a while. The doctors say her injuries are not life threatening and she could wake up anytime. When she does, I'm going to be there and figure out what the hell she's been up to."

"You think she can finger Omar?"

"I don't know, buddy. I've got to tread lightly. I haven't seen a lawyer near her room yet, but that's going to change soon. The truck driver died in the accident, so I'm not sure how quickly the investigation is going to go, but if they can find fault, she may get arrested by the local PD, which will slow me down."

Nick scratched his head. "One thing you have going for you is that her next of kin is not going to show up anytime soon. If Alejandro does, then you've got two in the bag. But what the hell was she doing in Seattle?"

"State troopers said they found luggage and a bunch of cash, some of it Canadian. She was on Interstate 5 heading north and looking to the border, my guess. Seattle is only three hours from Vancouver, Nick." Chad looked out the window. It started to rain. "I'm going to have to chase down my contacts here to get a warrant to search the contents of her stuff, or I'm going have to cozy up to Seattle PD, but I'm guessing there's going to be a passport with her photo under a different name in there somewhere."

"Will you give me a call when you've had a chance to talk to her?"

"Sure thing, Nick. If you get anything on your guy, give me a call. Perhaps we can use that as leverage on her as well."

"Stay dry, Chad."

"Ain't going to happen. See ya."

Nick followed the corrections officer down the long, shiny clean, and well-lit corridor to an empty interview room where he was ushered in and told not to leave, even if there were an emergency. He nodded to the man who quickly disappeared and then remained standing and watching through the corridor window as other visitors and inmates of the LAPD Metropolitan Detention Center were brought to or taken from rooms after discussing details of incarceration. He didn't have to wait too long, as the officer who escorted him returned with the prisoner that Nick had come to see.

He eyed the prisoner as he was unshackled, placed in a seat, and then cuffed to a steel loop affixed to the table in the center of the room. While this was taking place, Nick made a quick analysis of the man in the orange jumpsuit who was brought in. *Large for a Filipino, dark but graying hair pulled back in a bun. Hands are worn, thick, not afraid of labor. Face sagging, eye bags drooping. Eyes on me, then the officer, then me. He's inquisitive, doesn't know who I am or what is going on. He probably thought I was a lawyer, no papers or briefcase, has likely figured out I'm law enforcement by now. A sliver of a smile. Silence, he's defensive.*

Nick kept his eyes on Romeo Washington as the corrections officer left the room in silence.

"Mr. Washington, my name is Nick Seymour, Special Agent FBI." He let the statement prod a reaction, which it did, resulting in a more effortful smile.

Washington wondered why the FBI had come to see him. He didn't respond. He didn't need to. Seymour knew who he was and what he was doing here; there was no point in needless pleasantries.

"I understand you worked for the Saudi Consulate for a while?"

Washington smiled fully for the first time, showing off his missing teeth from both his upper and lower sets. He leaned forward to engage with Nick. "Yes, that's true, but what are you going to give me?"

Nick was confused by the quick turnaround. He hadn't been in the room two minutes, and the prisoner was ready to bargain. "Give you?

Give you what, Washington?"

"Immunity. I need immunity before I talk to you. You have to promise me that."

"I can't promise you anything, and I certainly can't promise you immunity."

"Then why did you come here, Mr. FBI Man?" Nick thought Washington already had forgotten his name, which was fine by him, less recrimination later. It seemed Washington wasn't all that bright; however, all he needed was one nugget to move forward with his investigation. "I'm hoping you will show your patriotism for your adopted country, Mr. Washington."

Romeo was perplexed and didn't know what this man wanted. He listened, but his confusion was putting him on his back foot.

"America is in great peril. We have been attacked, and we are not sure if another attack will come." Nick continued, "We are looking for good citizens to help fight these terrorists and prevent another attack like New York. Did you know that a number of Filipinos were killed in New York?"

"No, no . . .," he mumbled.

"Men and women with brothers, sisters, fathers, mothers, all perished because of these cowardly terrorists."

"That's very sad . . . but—"

"And let's not forget that the Philippines has also been a target of terrorism, Mr. Washington, and it seems that now that those same attackers have come to our shores. I'm sure that when you were in the Philippines you thought you could be safe in America, and we welcomed you in. But now . . . now we are not safe anymore. You and I and other Americans, our friends and families, we are all under threat."

Washington nodded his head. He didn't know what to say, but the FBI man made sense. He let him ramble on so he could buy some time and try to weasel his way out of being in a cell for no longer than necessary.

"Now, I understand why you are here, Mr. Washington, and I understand why you did what you did."

Washington raised his thin eyebrows. He thought at last they were getting somewhere.

"And I can tell you are a benevolent man, Mr. Washington."

The Filipino didn't understand what that meant, but he could tell the FBI man was being friendly, even sympathetic.

"You only tried to help people, other people from other countries who only want a better life. I completely understand that; you really are a good man." Nick was throwing it all out there. He knew the man was a criminal and his ultimate goal was greed, but he was pissing in the wind with his investigation, and if it took a thick slice of patronization to ease his worries and help his cause, then that was what he would do. Nick was running out of time, and his support from the LA office was getting less and less as each day passed.

Although the FBI was being stretched thin, there was even talk of bringing in retired agents to pick up the slack. Despite this, his head was still on the chopping block to be let go. His loyalty to his friend Chris had outweighed his better judgement, which had resulted in the death of an MI5 officer. The concluding inquiry into the incident found that Nick Seymour breached high levels of confidentiality with an ally, acted unprofessionally, and lacked good moral judgement by not presenting himself for questioning with the British authorities. FBI managers tried in vain to protect their man and allowed him to remain in the UK for a short time while being demoted, but the British still feeling the loss of a senior officer, asked for him to be replaced. Embarrassed by Seymour, the FBI had no choice but to call him home to the United States and give him a low-key assignment until management could figure out if he was worth keeping. Nick now felt as helpless as a rock climber using only his fingernails and toenails to climb an impossibly high, sheer cliff face, expecting any minute to fall.

"But these Arabs." Nick leaned forward with a stern look. He could see Washington's eyes were beginning to droop. *He's getting bored.* "Perhaps even some of the people you have worked for are trying to kill us, trying to change our way of life, our freedom, Mr. Washington, our freedom." Nick banged on the desk to emphasize his point, startling the

Filipino. Nick was out of his comfort zone acting forceful, but he was willing to try anything.

"Okay, okay, chill out man. I haven't done anything to hurt America, you know?" he bleated in defense.

"But what about the Saudis, Mr. Washington? You know that most of the hijackers were from Saudi Arabia. Did you know some of them?"

"No, no. Are you shitting me? How would I know them? I mean that shit in New York, man, it was wrong, I mean really wrong, and I wouldn't get involved in any of that shit."

"Are you sure? If it turns out that you helped those guys in any way, you are heading for the chair. You know that, right?"

Washington started to sweat. This was getting serious. "What the fuck, man. I ain't done any shit like that, and I ain't hurt anybody. I don't want to hurt anybody. Like you said, man, I came to this country to be free. That stuff was bad, really bad. I didn't know that Filipinos were killed." He looked sad and a little withdrawn with his last statement.

Nick didn't know if Filipinos were killed either; it was something he made up on the fly trying to win some points.

"You want these terrorists to come back again, these Arabs?"

"Hell no, man."

"Then you can help me, right? You want to serve your country, you want to protect your friends and family right?"

"Shit, if I could join the army, I would be out there, man. I would kick some ass, believe me."

"I've no doubt you could," Nick said, lathering it on. As large as the man was, he was still a flat slob who probably couldn't punch his way out of a wet paper bag. "I wouldn't mess with you, Romeo. I can call you that, right?"

"Sure, boss, no problem." He nodded.

"Listen, Romeo, I need your help." Nick was happy. Romeo seemed calm, and it looked as if he was buckling; he wasn't asking for anything, at least not yet. Nick proceeded forward, not giving the prisoner time to reflect, and spoke with haste. "You know Omar

Abboud, right?"

"Sure, he's an asshole."

Nick crunched his face a little. That wasn't what he was expecting, but it was a good comment from his point of view. "He's a diplomat, and it's kind of difficult to get to talk to him, so I'm looking for him."

"I know he's a diplomat, and he likes to tell everyone around him that he is. He never talked to me, even if I stood next to him. He would talk to someone else to tell me what to do. The guy is an asshole."

"Really? Do you know where he is?"

"I don't know. He is gone for a long time. Then he comes back, he doesn't look at me; he thinks I don't exist."

"Yeah, I know how that is, Romeo. Some people don't understand the hard work people like you do."

"You got that right, man. Shit wouldn't get done without me there."

"Where did you see him last? Did you ever see him down at the motor pool?"

"No, he treats those guys like shit too. They don't like him either. I think the last place I saw him was at the warehouse."

"Where's that?"

"Over in Long Beach, you know the one just at the end of 710."

Nick pulled out his notebook. "Don't know that one. Why don't you give me the address?" Which Romeo gladly did. "What was he doing down there?" Nick asked.

"He got me to set up some beds and other furniture. Then I was told to hang around for some shipments after he took off."

"What furniture?"

"It was like five beds, you know, more like camping cots, then some comfy chairs, and a sofa. I even got a fridge set up and a small stove."

Five? Holy shit! "What about the shipments?"

"The truck showed up with three pallets. They offloaded them, and I was about to unwrap them, and these five guys showed up. I never saw them before. They told me to leave it and get out."

"Who were they, Arabs, Americans, who?"

"Arabs. One of them spoke good English, but the others didn't even look at me."

"Do you know what was on the pallets?"

"They were like three or four blue steel drums, must have been fifty-five-gallon."

Nick's mind was in a spin, his heart rate was pounding in his ears. "What else?"

"Some boxes, some kind of pump, but I couldn't get close to those."

Nick scribbled madly. "And then you left. Did you see Omar after that?"

"No man, I ended up here," he claimed with a goofy smile.

Nick returned the warmness and gave Romeo a small smile back. "Is there anything else you want to tell me, about Omar, about the warehouse. You told the police you had some information about the Saudis."

"Don't trust them. You tell the rest of the FBI not to trust them."

"Okay, Romeo, I get that message. I will pass that along, but why?"

Romeo went into a rant about how he was treated at the consulate. Omar wasn't the only one who treated the hired help with disdain. He complained about almost all the diplomats that he came across. He whined about not getting a raise and the hiring's, the unjust firings, then the run-ins with the police, the unpaid contractor bills, unpaid parking bills in the tens of thousands, crimes the diplomats got away with.

The list went on and on, and what he thought was dirt was of no importance to Nick. Virtually the whole time Romeo babbled along, Nick was elsewhere. He'd found his gold, he had an address, and more importantly, he had a connection to five Arabs and a possible location of Omar. Nick felt at ease, content. *At last, a good day in the office.*

"So what you going to do for me, man? I helped you out, right?"

Kapisa Province, Afghanistan

Chris was getting tired of the same drill. It was the third village they had been to since their overnight stay in the no-name hamlet, and it seemed that every place they visited since was as bleak and dreary as the first. Each time they came to a stop, the imam got out of the Land Cruiser and did his spiel, Chris stood one-legged out of the door, weapon in hand, Alex took up the rear gunner position, and Nash robotic like, stared forward in his seat and didn't add anything to the exercise.

As this visit became drawn out, Chris called Alex over for a chat with Nash, sharing his concerns while out of earshot from others. "Mr. Nash, I don't like where this is going. This bouncing around is only advertising to the locals that there are westerners asking questions. Are we still supposed to trust this guy?"

Alex nodded in agreement. He was glad Chris brought it up, but Nash replied, "I share your worry, Chris, but he has gotten us this far, and there hasn't been anything but friendliness towards us. He's got to ask questions for us, or we are not going to get anywhere, and I'm sure we are going to be visiting a few more places like this before the day is out."

"I get that, Mr. Nash, but the further we dive into Taliban country, the more my balls itch."

Alex smiled. He knew what Chris was feeling, that they were as far out on the edge as possible, and he could tell the Brit was getting further away from his comfort zone. Alex, on the other hand, was at ease. He was in enemy territory and was happy to be involved, ready to make a difference.

They were gathered around Nash's passenger window. Chris leaned in. "I mean we don't even know what the imam is saying to these people, how's he selling us, what's the story."

Nash looked seriously at Chris. "Your balls are going to itch a bit more, Chris," Nash replied deadpan. "He is telling people I am a drug dealer from Amsterdam."

"What the fuck?" Chris almost shouted. Alex took in a deep breath. He wasn't too happy to hear that either but did a better job of keeping his emotions in check.

"We are looking for opium and a partner to process and ship heroin."

Chris ran his hand over his face, closing his eyes and then swallowing hard. He looked at Nash his eyes widening in denial as he tried to find the right words. "Whose bright idea was that?"

"Mine." Nash was agitated with the question and sat up straighter and leaned closer to Chris. "I don't need to explain myself to you, so drop the attitude. We have a job to do, and I need you to stop throwing tantrums."

Chris was shocked but knew not to interrupt. *Jesus, who took the jam out of your donut?*

"I'm open to discussion, Chris, but don't forget that I am making the decisions for us. You are here to follow orders. Understood?"

Chris felt as if he had been slapped down; he felt disheartened and admonished. "Yes, Mr. Nash," he replied. He wanted to storm off but held his ground. He was already embarrassed in front of Alex and didn't want to make things worse. Before he could say anything else, the imam returned.

"Onwards, my friends, not much further this time. I think we are close to finding the people you seek, Richard."

Nash nodded solemnly and didn't reply. Everyone mounted up, and they were back on the poor excuse for the pockmarked track that locals called a road.

It took the small convoy another hour and a half to reach the next settlement. This time, however, it seemed to Chris that the place had a little more infrastructure, and the main thoroughfare through the village was better maintained. He also noted power lines and sparsely posted light poles, and to boost his mood, he spotted a makeshift mechanics workshop complete with barrels of fuel and a pump.

The imam caught Chris's look, "Yes, we will be here for a while, my British friend. You may take advantage of fueling up. I think we are in need, yes?"

Chris nodded. He wasn't in the mood. Instead, he was busy check-ing out the donkeys and carts, the staring eyeballs, the old men sitting on stoops smoking, the pack of children looking for handouts, the motionless men who froze and then whispered to each other that strangers were amongst them. *Fucking great way to advertise, fucking great,* he privately remonstrated.

The imam took over the direction once again, telling the driver which turn to take and where and when to slow down. The convoy passed by a number of houses and small hovels, which became more sporadic as they drove on and eventually dissipated. When they reached the southern edge of the village, which was the beginning of a long slope down towards a stream, the two Toyotas turned right and towards a large walled-in house festooned with lush trees and shrubs. As they made the turn, Chris could see women in the river washing clothes and small children playing on the rocks, all stopping to look at the dust cloud that was created when the two Toyotas came to a halt. The imam got out and walked quickly through a decorative wooden gate that broke up a continuous six-foot-tall mud wall that stretched one hundred feet in both directions. Chris tried in vain to look over the wall but was hindered by trees and bushes that were attempting to escape from the compound within.

Chris and Alex took up positions and went through the well-practiced motions of hurrying up to wait. Much to everyone's satisfac-tion, the imam came out quickly and jumped back into his spot next to a lethargic Nash.

"We must move these vehicles," he announced, giving instructions to the driver who complied and drove around the thick wall to find an opening. Once there, a waiting man held two large, wooden gates open for the visitors to enter into a expansive, open area surrounded by the same height walls as in the front.

The gates closed promptly behind them, and Chris grabbed his Makarov tightly, not knowing what to expect. His level of anticipation was high, but his mood was still low. It wasn't a good mixture, but at least he was alert.

"We will be here to rest," the imam reassured them as he exited the Toyota. His outlook had changed, and he appeared to be joyful, even excited. He motioned to Azzami, who scurried after his master with his baggage held tightly to his chest.

Neither Chris nor Alex could share the imam's disposition. They were conducting their methodical analysis of the situation and gauging their surroundings, looking for cover, concealment, angles, lighting, open doors, closed doors, windows, other openings, obstacles that could be used for and against them, a process that was taking only seconds to form conclusions. Within a minute of having both feet on the ground, each former soldier knew their advantages and disadvantages of the current situation, but they still needed to conduct a more thorough survey before they could relax.

Chris, scanning the courtyard, spoke to Alex without looking at him, "Let's get turned around when we get the chance."

Alex agreed. He was already thinking along the same lines. "We'll need fuel pretty soon. You see the pump on the way in?"

"Yeah, we'll do one at a time, but let's see what's in here first. I'm going in." Chris held up his hand to Nash, ordering him non-verbally to stop and wait at the Land Cruiser while he secured the interior of the building.

Alex felt secure enough to leave Nash alone and moved to find a good defensive position near the double gate. He didn't like the fact that they were shut in, but no threats had appeared thus far. He checked the security of the ramshackle gate and quickly surmised that it wasn't designed to keep people in or out; it was just a barrier to define territory. He walked back over to the two Afghan drivers to get them to point their vehicle noses outward and then began his own review of the rest of the compound.

Chris returned after a few minutes and approached Nash. "We're good. Everyone is playing happy families in there; it looks like they know each other pretty well."

No sooner had Chris finished his thought than the imam appeared with another pious-looking man following close behind. Introductions were made, and Chris's supposition held true as the imam introduced a colleague and friend. During the formalities, the host invited Nash to join them for tea and refreshments, which threw Chris for a loop. Incredulous, he looked on, mouth agape. *Deep in rag-head country and they want to have tea and crumpets. Only the Queen is missing. What a shit show.*

"It's called being hospitable, Chris," Alex whispered behind him, reading his colleague's body language. "It's traditional for Afghans."

"Yeah, I know, but the clock's ticking. Hope he realizes it; we are running out of time."

Alex didn't want to rehash the earlier heated conversation between Nash and Chris. The moment had passed, and it wasn't his job to play human resources. He wanted Chris to be on his game. "Could be worse places to shack up for the night. You want to survey?"

"Yeah, I like the walls, by the way."

"Me too. The gate isn't worth shit, but I think this place is bigger than we think."

The pair strode away taking in the sights and making mental notes. When they circled back to the front gate of the house, they spotted a few hundred feet from the road several structures that looked abandoned. They were the nearest buildings to their new abode. Alex cocked his head as he looked. He then drew out a pair of small binoculars from his side pocket and took a closer look.

"Empty by the look of things. Nice spot for an OP," Alex noted.

"Sucks chunks actually. If we've got to get out of here quick, we need to cross that river. Those buildings will have a perfect view over the crossing. We may need to go check on that."

"I didn't see any real threats going through the village, but then again, we weren't expected. We got more surprised looks than disapproval," Alex added reassuringly and then threw out a touch of trepidation, "But then again, I don't think it would take much for one of the locals to go find the nearest Taliban post and blow this thing for us."

"You think this drug lord story will stick?"

"That kinda shit has legs for only so long. The guy we are travelling with is an imam. Unless it is normal for religious leaders to be involved in the drug trade in these parts, our story is not going to hold water for long."

It was an ominous statement. Chris looked at his watch trying to figure out if the CIA director's orders were going to be followed by Nash. He looked hard into the distance and thought not. "Guess we need to make do, make the best of a bad situation, soldier on, keep smiling, turn your frown upside down, always look on the bright side of life, don't worry, be happy."

"You got any more clichés, Chris? I've got a thousand I can call up if you want a contest."

"Sorry, Brit army humor, I suppose. When you're eating a shit sandwich, the best you can hope for is that it's your own shit."

Alex shook his head and laughed as he walked away. "You win . . ."

CHAPTER FOURTEEN

Nangarhar Province, Afghanistan

ALEX FABER'S ASSUMPTION that their latest port of call was larger than others they had been to was correct. The host imam's home was in fact a guesthouse used as a retreat for religious seminars or a location for religious scholars to meet with like-minded individuals to discuss issues of the Koran or religion in general. The space had enough room for each of the small party to have his own area, inclusive of a bathroom with shower and a clean bed. In the scope of things, these were luxuries that none of the group had encountered for days. Richard Nash took full advantage of the hospitality and, after a long, hot shower, crashed out on the bed as if he had never slept in his life. If a Taliban tank were to drive straight through the compound, he would not have heard a single chink of armor hitting stone walls. He was dead to the world.

Chris took up his guard station at the head of the long corridor that led to each of the guest rooms. Alex sought a different set of priorities and used the down time to power up his sat phone and make a few calls back to JAWBREAKER and beyond. After an hour, Alex met with Chris, map in hand.

"You get a shower yet?" Chris asked pondering how good a hot shower in the middle of Afghanistan would be.

"No, will do soon. I've been plotting our location."

Chris got out of his chair and joined Alex on the tiled floor.

"We are in the Hisarak District, here." He pointed with a pencil. "To our immediate south is Mount Sikaram, or Sikaram Mountain, depending on whom you ask. I gauge that to be about fifty miles in a straight line, and that is the zero line." He pointed again. "This is as close to Pakistan as we have been. Beyond that are the Tribal Areas of

Pakistan. If we ever end up going that way, we won't be getting a warm welcome."

Chris, crouching over the map, went down on one knee, let out a sigh, and then stroked his dirty beard. "I remember seeing a snow-capped peak on the way in. At least we have a bearing. I don't suppose there's a triple-wide freeway to take us over the top?"

"I wish," Alex answered, now sitting cross-legged on the floor next to Chris. They kept their conversation to a whisper. The corridors in the guesthouse were long with some sharp corners that could easily conceal a person listening in. "I've been thinking about our lack of an escape plan," Alex continued. "We are so deep in that it's not funny anymore. I know I said I wanted to go after the big man, but I don't see our situation changing for the better anytime soon. Nash is out of it. He's become a non-player. I'm not sure if he will perk up if we find TRODPINT, but I am not feeling too optimistic."

Chris was taken a little bit aback. He knew Alex was capable of operating behind enemy lines alone, but he was starting to become more cautious for their own safety. Chris felt the same way he did from the get go. He liked the less than gung-ho attitude and pragmatism that his new friend was showing.

"I made some calls; the good news is the bad news for us."

Chris winced, "Do I want to hear this?"

Alex nodded solemnly. "The bombing campaign has started in the north."

"Meaning we are behind an active enemy front line," Chris finished Alex's thought.

"Yes."

"So the drive in was the easy part. The drive out may not exist, and that's why you're showing me a mountain."

"Right. But here's a bit more news. An ODA has reached JAW-BREAKER. They have air assets on site. If we call it in, we could have someone here in a reasonable amount of time."

"Does reasonable amount of time mean how long our ammo can hold out?"

Alex smiled, showing deep lines around his face. He didn't think Chris's comment was sarcastic; he thought he was being practical, and he wasn't flapping about it. Alex was getting to like Chris more as time went by. "The easiest day was yesterday, Chris."

"Yeah, well tomorrow doesn't need to be a shit storm either. We can still control some of this," he said with confidence.

"How so?"

"Let's give the ODA a heads-up that we will need extraction within the next twenty-four."

Alex nodded. He agreed in principle.

Chris added, "You've seen the state Nash is in. I've said it before. He's not himself. Everyone from here to Kabul can hear him snoring."

"Ed Guild wants to pull him too. He's making his case with Langley right now. He thinks that, with the distraction in the north, we can slip the ODA in to get us."

"Won't that encroach on the Pentagon's mission?"

"It would, but if an American throws up a flare in a war zone, the military is duty bound to help."

"Even if we don't exist."

Alex shrugged his shoulders. "It's not like I haven't been in this situation before."

Chris was about to continue the conversation but stopped himself as he heard footsteps on a nearby walkway. Alex rushed to pick up the map.

"Gentlemen, gentlemen, where is Richard? We must speak," asked the imam breathlessly, having rushed down the corridor.

"He's sleeping. We don't need to wake him," Chris replied.

"But we must. I have news." The imam was insistent and moved to brush passed the two westerners.

Both Alex and Chris got off the floor. They didn't raise a hand or voice; their mere physical presence gave the imam pause for thought and stopped his train.

"What is it, Imam? We can pass the information on to him after he is awake. He needs his rest."

"Ah, true guardians, always willing to protect. I see that you mean well, Chris. I trust that he is feeling a little under the weather?"

Chris tried his best not to look surprised, unaware of the imam's keen perception. *Is Nash that bad that he sees it too?* "It must be important news for you to come rushing like this, Imam. How can we help?"

The imam relented. He wanted to be the one to break the news, but he could see he was not going to get past the two sentinels. "Chris, a man will come here soon, maybe today or maybe tomorrow. He is someone Richard is looking for."

TRODPINT, seriously? "I will pass that on. He should be awake soon." The imam was about to leave, but Chris thought he looked antsy. "Was there something else?"

"Yes, yes." He wringed his hands together, at that moment looking more like a street vendor selling a lame camel than a devout religious leader. "We are having a small party in my honor this evening," he explained quietly as if it were some state secret. "Unfortunately, and please understand this is not my idea, it was quite the pleasant surprise from my host to show his pleasure at my release, but . . . ."

Chris stared at the man who was becoming more nervous after each word he spoke. He watched as the cleric danced his weight from one foot to the other; he noticed how he began to look around in each direction as if expecting a wall to fall in or a dagger to fly into his chest. Chris recognized a man who was scared of something or at least trying to hide something.

"But this party . . . it is not for . . ." The imam struggled for words, which was out of character for the normally verbose man.

"You don't want us there," Alex pointed out.

The relief on the imam's face was obvious, as he beamed one of his famous pearly white smiles, "Yes, yes, unfortunately, my friends, this is a private party. You understand, I am sure. There will be some guests, but please don't worry. They are no threat to you. We will have some music and food, nothing to concern you, but your guns . . . ."

"You would like us to keep away and out of sight," Chris chimed in softly.

"Yes, I forget how perceptive you gentlemen are, and I see that you understand."

"Of course, Imam, we understand, and please thank your host for the hospitality he has shown towards us. I hope we are not putting anyone in danger here. We wouldn't want anyone to be harmed in anyway because of us." Chris pulled his Makarov out of its holster and made a feeble attempt to dust it off and then showed it to Alex, saying to him, "I need to clean this soon."

Alex nodded at the silent threat but kept his smile to himself.

The imam's eyes widened. The unspoken words were loud in the cramped corridor. The imam mumbled a few more incoherent words and then scuttled off back in the direction he came.

"Fucking pussy."

"He got your message, Chris."

Phoenix–Deer Valley Municipal Airport

The dark Arizona desert night covered the landing of the white Boeing 757 Saudi Arabian Royal Fleet aircraft as it taxied its way around the deserted Deer Valley Municipal Airport. The 757, unlike any other in the Saudi fleet, carried the designation HZ-HMED, which was fitted out as a mobile hospital, appropriate for the task of moving the ailing queen from the United States back to the Kingdom of Saudi Arabia.

Jawad was waiting patiently in the tiny Spanish-styled terminal as he watched phase one of his evacuation plans for the family get underway. He wanted to smile, wanted to feel happy that the plane was soon to be under his control, but his immediate concern was not only the security of the aircraft and the well-being of the staff on board, who had just completed a transatlantic journey from Geneva, but also of the secret cargo that should have been loaded in the kingdom. His sources in his home country assured him that the canisters were on board, but that was before the initial trip for the aircraft to the United States was postponed for a much more pressing need.

Alone, Jawad stood looking out the plate glass window in the terminal with his arms folded across his chest as he concentrated on the plane and the rush of ground crew vehicles getting into position to provide service. His mind was contorting in different directions knowing that the best-laid plans could easily flounder with so many variables in play. He was a master at flexibility and compromise, but he didn't expect or plan for his plane to be redirected at such short notice due to the attacks on the eleventh of September. Control of the situation was taken away from him when the royal family, fearing for King Fahd's safety and the potential of being stranded in the middle of a military crises arising from a pending US offensive in the region, secreted the chronically ill monarch out of the country in the airborne hospital. This bump in the schedule worried Jawad as the viability and the shelf life of the contents on board was diminishing as each day passed. To add to his pensiveness, he assumed that if he was not quick, the plane could be recalled to move the king once again.

When the aircraft finally came to a halt and the engines were turned off, the worker ants honed in to provide fuel, power, water, a mobile staircase, and catering services, all of which were foreign to the small airport and as such were outlined in Jawad's plan and organized and executed by Major Basrawi. Everything was moving along smoothly, even when the immigrations and customs officers boarded the plane to conduct their due diligence. Once the fueling was completed, the moment that Jawad had been waiting for had arrived. A Praxair hazardous-material flatbed truck carrying numerous tanks and canisters pulled up next to the loading hatch of the plane and began swapping out oxygen tanks with the onboard medical supply. With all the other activities happening around the plane, Jawad was fixated on just this one thing. The driver was conducting his duties as normal, swapping the canisters one for one, and then getting an airline representative to sign for the consignment. The driver secured his new load, backed his truck up, then headed for the exit gate where he was stopped and checked over by a lazy security guard, and then was left to go on his way.

Jawad continued to watch the plane for a few minutes as the pilots and crew exited the plane and a set of American contract security officers took up position around the aircraft to provide twenty-four-hour security. Satisfied the first part of the plan was complete, he walked out of the terminal and joined his waiting driver who was sitting in the parking lot with an idling engine trying to keep the interior cool. Jawad didn't have to instruct the man where to go, and he didn't feel the need to converse, so he remained silent, beset by thoughts of his precious cargo that was shipped out of the airport just minutes before him.

It was a quiet three-hour ride from Phoenix to the small city of Williams in northern Arizona, which locals called the gateway to the Grand Canyon. Jawad couldn't have cared less. He wasn't interested in seeing a hole in the ground and was too tightly wound up to sleep and too lost in his thoughts to talk to his companion about the sites the state had to offer. He'd seen enough cacti to last a lifetime. His driver was the type of subordinate every manager wanted; he did what he was told, he was discreet, and he only ever spoke when he was spoken to. As such, the journey was taken in complete silence.

Passing the Praxair truck on Interstate 17 at Black Canyon City, they were slightly ahead of schedule. However, Jawad was more interested in scouting the meeting place before the truck arrived and was pleased with the extra time he was getting. Close to their destination, they exited from I-40 where Jawad's driver crawled westwards along Route 66 towards the small city of three thousand. There wasn't a soul to be seen in these wee hours, which would normally would have troubled Jawad, but as they approached the center of town, he looked over to the north where a blaze lit up the night sky, which was taking place in the Canyon Gateway RV Park. He looked at the digital clock on the dashboard and mentally put a check mark on his list of things that needed to happen that night. He smiled. It was a small part of the operation, but it was needed. *That will keep the local sheriff busy for some time.*

Regardless of the planned distraction, they plodded carefully on keeping to the speed limit and played Johnny-good-citizen to the max. Passing through the sleepy town, the driver took a left turn into the mountain-view cemetery situated in a copse that ran almost parallel to the freeway.

He drove slowly and cautiously through the crisscross roads and walkways before coming to a halt at a predetermined junction. It was still pitch dark as Jawad got carefully out of the pickup, motioning his driver to follow. They walked slowly and deliberately around the gravestones and trees keeping a watchful eye and keen ear for any type of movement or mechanical sound. On occasion, Jawad stopped to look and listen. His driver matched his movements without question, also going through the same stealthy motions. As they moved deeper into the old graveyard, Jawad reminded himself that during the daytime rehearsal a month previous, he almost stepped on a rattlesnake. Now, he warned himself to step wisely and not panic if wildlife threw a wrench in his progress.

By the time they reached the edge of the burial grounds, their night vision and a full moon allowed them to see into a quarry where a Ford transit van was parked next to a small structure. Jawad signaled his driver to stay in position as he moved forward. His man held an Uzi down by his right leg, ready to unleash a barrage of automatic fire if events took a surprising turn.

Before Jawad could get close to the van, the passenger door opened. However, the interior light did not illuminate as a shadowed figure got out. Jawad stopped immediately.

"Jawad?"

He was surprised to hear a familiar voice. "Omar?"

The two Arabs approached each other, forcing themselves to not be cordial. They were on an operation, and they needed their wits about them in the darkness.

"Why are you here?"

"We have a lot to discuss, Jawad, but we must see this through first.

Where is the transportation?"

"It should be here momentarily. Where are the other vehicles?"

Omar turned and pointed behind him. "I put them together. I found another trail at the edge of the quarry. We can escape that way if we need to."

"If you had come here when I had asked you last month, you would know that trail is not passable by vehicle. It is merely a footpath to the hotel. I made specific diagrams where they need to be if we are compromised. What is wrong with you?"

"There's nothing wrong with me, Jawad, but why is Abdo in Phoenix?"

So that's why he's here. He's worried, Jawad concluded. "You really want to do this now? We are at a critical phase of this operation, Omar. We can talk about this later."

"We have to talk about this now. He was supposed to be here, not you." The tone of his voice was accusatory, as was the volume of his statement. "He is the one to test the chemicals. We do not have the equipment, and we do not know if during the delay of the flight they have become unstable or inert."

"Omar, we have nothing to worry about. Our contacts in the kingdom have assured me that everything is in order. We cannot change anything now; we must proceed."

Omar took a threatening step forward. "I ask you again, Jawad," he said with a raised voice, "why is Abdo in Phoenix?"

"Keep your voice low, Omar," Jawad demanded. "Every sound is amplified in this environment." Then he took a step closer to his colleague. This wasn't the time or place to have this conversation, but the younger man was pressing. Jawad's tone was easy, quiet, in control. "Abdo has made mistakes. He may not know what he has done yet, but the whole operation could easily fall apart, even now. The FBI was closing in on him because of his ties to Imam al-Hallak and his fundraising activities. It is the imam's fault that he is not here. I sent him to Phoenix to get on the plane with the family. We need to get him out of the country before he is picked up by the authorities."

"But Jawad—"

"But nothing, Omar. He is not like us. He is weak; he will not stand up to scrutiny or interrogation. I cannot allow him to be imprisoned. He is our friend. We need him for other operations. Surely you understand that?"

Omar pondered what he had just been told, but Jawad continued.

Surprised by Omar's presence, Jawad decided to take the opportunity to ask questions of his own. "Now I have a question for you. Abdo said he had papers; he wanted to stay here in America. Did you have something to do with that?"

Omar didn't have time to respond. The Praxair vehicle pulled into the quarry, lights ablaze, ruining everyone's night vision.

"Bring those vehicles over here now, Omar. Go. There is no time to waste," Jawad ordered and then went about marshalling the truck into place.

The truck driver followed Jawad's instructions to park his vehicle and then went through the motions of unloading some of his cargo onto the rear lift deck. The first white van, destined for San Francisco, pulled up alongside. Jawad opened the rear doors as the driver got out to assist the Praxair trucker who rolled four, four-foot, blue cylinders onto the lift and then gently lowered it to the ground. As much as Jawad was keen to rush through this part of the operation, he was happy to see that his Praxair man operated his equipment safely and was taking no risks or cutting corners. The last thing anyone wanted in this phase was for one of the cylinders to fall on someone or, worse, break open spilling its contents.

The San Francisco driver stood back to let the Praxair man roll one of the upright cylinders towards the back of the van. He tipped it over, and then they both lifted it into the rear, laying it flat and then securing it from rolling around. As soon as the doors of the van were shut, the Frisco driver jumped in his seat and sensibly and slowly pulled away. The second transport, destined for Portland with two drivers, pulled into place, and the same exercise was repeated, and then again for Los Angeles. Jawad looked at his watch as Omar joined him. There was nothing to say; they just had to observe and let their workers continue with their tasks. A few minutes more had passed when the last van, intended for San Diego, pulled in to pick up the last cylinder. Jawad was still happy; things were going smoothly. Omar's whining was the only kink in the program, but when Jawad looked over at him, he seemed content that their deadly cargo was finally loaded and being shipped. Both Arabs were satisfied that the distribution portion of Operation Najd was underway.

When the last van and the Praxair truck left the quarry, they turned to look at each other, then smiled, and without words Omar, hugged Jawad. It looked as if all reservations were put aside.

"Why did you come here, my friend?" Jawad asked.

Omar's pleasant disposition changed back to the offensive. "Because it was the only way I could see you," he fumed. "I needed to talk to you about Abdo. And now that I have heard your explanation, I must say that I strongly disagree with you, Jawad. Abdo is more valuable here."

"You mean for you he is more valuable if he is here, but not to the cause. Am I understanding that correctly?" Jawad let out a sigh of exasperation but quickly added to prevent Omar from answering. "Need I remind you that you are not running operations, Omar? We have already discussed this, and frankly, I don't like where your mind is. I feel like you are trying to take things into your own hands."

"Abdo and I . . . well, we both feel that we can do much more here in America. We can go on to greater things."

"Stop!" Jawad shouted. "You are going too far; that is not your call. I shouldn't have to explain myself—"

"I think you should explain. Where have you been all this time? What have you been doing?"

"THAT . . . is none of your concern." Jawad was losing his cool. He needed to retain his composure, but he squared off with the shorter man. "You don't know how shoddy Abdo's security was. Why did he have all the names of our soldiers? Why, Omar? Tell me."

"I gave them to him. I could not be caught with them."

"And that is what concerns me. That list should have been destroyed. If the FBI raided Abdo, this operation would have been over, we could have been arrested tonight . . . and another thing my, young friend. You should have taken care of your immigration contact. If that list is found and the men are arrested, then she would be under investigation and she would not be able to withstand interrogation. She would surrender your name."

"She left the country, Jawad."

"Are you sure, really?" he snapped. "You are putting all your future plans and safety on the hope that one woman will never talk about what she did for you, even after the attacks take place . . . you are naïve Omar. You are stupid. You are a risk."

The last statement stung Omar. He dropped his head, slumped his shoulders, and crouched back a step. "I will find her, Jawad. I will take care of it myself."

"It may be too late for that. Who knows where she is?" he hissed.

"Then you must help me Jawad, together we can find her."

"No, no, no, that is not what we are going to do. You will return to Los Angeles. You are deviating from the plan, Omar. You need to be in the consulate when the attacks take place. You cannot subject yourself to open conflict or harassment by the authorities. You need the protection of the diplomatic community. What are you thinking?"

"Then let me go to Phoenix with you," he pleaded.

"Again, no! Do as you're told. The consulate general is already with the family overseeing the logistics and working with the State Department. He will think it strange that you show up. You must go to Los Angeles and use the consulate for protection as we planned. When things die down, you will be called back to the kingdom."

Disillusioned, Omar looked to the dirt at his feet. "I need a ride," he whimpered.

Jawad shook his head. He had had high hopes for this man to be one of his more valued assets; instead, he was becoming more of a liability. "You have really not thought this out, have you?" he scolded but didn't wait for a response. "We will travel together to Phoenix, and my driver will take you to Los Angles, but you will not show your face to anyone, understand? He can drop me on the outskirts of the city, and I can make my own way." He thundered off, not waiting for a response. It was going to be another quiet ride.

Hisarak District, Afghanistan

Chris, still on duty, was fixing the bandage on his wound when Azzami coming from the main house barreled towards him. Behind him was another boy that he didn't recognize. Chris stood up from his chair not sure what to expect. Both boys, laughing and giggling like little girls, came to a skidding stop before him.

"Azzami, who is this?" Chris asked politely.

"My cousin Mateen." He beamed as he once again clutched his prized possessions close to his chest. Chris looked the visitor over, who looked a little more innocent and younger than his cousin.

"You look like you are up to no good. What are you doing?"

"We have to change for the party, get ready."

Chris wasn't sure what that meant. He thought the party was for the imam and guests, not the servants. He blew it off but wanted to get them out of the corridor and away from the westerners' quarters. "Well, you can't do it around here. Go find somewhere else. Go, go. I don't want to see you around here."

Mateen hid behind his cousin and put his hand over his face.

"He wanted to see a westerner, that's all." Azzami laughed.

"Okay, he's done that. Now go. Yallah, yallah," waving his hands in the air, "or whatever it is they say around here."

Azzami spotted the loose bandage around Chris' elbow. "But what are you doing? You are hurt. What is wrong?" his voice pleaded with genuine concern.

"It's nothing for you to worry about. Go on, get out of here."

"Please let me help, Chris. I can help, please." He dropped his bags noisily. It sounded like little bells clanging together. Chris cocked his head and squinted at the bundle on the floor, but before he could ask Azzami anything, the boy said something to his cousin and then ran back to where he came from.

Chris was confused and sat back down. Azzami never went any-where without his precious bags, and he wasn't sure where he went. He looked at Mateen standing in front of him, wide-eyed and shy. It was obvious he didn't know what to say or do. Chris stopped playing with his bandages and then stared at the young boy but was at a loss. "Umm," he mumbled, "what the fuck am I supposed to do now?"

Both adult and boy looked each other over, the youngster looking at the gun lying across the man's knees, the grownup staring at the charming, innocent youth. Neither could find words or make the next move; each was as uncomfortable as the other.

Mercifully for both strangers, Azzami returned with some hot wa-ter, a towel, gauze, fresh bandages, and a bottle of cleaning solution. He knelt in front of Chris. "Show me your injury," he ordered.

Chris complied and let his old bandage fall to the floor. "How do you know how to do this, Azzami?"

"I want to be a doctor one day, like my father."

"He showed you how to do this?"

"Yes, I can do many things. I was his assistant."

"Was he the one to teach you English too?"

"Some, but not all. The imam, he teaches too. Stop holding your arm. Go loose, loose," he insisted trying to make a wet noodle. Chris smiled and obeyed the order. Over the last few days, he and Azzami were getting on well. Every time they stopped, he ensured that everyone took water, had a snack. Even Alex commented that it was nice to have a travelling housewife. In the evenings, they chatted a little when he was on guard duty and others were sleeping.

"So what happened to your father?" Chris asked feeling bad that he had not enquired before.

Azzami didn't blink but concentrated on his work, though he hesi-tated before he spoke. Mateen stood quietly and simply looked on. "When the Russians came, he worked in the villages with the mujahi-deen. He move around a lot. Sometimes I go; sometimes I stay home with my mother. One day the Russians they come to my house to look for him. My mother . . . she did not tell them, but they hurt her, and my brother, he tried to stop them." Azzami's face was stone; he showed no emotion. He took his time with cleaning and dressing the wound. "They beat him, many of them, five or six, I think. I was too young to stop them. Relax, relax. How you say it, Chris? You are tense."

He nodded. "Yes, that's the right word, Azzami. Sorry." He blushed, knowing where this was going, and waited for him to continue. It took a second.

"But they took my mother. I tried to help my brother, but I didn't know how at the time. I had to wait for my father, but it was too late. He went to look for my mother, and he found her outside police station, but he was too late for her."

Chris had heard the story before of Soviet soldiers capturing and interrogating doctors for information about the local resistance. He looked into the blank face of his nurse, who continued to clean his wound.

There was silence, but Azzami coughed back an emotion. "Sorry . . . my mother was hanged outside the police station, but it was too dangerous to stay. We buried my mother and brother next to each other and then went to mountain for safe."

"Safety."

"Safety, yes. Sorry my English not so good sometimes."

"It's fine. You're doing good. How old are you, Azzami?"

"Eighteen."

Shit, he must have been four or five years old. What an age to bury your mother and brother, Chris thought sadly.

"We went to mountain for safety, and we stayed with different tribes until war was over. We come here too. But my father, he was sick. He had tubercle—"

"Tuberculosis," Chris finished for him.

He nodded. "He died when I was fifteen. But he made arrangement with the imam. He said no doctor for me, too dangerous if Russians came back. He wanted me to be religious scholar. He thinked it would be safer."

"He thought you would be safer."

"Yes, I must learn. He thought I would be safer . . . there, we have finished."

"You like what you do for the imam?"

Azzami stayed quiet and went about picking up his things. He was avoiding eye contact with Chris.

"Azzami, do you like the imam?"

"We have to go, Chris. I will change bandage for you tomorrow, okay?"

"Yes, that's okay, thank you." He reached out and grabbed Azzami's wrist gently to get his attention. "I think you would make a good doctor. You should follow your dream, Azzami."

The youth didn't reply. He shifted his eyes away again. Chris could see he was holding something back but didn't want to push; he let go. He wondered fleetingly what he could do for the young man, but at that point in time, it was fruitless.

There was another din from down the hallway. As Azzami picked up the last of his things, he stood in time to see the imam, robes billowing behind him in his wake, striding forcefully towards them. He spoke loudly in Pashtun to Azzami. Chris didn't like his tone and stood up to intervene if things were to escalate. The imam's berating of Azzami continued, and much to his credit, the youth did not answer back but bowed his head in subservience and scurried off to do whatever the imam's bidding was. *This ass-wipe has something over him*, Chris assumed as he heard little bells clink together again. *What the fuck is that sound?*

"I apologize, my young British friend. They should not be bothering you. They have other things they should be doing."

"They were not bothering me, Imam. In fact, Azzami helped me with my dressing. He's a talented young lad, that one."

"Yes, yes, you are correct, but our guests will be arriving soon. They must prepare. You will excuse me . . . I must also . . ." He didn't finish his sentence and turned away, preoccupied with something that Chris had no desire to explore.

Chris nodded and watched the flowing robes disappear down the corridor and thought with distrust, *Yeah fuck off, you muppet.*

"The band has arrived," Alex squawked over the radio.

"AC/DC?"

"More like the Backstreet Afghans."

"They got groupies?"

"Negative. Kettle drums, some weird-looking guitar, few trumpets, that sort of thing." Alex was speaking from a hide he built, monitoring the entryway to observe as the guests arrived.

"Five middle-aged guys," he continued to report.

Nash was sitting next to Chris in the front of one of the Land Cruisers. "Probably a dutar," he said, as if it mattered.

"Roger," Chris responded.

The plan was simple. They would wait out the party in the vehicle, ready to bolt if necessary, and then pick up Alex on the way out. Nash cradled the sat phone and attempted to make a few calls, but coverage was spotty, and after a while he gave up.

"More traffic. Stand by," Alex announced.

Chris held his focus towards the open gate. All he needed to do was turn the ignition and mash the gas.

"Three vehicles, multiple men exiting . . . looks like a few Azzami clones as well. Maybe all these guys have brought their servants."

Nash let out a short breath of air. Chris thought he was about to say something, but Alex communicated again.

"I count six visitors, plus four servants. They are all going in."

"Ten-four," Chris replied confirming he heard the transmission. He started to do the math. *Two imams already there, Azzami, Mateen, two houseboys, two cooks, five Backstreet Afghans, six visitors, and four servants; twenty-three already. That's a handful. Alex would have said something if there were weapons on show. Is anyone concealing something? Are any of these guys Taliban?* His suppositions were starting to accelerate.

Nash was reading his mind. "I make twenty-three so far, Chris. More on the way?"

"I don't know, Mr. Nash. The imam was pretty vague with details."

"These affairs can last a while, well past midnight, I would say."

"So we will have to play cards for the rest of the night because we are here for the duration."

"We have cards?"

"I was being facetious."

Nash gave him a smile. "We've sat and waited like this in the past, you and I."

"That was a long time ago, Mr. Nash, and things were a little different then."

"Germany was a great place to be. There was so much going on . . ."

They began to reminisce. Chris was happy to chat with him again. Over the last few days, his boss had seemed withdrawn, almost reclusive and non-communicative. By his fresh appearance, it looked like all he had needed was a decent night's sleep, warm food, and hot water. His good mood was also lifted by the news that someone, possibly a member of TRODPINT, was on his way.

Their warm and fuzzy conversation was broken for a second by Alex. "I hear light music. Sounds like it should be in an elevator. Perhaps dinner is served. Maybe all guests have arrived."

Chris and Nash were too far from the main house to hear the progress of the party.

"Roger that," Chris replied.

Nash let Chris concentrate on his job for a few minutes before he continued his chat. He was proud of his protégé and his affable character. He had to admit that Chris had some rough edges and did from time to time exceed his boundaries, but Nash liked him, had confidence in him, and was eager to be part of what Chris could become. He especially liked how he was handling things here and now, behind enemy lines, and how he formed a solid bond with a member of the coveted CIA SAD team. He knew long ago that Chris would never be some desk-jockey, analyst, manager, or administrator. Nash knew he had found the real deal. All he had to do was protect Chris, teach him, guide him, and support his actions just for a few more steps in his career. He surprised himself when he looked over at his friend and thought, *It's never boring around this guy. There's always something happening, always trouble around the next corner, but here he is, still soldiering on. You have to respect that.*

"What's wrong, Mr. Nash? Wish you'd brought your banjo?"

"I left it with my cards."

"Touché, Mr. Nash, touché."

"I need to stand and stretch for a while. Join me."

They both exited the Toyota and met at the front of the vehicle. Nash leaned against the hood, arms thrust down into his jacket pockets. They stood there in silence.

Nash looked at the stars, breathed in the fresh air, and listened to nature take over the night. He was sentimental for a second. "You could easily forget that we are in a war zone."

Chris followed Nash's gaze. "It's pretty sad; that it is."

It was about two hours after Alex's last report that the Backstreet Afghans cranked up the tunes. The trumpets were blaring, drums were banging, and then there was a whole lot of cheering, shouting, and excited singing. The racket went on well past midnight as Nash predicted, but his mood changed somewhat, and he began to shut down. He became withdrawn, as if there was some foreboding event that would ruin the evening but was not letting on the secret. Chris noticed and felt disappointed in the change. He couldn't figure it out, so he reverted to his full-time duty of being vigilant from the relative safety of the Toyota and checked in from time to time with Alex.

The music was continuous. Sometimes Chris couldn't figure out if they started a new tune or the one he had just heard was a conglomeration of another, but the drummer kept hammering away on the kettle drums, and the songs kept being sung. It must have been around two in the morning that, one by one, each of the instruments ceased to play. All that could be heard was the slow beat of a drum. It alone was beat for a minute. There was no more hooting or hollering. It was just the drum announcing that peace was on its way, it was time to finish and close out the night.

"Sounds like their wrapping up."

"Roger," Alex replied.

Nash sat up from his slumped posture, wide awake but still quiet.

"Backstreet Boys are mounting up." Alex reported.

"They been promoted?"

"Kept me interested; stayed awake the whole time."

"If you want to be their agent, then go for it."

"Looks like they are the only ones heading out so far."

"Roger." *Eighteen left inside*, Chris calculated.

Everything went quiet. If a donkey had farted in Kabul. they would have heard it from where they were. It was eerie, but the cacophony of the musicians killed their hearing, just as a bright light would kill night vision. It took Chris, Nash, and Alex a while to readjust to the total silence.

"Do you hear that?" Alex whispered over the radio.

Chris strained his ears. He concentrated as hard as he could, hearing something unusual. He thought it was an animal, perhaps a screeching cat, but it was not. "I got something, not sure. Stand by, Alex."

As Chris spoke, Nash leaned over and held his head in his hands. *What the hell is wrong with him?*

But then the sounds became screams, screams that came from within the house.

CHAPTER FIFTEEN

Hisarak District, Afghanistan

CHRIS SPRANG OUT OF THE VEHICLE quicker than a burning rat running up a drainpipe. He retrieved his rifle from the seat behind him and then froze in place waiting for the next indicator of risk, but for some reason he was feeling different sensations from when he was shot at or in other forms of danger. This time he felt it strange to hear screams. He was confused as he wasn't sure what the source of the distress was or where it was coming from. His stomach fluttered, his body temperature began to rise, all his senses were alert, but he didn't have a grasp of the situation.

"Chris . . ." Nash began, but was waved off and not offered a reply. Nash insisted again, "Chris, leave it alone."

Chris ignored the request and took a step forward when he heard yet another cry. *That's not a woman. What the hell?* "Alex?"

"I don't know, Chris."

He slung his rifle over his shoulder and drew his Makarov. "Close in on Nash. I'm going in."

"Roger. Wait for me to have eyeballs on you."

"Make it quick."

"Chris, you can't go in there. Let it go," Nash pleaded.

"Are you deaf? Someone is screaming in there. You stay here. Wait for Alex."

Nash ignored him and got out of the Toyota and rushed around to the front to stop Chris from going. He reached out and grabbed Chris's arm and jerked him around.

Chris swung his arm violently away. "What the fuck's wrong with you? Wait here!" Chris spotted Alex jogging towards him, prompting him to begin running into the main building. While he ran, he noticed their Afghan escorts sitting casually in a tight circle on the ground, paying no heed to the distress that Chris was hearing. *Am I the only one who gives a shit around here?*

He reached the door to the main corridor and paused, waiting for a sign or sound to enable his next act. He didn't have to wait long. The sound of a boy screaming and an opposing male voice shouting something he couldn't understand thrust him into action. He found the door where the disturbance was coming from, and without hesitation, he kicked it in. The door flung open, and to his horror in the dim light of the candlelit room, he saw the imam's naked form step away from a bed where an equally naked young boy was bound by his wrists to the headboard. The imam began to shout at the top of his voice words that Chris could not understand or even hear. Chris was so incensed, his jaw was clenched tight, his eyes were wide, his pulse was racing, racing too fast. He stood shocked for a moment not fully understanding the spectacle. In denial, he could not believe what he was seeing, but it was only when the young boy turned around to see the commotion that Chris recognized Mateen on the bed. The familiarity of the face brought him back to reality, and without thinking about what he was doing, he moved forward into the room. When he did, the imam, who was still shouting at the intruder, backed up to grab his clothes. As the imam moved a pile of clothes from a corner of the room, a body stirred underneath.

Chris was distracted by the movement as the figure came alive and attempted to stand up. Chris held off making his next move until the potential threat manifested itself. He held his Makarov in his right hand. All the while, the imam continued yelling, now in English, for Chris to get out. The shape in the corner stood up and began to straighten its clothing and affix a woman's headdress that had come undone. As the figure continued with its back to Chris, he heard the sounds that had haunted him earlier in the day, bells.

What the fuck is going on here? Where did this woman come from? His thoughts were moving too fast. There were too many things in the room going on. The begging eyes of Mateen, the furious imam, the smell of pot, and now a woman wearing bells, straightening herself up. She needed to turn around.

Chris managed to rationalize one thing. *Is there a threat here? No matter, the kid is coming with me.* He was about to move forward when a strong hand grabbed his shoulder.

"Chris, drop it; let's go."

Chris spun around to face Alex as he felt the strength of the request get stronger. He tried to struggle away, but Alex wasn't letting go. "Are you seeing this?" Chris said. "This isn't happening."

Alex's face was distraught. He was trying to avert his eyes from the shame he felt, from the disgust and the depravity of it all. "We've got to go, buddy. This isn't our problem. We've got to go."

He tried to pull Chris away by the scruff of his jacket, but he wasn't having any of it and resisted. A pushing and shoving match ensued and was interrupted only when the woman in the room got in between the two men.

"Chris, Chris, it is all right. It is all right. We are okay. You should leave."

Both Alex and Chris let go of each other simultaneously.

"Azzami?" Chris muttered.

"Chris, you need to leave. We are okay. Everything is fine."

Chris stood back in disbelief and looked incomprehensively at his young friend who was dressed from head to foot in bright women's clothing.

Alex took two steps back, not comprehending what he was seeing, staring without saying a word, feeling a movement in his stomach that he couldn't explain. His right hand uncontrollably went to his mouth to cover his surprise; the battle-hardened, ex–Delta Force warrior was speechless and horrified.

Chris looked at Azzami from head to toe, backtracking away from him as he did. If the woman's clothes weren't enough to send him over the edge, the makeup, the bloodshot eyes, the faraway, drug-induced lost look did. He raised his Makarov and took a wild shot at the imam hitting the wall above his head. He was about to release a second shot but was prevented by a strong yank on his collar from Alex who pulled him forcibly to the ground.

Both men struggled on the ground for a few seconds, but the American got the better of the Brit, who tapped his hand on the ground signaling he had had enough from the chokehold he was in. Alex dutifully released his grip and pushed away from Chris, who appeared to have calmed down. They got to their feet, but Chris was breathing heavy. A mixture of wrestling and raw emotions had gotten the better of him. He wasn't sure what to do next, but new raised voices in the corridor made him wish for silence. He looked all about him, and all he could see were more faces, half-dressed men, boys dressed as women, Alex, and Nash. Chris wanted to drag Azzami out, rescue Mateen, and kill the imam, but everyone else had other ideas.

Nash was shouting at him, but he didn't hear it. Alex grabbed him by the jacket and started to drag him out of the melee. Other guests of the party began to hurl abuse and fists in his direction. The imam chased and kicked Azzami out and slammed the door in frustration. It was pandemonium.

On the way out of the door to the courtyard, Nash had somehow wedged himself in between Chris, Alex, and the riotous guests. For his intervention, he was punched hard in the face, making him stagger and fall to the ground. Chris saw him fall. Coming to his senses, Chris wrangled his way out of Alex's grip and rushed to Nash's aid. Alex, realizing things were getting out of hand, raised his handgun and pointed it at the mob, covering Chris and Nash. Seeing the weapon was enough for the irate visitors who, despite their vociferous furor, backed down, hands raised, but scorn on their faces.

Chris managed to get Nash back to the rear of the Toyota where he sat him down on the rear of the vehicle. Alex maintained cover with his pistol in its holster but rifle at the ready. Nash bent over and held his head, and a small rivulet of blood trickled out of his nose. Chris found the first-aid kit, fished out a piece of gauze, and handed it over to him.

"Lie back, Mr. Nash."

"I'm okay."

"Just humor me and lie back for a while, okay?"

Nash reluctantly replied and scooted further into the rear of the Toyota, making himself comfortable and began concentrating on the inner roof of the vehicle.

Nobody in the trio could begin the conversation. Not merely one elephant but a large herd of them was vying for space in the small courtyard.

Chris began to square himself away, checked his jacket to see if he had lost anything, then his trousers, and then his body. Satisfied everything was still in place, including his weapons, all his blood, and teeth, he deemed himself ready for action. He wasn't sure what was to come next, but killing the imam was his first priority.

The Platinum House, Paradise Valley, Arizona

Jawad Halabi stood back in the shadows of the villa five steps away from the balcony that overlooked East Sierra Vista Drive. He was glad things were progressing with Her Majesty's departure but frustrated with the fuss and overkill of the moment from so many people and so many vehicles drawn in to make it all happen.

He sipped his coffee and took long drags on a cigarette, watching each minute pass by as the minions below him went about their work to get the queen safely to the airport. Thirty minutes earlier, Abdo Ihab had left for the airport with his family. Jawad felt it safer that he should not be in the convoy and sent him to the plane with orders not to talk to anyone about his role or the reason he was on the aircraft. Despite Abdo's late protestations, Jawad ordered to him to get out of the country lest the FBI dragnet snatch him up. Jawad explained once more that Abdo was too valuable to the cause for him to be caught because he filed the wrong piece of paper at the wrong time or had his picture taken once too often with the wrong type of person or was associated with some other banal issue that a keen officer of authority found questionable.

There was a knock on the door behind him.

"Come," he instructed.

"Jawad, you wanted to see me?"

"Yes, Saleh, please come in. Sit, have some tea, join me."

Jawad watched with displeasure as the fat banker bumbled his way to the sofa, sweating not just from the oppressive Phoenix heat but also because he was summoned to a meeting when he had hoped to have created enough distance from the intelligence man.

Jawad moved to the comfort of a chair. "I see things are moving forward well."

"Yes, Jawad, it seems your plans are being carried out in a well-organized manner, almost military like."

"Yes, quite. We can thank Major Basrawi for that." Jawad poured himself a strong black tea and then leaned over to fill his visitor's glass. He concentrated on this menial task and did not make eye contact with the slob. Sitting back in his chair and enjoying his drink, Jawad let his visitor stew in a minute of silence before opening the conversation. "Saleh, you must pack all your things, and I must insist that you pack all your documentation first. I will send you an assistant to collect the material, but you will get on that plane this evening. A seat is reserved for you."

Saleh was in the middle of picking up his cup, and his nervous hand shook, spilling some of the contents onto the coffee table. He picked up a napkin and dabbed his mess away, then replaced the cup on the table, and took another napkin to mop his brow. "Jawad, with all due respect, I must object. I am needed here. There is so much to do, her Majesty's affairs—"

Jawad raised a hand. "That is of no concern now. Her Majesty is leaving, and this location will be dissolved. We will have no further interests in this community. I am sure one of your staff can take care of the outstanding payments to the Americans, any leasing agreements we may have, the doctors, the lawyers . . . but honestly, Saleh, I believe that is all beneath you anyway. Leave that to one of your people. You said yourself that the Americans are, how did you put it, immature, uncouth, and without respect for our family. So why put yourself in that uncomfortable position again?"

He remembers everything. What does he want from me? What game is he playing? Saleh mused as his nervous hand trembled again as he held his tea.

Jawad gave him the same briefing as he had for Abdo. "Now while you are aboard that plane, I want you to sleep. It is, as you know, quite comfortable, so please take some rest. I don't want you to talk to anyone."

"Of course, Jawad, but there are many things I need to do if I leave. Perhaps in a few days I can take another flight," he implored.

Remaining composed, Jawad stared at Saleh and flicked some ash into a nearby silver tray. "Saleh, my friend . . . you are indeed a loyal servant of the crown. I am sure the court will sing your praises for all your efforts over the time that Her Majesty was convalescing here; however, you are leaving on that plane. I will not hear another word."

"Jawad—"

"What did I just say to you?" Jawad's was tired of buttering the man up, but his voice was not raised in anger. It was deep but menacing. Still relaxed in his chair, he extinguished his cigarette. "Are you really that stupid?" The sentence was delivered as if by the devil himself, smooth, deliberate, menacing.

"W-wh-what?" Saleh stumbled over his words, scared of what was to come next. He didn't want a repeat visit to the garage.

"You have become a liability, Saleh, and you are putting us all in jeopardy." Jawad's hushed tone put genuine fear into the fat banker. "Why did you converse with the five men? Why did you involve yourself . . ." He cut Saleh's attempt to interrupt with a dismissive wave. "Don't think about answering, you fool. I don't need your idiotic explanations. You may have compromised our entire operation, so your pathetic excuses are not what I need right now." Jawad pulled out a crumpled piece of paper from his shirt pocket. "This . . . you idiot, is the number you gave those men, your number," he hissed. "What if the FBI intercepted them and found this? What if they retrieved it from the wreckage had they boarded that plane? What were you thinking?"

How did he get that . . . how? Saleh cringed but wisely kept his mouth shut and came to terms with his mistake. He dropped his head in shame, a tear ran down his cheek.

There was a moment of silence between the two.

"I have every right to end your life right here and now, Saleh, and I should for nobody would fault me for it."

Saleh's face turned ashen, and his eyes almost popped out in fear of what Jawad just announced. Sweat from his forehead met with the tears on his cheek.

"My only regret is that I did not come to see you sooner. If you were this careless to leave an open trail like a wedding invitation, what else can I expect from the other things that you were entrusted with?"

Saleh put both his hands between his knees and squeezed them trying in vain to make himself as small as possible. He wanted to say something, wanted to answer, but he kept his gaze affixed to a spot on the carpet.

"You are wise not to answer me; however, I must have your papers, and that is everything, Saleh. You need to have everything on that plane this evening, or we are doomed. The FBI is getting close, and I don't want you to be stuck here for months or even years trying to clear your name and give up operational details and members of the cause. You and I both know that you cannot keep your mouth shut, and your value of your own preservation is sickening. You are not a true believer; the cause, this mission is second to you. You disgust me." Jawad leaned forward and lit up another cigarette. His dark, piercing eyes bore through the smoke. Inhaling, he leaned back again studying the burning ember in front of his face.

"My objections to your continued existence have been overruled, and you are to be given a chance to redeem yourself, but I will not take the risk of compromise, and that is final. An associate of mine will be meeting you in Riyadh. He is to be trusted, and you must tell him everything about the documentation that you take. As trivial as this seems, everything will be analyzed. I don't care how long it takes, but it is needed, needed for our security. I know you understand that. We cannot take any risks, not now as we are so far along, Saleh."

The fat man nodded to show his understanding.

Jawad lit the piece of paper with the telephone number with his cigarette and then carried on. "This meeting will happen as soon as you get off that plane, Saleh. I will join you when time permits." He let the paper fall into the ashtray and continue to burn.

For a second, Saleh thought Jawad was in a trance, watching the flames in silence, as if he was elsewhere, but he too got caught in the peacefulness of the burn. When Jawad stood quickly, it made Saleh wince as if expecting a blow from a fist, but nothing came.

Jawad made for the door and opened it. "Major Basrawi," he shouted to the innards of the house. He left the door open and returned to sit opposite Saleh.

The major promptly arrived. "Yes, sir."

"Major, you will find one of your trusted men to escort Our Highness's trusted banker to his quarters and his office. He is not to leave Saleh's side until he has boarded the plane this evening. You will also need to organize a vehicle for all his documentation to be placed in the hold of the aircraft. Now, Major, listen carefully to what I have to say because you need to understand this. I will hold you responsible for this task, and if I find one scrap of paper, even if it is this large," he held up the burned note in the ashtray, "anywhere in his work or residence, you, my friend, will suffer. We have an understanding?"

"Yes, sir."

"Good. Now be on your way. Mr. Bahar will join you as soon as your escort is here. Thank you. Please shut the door after you."

Jawad took to the comfort of his chair again, carefully brushed off some fallen ash, totally cool and in control. He wanted desperately to lash out at the slovenly man and cause him some pain, but it was pointless. Jawad needed him whole. He'd achieved his aim of scaring the man to compliance. It would only draw attention to him if he sat on a plane needing medical treatment.

"Saleh, my friend, I really wish you no harm, but you have left me in a tough predicament." His manner was now conciliatory; he still wanted him to fulfill his remaining obligations. "I have said as much to others that this is only one battle. This mission is moving ahead, and we will succeed, but only if we are all disciplined, Saleh. You must appreciate that I have my responsibilities to the sheik and a higher calling. You do understand that, don't you?"

Saleh nodded hoping his day would end while still breathing air. He kept his mouth from opening and his tongue from wagging unnecessarily.

"Good. Now please follow my orders. We will have other battles, you and I. The sheik has great confidence in us, and if it is Allah's will, we will be joined in the fight once again against the great Satan. Please be helpful with the major's men and make sure nothing is left behind for the FBI. For I fear that if we are caught, Saleh, we will both be killed, and it will not be by the hands of the Americans."

Sea-Tac Airport, Seattle

Chad Peters called the FBI LA Field Office looking for Nick Seymour but, to his frustration, was transferred to a female switchboard operator.

"FBI Los Angeles. How may I help?"

"This is Chad Peters. I'm an investigator with the INS. I'm trying to locate Special Agent Nick Seymour."

"Let me see what his status is. Please hold . . ."

Chad dreaded losing a human on the other end of the phone. He'd already been spun around in perpetuity from office to office, hold to hold, strange person to strange person. He was running out of patience, but his information was too important to not pass on.

"Sir, his status is marked as out of the office."

Well duh! Wouldn't be talking to you if that were not the case, he wanted to say but refrained. "Any indication of where I may find him or when he will return?"

"Sir, I'm not at liberty to give you that information. All I can tell you is that he is out of the office. Is there someone else I can put you in touch with?"

"No, no, thank you . . ." He was about to hang up when he had an idea. "Does he have a voice mail?"

"Yes. Would you like me to connect you?"

He rolled his eyes but kept his cool. "Yes, please and thank you for your help."

"You're welcome. Please hold."

"No, don't make me hold," he said into an empty line. However, he didn't have to wait long for the automated voice recording system and followed the prompt after the tone.

"Nick, Chad Peters. Listen I need to talk to you as soon as possible. Louisa woke up, and I have had quite the chat with her." He was talking quickly not knowing how long the voice mail would record. "Here's the rub, dude. She has passed on twenty US passports to your man Omar. I'll say that again, twenty valid US passports have gone to Omar. If I'm hearing the same warnings as you are, then this could be the next cell that we are being warned about, Nick. I'm at the airport but heading back to LA on the next flight so I can do some digging when I get to my office. Perhaps we can go through our system to identify passport numbers and set flags against them. If the next cell hasn't already arrived, then there's a chance we can catch them at a port of entry. If not . . . we are up shit street. Call me, buddy."

Chad hung up the phone, hoping Nick would get his message soon as his flight was about to board. He had gotten the result he was hoping for, and with the threat of federal charges for immigration fraud and a manslaughter charge for killing a truck driver, Louisa Chavez was willing to plead and chat her way out. Chad only hoped it wasn't already too late. All he could do was pray that Nick would call him back in the next few minutes or show up waiting for him at his office.

Long Beach, California

Nick Seymour took two steps back and placed his right hand on his handgun without drawing his weapon out of its holster. Although scared, he maintained his self-control as he stared intently at the threat in front of him and was ready to escalate the situation if the dog broke free of the chain around his neck.

The hound barked with a ferocity that would have made a pack of wolves think twice about entering his realm. Nick concentrated on the chain and tried to see if it was as strong as it looked or if one link was about to snap. He had parked his car outside the towing yard and then entered the dust- and debris-strewn property on foot. Now after seeing a larger version of Cujo, he tried to gauge how fast he could run back to his car or if the beast would take a chunk out of him in the process. He stood his ground while the part pit bull, part mountain lion, part bear strained and twisted on his restraint. Nick took a step back fearing the worst. The beast stopped barking only when it twisted so violently trying to get to him that he fell on his back but immediately sprang up and foamed at the mouth, letting the world know that fresh meat was in sight.

A large man dressed in dirty overalls and a once-white T-shirt came strolling out with a dirty rag in his hands. "Toodles, Toodles, give it a rest, dude." The dog did not back down. "TOODLES! Goddammitt!" he shouted at the top of his voice. Then he reached down, picked up an old tire lying nearby, and lofted it at the dog. Nick guessed the man must have weighed close to three hundred pounds as the tire flew through the air as if he was throwing a beer to a buddy. The man got between his guard dog and Nick. "SIT!" he shouted at the dog, and Toodles, feeling threatened by his master did as he was told. The man fished out a piece of beef jerky and tossed it towards the canine, who gulped it down without chewing, but the dog kept his eyes on the intruder and licked his lips.

The giant man drew his attention to the visitor. "You don't mind taking your hand off that for me, would you?"

Removing his hand from his gun and relaxing his tense posture, Nick reached into his jacket pocket and pulled out his identification. "Nick Seymour, FBI. I'd like to ask you some questions if you have a minute, Mr. . . .?"

"Everyone round here calls me Arnie on account I look like Schwarzenegger." Which he did in some respects—gapped teeth, fat head, no neck, and biceps twice the size of Nick's thighs.

"Well, Arnie, don't mean to intrude, but is there somewhere we can chat? I don't have much confidence in the chain that Toodles is wrapped up in."

Arnie smiled. "Ah, Toodles is a sweetheart. He means well. He's harmless really, ain't ya, boy?"

The dog let loose a blood-curdling growl.

Nick, feeling goosebumps, thought, *Easy for you to say.*

"But if you're scared, Mr. FBI, let's go to my office."

After zigzagging their way through a parking lot of about twenty cars, old engines, piles of tall tires, car hoods, and rust-bucket cars, they found their way to a large workshop where two other men were busy working on a new-looking Mercedes. Nick quickly pushed aside the thoughts of chop shop. He wasn't here to bust balls; he wanted help.

The office was a complete mess, and Nick felt out of place being the cleanest and most organized thing in there. Arnie took a seat behind a desk that was cluttered with papers, car parts, and small electronics. Nick took a quick look around and spotted a few small US flags, a military calendar, a few pictures of men in combat dress, and a picture of Ronald Regan. He also noted the 12-guage shotgun in a corner. It looked spotless. He wondered what other handy tools were lying around and also if the two mechanics were still working on the Mercedes or getting tooled up for trouble with a suit.

Arnie motioned for him to sit. "What can I do for the FBI?"

"I understand that you are leasing out some warehouse space."

"That's right. Do you have a warrant?"

"Arnie, listen, I'm not looking for trouble, okay? I really don't care what you do here. It's not my business. I'm just interested in your lockup."

Although Arnie showed a little uneasiness, he didn't come across as being combative but was still full of curiosity. "What's it to you?"

"I know who is leasing it from you. They're the ones I am interested in."

"I'm leasing it to some realtor from Bellflower. So what's the problem?"

This was news to Nick, another chain, another link to hunt down. "Can you show me the lease agreement?"

"Why should I? What the fuck do you really want, Seymour?" Arnie was becoming cross and getting bored with simple questions.

"I don't want to piss you off, Arnie, but this is of national importance. You may be leasing to some realtor, but that is not who is using the space."

"What the hell are you talking about? I run a legit business here. I don't dick around."

Nick heard footsteps behind him. He wanted to turn around, but he knew that one or both the mechanics were a few feet behind him. The problem was he didn't know what tools they were carrying. "We have reason to believe that someone from the Saudi government has been using your lockup." He wanted to let the statement settle for a minute, there was no "we"; he was running his own hunches down. He continued, "I know you guys haven't been hiding under a rock for the last few days; everyone knows that most of the hijackers from 9/11 were from Saudi Arabia, right?"

Arnie stirred. His face was grave. One of his men shifted his weight behind him and brushed up against something that almost fell over.

Nick wanted to keep the ball rolling and gain control. "I'll spell it out for you, Arnie. I need to take a look into the lockup. The FBI is trying to prevent the next attack against this country, and we don't want to be blindsided again. I'm not saying the Saudi government was behind the New York attacks, but if some Saudis have things stashed away down here, I may need to know about it. It may well be all above board, but it's my job to investigate each and every lead, and right now this is a lead that needs a close look. Now I can run off and get a judge to issue a warrant to me to talk to the realtor and then come all the way back down here with a bunch of uniforms and dogs and all that shit, then pull this place and the lockup to pieces, or you can let me have a look. If I don't find anything that interests me, nobody's hurt, I didn't see anything, we all move along . . . how about it?"

Hisarak District, Afghanistan

Chris had finished pacing. Throughout the rest of the night, he had paced, sat alone, paced, and then sat alone again. When he got control of his temper, he made his way back to the Toyota just in time for the sun to begin its rise in the sky. He looked at Nash who was wide awake. Alex was sitting on the tailgate fighting the urge to lie back and sleep, but none of the group was willing to go that far.

The trio exchanged glances at each other as Alex ambled his way around to the passenger side of the vehicle. It was time to talk.

"What happened here last night, Mr. Nash?" Chris began.

Nash stoked his forehead struggling to find the words. The last thing he wanted was for Chris to fly off the handle again. "Chris, you have to understand something. This is not our country. There are things here that we don't understand and can't hope to comprehend." Nash had been mulling his speech over for hours. "There are traditions, customs, and certain things that these people have being doing for centuries. To them we are invaders, conquers, armies of oppression who only want to rape the lands and rule with iron fists, and most importantly of all, we are just visitors."

"I don't need a history lesson, Mr. Nash," Chris interrupted, cool but direct.

"Granted, but you have to understand the context of it all. Long after we have gone, long after the Taliban or any invading force is ousted, the Afghan will still be here. They will struggle as long as it takes, and they really don't care for our morals and values."

"Like I said, Mr. Nash, history is not why I am standing here. I am trying to figure out the best way to string those fuckers out and nail their dicks to a chunk of wood."

Alex shifted and looked away. A similar thought had crossed his mind. He didn't want to engage with the conversation, though; he felt he needed to listen.

Nash didn't look in his direction; his words were meant for Chris. "If you were in London, DC, Paris, or elsewhere in the world that would be reasonable, Chris, I'm sure there would be a thousand people like you standing in line just waiting to do the same thing, but we are not in Europe or the US. Look around you. Look at these other men, the other Afghans. Do you think they care? Why didn't they get up off their butts last night?"

Chris had no reply. He looked over at Alex who was as much perplexed as he.

"This thing . . . what we saw last night has been going on for years, perhaps even as far back as the 1800s. It's been outlawed by various rulers. Even the Taliban have tried to put a stop to it, but the practice still continues."

"Are you trying to defend pedophiles, Mr. Nash?"

"Slow down, you shit." Nash got out of the vehicle in a rage. "You had better watch your tongue. I saw the same as you. I was just as disgusted, but there is nothing we can do. These batchas, or dancing boys as they call them, are a recognized institution throughout many parts of Central Asia, meaning it's organized and accepted in certain circles. What I am trying to say is that it is rampant and a pissed-off Brit with a gun is not going to change that. Sure, go ahead use all your bullets on the imam. Where will it get us? Killed by the Taliban is my guess. We are one step away from being turned over, and we are as close as we have been from finding someone from TRODPINT."

Nash took a step forward and got in Chris's face. He prodded him with his index finger. "Listen, you had better wind your neck in. You will not compromise this mission, and you will distance yourself from the imam. We can't ignore what happened last night, but we still can't do anything about it either. Focus on the mission, Chris."

"Young boys dressed as women, dancing for old men, only to be fucked and passed around. That's accepted in certain circles? You have got to be fucking kidding me." Chris was loud and getting animated.

Alex moved in between the pair. He didn't touch Nash but nudged Chris backwards to get him to calm down.

Chris was about to say something else but was stopped by shouts of his name.

"Chris, Chris?"

The three men looked over to the main building and saw Azzami running towards them.

"Chris, Chris . . . you have to help me, please, please."

Chris turned to face him.

Azzami was in a fluster. His eyes were as wide as dishes, and he was sweating profusely.

"What the hell's wrong, Azzami?"

"It's Mateen. Mateen, he has gone missing. You must help me. You must help me find him, Chris. Please. Come, come. We go, come," he beckoned.

Chris turned to Nash. "This conversation isn't over, Mr. Nash. Alex you got this?" Chris asked, motioning to Nash.

Alex nodded in return.

"Please, please, we have to find him, Chris. Please."

CHAPTER SIXTEEN

Hisarak District, Afghanistan

CHRIS ASKED THE OBVIOUS, typical questions when he searched for Mateen. He wanted to know who had last seen him or where he was seen, if someone had checked everywhere in the immediate area, did they check down by the river, did he run back to someone he knew in the village, but all answers from Azzami provided no clues. He had been looking for his cousin for almost three hours, and there was no sign and nobody was willing to help in the search. It was as if nobody cared.

Standing with his back to the villa, Chris pulled out his binoculars and scanned the abandoned buildings that he and Alex had identified as interesting on their arrival. He was loath to tread across the open ground without any cover or concealment but rationalized that if someone was willing to do him or Nash harm, it would have happened already.

"What is in those buildings over there, Azzami?" Chris pointed across the way.

"I do not know. They have be empty for many years. People say they ghosts there."

Now was not the time to correct his English. "Have you been there to look for him?"

"No, we should go now." Chris's reluctance to cross open terrain was quashed when Azzami took off at a quick pace.

In for a penny, in for a pound. Chris sighed and then marched swiftly behind him. When they got within forty or fifty feet of the first squat building, he slowed his pace as he saw something strange in his path. *What the hell is that?* He stooped over skeletal remains but couldn't make the shape out other than to realize that it wasn't human. He passed it by not thinking too much about it until he found two more skeletons. However, this time they were more intact than the previous find. Continuing forward with his head swiveling in the search for Mateen, racking his brain to make sense of what he saw, he thought, *Too small for a donkey, too big for a cat . . . dog! That had to be dogs. I never saw any in the village. What the hell's this bollocks now?* Then he found yet more remains. *If this is a gravesite, then they didn't bury them; they just let them rot. Is that normal around here?* He didn't know the answer but thought to ask Nash later.

Azzami was out of sight by the time Chris reached the wall of the first building. It was open to the environment and looked as if the window that was supposed to be there fell in on itself leaving a gaping hole. He stuck his head inside and did a quick left and right scan and saw nothing. Moving on, he could hear Azzami shouting for his cousin and took the opportunity to update Alex on his location.

Chris passed through a wide alley between two structures and towards the front side of the abandoned hamlet. A moment of déjà vu ran through his mind when he looked at the buildings before him. All were built in straight lines with even numbers of structures on each of three sides, almost forming a square. Some of the buildings had windows, some had doors, but one or two structures had no roof or coverings, leaving them open to the elements. The fourth leg of the fourth side was missing, leaving an open area that ran down to the river that Chris was familiar with. He walked to the center and did a complete 360-degree turn and knew instantly where he was. He had found a parade ground. It was flat, even, and at one time well maintained. All that was missing was a flagpole. He stood still for a moment. *Who the hell built this place?* His reverie was broken only when he heard Azzami off in the distance, still shouting for his cousin.

"Alex, found a disused barracks across the way from the villa. It's the building we spotted yesterday. We're still searching," he reported over the radio.

"Any signs of the boy?"

"Negative. I'll give you an update if we do."

"Roger."

Chris was drawn back to the search by Azzami's shouts. At first, his young friend's calls were loud and constant, but as time wore on, his voice became fainter and the cries for his cousin's name more infrequent. He spotted Azzami running towards one of the buildings, and catching sight of Chris, the Afghan gave him a wave and trotted onwards in his quest. Chris, duty bound to help his friend, walked off to the other side of the parade ground towards a building with doors and windows. He gave the door a kick, and it moved quite easily allowing him entry. As he moved inside, he realized he was in a classroom with a few tables and chairs all facing the same way towards a wall, where the remnants of a chalkboard could be seen in a frame. Finding nothing of importance, he moved on to the next building in the row. Again finding nothing, he repeated the exercise in the third building. This time, however, he found an open trap door leading to a stairway and then down to a basement. He took out his knife and wedged it between the trap door and door frame.

Retrieving his small flashlight out of his right leg pocket and using it to illuminate the way down the stairs, Chris slipped slightly on debris and brushed up against one side of the stairway, hurting his shoulder on a solid object protruding from the wall. He flashed his light over to see a switch, which he flipped and turned on a set of lights that ran down the steps and onwards to a passageway below. *Power, there's power out here. Why didn't I see the lines outside? Were there poles out there?* He considered pulling out his Makarov but thought it pointless as he once more rationalized that if bad guys were coming, they would have gotten him by now. He turned off his flashlight but kept it in his hand, ready for an outage.

"Alex, found a staircase leading downwards. Could be a storage. Going in."

There was no response from Alex. He tried twice more but was fruitless. *Great, no comms. Is this concrete?* he questioned as he stepped off the last step to the passageway. Chris moved slowly and silently through the passage, and within twenty feet of the stairway, he came to a room that was lit up. When he entered, he found a strange sight before him.

Long Beach, California

Arnie fished out a key from his desk and beckoned Nick to follow him if he wanted access to the lockup. Nick thought they would exit the yard the way he came in and then loop around to the unit from the street but was surprised when Arnie led him through his workshop and pointed at a set of shelves full of car parts that was blocking a door.

"Hope you don't mind getting your hands dirty, Mr. FBI, but there's the back door to the space. If you want in, that's the only way to go. You up for a workout?"

Nick looked up and down and then left to right. The shelving must have been close to ten feet tall and twenty feet wide. Each shelf had some part of a car or truck or engine parts that he didn't recognize.

Arnie caught his gaze and sympathized a little. "We can't get the forklift in here to move all this until we have cleared a path, so get to work."

"We can't go in from the front?"

"Only if you have a warrant, and they have changed the locks on the rollup and the side door. This is it. You change your mind?"

Nick took off his suit jacket and tie and then rolled up his sleeves to show he was serious about gaining access. As he did, he asked another question. "What if they have shelves on the other side of that door?"

"Not my problem."

"I'm not feeling the love, Arnie. I think you're treating Toodles better than me right about now."

"Want some jerky, or do you want to pump iron, little girl?"

He watched Arnie walk away, then smiled, and picked up the smallest item on the nearest shelf to the door. *Now where the hell do I put this?*

One hour into the shelf clearing, the forklift finally found its way in through the labyrinth of engines and faced off with the tall shelves in front of the door. One of Arnie's men was at the controls. Arnie gave Nick a bottle of water and squeezed his right bicep.

"You need more form, more definition, more powahh," he said in his best Austrian accent.

"So I can move as slowly as you? No thanks, Arnie."

Arnie pushed Nick back just in time to miss an exhaust manifold fall off one of the shelves as the forklift maneuvered its way through the mangle. "I've been looking for that," he quipped.

Nick couldn't help smile. Although he was going out on a limb with his hunch, he felt at ease around the big lug nut of a guy, and it felt nice to have a little comic relief. He took a long drink, gauged the progress, and then looked at his watch. He didn't know if Omar was still using the lockup, stored equipment there, or was even there himself. There were too many suppositions to count but felt relief as he saw the outline of the door clearly and the hinges that were affixed on Arnie's side of the warehouse. While he was digging through the mess earlier, he prayed that the door didn't open inwards towards the lockup and, if so, that it wouldn't be barred from the other side from opening. As the last shelf was removed, he had his answer. Then Arnie inserted the key into the lock.

At first, Arnie couldn't open the door, until he used his three hundred pounds of brute strength to yank it open. Nick strode towards the door, peeked inside, but only saw darkness. Arnie dispatched one of his men to retrieve a flashlight and, when he returned, handed it over to Nick. Shining it into the opening, Nick was greeted by a wall of wood paneling. Touching the makeup of the wood and pushing gently to see if there was any give, he heard something from the other side move or drop to the floor. It wasn't mechanical but more of a rustling of a bush or plastic bag. Nick prodded again. This time the thin panel moved more and fell inwards revealing the innards of the lockup. It was pitch black inside.

"Where are the light switches, Arnie?"

"Walk about thirty feet straight on. Then you will come to the rollup door. Turn around then with your back to the rollup. Go right until you find the wall. There is a switch over there."

Nick wasn't sure about what to expect inside. Hesitating and questioning his motive for doing what he was about to do, he ran through a list of things that were wrong and another list of what was right. But his inner battle was defeated when his mind flashed back to the images of the two towers collapsing. *Right or wrong, I need to do something.* He turned to Arnie. "Thanks for the help. Listen, in my jacket is the number of the FBI Field Office in LA. If something goes wrong while I am in there, you give them a call for me, okay?"

"You want me to come in?"

"You've done enough, Arnie. You gave me permission to enter. That's all I needed." He extended his hand. "Look after Toodles for me, okay?"

Arnie squeezed his hand. "You can come and visit him any time, Nick. I'm sure he'll be happy to see you."

Nick looked back into the darkness and went in, crouching through the hole he had made, shining his light upwards looking for hazards, but missing what was on the floor. His feet were caught in some type of textile material that he tripped over and fell to his knees. He turned around and flashed the light back towards the hole to see Arnie looking through.

"You okay, man?"

"Sure, all good," Nick replied and then saw what he had tripped on. There were three or four leather jackets on the ground. *What the hell? Fashion show?*

Chris walked into the small room and squinted at what he saw. On a line strung across from wall to wall were several neatly hanging jackets. On closer inspection, he saw that a few of them were leather, one or two were heavy wool, others were heavy nylon and weatherproof. He stared for a minute trying to comprehend why the jackets were there and then pulled one of the weatherproof jackets off the line and gave it a more detailed look. There were no markings on the jacket, no logo, no manufacturer's label, no washing instructions. *Hmm, custom made,* he surmised. He found a zipper on the inside of the jacket and on the inner side back, as well as the standard pockets front left and right. Confused, he opened up the zipper but found nothing inside, only a compartment. He then hung the jacket back up, inspected others, and found exactly the same configuration. *Someone is trying to hide something*, he supposed again and then began looking around elsewhere. Finding a box on the floor, Chris bent over, and before opening it, he examined it cautiously. *We're in a war zone, dumbass. Don't go opening any suspicious packages.* Despite his own warning, he pulled the flap of the box open and found multiple pairs of gloves of differing styles inside. Some were like the jackets he found, and as he was about to put them back in, he felt the thickness of one of the gloves, drawing his attention to a plastic port that was sticking out the back of the glove near where the inner wrist would be. He looked at it carefully, squinted as much thought process as he could manage out of his brow, but drew a blank. He picked up another pair of gloves out of the box. However on this pair, he found only the right hand had the plastic port. He did the same with another search of three other pairs, but came to the same conclusion.

Chris grabbed a jacket off the line and a pair of gloves. He needed to see what he had found in the light of day.

Nick made his way over to the light switch and turned on a string of fluorescent shop lights that hung from the high ceiling. Blinking his eyes to readjust, he was finally able to see what was stored in the lockup. At first he was disappointed. He wasn't expecting to see a battle tank or rocket launchers lying on a table, but at least there should have been something tangible to work with other than a bunch of leather jackets on the floor, a drum in one corner, another drum in another, a small electrical pump that was plugged into a wall, a blue cylindrical canister that stood about four feet tall, and a number of boxes laid out on the floor. The sheer volume of the lockup paled in comparison to the items inside. The information that Romeo Washington gave him about furniture being stored there was false as no comforts could be found. It seemed a complete waste of time, until the stench hit his nostrils.

"What the hell is that smell?" Arnie asked.

"You are not supposed to be in here, Arnie," Nick answered half knowing the answer, half not wanting to confirm his suspicions but then walked over to one of the two drums. He stopped halfway to look in an open cardboard box and then bent over to inspect the contents. Again, he was surprised to find it full of men's gloves. In his frustration he tipped the contents out, not thinking about the mess he would need to clean up later. He stood with both hands on his hips. His eyes were straining to search for something that was not there, but the problem was he didn't know what it was he came to find.

Looking around the almost empty space, his gut was telling him that something was wrong. He looked at the gloves, the jackets, and back again at both. His curiosity got the better of him, and he inspected the jackets on the floor, picking one up and thinking it odd that there was no label on the inside but only a strange place for a zipper on the inside back of the coat. He then walked over to the box of gloves and pulled a couple of pairs out. The first thing he noticed was a strange plastic port sticking out of the back on the inside. Perplexed, he dropped both items. *What the hell is this shit?* Then he concentrated on another box that was closed but not secured.

"What the hell is that smell?" Chris blurted out loudly to himself in the passageway. Knowing he was alone didn't prevent him from speaking his mind when he was disgusted. He stopped outside another room in the basement, but the stench was assaulting his nose. He had encountered the odor before, but he couldn't quite place it. He was feeling a little giddy, a tad weak. *No ventilation down here. Where have I smelt that before?* But before he could worry about it any longer, he scanned a new room that he found and saw something equally intriguing as the gloves and jackets. Along the wall on one side were a number of empty IV bags hanging off hooks. *This isn't a hospital or aid station, so what the hell now?* He looked around the room for saline, blood, other medical equipment, or some reason for why the bags were there but came up empty. All he could find were more IV bags in boxes. Since he wasn't a trained medic, he missed an important clue to the use of the bag and was about to dismiss the items and move on, but when he studied the bag from a distance, it dawned on him that there were two ports on the bag. To his recollection, an IV bag needed only one port that attached to a tube that was then directed into the body. *Why two?* He picked up one of the bags and followed one line, which to him looked pretty standard for an IV. He then picked up the other line and followed it to a ball pump. It looked much like a nurse's blood pressure kit ball that was squeezed to get a reading. Chris was beginning to get pissed; he couldn't figure out the puzzle. *What is going on here? IVs, ball pumps, gloves and jackets, these are going with me.* He walked out of the room and went in search of the smell that plagued him. As he rounded a corner into the next space, he saw two steel drums sitting in the center. He backed away as quickly as his two feet could take him.

Nick walked over to one of the steel drums and before kicking it, he looked around it for something suspicious that would tell him to run like hell. Not finding anything except for a stronger stench, he played with the top of the drum to see if it would budge. It did and came away easier than he thought it would, but the smell pushed him back a step. During his career as an FBI agent, he was required to be present during an autopsy, so seeing a dead body, while repugnant in thought, was part of agent training and expected to witness out in the field. His intuition had been correct when he had entered the lockup and thought he could smell a dead body. Still, when he found the decomposing body of Omar, his heart dropped to the floor. He looked down at the lifeless Arab and could see a bullet hole in a socket where an eye used to be. He wanted to look closer but was distracted by a loud clang. He turned around in time to see Arnie open the other drum. The next thing Nick Seymour saw was a bright flash and then darkness.

—————◦◦◦◦—————

Chris sprinted down the corridor from where he came, booty in hand, but panic on his mind. "Almonds, fucking almonds, Jesus Christ," he cursed as he ran. As he got to the bottom step, he heard Azzami calling his name in the distance. "Don't come down here, Azzami," he tried to scream between breaths and then bounded up the stairs two at a time. Azzami was waiting at the top of the stairs for him, but Chris hustled him back not looking at him and then withdrew the knife he was using as a wedge from the trap door. It slammed shut. Chris grabbed Azzami roughly and dragged him out of the building. When they were outside, Chris took a real look at the young Afghan for the first time. He was about to warn him not to go down there but saw the face of someone who was in shock. His eyes were totally bloodshot, his happy smile gone. He was standing loose like a wet dishrag. Chris dropped the items he was carrying and held both the boy's shoulders at arm's distance and looked at him, knowing there was only bad news.

"Azzami, Azzami, where is Mateen? Did you find him?" he asked. He got no reply, but Chris needed an answer. If he was right in what he had found in the basement, then they were going to have major problems on their hands.

"Azzami, you need to tell me. Show me, okay?"

Azzami dropped to the ground, beginning to cry and then whimper. He was distraught and spent. Chris took a knee beside him. When he did, Azzami fell into his chest and cried. Chris wrapped his arms around him and gently rocked him through his pain.

The pair stayed like that for a few minutes, neither saying a word, but Chris's mind was racing. He needed to find Mateen. He needed to see his injuries to confirm his fears. He needed to get Alex and Nash to see his discovery. He needed a plan to do something. And he so needed not to be here, but he was. *It's a shit sandwich. Deal with it, soldier,* he ordered himself. He asked Azzami again, gently, "Where is he, Azzami? Can you show me?"

Azzami pushed back and shook his head. "I can't go in there again, Chris. I can't see him like that."

"Okay, okay, I understand. If you take me to the building, you can stay outside, okay? Just show me."

The young man nodded and wiped away the tears from his face with his sleeve. Chris helped him off the ground and put an arm over his shoulder to reassure him that he was safe. They both walked slowly across the parade ground, but as patient as Chris was with Azzami's grief, internally he was beside himself. He wanted to run, he wanted to call for Alex, he wanted to do something quickly, not saunter like two friends heading home from a pub after closing.

They reached one of the outermost buildings where Azzami stopped dead. He pointed a shaky finger and then held his ground. "No go in, Chris. I stay, I stay here."

"Okay, it's all right. I will go in alone. You just wait here. I am going to call Alex. You tell him where I am when he comes, okay? I need your help, so please do as I say. Stay here, Azzami, okay? It won't be long."

Azzami nodded, dropped to the ground, sat cross-legged, and let his head fall down. The tears had started again.

I'll take that as a yes then, Chris assumed. He entered the structure, which was much the same in size as the rest, but the only difference was that it was a little more split up on the inside, more like an administration setup. There were more rooms, though smaller with a few desks and chairs that had seen better days. He trudged through the dust and emptiness of the space, anticipating a fearsome sight around the next corner, and when he found the last open office, he saw the naked, beaten, bloodied body of Mateen hanging by his neck from a rafter in the ceiling. He was astonished and relieved but at the same time saddened by the boy's obvious painful death when he noticed the tightly bound hands and a gag in his mouth. As much as he wanted to despair, he had work to do.

"Alex, Alex, Alex, come in Alex." He spoke concisely, managing his rhythm, speed, volume, and pitch but wanted to scream at the top of his lungs.

Alex was short and to the point. "Go Chris."

"Get over to the barracks now. Bring Nash. Drive over and make it quick. I've found the boy deceased, but we have bigger problems. Now, Alex, need you now," he ordered while picking up a stool that was used by someone to hang Mateen.

He pulled out his knife, stepped up on the stool, and then went to work on the makeshift hangman's noose. He felt the boy's cold body against his skin making him wince but didn't prevent him from taking him down. He knew in his mind that if he had to, or was able, he would dig the child's grave. But the thought led him to his next problem. How was Mateen to be buried? How soon would that happen? He also wondered if someone from the village would investigate the death or if it would attract the attention of the Taliban. He had no answers, just more worries to add to his list.

By the time Chris laid Mateen carefully down on the ground and covered in an old curtain that was swinging lonely by itself in the wind, Alex and Nash arrived and met him in the building. Without uttering any words, Chris pulled back the covering and showed them the corpse. "I pulled him down from there." He pointed to the rafters.

But Nash's attention was drawn to the other items in the room. "What are all these?" he asked kicking the pile of jackets and gloves lightly with his foot.

"We have a serious problem, Mr. Nash, and I don't just mean Mateen." Chris wanted to play out a theory about the boy's death, but there was a more pressing matter to discuss. He bent down to kneel and picked up a jacket. "I found this lot across the way there in a basement. I found three rooms. In the first one, I found the jacket. Looks normal but check out this zipper." He opened it to show his colleagues who had now joined him kneeling on the floor. "There's a compartment in here like someone was trying to hide something, obviously custom made." He picked up one of the gloves. "Check this out, Alex."

Alex tried to pull on the glove but stopped himself when he found the port. "Umm, what's this?"

"That led me on to the next part of the puzzle. Look at this . . . looks like a normal IV, right?"

"But it has two ports," Alex answered for him.

"That's not the scary part. I found a room down there with two steel drums, and it smelled like almonds."

"Holy shit!" Alex blurted.

"Oh my God!" Nash gasped, "Are you sure, Chris?"

"I ran like hell. I wasn't sticking around to do a taste test. I know almonds are found in this region, but do you see any almond trees around here? I haven't been looking, but I'm sure as shit that they're not storing fresh almonds in a basement in two steel drums."

"Chemical agent?" Alex asked anxiously.

"That's my best guess, but which one?"

"Let me see all that, Chris," Nash requested before a debate ensued. Chris passed everything over to him as he began to put things together on the floor.

Before Alex handed his glove over, he noticed something else. "Did you take a close look at this glove, Chris?"

"Haven't had time. Why?"

Alex turned the glove palm side up, "There are tiny holes in the glove, but only in the palm and fingers."

Nash took the glove from him without a word, scrutinizing it for a moment and nodding affirmatively to acknowledge Alex's findings, and then went back to his task. First, he opened the zipper and stuffed the IV bag into the back of the coat into the compartment. He then fed one end of the tube down the right sleeve and did the same with the left, forcing the pressure ball down to the cuff. Next, he turned his attention back to the right arm and pulled the tube out and attached the glove via the port. He sat back onto his butt and looked astonished at what he had created.

Chris was as much shocked at the conception as at the pale look and genuine fear on Nash's face. It unnerved him to see the man that he had come to respect, admire, and look up to now show true distress. *If he's shit scared, what the hell am I supposed to feel?*

"Gentlemen," Nash started slowly and dramatically, "what we have here is an individual chemical weapon delivery system."

The three men sat around the jacket for a minute. Nobody wanted to speak. Each was involved in his own mind with multiple scenarios of what the discovery meant.

"We have to get this back." Chris was the first to open the discussion. Both Nash and Alex nodded in agreement. "Mr. Nash, I can see that your gears are working, but we have to have a mutual understanding what this all means and what our plan is to get it out of here."

"I agree, Chris. This does change things. It adds a new dimension to the battlefield, so to speak." Nash didn't want to admit it, but Chris was right. This system needed to get back to the United States, or at least out of Afghanistan, and he was also right about coming up with an immediate plan. He was used to being surrounded by like-minded strategists, managers, politicians, think-tankers, and a whole host of other experts for this, that, and the other. Now he was in the field, and he had only two men at his disposal. While experts in the art of security and combat, they were not policy decision makers. The time for high-level possible, probable, wait-and-see approaches from afar was null and void now. He needed to come up with decisions that would get them and the weapon system back to safety, and to do that, his in the field advisers were sitting in front of him, waiting for instructions.

"Let's walk this whole thing through," he began. "We know we have to get this out of the country. We don't know if there are chemicals here or, if there are, what their makeup is. Additionally, add this to your food for thought: chemical weapons are not typical for the Taliban. They can cook opium, and that's the best science they can muster. That leads me to believe this is al-Qaeda's handicraft."

Alex and Chris were leaning forward listening to every word, nodding, and supposing. Chris started forming his what-if scenarios, but he was pleased to see that Nash was leading the conversation.

"What I don't like, however," he continued, "is that this stuff was simply lying around for us to find. Granted we weren't expected here, but you would think that if there are live chemicals down there, someone would be here to guard it."

"I asked Azzami if he knew what was going on out here. He didn't know, but he's been locked up for a while with the Northern Alliance, so he hasn't been here in a while," Chris responded.

Nash pondered that for a second, then frowned, and stared at the equipment. "Let's say there was a guard or two here, and those are live chemicals. Could they have been affected by the solution, and are we going to find a body or two somewhere around here?"

"You want me to go look?" Alex asked.

"Not yet."

Chris jumped in before Nash could continue, "I'm guessing what's in those drums is live. I came across some dog carcasses on the way over here."

Nash rubbed his left arm and then held on to it for a while. "Hmm, interesting. Let's suppose then this is a testing site, al-Qaeda has experimented on dogs, and this jacket is either a prototype or the real thing. If it actually worked, then who the hell knows how many of these things were made and if they were shipped somewhere."

Chris threw out a hypothesis, "We've already had a major attack on the US, Mr. Nash. Is all this a precursor to a new wave of attacks, another active cell with chemical weapons?"

"I'm thinking the same thing, Chris, but—"

"This isn't a precursor," Alex interjected. "If al-Qaeda has left this behind without destroying it, then they intend to use it and use it again."

"Exactly. I think we have to think worst-case scenario in that this system is already out of the country and on its way to a target," Nash opined. "Obviously, we don't know for sure how far they are along with that type of mission, but we have a start point, gentlemen. We have tangible intelligence in our hands and chemical weapons nearby. We have to get it tested."

"I don't disagree with that, Mr. Nash, but we are not rolling out two drums of weird science and lashing them onto the top of the Land Cruisers."

"We have the ODA at JAWBREAKER," Alex offered. "It's possible they have chemical testing equipment, but if they do, then it's going to pretty rudimentary."

"How soon can we get them here?" Nash asked.

"I don't know if they are even available to help out. They could be tasked out already."

"Well, we will have to override and second them here. You will take care of that, Alex. That's your first assignment," the senior officer ordered.

"I can do that, but let's be realistic for a minute," Alex countered. "The last thing we want is a Chinook landing here in daylight looking like an invasion force. They need to drop in at night, do their thing. Then when we are ready to exfiltrate, we call in the helo for a pickup."

"Makes sense," Nash confirmed.

Chris threw up his hand as if he was in class. "I hate to rain on anybody's parade, guys, but there is something else to consider. This place was an old barracks. If some young lieutenant back in the Pentagon has a hard on for al-Qaeda training camps and this place is on a target list, then he may drop in a Tomahawk to light it up. I don't want to be on the wrong end of one of those. But maybe that's just me."

"Good point, Chris. Alex, you will be busy for a while. Let's see what we can do to prevent that from happening. What else?"

"We still have this to take care of, Mr. Nash," Chris added and then looked over at Mateen. "He's going to have to be buried. Someone's going to have to inform any family he has around here. Azzami, poor kid, can't cope."

Alex looked hard at the ever-so-young corpse. *We should bury him ourselves. Will cause is less drama that way*, he considered but pushed the idea of openly talking about it out of his mind. "He will need to be buried in the next twenty-four/forty-eight hours," Alex suggested, "and we should not be anywhere near this when it happens. I suppose you have a theory about how this happened, Chris?"

"Yeah, but don't get me started."

"Speak your mind, Chris. It is between us," Nash pushed.

Chris's voice was full of hate and rage. "That fucker the imam did this. Something went wrong after we busted open that party last night.

You heard the screams, you saw what I saw, you know it wasn't going to end well. We should lock that bastard up with the drums in the basement. That will be enough of a chemical test, if you ask me."

Nash tried to make himself comfortable on the floor but was struggling a little.

Chris pulled over the stool, offering it to his boss.

"We still need him, Chris."

"Are you shitting me? Are you still thinking about TRODPINT after what we've just been talking about? Really, Mr. Nash?"

"It's more important than ever. We have solid intelligence, but we need more. We need to find out if al-Qaeda is really active with chemicals. TRODPINT may help us establish that."

"Then nobody gives a shit about Mateen," Chris bit back. "We go about our business as if nothing happened to him or those other kids. Meanwhile, a pedophile wanders on to the next village and fucks some more kids."

"Focus on the mission, Chris, goddammit! You're a pain in my butt sometimes. Look, we are not going to be able to do anything about their ways; it's beyond our control. We need to take emotion out of the equation and concentrate on what we see before us. Leave the imam alone, at least for now until a plan is solidified. Alex, take Azzami back to the villa and convince him that he needs to find family, friends, or whomever to tell them what has happened to his cousin. Don't go with him. I have no idea of how many people know we are here, and if someone takes this the wrong way, then we could get blamed. Next thing we know we'll have the Taliban smoking us out. When you get there, pack up anything of ours and bring back the other vehicle and our Afghan friends. We'll get them to take care of Mateen's body. This is going to be our new home for a while. If you run into the imam, give him some bullshit excuse that we will be back for him later. Chris, you and I are going walkabout. Let's see if we can find a dead terrorist around here somewhere."

CHAPTER SEVENTEEN

Hisarak District, Afghanistan

IT TOOK EIGHTEEN HOURS for the US Army Rangers of ODA 575 to arrive at the disused barracks. Earlier in the day, Alex had marched three miles out and away from the villa to identify a suitable drop zone for the team to parachute into and then had waited patiently for the team to arrive. Although he never heard the Chinook CH-47 flying high at ten thousand feet, nor did he see or hear the team in the darkness conduct the HALO jump, he knew exactly when to turn on his strobe, invisible to the naked eye, to guide the team to a secure landing site.

Standing in the barrack room where he had left Chris and Nash, he introduced the team leader to the CIA officers, "Nash, Chris, this is Captain Stone. The rest of his team are deployed in a perimeter around us."

"Captain, welcome on board. How many are you?" Nash asked.

"Six including me. I understand you have some chemicals you would like me to check out for you."

"That's right. Chris here will take you over there. How soon can we get your Chinook back?"

The question surprised Chris. *Keen to go home for a change, unless he has an ulterior motive.*

"It's probably a five-hour turnaround. Two back from here, one hour or less to refuel, and another two to come for us."

"I assume you have a good line of communications back to JAW-BREAKER?"

Stone was all business. "I have my team working on that right now. Can you give me a situation report, sir? I understand we are in Taliban country. Is there an immediate threat?"

Alex took over before Nash became too optimistic and frugal with the truth. "Chris and I are the only American personnel that are armed. We have four Afghan Northern Alliance soldiers, armed. We have two Toyota Land Cruisers, which are fueled and have good mobility. We are very light on arms and munitions. We have little in the way of food, some water, money. There are two other non-combatants that may be joining us and possibly an agent who will meet us here."

Stone nodded a few times but showed no other emotions. He didn't need to; it was straight talk that he wanted. He was about to ask a question, but Alex continued.

"There is no known enemy in the area. We haven't come across any since we have been out here; however, there is another dimension that may escalate matters." Alex looked straight on at the soldier. He didn't need eye contact from either Chris or Nash to sway his words. "A young boy was killed here in this room last night; his body was retrieved, but we're not sure if he has been buried yet. Our issue is that he was beaten and hanged . . . we have our suspicions but are trying to keep our noses out of it. The reason I'm bringing this up now is we don't know how many of the locals know of us being here, but we have been under the protection of the local imam who has a villa five hundred yards away to the east. I really don't know how long that will last or if we will be blamed for the death, but one of the non-combatants in our party is another imam who has been with us for a while. It's a fluid situation, and we hope it stays local, but we have no idea if there are Taliban forces in the area, who may get interested, especially if they know that foreigners are on the ground."

Stone nodded again and gave Chris the once over. Then he looked at Nash. Chris could tell he was sizing the group up. Stone had already made his mind up about Alex on the march back to the barracks, but now he had two men, one who seemed capable and the other a shiny-ass desk jockey who looked permanently tired and out of his depth.

"Our Land Cruisers are good for an emergency evacuation, but if we do," Alex went on, "then you guys are going to be on the roof. Comms, I have my sat phone—I hope you brought me some batteries—and Chris and I have a two-way. That's about it."

"Next steps?"

"Test the two drums in the basement, evaluate results. Then we call for the exfil—"

"Hang on a second there," Nash chimed in. "We still have an agent heading this way. We will need to talk to him before we go anywhere."

"ETA?" Stone asked.

"Unknown, supposed to be here already," Alex answered quickly.

Stone wanted to get down to work. "It sounds like we have a few things that still need to be worked out. We will get on with the tests at hand and then regroup. I estimate sunrise in about an hour. Maybe the locals will make our decisions for us, and we will have to evac in the Toyotas. I will brief my guys on the situation and see what our commo is like. Now, Chris, was it?"

Chris nodded, happy for the attention.

"You want to show me what we got?"

"One more thing before you go, Captain," Nash added and held up his zipped-up bag of money and the chemical weapon system. "This bag will be with us at all times. I can't emphasize this enough, but if only one man walks out and across the border, then he needs to be carrying this."

The oil painting that Chris saw in the American Club in Peshawar flashed before his eyes, the only survivor of the retreating British army. He scoured his memory. *What the hell was that called again . . . Messenger of Death . . . Jesus, isn't that just about right!*

"You want to tell me what's in there?" Stone inquired.

"Go and do your tests, Captain. We'll meet back here."

<hr/>

Chris and Stone returned after half an hour. Alex was going over a map with a small flashlight camouflaged by his hand when they walked in but extinguished it as soon as he saw them. The four men circled around a handheld device that Stone was holding. The LED display was powerful enough for everyone to see.

"AC, strong indications, potency of plus or minus 75 percent."

Nash looked at the device but was none the wiser. Neither was Alex or Chris. "What does that mean, Captain?"

"Otherwise known as hydrogen cyanide, HCN in the civilian world."

Nash almost stumbled backwards when he heard the news. He sat himself down on the only stool in the room. The one that was used to hang Mateen.

Chris went to his side. He was concerned. "You okay, Mr. Nash?"

Nash ignored him. "Captain, you said it has a potency of 75 percent. How much is there in those drums?"

"I can't tell you exactly, but they were both seeping at the base. I'm no chemist, but I would say it's losing its effectiveness the longer it sits there. I'm guessing they are fifty-five-gallon drums, and they were both about 90 percent full."

"Jesus Christ!" Nash blurted out.

"I saw some other things down there. You want to explain to me what we have here?"

Nash remained silent. Nobody said anything.

Chris decided to keep the conversation going, opening up Nash's bag to reveal the contents. "What you saw in the basement is what is in here. We are calling this . . .," he pulled out the jacket, gloves, and tubes, "a chemical weapon delivery system. Like the man said, this needs to be taken across the border. We need to get this back to the US sooner than yesterday."

Stone knelt down to check the items thoroughly, throwing out a few cusswords and then lapsing into silence himself. He looked at Alex. "Now I know why you asked us to bring C-4."

"We think this place is a test lab. We found some dead dogs and a dead guard near the river. My guess is," Chris supposed, "he was left here to guard the place but he got close enough for his own sniff test and started feeling the effects, panicked, and ended up near the river. We discovered him face down, nothing but bones."

"Is someone going to come looking for him?" Stone asked but knew that nobody could really answer that.

Chris shrugged his shoulders. "He's been there a while. My guess is he's not being missed, but who knows."

Stone stared at the contents on the floor. "Whoa! Wait a minute. Have you guys been handling this stuff?"

Nash looked up from his gloomy downward view, Alex's eyes popped, Chris twitched his lips and one eyebrow went up sharply, but nobody said a word. Stone reset his chemical detector and scanned the items on the floor. Everyone looked on in anticipation for the worst, but the detector pulsed green, and the screen digits remained at 000.000.

"You're all a bunch of fucking amateurs," Stone cussed. "You could all be walking bio hazards or dead. Either way, you could have put me and my men at serious risk . . . and you," pointing at Alex, "you should know better. I know who you are, or were, you ass hat. Did the fucking CIA bleed your brain?"

He was about to storm out, but Chris headed him off and got in front of his face. "Hang on a second there, mate." He wisely refrained from putting his hands on the man but stood his ground. Chris didn't appreciate being ridiculed, even if the man was right. "I was the one touching this stuff. Alex had nothing to do with it. If anybody's at risk, then it would be me. I brought it in, and it's been almost twenty-four hours since I pulled the stuff off the rack not from the bundles on the floor. I thought the risk was low, and I'm still pissing and shitting just fine, and I'm talking to you and you don't look like a jolly green giant, so I'm guessing my body and brain are just fine. So if anybody is an ass hat, it's me. Wind your neck in for fucks sake. We're all good. Let's just focus on getting this shit out of here and off our hands."

"You motherfuckers need to keep your distance from me. You could still have minute traces in your system. I don't want what you got, but I hope your dicks fall off one day!" Stone walked out in a huff. He didn't look behind but went in search of the man with the commo gear.

He needed his airborne taxi to be in the air; he'd had enough of the three amigos already.

The Platinum House, Paradise Valley, Arizona

Jawad had the TV on and tuned in to CNN. The rolling coverage of an explosion in Long Beach had his full attention, but he was tiring of the incompetent reporters who asked the dumbest people the dumbest things. His phone rang, and he was relieved to hear his driver on the other end. He didn't need any preamble. "What of Omar?"

The driver explained that he was taken care of after the encounter in Williams and that he was dumped in the storage unit two days prior.

"Good, good. The explosion, explain that to me."

He had no explanation, only supposition. He thought Omar had planted the charges in order to cover their activities once the team had been there to retrieve their operational attire. He confirmed that the five-man team had reached the warehouse and each had walked out carrying backpacks with what he again supposed were the jackets and gloves for the operation.

"And the injured FBI agent, how did he get so close?"

There was more guessing by the henchman. He wasn't sure how he got into the warehouse, but he explained to Jawad that he did not enter the premises from the front and probably had assistance from the property owner who died in the incident.

Jawad looked at his watch. It was just a matter of hours before the daily commute would begin in Los Angeles, San Francisco, San Diego, and Portland. "Have your sources confirmed the deployment of the teams in the other cities?"

The driver confirmed that each of the five-man teams had followed their orders and were in place waiting for their own early morning start times.

"Then, my friend, I believe our business in complete. I must say it has been a pleasure working with you again. Your account has been stocked with the agreed amount, and as a gesture of goodwill, I have included a small bonus for taking care of our mutual friend. . . . Yes,

yes, I will be in touch. Goodbye."

Jawad hung up the phone and then continued to watch the TV. He looked at his watch again. He was getting a little anxious. *It's time to go,* he mused. He looked around the room and gathered some of his things but was distracted with the thoughts of completing his mission. Events now were out of his hands. It would be up to the twenty martyrs to pave their own destiny and for him to retreat and ready himself for the next battle. He opened his office door and shouted down the corridor, "Major Basrawi!"

Basrawi came rushing up the stairs with a notepad in hand, knocking on the open door, and stood at attention waiting to be invited in. A slight sliver of sweat ran down the side of his forehead, not because he had exerted himself but because he was nervous around a man that held his daughters' lives in his hands.

"Come, come, Major. Please take a seat. This won't take long."

Basrawi sat on the edge of the couch, stiff as a board, not sure what to expect. He looked down at his notepad pretending to scribble something and then stopped himself realizing that Jawad might see he was writing something, thus opening a door to interrogation. He flicked his eyes over to Jawad, who was sitting behind his desk, but as soon as Jawad looked at him, Basrawi looked to the ground.

"Major, I must compliment you."

The soldier looked up and frowned at the unexpected compliment. He held his breath for a second, expecting some kind of trap.

"Her Highness has successfully left American airspace and will soon be home in the kingdom. I think we can all breathe a sigh of relief once she is safely at home, but I believe it is down to your expert planning and coordination that the move from here to the aircraft was seamless. Congratulations, Major. You can be quite proud of yourself."

Basrawi nodded his head like a serf being praised by his evil lord but expected a large mace to swoop down on his head at any moment. He didn't utter a word. He was more afraid now in the empty house than he was before. Everyone was gone, all the members of the royal family, their servants, the cooks, cleaners, the police, the American security company, even his soldiers. Only Jawad and he remained, no supporters, no witnesses. His only saving grace was the fact that Jawad's henchman was nowhere to be found. "Thank you, sir," he uttered feebly, not knowing if these were his last words.

Jawad got up from behind his desk and approached him with a large envelope. He leaned back on the desk with his butt to face the major. "These are your orders." He waved the packet tantalizing with his right hand while tapping it into his left.

Hope danced in Basrawi's eyes at the prospect of an order. His demise would not be forthcoming.

"I want you to know that I have given this a lot of thought . . . it hasn't escaped me that you were acting in concert with the FBI, my friend. It offends me still that you considered betraying us . . . however, we must move forward. We cannot let your lack of caution halt progress. By that I mean you and I must move on from here. Take this . . ." Jawad handed him the envelope with one hand but held on to it firmly before releasing. "But you will not open this for forty-eight hours. Inside are your instructions for your next task. I will not discuss the details of this with you for I need you to obey my orders and not open it until the appropriate time." He let go of the instructions. "Now look at your watch, Major. Make the calculations. Open in forty-eight hours from this time. Do we understand each other?"

"Yes, of course, sir," Basrawi replied suppressing a thin smile.

Jawad moved back from the desk and went to the window where he looked across to the empty street. He talked to his visitor over his shoulder. "Your house arrest is lifted, and as you can tell, you are the only remaining Saudi. I highly recommend that you do not leave this house. However, if you want to leave, please do so, but that envelope cannot fall into the wrong hands. Your instructions will cover all details of your departure."

Basrawi nodded but still perspired. He had no idea what was so valuable in the packet, but he knew how to follow an order. Although Jawad's man was not visibly present, Basrawi feared he was waiting somewhere for him to falter. He vowed to himself that he would follow his orders and remain in the house until the commanded time.

Jawad spun around, walked over to Basrawi, and offered his hand. The soldier stood up and inhaled sharply. Jawad could see that he was terrified. As they shook hands, Jawad felt the clammy skin of the man. He began to feel slightly sorry for him, seeing the terror in his eyes, but he didn't want to become his friend or therapist.

"Karim, you and I will meet again for there is much for us to do. I will see you in a time and place of my choosing. Please do not be offended or hesitant if I ask you to undertake another task. It is God's will that we have been brought together. Go in peace, my friend."

Hisarak District, Afghanistan

Nash's team of warriors made themselves relatively comfortable while waiting for the CH-47 pickup. There wasn't much to do or say, and just like any other soldier in a war zone, all they were doing was waiting, shooting the shit, and waiting some more.

Azzami came looking for Chris late in the afternoon. Still upset, he had calmed down enough to have a conversation with him and to let him know what was happening with Mateen.

"He is with family now Chris."

"I am truly sorry for your loss, Azzami. We all are."

"Tomorrow he will be laid to rest . . . I think that is the correct words, yes?"

Chris nodded. There wasn't much to say as they sat on a stoop of one of the buildings at the barracks.

"The family are asking many questions. They know that you are here."

"Do they know how he died?" Chris didn't get a response. He wasn't looking at the young Afghan, but he could see in his peripheral vision that Azzami's shoulders were moving involuntarily as he began to sob. Azzami hunched over and held his face in his hands. Chris put his hand on his shoulder and let him cry. He sympathized, but he just didn't know what to say. A few minutes more of silence divided the two, but Azzami regained his composure. "They think he was tortured."

Chris blinked and stared off in the distance. He felt a warm sweating sensation in his face. *Shit!*

"And this only came to pass when you came."

"Do they think it was us?" Chris asked already guessing the answer.

"Maybe, I don't know, but the imam he talks to them now."

Chris was becoming irate. *That ass-wipe is stirring up the shit and covering his arse. We'll be lucky to get out of here.* "Is he there now?"

"Yes, he is talking to the elders and the family."

Chris had a feeling that he knew the answer to his next question. "Has this happened before, Azzami?"

"Yes, many times."

"And what was the outcome?" Azzami didn't answer, but Chris could tell Azzami didn't understand. Chris tried a different tack. "What will happen after the imam has talked to the family?"

"Someone will be hanged."

Jesus, that could easily be one of us . . . motherfucker. Chris was lost in his thoughts and watched as Captain Stone scurried around in the distance talking to his men. Azzami saw him too.

"Why are these soldiers here?"

"They have come to take us out of here, Azzami. It may be soon."

The young Afghan was silent.

Chris turned to look at him and could see he was holding back his emotions. Chris wanted to reassure him, wanted to make him feel that he was going to be okay, though he could not guarantee anything, especially his safety. He too remained silent, struggling to come to terms that after what he saw, what he witnessed, the confusion, the fighting, the aftermath, but there was little he could do or say that could make a difference. What made things worse was that Nash still had not made up his mind if the imam and Azzami would be going with them.

He swallowed hard as if about to say something profound when Alex squawked over the radio, "One hour to exfil, Chris."

"Roger that," he replied, staring blankly out across the parade square. "Wait here, okay?" he ordered his young friend.

Chris hastily made his way to the makeshift command post the

ODA had created in the room where they had found Mateen. Nash was sitting on the stool, and Stone was kneeling beside him looking over a map. They both looked up as they heard him come in. He came straight to the point, "What are we doing about the imam and Azzami?"

"They are coming with us," Nash answered.

"Do they know that?" Alex piped up as he appeared from around a corner.

"You two are about to go and tell them. What's our timeline for detonation, Captain?"

"Fifteen minutes before the helo touches down. That's roughly forty-five minutes from now."

"Good." Nash turned back to his men. "Go round them up, make it quick, but we don't need a parade through here. Keep it quiet, Chris."

"In all due respect, Mr. Nash, I don't see why we need the imam anymore, but Azzami, yes, let's take him out. That other piece of shit can be stuffed in the chem room if you ask me."

"Nobody is asking you, Chris. I am not going to debate with you. Go and do what I ask or I will find someone else, clear?"

Chris stomped off. He was satisfied that at least Azzami would get out of this immediate situation, but he didn't want anything to do with the imam.

As Alex was about to follow Chris, Nash said quietly, "Alex, keep an eye on him. Let's get the imam back here with all his blood inside his body, okay?"

Alex stared back at Nash and didn't say a word. In principle, he agreed with Chris that the imam needed to die a violent death, but he also realized that even killing one child abuser would not stamp out the widespread practice that would continue long after they had disappeared. Alex couldn't figure out why Nash wanted to protect the cleric, as the mission to find TRODPINT was all but over. Finding the chemicals and the other paraphernalia trumped all other priorities, and the mission to get the discovery back to the west was now paramount, but in his mind bringing the imam along was pointless. Plus, Alex balked at Nash's order; he didn't need to be told to watch out for Chris. He knew he could be a handful, but he also thought the Brit had the discipline to carry out an order.

When Alex walked outside, he saw Chris talking to Azzami. Out of the corner of his eye, he saw some movement to the north of the barracks. He stuck his head back into the command post. "We got some movement to the north at the edge of the village. Your boys got eyeballs on that?"

Stone held up his hand listening in on his earpiece, nodding a few times, and acknowledging the radio report, and then answered Alex, "There's a small gathering in the village. We have no high ground to speak of, so we have limited line of sight to any potential hostiles. Right now, it's a bunch of old men milling around. We'll keep eyes on."

Alex looked passively at Stone but said nothing. He left the command post and racked a round into the chamber of his rifle. *It's going to escalate.*

Portland, Oregon

The man in the leather jacket boarded the MAX Light Rail Service at the Blue Line Gresham Central Transit Station. The clock ticked to 07:01 before it moved off westwards towards the city. He made his way to the rear of the second car and scanned the passengers who got on with him, hoping to identify any police officers before they spotted him. Although a warning of possible terror attacks that could happen circulated the news channels, no specifics were issued to the public or local authorities.

Satisfied that he was not being sought after or looked at suspiciously, he removed a glove from his left pocket and fitted it onto his left hand. He took the tube, which was dangling loosely out of the left sleeve of his jacket and attached it to a pressure ball that he also retrieved from his pocket. As soon as he made sure of the fit, he extracted a right-hand glove from his right jacket pocket. *Allahu Akbar, Allahu Akbar, Allahu Akbar,* he chanted to himself, then put the glove on his hand, and clipped the tube from the sleeve to the glove. *Allahu Akbar, Allahu Akbar, Allahu Akbar.*

He continued his mantra, and by the time he reached the Civic Drive Max Station, he was ready. He walked down the isle of the car touching each of the handrails. As he did, he pumped the cyanide from his hidden backpack down through the tube, through his glove, and on to the surface of the aluminum. *Allahu Akbar, Allahu Akbar, Allahu Akbar.*

At 07:04, a man in a waterproof jacket boarded the MAX Light Rail Service at the Red Line Gateway/NE Ninety-Ninth Avenue Transit Station. *Allahu Akbar, Allahu Akbar, Allahu Akbar.* He too went through the motions in the same fashion as his comrade on the Blue Line, but his destination was Beaverton, headquarters of Nike, but he didn't know if his toxic agent would last that long.

At 07:15, 07:22, and 07:34, three other terrorists boarded the MAX Light Rail Yellow, Green, and Orange Lines. The next cell had mobilized. Portland was under attack.

Hisarak District, Afghanistan

Chris walked back to the villa with Azzami purporting to search for the imam but in actual fact was just going through the exercise of picking up what the young Afghan needed while disregarding the whereabouts of the abuser.

Alex caught up with him. "Convenient that he's not here?"

"That fucker is rousing a rabble over in the village. If we don't get out of here, one of us is going to get lynched."

"What makes you say that?" he asked. Chris gave him the same story that Azzami had given him earlier, and by the time he had finished, Alex was more convinced that the day was going to end with hostilities.

"Okay," Chris added, "we looked around, can't find him, too bad, so sad, let's get out of here. They're going to blow the basement soon, and I want to be standing nearer the landing zone when that happens rather than stuck out here."

Azzami grabbed his paltry possessions and tagged along behind the two men, struggling to keep up as they marched quickly.

Alex caught sight of more people from the village beginning to congregate not far from the entrance to the barracks. "You see what I see?" Alex asked.

"Yup, I don't think they are selling Celine Dion tickets, so I think we should piss off pretty quick."

Alex broke into a jog. Chris easily matched his pace, although the lanky SAD operator took longer bounds. Chris dropped back a little, coercing Azzami to keep up.

They reached the command post just in time for Stone to announce that the chopper was inbound and twenty minutes out.

Before Nash asked about the imam, Alex faced off with the Ranger. "I think you should go loud now. There's a large crowd gathering near the edge of the barracks. They may be heading in this direction. We need to keep them out of the landing zone."

Stone looked at Chris and then Nash and was about to make his decision when one of his team called in that someone was approaching and someone needed to ID them before they got too close. He pulled his earpiece out and switched his radio to the open speaker mode. "We've got someone approaching. Would one of you two go and ID him before he gets a 5.56mm for lunch."

Chris motioned for Azzami to join him, and they both walked outside. From a distance, they could see the imam approaching. "He's a friendly." he shouted back to the inside, hoping nobody heard him and one of the Rangers would do him a favor.

They met in the center of the parade square. "Chris, my friend, there you are. How are you?" The imam was all smiles, open, warm, and inviting.

Chris didn't reply. He wanted an excuse to end the man's life, but there were a hundred sets of eyes on them. He wasn't stupid enough to ignite a possible volatile situation that could engage the entire team.

"I'm afraid we have a problem, you and I."

"I'm listening."

"For some reason, the villagers—and you must understand they are in mourning and are not of sound judgement at the moment—but for some reason they believe that a westerner killed that young boy. It's tragic, and I have tried to reason with them, but they will not listen to me."

Chris did not take his eyes off the imam and saw Alex circling around to his front right, providing an extra set of eyes. He got into a position behind the imam and within earshot. "That boy's name was Mateen!" Chris barked.

"Yes, yes Mateen, such a lovely boy."

Chris almost bit his lip; his knuckles were turning white. He wanted to rip the imam's throat out and drink his blood. "So what do you want from me?" he asked already knowing the answer.

"I would like you to come and explain to the family, to the village elders that you had nothing to do with this. Then we can all go on our way."

"Go fuck yourself!"

The imam was feigning being taken aback. His tone was almost childish when he spoke again. "Chris, why are you so hostile? I thought we were friends, you and I. We still have a mission to complete."

Chris looked at him sideways.

But the imam continued, "The man you are looking for, he is on his way. We can still meet with him, but we must talk to the villagers first to clear up this sad, sad death."

Chris was glad Nash couldn't hear the conversation.

Alex turned around when he heard the news. He shook his head at Chris, who nodded in return. The silent communication between the two former soldiers was enough; they both had the understanding that they didn't need to rehash the TRODPINT angle.

Stone marched over to the group in the center of the parade ground. "You ladies finished swapping recipes? I have work to do, and you are in the way. Let's go, let's go!" Then turned back towards the command post expecting the train to follow him.

Chris and Alex followed his orders. "Azzami, you coming?" Chris shouted.

The imam grabbed Azzami roughly and began to berate him, almost coming to blows with the young man. Alex headed Chris off and got in between both antagonists. He dragged a sobbing Azzami back to the command post, but it didn't take long for the imam to invite himself into the westerner's new residence.

"I don't give a shit what's going on here. I don't want to know. Everyone back behind the wall at the rear of the building," Stone ordered and pointed to the direction he needed them to take. "I suggest you hold on to your nuts."

The imam was genuinely bewildered. It was the first time he saw Stone and was just as surprised when he saw the communication gear and the weaponry. His eyes were struggling to take everything in. He saw Nash plod towards a door at the rear of the building and followed. When he got there, he saw that everyone was hunkered down. Azzami was firmly held by Chris, and the imam still didn't know what was going on but sat down near them.

"Helo inbound fifteen minutes," Stone stated as he plunked down next to the gang. "Blow it, Chuckie!" he ordered one of his men over the radio. Two seconds later, there was a loud CURRUMPHH that sent a large cloud of brown and gray dust up into the air.

Chris opened his eyes and looked to the sky to watch the cloud get swept away by the wind. *Did you use enough? Jeezuus!*

The group moved back into the building, which didn't suffer any damage from the blast. Stone sent two of his men to break cover and assess the damage. It didn't take long for the Rangers to call in a positive detonation. Stone wasn't waiting for his congressional Medal of Honor and ordered his men to check the landing zone for debris. Just as he finished talking, his loudspeaker came to life.

"Utah One Zero, Utah One Zero, this is Lima Two Two Charlie, five minutes."

"I'll take early over late," Stone said aloud to nobody, happy to hear his team's call sign. "Lima Two Two Charlie, Utah One Zero, roger. Stand by for green smoke, over," he responded to the Chinook.

Stone turned to the group, "Here's what's going to happen. The helo will touch down. One of my men will secure the ramp. Nash, you will be first. Chris, you will hold his hand. Alex, you bring up the rear.

Then your Afghans will follow. We will collapse on the helo and lift. Questions?"

Before anyone could say anything, Chuckie the Ranger blasted over the radio, "Hostiles, hostiles. Stand by for contact!"

"Utah One Zero, Lima Two Two Charlie, I have multiple fast-moving vehicles moving towards your location. Armed men in five pickups."

"Roger that Lima Two Two. Stand by for smoke."

Alex turned to Chris, but before he could say anything, the first shots rang out. Stone was calmly talking to his men over the radio trying to gauge the enemy's location and strength. Chris was impressed. It was as if he was ordering a happy meal at a MacDonald's drive-through. Through the commotion of radio traffic, Alex found time to speak to Chris, "You need to stay here. You need to get that shit out, get Nash out. Stay by him, understand? Don't follow me." Without waiting for a response, Alex sprinted out the door, weapon at the ready.

Chris held himself back. He wanted to rush into the battle, but his responsibilities were with the bag on the floor and his boss.

"Make yourself useful, Chris." Stone gave him a smoke canister, "Pop that sucker out there; get back in here."

Chris stuck his head out of the building, ran a few feet forward, and lobbed the canister towards the south end of the parade square. He was about to run back when he heard someone shout at the top of their voice, "RPG!" He dropped to the floor immediately, waited a second, and then scrambled back on all fours towards the command post, making it inside just in time for the RPG round to hit the dirt where the green smoke was wafting into the air.

"Lima Two Two Charlie, Utah One Zero, hot LZ, hot LZ, abort, abort," Stone once again casually announced over the radio.

"Utah One Zero, hot LZ, roger. Lima Two Two Charlie on station three miles from LZ, standing by."

"I like to drive anyway," Chris said to Stone, who simply returned his comment with a smile.

CHAPTER EIGHTEEN

Hisarak District, Afghanistan

THERE WAS A BRIEF LULL in the firefight that had taken Nash's warriors by surprise. No more RPGs were fired; however, some potshots were taken at the Rangers. Stone informed the group in the command post that the enemy was probably sizing up the opposition and strategizing for a concerted attack. The imam shuddered at the thought of the Taliban closing in. Chris saw him squirm and was sure if he got closer to him he would smell the piss running down his legs.

Stone's men were calling in the movements that they could see before them. Although Alex wasn't on the same radio frequency as the Rangers, he relayed his observations through to Chris, who in turn passed on the information to Stone.

It was quiet in the command post until Nash opened a conversation with the imam. "Imam Alim, I can't help but notice your concern. Are you worried about us or the Taliban?"

The imam didn't respond. His jaw was clenched tight, and he jumped every time a shot was heard near or far. He wrung his hands and wrists as if he was trying to wrench them off. His eyes darted furtively from opening to opening, from body movement to body movement. Everyone could tell he was frightened.

Nash's question was subtle. He knew what was bothering the imam so much, but he wanted to hear it from him, wanted him to admit he was petrified, wanted him to show his weakness. "Imam, please clarify something for me."

The imam was confused. They were in a battle, and this man wanted a fireside chat. It was bizarre, but again he held his tongue.

"Is it true the Taliban have strict rules with the dancing boys?"

Azzami looked up in amazement. Chris shut down the smile that was forming on his face, but Stone didn't know what was going on.

Nash continued, "I believe it is forbidden under Sharia law, by penalty of death. Am I correct?"

The imam crushed his lips together giving the impression that he had none or that they were lost in his well-manicured beard. He nodded quicker than the man tapping in SOS in Morse code on the *Titanic*. A loud bang made him quiver and search for the intruding sound.

"LOOK AT ME!" Nash screamed. Chris jumped slightly. He hadn't heard this type of thing from Nash in all the years that he had known him. It was out of character, but Chris liked it.

The imam made eye contact with Nash.

"Now is the time, Imam Alim. Now you will tell me what you promised me at the prison. Tell me where bin Laden is. Tell me now."

Nobody was sure if the imam was going to say anything. Even if he were, the silent radio burst into voice, "Utah One Zero, Lima Two Two Charlie, I am one-five minutes to bingo fuel. If you want to go, your window is closing."

"Lima Two Two Charlie, Utah One Zero, roger. We are assessing enemy contact. Stand by."

"What about it, dickweed? Do you know where bin Laden is?" Stone asked of the imam.

Nash held up his hand. He wanted to control this. Time was running out. Name calling wasn't going to help. "Imam, it is simple. We are getting on that helicopter. You can come with us, or we will leave you for the Taliban." Nash wanted to hit him hard, but he had a better idea. He would take his plaything away. He turned to the young Afghan. "Azzami, take this piece of paper. Write this in Pashto, 'I fuck little boys. I killed Mateen.'"

Azzami shook his head. He couldn't believe what he was hearing.

"Azzami, do as he says. You are safe. You will come with us. Don't worry," Chris assured him.

Azzami complied, and when the young Afghan was finished, Nash stuck the piece of paper in front of the imam's face. "If you don't tell me now, I will have you tied up, gagged, and I will pin this piece of paper to your head." Chris liked where this was going and looked over at Stone who produced a pair of plastic cuffs. The imam started backing into a corner like a scared rabbit, only showing one eye to the world but holding his knees tightly to his chest.

"WHERE IS BIN LADEN?" Nash screamed at the top of his voice again. Chris looked over at him and thought he was going to burst a blood vessel. Nash's face was flushed, his throat was swelling up, and his hands were shaking." Now Chris knew why he wanted to hang on to the imam so badly.

The imam shook his head once again, but before anyone said anything, Lima Two Two Charlie spoilt the party. This time the message was harried.

"Utah, Utah, T-72 tank closing in on your location. Repeat, T-72 closing in on you. I'm inbound, two minutes for exfil."

Stone cursed and informed his men, Chris relayed the information to Alex who also let loose a storm of expletives over the radio, the battlefield had just changed. Light troops versus heavy armor does not a fun day make.

The leader of the Rangers prepared his men and turned to Nash. "You've missed your chance. We are out of here." He pointed to the imam. "Drag that prick with you, Chris, same order as before. One of my team will secure the ramp. He will signal for you to go. Walk fast, do not run. Nash you go first. Chris bring ass-wipe and the boy. The Afghans will follow you. I will come out as my men close in."

The clatter of machine gun fire became sustained. The battle proper had begun. Messages from the Rangers were coming in, reporting heavy contact.

The sound of the Chinook overhead prompted Stone to grab Chris and pull him towards him, "Relay message of T-72 to Alex. Get him back here now. We are leaving with or without him."

Chris followed the order, and then everyone staged in a crouched formation near the door. Nash held on to the bag for dear life. He was sweating profusely and rubbing his left arm. Chris wondered if he fell over but didn't have time to think about it. He grabbed the imam and then stuck his rifle in his face as a gentle method of persuasion to take his place in the line.

No sooner had the CH-47 landed in the center of the parade ground than the first shell from the T-72 hit one of the buildings that housed one of the Rangers. "Man down, man down," came the calls over the radio. Stone concentrated on the Chinook; his men would have to look after themselves for the moment.

A Ranger sprinted to the back of the helicopter as its ramp was deployed. He took a few seconds to scan the area and then waved at Stone, who shouted at the team before him, "GO! GO! GO!" Nash, first in line got up too quickly from his crouched position and fell back slightly onto Azzami, who in his will to get out of the battle, pushed the slow Nash upwards and onwards to the safety of the helicopter. Chris grabbed the imam by the scruff of his neck and dragged him out of the door.

The group was about half way between the helicopter and the command post when Chris saw movement to his right. Releasing the imam and taking a knee, he shot a man who was carrying an RPG running between buildings. The distraction however, proved to be costly. The imam had caught up with Azzami and forced him to kneel on the ground. When Chris turned towards the helicopter again, he saw the imam holding the young boy's hair with his left hand and pressing a handgun into his temple with the right. Before Chris could do or say something, the imam shot Azzami, throwing his limp body to the ground.

Chris almost dropped his rifle in shock. In the background behind the imam, he saw Nash stumble and fall onto the ramp and was subsequently picked up by one of the aircrew. He was about to react to the imam's action, but the Ranger who was stationed next to the ramp, let loose a burst of automatic fire just twenty feet to Chris's right. Chris spun and went down on one knee again to engage the enemy. One of the four Afghans joined him in the fight, but it was senseless without cover or concealment. Although they were taking a few of the Taliban out, they were easy targets.

Motioning the Northern Alliance soldier to get on board, which he readily did, Chris then also started to march quickly when he saw Alex carrying an injured Ranger over his shoulder. The ex-Delta operator was moving quickly under the weight but was coming under fire. Even though the Ranger he was carrying was engaging the enemy by firing his pistol as they were heading to safety, one lucky shot could have ended their chance of escape.

Chris halted his movements and ran back towards his friend, opening fire with his rifle. Stone came up next to Chris, who was in the middle of a magazine change, and let loose with everything he had covering Alex's progress to the helicopter.

The T-72 let loose a round destroying the command post and was closing in fast. The three remaining Rangers showed up and traded cover, maneuver, and fire between them. As they closed in to the LZ, heavy machine gun rounds began to make life miserable for everyone and the Chinook. Rounds of tracers were flying amongst normal lead, and though seldom accurate, being safe from the projectiles was becoming difficult. One or two rounds hit the helicopter, and though the din, Chris could hear the radio communication from the pilot, "Let's go, let's go." Chris peeked backwards, straining to see through the dust storm the helicopter was spewing, and saw that Alex had made it aboard with his charge. He also noted that all the Rangers were on board. He tapped Stone's shoulder and nodded in the direction of the helo Stone nodded back, and both made their move.

They broke into a run as the Taliban's fire increased. It was now useless for them to return fire as it would only waste time for them to stop and take aim. Running and shooting was Hollywood; running to survive wasn't.

It didn't take two seconds after both Stone and Chris set foot on the ramp for the pilot to lift off. The crew chief of the helicopter sat down behind a .50 caliber machine gun that was bolted to the floor of the ramp and let loose with nonstop fire. Chris, still facing the front of the helicopter, noted that someone was on the floor receiving chest compressions. He couldn't look for long as enemy fire from below strafed the inside of the Chinook, causing the gunner to stop what he was doing forcing everyone on board to hit the deck.

As they gained elevation, Chris stuck his head up only to receive a stream of red hydraulic fluid piss into his face from a device on the wall. He reeled back from it and then wiped his sleeve over his face. As his vision restored, he could see they had made the lift off just in time, as the T-72 had burst through a building and was sitting in the very center of the parade square, surrounded by a horde of Taliban soldiers. He saw a puff of white smoke emitting from the barrel of the tank the same time an RPG was fired. "Oh fuck!" he shouted. Stone heard him and peered outside. He too had red fluid on his uniform. "Climb, climb, you piece of shit!" willed Chris.

As much as Stone wanted to steal elevation and outrun the incoming shell from the ground, the pilot had other ideas and banked sharply away and mysteriously downwards. Alarm bells were ringing solidly in the cockpit telling the crew that a missile was locked on. The Special Forces helicopter from the 160th Special Operations Aviation Regiment was fitted with primitive anti-missile defenses, so one of the first things it did was deploy chaff. It wasn't needed, however, as the RPG missile fired from the Taliban soldier didn't have enough of a brain to seek and destroy a moving target, even if it was an airborne bus. It was simply a fire-and-forget system that could be defeated from the air. Chris and Stone watched the projectile on its death spiral towards an innocent hillside, while the T-72's round fell near the riverbank mercilessly killing a mound of rocks and shrubs.

If the Chinook pilot thought his maneuver was sound, Chris and Stone had other opinions as they tumbled around on the limited space between the eight-foot-long ramp and the cargo deck. Chris found something stationary to hold onto as the pilot continued to play hard target and bob and weave as best as he could, with close to thirty thousand pounds of steel, aluminum, plastics, fuel, and bodies hindering his acrobatic performance.

During the tumble-dryer ride, the crew chief moved away from his machine gun and tried his utmost to close the rear ramp of the chopper. He used both hands to try to maneuver the yellow lever that controlled the opening and closing of the ramp, but the device wouldn't budge. The airman took his hands off the lever, looked up to the connecting rods and pipes, and realized that the amongst the pock-marked ceiling from the Taliban rounds, the lines were severed leaving a steady flow of red hydraulic fluid running down the inside workings of the aircraft. The three thousand pounds of pressure used to control the ramp were voided leaving both Chris and Stone feeling vulnerable as the pilot continued to twist and turn the huge helicopter through the valleys and peaks to escape the enemy with the ramp open to the elements.

By the time the pilot had leveled off, the jumble of bodies began to sort themselves out. Chris was still looking out of the back of the chopper not paying attention to what was going on around him. He couldn't figure out why they hadn't gained any elevation, but he supposed the pilot knew what he was doing and had the route planned out to get over the higher elevations or avoid them completely. He really didn't know how low they were, but it was enough to get the attention of people on the ground who looked up in amazement as they passed over. One particular man on a motorcycle became animated waving his hands frantically at the helicopter. Chris was tempted to wave back but he wasn't on a joy ride. They had just extracted themselves from a firefight; men were killed, injured. He too could have been shot, but then he began to think of Azzami.

When the man on the motorcycle followed the helicopter's path, Chris squinted and gave the sight a closer look. *What the hell is his problem?* But the wild man, though getting distant, was still waving, and at one point fell off his bike, only to stand up and keep on waving. *TRODPINT!* Chris realized, but it was too late.

The stress of battle had finally taken its toll on Chris. All of a sudden, he felt tired and needed to sit down properly and rest. When he turned to face the cabin, he looked at all the faces that looked worn and battered. He saw Alex tending to the Ranger whom he had carried into the chopper. From where he was, Chris couldn't tell what type of wound he had received, but it looked like he was coherent enough to have a conversation with his buddies. He looked at Stone who was fiddling with the radio and chatting to one of his men at the same time, ignoring him as they were preparing for the next eventuality. He saw the imam had made it on board and was sitting in the last seat before the ramp opposite him. They exchanged looks, but neither said a word. Chris was still dubious. *Does that bastard know where bin Laden is, or did he just want to get out of prison to fuck young boys?* Chris averted his eyes from the man and then continued his search around the cabin, but he didn't see Nash. He found the four Afghans who were no worse for wear, but he got a feeling that he had never felt before. Something was off . . .

Nash wasn't there.

Chris felt a wave of panic wash over him. He had seen Nash get on the aircraft, but he couldn't see him anywhere on either the port or starboard red bench seats that lined each wall. Chris was getting frantic. His breathing was becoming labored. He wasn't sure if it was because the Chinook was finally gaining altitude or dread. *Did he get off? I saw him get on. Where the hell is he?* Towards the front of the cabin, there was a pile of Rangers' equipment, but there looked to be some space between that and the cockpit. He struggled forward trying to find purchase on an overhead handhold. While stepping on feet or other body parts, apologizing as he moved forward. When he reached the center of the aircraft, he stopped, feeling a weird sour taste in his mouth, a shakiness in his limbs. He saw Nash's face. His eyes were closed, and he was lying flat on his back. Chris took another few steps and saw that his shirt had been ripped open; a used AED was lying next to him. An air force gunner who was manning a machine gun in a door behind the cockpit saw Chris's expression. Their eyes locked, and the airman shook his head. Chris fought back the urge to vomit; bile rose in his throat, but he swallowed hard to prevent the upward motion. He used the bucking aircraft's motion as an excuse to fall into an empty seat next to Nash's body, slumping down and letting his head fall down into his hands.

Chris had no idea how long he had been sitting in the same position. When he raised his head, it spun fast enough to give himself a headache of mammoth proportions. He rubbed his eyes as hard as he could to erase the pain, but to no avail. His nausea was taking away his sense of equilibrium as if he was riding on a rough sea and getting seasick. He wanted to throw up, wanted to sleep, wanted to drink, wanted to walk away, all at the same time. He couldn't comprehend what was going to happen in the next two minutes, but each second was turning out to be an emotional battle as ferocious as the one he just left.

He took off his jacket to cover Nash's body. Alex saw the motion and watched Chris kneel by the body, lean over to whisper something in Nash's ear, and then place the jacket over his head.

Chris stood up again. However, this time he didn't return to his seat. He scrambled towards the ramp of the helicopter. Alex looked on trying to figure out what he was trying to do. All the other combatants in the aircraft were too occupied either snoozing or staring off into the distance to pay much attention to Chris.

When Chris reached the rear of the ramp, he stood in front of the imam as he held on to a piece of the aircraft's framework with his left hand above his head. After a second, he pointed to the imam's right shoulder and back to his brushing his own as he did it. The imam was confused and wasn't sure what he wanted. Chris repeated the move twice more. On the second hint, the imam looked at his shoulder and realized that it was red, Chris pointed to the ceiling that was still oozing remnants of the ramp's hydraulic fluid. The imam looked up, saw the problem, and then looked at Chris again, who was now motioning him to move to the other side where there was an empty seat and no leak. Chris reached out his right hand to help as the imam struggled to get out of the bucket seat and managed to stand up to grab Chris's offered right hand. Chris let go of his handhold above his head and placed his left hand on the imam's right elbow and pulled him gently towards him. When Chris began to maneuver him toward the empty seat, he shifted his body weight to pivot on his right foot forcing the imam to topple towards him. As the imam stumbled, Chris grasped the man with all his strength, took two steps to the rear of the ramp, and spun his whole body around quickly causing the imam to run in the direction of the opening.

Chris watched the man fall for a second and then grabbed the overhead hand hold. When he turned around, two pairs of eyes were staring at him, Alex's and Stone's. Neither said a word or gave a disapproving look. Chris took the empty seat where the imam was supposed to be. He looked out the back again and hoped they were flying at five thousand feet.

Nogales, Arizona

Jawad kept his rental car's speed at just one mile per hour over the posted speed limit as he reached the outskirts of Nogales and the border between the United States and Mexico. He'd been scouring the car's radio for news channels, but as he got closer to the border, the options for English-speaking stations were getting few and far between. Not three miles to the border, he found what he was looking for.

"Reports are coming in from San Diego that police have arrested two men in separate instances on the San Diego Metropolitan Transit System during the morning commute. Unconfirmed reports allege that the two men were acting suspiciously, and one was approached by a police officer at the Courthouse Station in downtown San Diego. After a brief scuffle, one of the men attempted to spray some kind of substance at the officer but was arrested. The second suspect, who was apprehended roughly at the same time at the Spring Street Station, refused to answer officers' questions. Sources claim that the man allegedly began shouting something in Arabic and became belligerent when approached by concerned passengers. The San Diego Police Department has not issued a statement on the incidents or whether the two arrests are connected. More on this update to follow at the top of the hour. In other news—"

Jawad turned off the radio and pulled out his Maltese passport from his shirt pocket. He tried his best to control his smile, but his excitement was getting the better of him. Operation Najd was underway, the next cell was engaged, his mission was getting closer to being complete.

He slowed his car as he approached the border. An overweight Mexican border guard saw him approach, looked at a clipboard, and then waved him through. Jawad was free of the United States.

Panjshir Valley, Afghanistan

Chris was sitting once again in Ed Guild's office; however, this time a new face was taking up space on the sofa in the confined study. He noticed that the pile of boxes full of money that he had sat on days before had increased in size. Looking at it, he wondered how much the CIA had already spent on the campaign and how big of a money hole there was in the country that could swallow up this mere speck of what was needed.

"Chris, this is Ted Bechous. He will be taking over from me. My old bones and bowels have not stood the test of endurance, and it's time for me to leave. You and I will be leaving on the next transport to Task Force Dagger in Uzbekistan. From there, we are going to get on a C-17 bound for Ramstein, then home." Chris nodded. He was too tired to have a meet and greet, but he knew the mission he had been given by Gene in Maryland was now complete. He remembered the words the CIA SAD chief had said to him before he left the United States: "Chris, if he's dead or alive, you are leaving the country with him, and I don't really care if you are in the body bag next to him. Understood?"

"What time are we leaving? I'm guessing we are taking Mr. Nash with us." Both of the CIA men before him looked at him strangely, unable to figure out why Chris used such a formal name, but neither of them wanted to query the issue. Ed answered his question, "Yes, we will. We are scheduled to leave at 0730, but that could change with the weather. We have fair conditions as of right now, but when it changes around here, it changes quickly. More than likely we will have a rough ride, blue or gray skies, no matter."

Ed looked at Chris's soulless face. He could tell the young man was grieving, but he didn't know him well enough to give him words of comfort. However, they needed to pick his brain and get a full debrief of all the actions of the last few days.

"Chris, I can tell you are tired and probably not in the mood, but we need to have you debrief. You need to give us a full action report. I have a rough understanding of what happened, but Ted and I need to hear it from you. I will bring Alex and Stone in to get their perspectives and one of the team to take notes. You good with that?"

Chris wanted a beer while taking a long shit and then another drink in a hot shower. He didn't care for reports, opinions, recommendations, and all the blah, blah bullshit that went along with it. He wanted to be left alone to regroup on his own time in his own way. However, that meant getting drunk and getting into a fight. He rationalized that none of those things was going to happen any time soon, and more seriously, he owed it to Nash to play nice. The time for being a smart-arse was over.

"Sure, Ed," he said with feigned enthusiasm. "Let's get them in here and crack on. There's a ton of stuff we need to talk about. We can sleep on the plane tomorrow."

Ed nodded with a thin smile. He knew the young man was close to Nash but was glad Chris was ready to keep on working and not fall into a sullen, distant mood.

After a few hours of discussion about how Chris got into country, how he met with the SAS, and how he rescued Nash and Guy Trimble from the Taliban, Ed stood up in the meeting room and announced that he had a bio emergency and basically sprinted from the debrief to take care of his burning bowels. It was a welcome break from the proceedings, but there was still much to discuss. Dinner was one of the freshest MREs that the Rangers brought with them—a few apples brought in from the nearby village and a few cans of beer disguised as Coke to wash down the delicacies.

Ted left the room during the meal to check on communications while Ed returning from the latrine claimed he felt better and well enough to join the meeting. He looked whiter than a ghost's ghost and refrained from eating lest he involuntarily pass around the remnants of his last meal to anyone who was sitting near him.

Chris waded back into the debrief and finally got down to the meat and bones. They reached the point where he discovered the jacket, gloves, IV tubes, and chemicals. He retrieved the bag holding the booty and displayed the items on a table. He assembled the contraption the same way Nash had done while giving him complete credit for figuring out the weapon.

Ted stopped Chris's narrative when he walked back in. "I hate to bust everyone's bubble here. I've just been reading some traffic. This isn't the only system out there."

Everyone looked at him in bewilderment, surprised at his comment.

"You care to explain?" Ed requested.

"There's been a number of incidents on the West Coast. Los Angeles, San Diego, San Francisco, and Portland have all had arrests on their mass transit systems. So far six Arabs have been apprehended for wearing this thing or something similar."

"We're too late." Chris added solemnly.

"No, that's not what I said. I said they had arrested Arabs; there are no reports of casualties."

There was silence in the room. Everyone looked at each other in confusion.

"What the hell, did they have cyanide or not, Ted?" Ed asked. The color was coming back to his cheeks but mostly because he was getting flustered. He thought the CIA had just discovered gold in Afghanistan, but now he was thinking he had found a bunch of chocolate gold coins instead.

"There's not much information on that yet. The substances they were carrying are being analyzed, but as of right now, they're non-lethal."

"We may have dodged a bullet, but we're still too late," Chris stated to nobody in particular. Everyone turned to him for a follow-up to his statement, which he provided. "So six have been caught. We don't know how many more are out there. Were there others that deployed at the same time? Or are they going to attack later? If they do, are the substances that they carry going to be lethal? Whatever the case, this system," he picked up the jacket of the table, "is already in the US. We are too late."

Alex agreed. "We haven't prevented an attack. So now we are going backwards into investigative mode. How did this happen, etcetera, etcetera."

"Right," Chris continued the double act, "and here's the shitty part. We have in our possession the distribution system, and some people think we dropped the ball by having it and not telling anybody about it."

"But we didn't know about it, Chris," Ed countered.

"And you're right, but someone will have to testify to that . . . Mr. Nash would have been the prefect person to do that with him on the ground, but to the government and the public, it's going to look like a failure on our part."

Alex pushed the conversation on. "The challenge is not knowing how many operatives are out there. So we have six. Are there twenty-six or fifty-six waiting in the wings for a signal of some kind to deploy?"

"So we have missed an opportunity," Chris added immediately, preventing anyone else from interjecting, "to prevent what has happened or is happening on the West Coast. I don't think we can worry about that now. But what we can do is figure out how this even happened."

Ed was impressed that Chris was somehow taking the lead in the discussion. This was supposed to be a debrief, not a strategy meeting, but he let him continue.

"Let's get down to basics. The IV, pretty simple; this can be sourced anywhere, but let's forget about the double port for now. The jacket isn't that sophisticated, so the questions are where did it come from, who made this, was it made in Afghanistan?" Chris wasn't expecting an answer, and he didn't give anyone the chance. He was on a roll and actually enjoying himself. "The gloves, now that's something different . . . these pores in the hand of the glove and the IV port, that takes some design, a lot of thought. Same questions, where was this made? Afghanistan?" He paused to let the group take things in and then sped along. "Now a critical piece to the puzzle, the cyanide, where did that come from? Afghanistan?" Although not expecting an answer, he wanted people, even more senior than he, to think for a minute. Nobody replied. They were rhetorical questions, and everyone wanted Chris to finish his thoughts.

"Nash said that chemical weapons are not typical for the Taliban. They can cook opium, and that's the best science they can muster. So let's rule the Taliban out for that. Who's big buddies with the Taliban who would use something like this . . . bin Laden? Okay, so now we know—"

"I see where you are going, Chris," Ted said, cutting him off, "but you are in no position to make a hypothesis or opinion on behalf of the CIA—"

Ed stopped Ted with a wave of his hand. "We are in a hut in the middle of a war zone, Ted. This isn't Langley. We're just spit balling here. Let's keep going, Chris."

Chris sighed. He was thrown off for a second by Ted, though determined to play his part. Nash would have wanted him to, and it was about time he stood his ground, but knew he had to be careful with people above his pay grade. "Let's say for argument's sake, and this is only my opinion," he looked over at Ted who looked placated for a moment, "that bin Laden was exploring the use of chemical weapons. We have found a test lab in Afghanistan with dead dogs that we can assume he tried out for his concoction. But where did he get the cyanide? It could have been from a chemical plant here in Afghanistan, but how is that controlled? Who controls it? Where is it? If the answers are that some chemical plants are in Taliban territory, then there's a good chance that they supplied it. If the plants are on the Northern Alliance side, then I'm guessing they didn't supply it so they got the cyanide from outside the country. Step one in our investigation should be where did the cyanide come from and how did it get to the US."

The Ted and Ed show went off in hyperspeed about the possible locations of the cyanide, if it was sourced in the country for testing or elsewhere, and the larger problem of how it got to the United States. The remainder of the group just looked on silently exchanging glances at each other.

Chris could tell the conversation wasn't going anywhere. In a different setting perhaps it would, but he wanted the focus to be a little more tangible. "Gents, gents, can we skip all that for a minute? There are still some other things we need to put on the table."

Both senior officers quieted down for Chris to continue. Ed nodded for Chris to begin.

"Okay, the next question is this stuff . . ." He picked up the jacket and gloves again. "Was this made in Afghanistan? I think this is too sophisticated for the Taliban, so the same question comes up . . . Taliban territory or Northern Alliance territory? Before you guys go ballistic, let's really strip this back. I saw three types of jackets, wool, waterproof, and leather. Could the wool jacket be produced in this country? My guess is yeah, sure, why not? Could the leather jacket be produced here? Probably, but maybe not. But the waterproof jacket . . . I don't think so. And the gloves, my opinion, Ted, no definitely not."

"You're so full of theories, Chris. If this stuff wasn't made here," Ted asked, "then where?"

Chris scratched his beard and then fiddled with his ear lobe. All eyes were upon him. His audience was going to either crucify him or give him the keys to New York City. "Pakistan," he simply offered.

"Are you serious . . . Pakistan? Where the hell did you come up with that?" Ed asked almost laughing as he did.

"You forget that he comes from the school of Richard Nash, Ed," Ted joined. "He's been listening to Nash's disdain of the Pakistanis. It's illogical. He doesn't know what he's talking about."

Chris knew he had to be firm. It was a chance to prove his worth with these two men. "It stands to reason that it can't be any other country. I've seen enough material to know that Afghanistan cannot stand alone as a viable country anymore. The Taliban have destroyed everything and are getting closer and closer to being in the medieval age. They don't have the infrastructure to support themselves, so they have to rely on outside sources. Pakistan is the only country in the world that has diplomatic relations with Afghanistan, and I think you both know the only way goods or products get into the country is through Pakistan."

"I appreciate your insights, Chris," Ed offered almost sympathetically. "But don't you think you are punching above your weight class here?"

"Nash didn't hate the Pakistanis; he just didn't trust them."

Ted ignored the response from Chris, looked at his watch, and then shuffled some papers together.

"He would at least be listening to me right now instead of dismissing me like some errant school boy."

"Chris, that's not—"

"Forget about it Ed. Run it up the flagpole or not; I don't give a shit."

"Now hang on a minute—"

"Leave it, Ed. He doesn't know what he is talking about."

"We need to think about this, Ted. He may be onto something."

CHAPTER NINETEEN

Karshni Khanabad Air Base, Uzbekistan

THE CIA'S MI-8 RUSSSIAN-MADE transport helicopter touched down at almost midday at the Uzbek Air Force Base. Chris looked out of the window and felt as dismal and grey as the weather. For company on the perilous journey over the Hindu Kush and out of Afghanistan was the wounded Ranger, the CIA flight crew, a deep-thinking, non-talkative Ed Guild, and the body of Richard Nash.

Chris was lost in his thoughts and primarily concerned with the unfinished business of the night before. As soon as he had made his case for mischievous Pakistan, he struggled to get a word in edgeways as Ed and Ted went at it like cat and dog, shouting and screaming like little girls at a boy band concert. Neither of them could come to any form of agreement, compromise, or answer to Chris's theories. The arguments only escalated as more of the JAWBREAKER team got involved and really started to spiral out of control when someone in the room said something to the effect of "why should anyone listen to a driver?" Alex jumped in to defend Chris with Stone close in support. It was at that point Chris left the room and went in search of a few Afghans circled around a fire who cleaned guns for a living. The next morning still lying next to a warm hearth, he was nudged by Alex from his restless slumber and informed him that his journey home was about to begin.

Neither of the men dwelled on long goodbyes, each recognizing that everything they had done over the last few days was just business and there was still work to do. Nevertheless, each could tell that a bond had formed and that they would welcome the opportunity to do it all over again, even agreeing, when Stone approached to shake Chris's hand, to work with the ass-hat Rangers if push came to shove.

When the rear bi-fold doors of the helicopter opened to the tarmac, Chris was surprised to see four US soldiers board the aircraft and, without being prompted, picked up the body bag and carried Nash away to a waiting pickup truck. Chris got up and assisted the wounded Ranger off the helicopter, Ed following close behind with the black bag containing the chemical weapon system over his shoulder. Whatever other possessions he had taken into Afghanistan were in his right hand. Chris walked off the chopper with nothing but an almost empty backpack and two empty hands, feeling naked without his Makarov and AR-15.

Another American soldier was waiting for the injured Ranger and assisted him into a Humvee, leaving the two CIA officers to themselves. Chris didn't think too much of it and welcomed a walk after being cooped up and bounced around in the helicopter for hours. He watched the direction the Humvee took to get to a hangar and marched in the general direction hoping to find someone who would tell them where to go or what to do next. He spotted a Globemaster C-17 aircraft that was being hastily unloaded and figured that, as soon as it was refueled, it would be his ride home. Ed struggled behind as Chris walked briskly over the tarmac. After a sizeable gap appeared between the two, Chris, knowing that Ed had been struggling with his health over the last few days, turned around and took a bag off him to ease his load. Ed nodded his thanks, but again, words were missing. It wasn't a situation Chris relished as he felt he had done nothing wrong. All he did was put a theory on a table, though he received nothing but hostility in return. He could tell he wasn't wanted amongst the JAWBREAKER team, so he decided to put things behind him and hope that once he got back to the United States, Gene would have something worthwhile for him to do.

When they neared the hangar, a familiar face to Chris waited outside a door with his hands on his hips. Guy Trimble smiled at Chris and stretched out his hand as they approached. "Good to see you, Chris? How are you?"

"Hello, Guy. Didn't expect to see you here. This is Ed Guild . . .

Ed, Guy Trimble MI6." His voice was flat and unenthusiastic.

"Ed, pleasure . . . welcome to Task Force Dagger. We have a liaison team here with your Special Forces. There's only a few of us, but there's a whole bunch of your guys."

Chris caught a movement out of the corner of his eye as he saw Ed wavering slightly. The high altitude and bumpy ride had gotten the better of him. "Can you show us where our team is?" Chris asked. "I think we need to catch a breath."

"Sure, sure, come on. Let's get you some tea. I think we can find a sandwich or something too if you want."

Guy opened the door to the hangar, which led down a narrow corridor with a door at the end that led into the hangar itself. The usually vast expanse of a hangar was taken over by temporary walls and ceilings with spaghetti runs of black, blue, red, and white cabling, strung over the makeshift ceilings and up and down walls. Guy navigated his way through the maze of temporary rooms and came to a halt outside a door that led into a canteen of sorts.

"You want to camp out here for a bit. I'll go find some of your chaps. I think this is where they wanted you anyway."

Ed and Chris stood in awkward silence. This wasn't the reception they had been expecting. Ed made a beeline for a couch near a TV and hit it hard.

Chris dropped his bags and headed for a Coke machine. He didn't have any cash, but after he gave it a shake, he realized the door was open, and he grabbed a couple of red ones and handed one to Ed.

They sipped on their cold beverages for a while until a tidy-looking CIA officer, who obviously to Chris hadn't seen dirt since he'd left kindergarten a week earlier, beckoned for Ed to join him. Ed grabbed the chemical bag and strode heavily after him. Chris stood to follow but was waved off. He gave the orderly man a look of death and held back a belligerent thought, *You want to tell me where the motor pool is? I'll go and wash your car for you . . . pasty face ass fucker.*

Chris took Ed's spot and made himself comfortable. He closed his eyes but didn't sleep. He'd been that way for a few minutes when Guy reappeared.

"If you want to get some kip, I'll leave you to it."

Chris opened his eyes, sat up, and sipped his Coke. "It's okay. Nice to see a friendly face. How are you?"

"Not one to complain, Chris, you know, stiff upper lip and all that."

"Yes, for Queen and country, to Her Majesty." He raised his Coke and then drained it.

Guy looked on, not sure what to make of the strange comment. "Sorry to hear about Nash. I understand you were close."

Chris looked down to the ground. There was nothing to say. He bobbed a little but showed no emotion.

Guy didn't know Chris very well other than what he'd seen of him during the SAS rescue and what others said of him. He was impressed with the man's operational skills but hadn't worked out how he came to being a Brit working for the CIA. He wanted to get to know him a little more but was confused about something that was on his mind since he heard Nash had died.

"Why didn't he leave Afghanistan when he had the chance with us?" he asked Chris.

"He had this thing about finding bin Laden. I don't know what his real motivations were. I was just along for the ride. He had a habit of that, taking me with him."

"But he was sick. He should have come out with us."

Chris looked hard at the MI6 officer. He didn't quite understand what he was talking about. "What . . . what are you talking about, Guy? He had a heart attack during a firefight. It happens."

"But . . . wait, didn't he tell you about the other episodes he had?" Guy receiving only a blank stare continued, "When we were picked up by the Taliban, he had a heart attack then. They found him a doctor, but they decided to transport him to Kabul for treatment. We were on the way there when you found us. He actually said that it added to their cover of being missionaries, and the Taliban believed the CIA wouldn't send a spy to their country with a heart condition. He strung them along. He was sick, but he played it out to buy time. He didn't tell you any of this?"

Chris squeezed his eyes closed, pinched the bridge of his nose, then scrubbed his face with his hands and let out a long sigh. "No," he whispered as his head drooped closer to his chest. He began to regret his past actions and remembered some of the harsh words he and Nash had had over the last few days. *Why didn't I see it? Why did I give him such a hard time? Gene had mentioned his heart issues to me years ago. If anyone knew what was going on, it should have been me. It was my job to protect him. I failed, I fucking failed again.*

Guy could see from his pained expression that Chris was dealing with some inner turmoil. He wanted to give him some words of comfort but let things lie and got up to make some tea. Guy asked if he wanted British army standard, "Milk, two sugars?"

Chris nodded and then leaned back in his chair and held onto his forehead, rubbing it slowly and hard, trying to erase some memories, fighting back a tear for the first time since Nash died. He berated himself again and tried to justify his actions from the last few days, but all he did was shake his head in silence.

Guy returned with the promised tea, passing a cup over and pulling up a chair in front of him. He leaned forward onto his elbows still holding the warm beverage. "We went back a long way, Richard and I. He mentioned you often."

Chris didn't say anything. He was actually relieved to have someone not talk business, at least not directly. Guy continued with some old war stories from the Cold War that Chris enjoyed hearing about and marveled at some of the capers he and Nash got away with. In every scenario that Guy painted, Chris could vividly see in his mind Nash working undercover, one step ahead of the bad guys and changing the world, one agent at a time.

Chris shared some of what he did and how he came to meet Nash when he started out as a simple driver at the US embassy in Germany.

"You've come a long way, Chris. What's next?"

"I really don't know. Right now I guess I'm surplus. Ed is off talking to his people about stuff I don't need to know. I suppose when the plane back to the US is ready, I'll be on it, and then . . . who knows? What about you? What are you up to, not meaning to be too nosey that is."

Guy didn't have to tell him what he was up to but shared just a little. "We're good, Chris. You're not nosey. I'm actually waiting for a plane ride to Pakistan."

That got Chris's attention. He sat up a little straighter; his eyes became a little brighter. "Did you hear about this jacket we found?"

"Yes, it's all over the intelligence community. Now everybody and his donkey is on the alert for the stuff," Guy answered.

Chris went on to tell the story of the night before and his suppositions about the chemical weapon system. He wasn't sure if he was supposed to do it, but he was at a point where he didn't care. The CIA was ignoring him; he needed someone to hear his story and give him a decent response. Guy listened but did not offer anything in return.

Chris wondered during the silent few minutes between the two as Guy processed the information if he could trust him and hoped he had not stepped too far overboard by passing on classified information. He wanted to keep the discussion going and didn't want to lose the momentum. "Any new developments from the US? The last I heard was that six Arabs were picked up."

"Make that eight, old boy."

"Casualties?"

"Not a single one."

"Doesn't that strike you as strange, Guy, the chemicals not really being toxic?"

"Yes and no."

Chris thought the answer as odd. He wanted more. He could tell the MI6 officer was holding something back, but it wasn't his business to push. Chris rocked in his chair contorting his face hoping that Guy would read his body language and answer the question properly. He did.

"I have a source in Pakistan that may help me out with that very question."

"When does our plane arrive?"

"Now hang on a minute, Chris . . ."

Riyadh, Saudi Arabia

Abdo Ihab sat in the rear of the police van with his hands handcuffed behind his back and a black hood over his head. To both his right and left were uniformed officers from the Mabaheth, the Saudi secret police force in charge of domestic security and counterintelligence affairs. On this day, however, the officers were escorting their prisoner from the Ulaysha Prison in Riyadh to Deera Square that lay near the center of the country's capital city, which the locals called Chop Chop Square.

Unbeknownst to Abdo were the five other vehicles behind him in convoy with other prisoners on board heading in the same direction to receive the same punishment for crimes against the state or against Sharia law.

When Abdo's vehicle came to a halt on the edge of the square, he was grabbed firmly by the two officers as the double doors opened and a small step was produced for them to exit from the van. He was forcefully marched one hundred steps to the center of the square and then pushed down hard to his knees. His hood was removed. The two officers stood a close distance away as a prosecutor approached the prisoner from behind and removed a tag from the offender's wrist. He checked a clipboard against the tag and then looked over at a nearby man who had a long decorative sword known as a sulthan at his side. The prosecutor gave him a nod, and the executioner beheaded Abdo Ihab with one fell swoop of the long sword. The prosecutor watched the head of the prisoner roll in front of the criminal's lifeless body and then read the charges to the public.

The prosecutor and the man with the sword repeated the exercise five more times in the space of an hour. The Saudi royal family's banker, Saleh Bahar, was the last man to be executed.

Karachi, Pakistan

Chris was able to find a new set of clothes at the Madina City Mall in the center of Karachi. He left the clothes that he wore in Afghanistan behind in a shop and asked the proprietor to burn the clothes if they didn't want his underwear to start dancing like John Travolta on a Saturday night. The shop owner didn't get the joke, though Guy got the reference. His clothes were so dirty, torn, and stinky, not even the bravest of rats would have stolen them for the promise of food. The only things he didn't want to part with were his boots.

Satisfied that he didn't look too much like a muppet or snap-happy tourist, Chris paid for the clothes with Guy's money, and they both set off for a meal before meeting the MI6 officer's source in the city.

"It won't take long until we have eyeballs on us," Chris noted as he looked around the mall for surveillance.

"I think you're right, Chris. We've already had a few curious glances."

"I can pass for German. You?"

"French, Russian."

Chris spotted a quiet-looking restaurant near an emergency exit. "Let's dive in here, get some grub, and talk this out."

The pair discussed over dinner the layout of the city with a map that Guy provided, the various points of interests, and the locations of friendly consulates, only stopping their conversation each time a waiter attended or another patron came within earshot. Only once satisfied each knew where they were and where they were going did they concoct an on-the-fly escape plan. Guy was unsure of Chris's situation, as he left Ed Guild at the Uzbek Air Base without saying a word about his intentions or where he was headed, but told Chris that his first stop would be the British consulate if things turned sour.

"I can go to the US consulate, but I'd rather we stay together. You have more pull than I do at your place, and you can wake someone up if it's the middle of the night. Me they don't give a shit about, and all they will do is tell me to come back tomorrow and get in line."

"This city isn't friendly to either of our countries, Chris. The last thing we want is to be picked up by the Pakistani intelligence services, who are very active here, by the way."

"I know how dangerous those guys can be, but I'm more worried about the Joes on the street anti-western attitudes, especially after the New York affair."

"Mob mentality and all that?" Guy queried.

"Yeah, I don't know what the political feeling towards the attacks in the US are in this country now, but I think we can both agree that the madrassas here are breeding grounds for new, young terrorists. If we walk down the wrong alleyway tonight and come across one of these schools and the class topic is death to America, we may end up hanging from a lamppost and being used as a piñata."

"Well I suppose we had better be on our best behavior then. If you start to feel a bit furry, you break into German and I will switch to French, and that will be our sign to do a runner."

Chris, for the first time since he had met Guy, gave him the once over. He thought the fifty-something, lithe-looking man could probably hold his own. Guy had that sinewy look of a man who regularly exercised or ran marathons. He maintained a good weight, and his hands weren't homosexually manicured, and he looked as if he had been around the block a few times with his firm grip, graying short hair, and deep-blue eyes that kept secrets dark within.

Chris wondered how much actual hand-to-fist training Guy had, if he was ex-military or Oxford or Cambridge. It mattered not. Chris liked him and was glad he was the one that listened to him and his theory that Pakistan had a hand in the cyanide attacks against the United States.

Night had fallen by the time they had finished their meal and started to make their way to the meeting point. They took a mixture of taxicabs and rickshaws, getting out often before their ride was complete so they could assess the immediate area for signs of surveillance. Satisfied they were not under any formal method of observance, they made their final part of the journey by rickshaw to the Port Grand market on Chirma Creek. Once there, they walked casually towards the still-under-construction new Fisherman's Wharf.

Chris didn't particularly like the location as the causeway only offered a thin walkway of about thirty feet with an entryway on one end and an exit on the opposite end. If they were caught in the middle, the only escape would be to swim in the bug-infested Karachi waters. He hoped the only reason this location was chosen was that Guy's source was practicing good counter-surveillance and would warn if a threat appeared.

Both Brits had to dodge the evening construction workers who were navigating the slim walkway to their work sites with a smattering of street vendors and local shoppers all vying for scant real estate. The atmosphere was electric as music of all kinds was battling with the sounds of drilling and hammering and the shouting of vendors selling their wares. Chris caught sight of something that gave him a chill. He stood longer than he should. He knew one of the first rules of surveillance was to act natural; to stand mute like a frozen fish was asking for trouble. Guy was directly in front of him so he didn't see what Chris was up to. As Chris tried to process the information he was just given, a large piece of corrugated steel fell from a scaffold making Chris jump for his life; the only way he could go was into the water.

Chris surfaced from his involuntary dive into the bay and vigorously spat out whatever godforsaken sludge, shit, or fish detritus that he ingested. He began to panic, not because of his inability to swim or becoming swept away but because of the potential diseases that he could pick up from the water. He made his way back towards the causeway structure, and reaching up to find a handhold of some kind, hearing dozens of voices shouting in Urdu, only Guy's stood out from the chorus.

"Jawad, Jawad, help him."

FBI Field Office, Phoenix

Major Karim Basrawi stood at the reception desk of the FBI Field Office and requested a meeting with Agent Leroy Lewis. The receptionist politely told him that he was no longer with the bureau; however, she would find someone to see him if he was able to wait. Upon asking for some identification, he happily opened his large envelope and produced the gift that Jawad had given him forty-eight hours ago. He placed his diplomatic passport on the counter and held on tightly to it as the young lady behind the desk copied the relevant information. Satisfied that she had all she needed, she asked him to take a seat and told him that someone would be along as soon as possible to see him.

Basrawi took a seat up against a wall facing the receptionist and stared at the door behind her desk, which led to the back of the office space. Within twenty minutes of him nervously willing the door to open, an FBI agent, wearing his badge around his neck on a silver chain, came across the lobby and stopped right in front of him.

"I'm Special Agent Corelli. How may I help you, Mr. Basrawi?"

The major stood up to attention in true military fashion. He was cordial and direct. "I have been instructed to pass some information on to you." He held onto Jawad's envelope with his right hand.

Corelli looked down on it and then reached out his hand. "Okay, thanks. Can you tell me what this is about?"

Basrawi was untrusting. He might have had a brand-new diplomatic passport that protected him from certain types of arrest by the authorities, but he was skeptical about entering the FBI office and not being allowed to leave. "I was hoping to talk to Agent Lewis. He is not available?"

"I'm afraid Agent Lewis has passed away, but I understand that you were working with him. Is that correct?"

"Yes, we had a mutual understanding, but that is of no consequence. May we talk outside?"

"It's pretty hot out there. We can go to my office if you want," Corelli offered.

Basrawi looked at the door behind the reception and then back at the main entrance. "Thank you for your hospitality; however, I would prefer not to enter your facility," he replied. "Let us sit. I believe this will take but a moment."

Corelli didn't take him up on his offer. He preferred to stand when he was confronting a confidential informant. Crossing his arms over his chest, he said, "Karim, we have been looking for you. We wanted to discuss a few things, but you disappeared. What have you been doing?"

Basrawi was getting uncomfortable. He didn't want to be there, and he definitely did not want to answer a whole set of questions about his potential charges. He opened his package and passed over a smaller letter-size envelope to Corelli.

"What's this?"

Basrawi was working from the script that Jawad had given him. "Some information that will help you in your investigation of the events over the last few days."

Corelli opened the envelope that held three sheets of paper. The first was a list of twenty names, the second a number of addresses in Portland, San Diego, San Francisco, and Los Angeles, and the third a list of men in the Los Angeles and Arlington Texas areas.

"What the hell is this all about?"

"A gift from the government of the Kingdom of Saudi Arabia. I wish you good day, sir." He turned to leave, but Corelli wanted to know more.

"Wait, now hang on a second. What are you talking about? What's this all about anyway?"

Basrawi looked towards the main entry door and started to make his way.

Corelli wasn't about to let him go so easy. He reached out to grab his arm, but the Saudi was too quick. Corelli raised his voice, "We need to talk about this. You are not leaving this building."

Basrawi looked back at him and then produced his diplomatic passport. He smiled broadly as Corelli closed in to confront him, but as the agent read the letters on the passport, he stopped in his tracks. He was unable to say a word. To Basrawi, the look on the FBI man's face was priceless. He replaced the document in his jacket pocket and walked confidently out of the door.

Marriott Hotel, Karachi, Pakistan

Chris exited the bathroom wearing a hotel bathrobe while drying his hair with a towel over his head. He walked over to one of the two large beds in the room and picked the nearest and sat on the corner. He looked over to Guy who was sitting at the desk and then over to Jawad who was lying relaxed on the other bed, leaning up against the headboard. His hands were holding a small bowl of nuts that he picked at. Chris didn't know what to say, and from the awkward silence in the room, neither did anyone else.

Chris put the towel around his neck, then headed for the fridge, scanned the inside, and pulled out a bottle of water. He sat back on down on his perch, and still there was no conversation. There were a few glances, a few movements of getting comfortable, or a stifling of a yawn, but the tense atmosphere trumped any form of verbal interaction. As he looked around the room, he noticed something amiss. He didn't want to start talking around the elephant in the room, but he was concerned. "Where are my clothes?"

"I took the liberty of having them dry cleaned. I assumed you had no other change of clothing nearby. They are quite hospitable here. I think we shall have them back to you within the hour," Jawad answered casually.

Chris nodded. Although robed, he felt uncomfortable without clothes nearby. He looked at Jawad carefully and came up with a plan that if things went sideways, he would take his clothes and he wouldn't care if he was taking them from a bloody or bruised dead body.

Guy broke the strain. He was getting fed up waiting for something to happen. "I'm guessing from our brief conversation at the wharf you two know each other."

"Know *of* each other more like," Chris replied, his voice harsh, cold.

"Shall we start with introductions? I don't know if you are aware of each other's names."

"It's your show, Guy. Fill your boots."

"Chris Morehouse, CIA, may I introduce Jawad Halabi from the General Intelligence Department of Saudi Arabia, but also known within MI6 circles as Agent FURLONG. Jawad and I have been working together for quite some time on behalf of our respective governments."

Jawad remained passive while staring into the bowl in his hands. He wasn't sure what reaction to expect from Chris, so he waited, but Chris didn't utter a word.

Guy could see that Chris was brooding. He obviously had things on his mind, but he wasn't sharing. Guy needed to get down to the reason he was in Karachi, but he didn't need a moody tag-along to disrupt his business. *Well he invited himself. If he doesn't like it, he can bugger off.* "Chris, Jawad is the reason I am here. If you're not comfortable with that, then I must ask you to leave."

Chris took a long drink of water, tilting his head back and almost draining the entire bottle. He wiped his mouth before he spoke. He wanted to go off the deep end, he wanted to tell Guy that the man lounging on the bed was a terrorist or he was working as a double agent. He wanted to shout, wanted to scream, wanted to interrogate the man, but he held back. As much as he wanted to get to the truth, beating someone half to death was not the right way, at least not yet. He thought that Guy was a smart man; he needed to let him do his job so he could gather intelligence the silent way, see, hear, note. "I'm still here, Guy."

"You don't have much choice, my friend," Jawad said, "your clothes . . ."

Don't tempt me, arsehole. I don't like what you're wearing, but it'll fit, Chris thought but answered a little more coolly, "I don't have a problem sitting in the lobby with just a robe and no underwear. Give them something to gawk at."

"Well, let's hope that it doesn't come to that," Guy added. He turned to Jawad and took a deep breath. "Now, Jawad, you asked me to meet you in Karachi. Why?"

"I have found the name and location of the chemist that we have been searching for. He is here in Karachi."

"It's about bloody time, but what about the clothing manufacturer? Anything?"

"Yes, also here in Karachi."

Excited, Guy stood up but turned his attention to Chris for a second. "It seems your feelings were well founded."

Chris gave the faintest of smiles. He didn't want to dwell on being right about something but thought, *Keep it going, Guy. I need more.*

Guy stood with his hands on his hips. He was in control and fought back his eagerness. "But before we start pointing fingers or starting an international incident with Pakistan, we need to back up a few steps. How did we get to this point, Jawad? Tell me about Operation Najd."

Jawad placed the bowl of nuts on the nightstand and used a small towel to wipe his fingers. He wasn't as excited as the MI6 man, though he did have an immediate concern. "Guy, my friend, we cannot wait for the international community or our intelligence services to act. I may have stopped the attack in the United States, but al-Qaeda will now be conducting its own investigation and soon will be looking for me. We must strike, and we must do it soon. We must find this chemist and interrogate him before he flees across the border to Afghanistan."

"Slow down, Jawad. Fill me in on the blanks. How did you stop the Najd? How did you get the information about the chemist and the clothing manufacturer?"

"Do we really have time for all of this? There is a man in this city that can answer more questions than I about al-Qaeda operations. We must get to him—"

"Jawad," Chris interjected, "answer the fucking questions. I'm not going to stick my dick in the wind for you until you tell us what's going on."

"Well I suppose you could put it as crudely as that, Chris, but yes, Jawad, let's have it. There is time for this."

Jawad withdrew for a second. He stroked his beard in thought. Though he needed technical and military help from the British and Americans to engage and destroy the terror network, he preferred to do it by his own means. But being in a hostile Pakistan, his chances of setting up a new line of informants and resources would be too time-consuming and dangerous. He conceded he should discuss his findings lest something happen to him but made his mind up that he could find the chemist with or without the men in his room.

"My information comes from a network in the United States that I destroyed. Contrary to belief, more intelligence comes from the sloppy security of data, rather than beating someone half to death. Part of my operation was to penetrate the American cell and their sympathizers and disrupt the attack on the mass transit systems on the West Coast. The information I found has led me here."

Jawad paused. He was glad he wasn't being interrupted, and he certainly didn't want a volatile CIA officer berating him every two minutes. "I, or should I say, my government stopped the cyanide attacks by simply removing the chemicals from the canisters that were loaded in the kingdom, replacing them with an inert mixture, and then removing the one man from the network who could test the substance when it reached America. The FBI is now in possession of a list of names of the men who attacked the transit systems and a number of sympathizers and supporters of al-Qaeda in the United States."

"So all we have left to do is to track down the chemist," Guy suggested.

"Yes, once more I have to marvel at the incompetency of these men. It was a simple matter of following a bank trail. It saddens me, however, at the audacity of one particular man who transferred money that was to be used for the royal family and funneled it back into supporting the Najd operation. However, some of the active participants have met their fates and are no longer a threat."

"You mean executed without due process?" Chris spouted.

Jawad glanced at the young CIA officer. "Chris, Saudi Arabia believes in swift justice. Those men received a fair trial and were deemed guilty. There was no need to draw out matters to benefit al-Qaeda."

Chris wasn't too happy with the Arab's statement. "But we have lost an opportunity to interrogate them further, gather more intelligence."

"That is neither here nor there, as you Brits like to say."

Chris was surprised but showed his best poker face. *So he knows who I am. What the fuck?*

"Those men were tiny pawns. They were of little importance, and they would have had nothing to add. I made sure that all their documentation was transported to the kingdom and my colleagues had enough to appropriate guilt, so please, do not lecture me on due process. I have achieved an objective. Another opportunity has come before me, and the time is now to act on that information."

"I saw you in Malaysia," Chris blurted as if it added something to the discussion.

"I saw you, Chris," Jawad replied, deadpan as if he was playing slow-motion Ping-Pong.

"You were with another Saudi. There was an al-Qaeda meeting there."

"Yes, I was shadowing Khalid al-Midhar, but this is no secret. The CIA had knowledge of this. That's why you were there working with the Malaysian authorities. Why do you bring this up now?"

"I don't trust you. I followed you to Malaysia and other countries around the world." Chris didn't want to give away all his activities. "All that I saw was that you were sipping tea in Paris with this guy or having dinner in Vienna with that guy. Neither of them was Mother Teresa or Nelson Mandela."

Jawad looked at Guy who just shrugged his shoulders. Jawad was surprised that Chris had seen him in those two places, wondering where else he was spotted. "Chris, I worked closely with MI6 and the CIA. They were quite aware of my activities. I'm sure Guy would confirm my assertions. Even your boss, Richard Nash, knew of my plans and actions."

Chris shot a look at Guy and jumped off the bed, almost exposing himself. *Nash knew about this . . . Nash knew?*

Before Chris could do anything else or say something, Jawad continued with a slight edge to his voice. He turned to Guy. "I should not have to explain my actions to this man. He is but a surveillance operative. Why is he here?"

"Because Richard Nash is dead and the CIA is too busy in Afghanistan to pay attention to us. If there was more time, Jawad, we could mount a formal operation to find this chemist . . ."

Jawad dropped his head and showed genuine concern. He had been unaware of the death, though now understood why there was a breakdown in communications with the CIA. "I am truly sorry to hear that. May Allah have mercy on his soul."

Chris composed himself and sat back down, watching Jawad who seemed to be in deep thought. The glancing and silence match started again.

After a minute, Jawad broke the quiet. "We are running out of time, Guy. I cannot emphasize this much more than I already have. We need to find this man and hold him accountable. He may have other information that we need, something that al-Qaeda is planning."

Chris wasn't so sure of Jawad. He moved the discussion in a different direction. "Why should I trust you?"

"Because neither of us has tried to kill the other," Jawad shot back.

Chris stared the man in the eyes. "Not yet," he responded icily. "Not yet."

CHAPTER TWENTY

Marriott Hotel, Karachi, Pakistan

CHRIS TRAIPSED DOWN the emergency staircase of the Marriot Hotel trying to relieve the stress of the last few hours. He was tired of the brainstorming session in Jawad's room and was pleased when his dry-cleaned clothes were brought back giving Chris and the others a welcome break. As much as he wanted to take a long walk, or better still a long run, he refrained from leaving the confines and security of the large hotel. When he made it down to the ground floor, he meandered the corridors and hallways looking for something to take his mind off hashing out plans to either abduct and interrogate, abduct and hand over to the authorities, or assassinate the chemist of Karachi.

None of the options seemed favorable to Chris chiefly because he was not a fan of ad hoc missions per se. He advocated for sustained surveillance, by both human and technical means. Jawad favored a more expeditious, direct, and admittedly riskier approach—leaving as soon as the sun came up and snatching the man off the streets. Guy, on the other hand, wanted a softer approach by involving the Pakistani government and the blessings of the British, American, and Saudi governments. The topic went around and around with each person in the room throwing out the pros and cons of each action or inaction. One of the main challenges that everyone agreed on, however, was how to identify a man by just a name and an address of where he worked. The only consensus reached was they needed to identify the man, his work location, and his home. But even this basic first step required a plan they didn't have.

On reaching the main lobby of the hotel, Chris did a 360 to find an avenue to explore. He spotted a wing where conferences were held, and for no other reason than boredom, he headed in that direction. When he reached the end of the highly polished marble corridor with shiny décor, he found an unmanned reception desk with a display showing conference events. He scrolled through the obscure names of companies and topics of seminars that he didn't recognize just to give his mind a nugget of something different to think about. Halfway down the page, he stopped as one name piqued his interest.

"Royal Dutch Shell, Gastech Exhibition and Conference. Aga Khan Room Third Floor,"

Shell, Shell . . . what can I do with that? he wondered. Chris stood in the empty space with his hands in his pockets for a few minutes longer, stared out at the city through the floor-to-ceiling windows and rocked back and forth on his heels. He was the only person in the area, which was a nice change for him, and after a while, he found a comfy chair and planted himself down to think of a strategy to nab the chemist.

———— ◦∞◦ ————

Chris woke with a jolt, unsure how long he had been out, but his eyelids felt like lead weights, and the drool down his shirt made him look like an eighty-year-old man. He rubbed his forehead and wiped his mouth. It was a welcome nap, and he was glad for the respite as it cleared his mind enough to help him focus on creating a plan.

He extracted himself from the comfortable chair and strode with purpose in search of the hotel business center. After navigating a few more empty corridors, he found the office open, despite the early hour. Greeted by a pleasant, young, female Pakistani staffer, who spoke impeccable English, he began his spiel. As he talked, he noted something draped over a chair in the room that supported a possible new legend.

"I've had a few mishaps along the way to the conference," he began trying his best to look forlorn.

"Which conference are you attending, sir?"

"I am with the Shell corporation. You see, the airlines lost my luggage, and that wasn't the worst part as I am sure they will get my things to me," he said trying to gain sympathy. "But I have also lost my backpack with all my items for the conference, my laptop, my wallet, all my things."

"That's terrible, sir. Have you notified the front desk? I am sure they will be able to help you."

"Yes, yes, they have been very helpful, indeed. They will notify me when my luggage arrives. However, they sent me here to see if you could print me some new business cards for the conference. My work with the exhibition is of utmost importance, and I have so many people to meet—"

"Of course, sir," she interrupted, not wanting a dissertation on the innards of a gas pump. "I can help you with that." She tapped away at her keyboard to find the appropriate software.

"Could you please give me your name sir?"

"Yes, Ben Van den Berg. Let me write that for you." He picked up a notebook and pen next to the desk and began to scribble. As she continued to type he added, "Royal Dutch Shell, Managing Director, Research and Development Gas Technologies."

She smiled at him and asked in an ebullient voice, "Do you have any contact details that you would like to add?"

Chris gave her some fictitious numbers and an email address and felt pretty good with his concocted title of managing director. *I should do this more often. She looks impressed.*

As the printer churned away a few dozen copies of the cards, he looked over at a chair with a jacket with the yellow Shell emblem on it.

His new legend was taking shape nicely with the outlines of a plan to abduct the chemist settling in his mind. Chris decided to be bold and simply walk up to the front door of his business in the guise of a Shell employee and persuade him nicely to have a chat outside. From there, he and Jawad would hustle him into a vehicle and whisk him away. The plan was skimpy on the details, but it was at least a starting point to put to his collaborators.

"Is that Ruud's jacket over there?"

"I'm sorry, sir. That jacket was left here yesterday. One of my colleagues was here when the gentleman left it behind."

"I'm sure that's Ruud's. He told me he lost some things on his journey; he left his jacket somewhere. That must be it. I can take it with me.
I will be having breakfast with him soon."

"Sir, I am sure the concierge will take care of that. It is not necessary for you to worry about it—"

"Nonsense, you have been very helpful to me, as has everyone else
here in the hotel. It's the least I can do . . . everyone should equally
bear the burden of the work we have to do, don't you think?"

From the look on the young girl's face, he could tell she was confused. She gave in to the eccentric Dutchman and allowed him to take
the jacket and shuffled the business cards together quickly to get rid of
him before he asked for something else.

∞∞∞

The trio pulled off the Port Qasim Road and into the parking lot of the
Ghandhara Chemical Pakistan facility in the white Land Rover that
Jawad had secured with help from the Saudi consulate in the city. The
vehicle without diplomatic plates was beat up and old enough for it not
to stand out in a city of almost fourteen million that was just coming to
life. Jawad parked the car, and Guy jumped in the driver's seat as both
Chris and the Arab entered the main building's reception area.

Chris was acting the lead in the play that the other participants
agreed would end when the chemist was handed over to the authorities.
He straightened his newfound Shell jacket. "Good morning," Chris
began, speaking to the male receptionist who was flanked by an old,
lethargic-looking uniformed guard. He produced his hastily made
business card and placed it on the counter. "We are here to see Dr.
Ghufran Malak."

"Do you have an appointment, sir?" the receptionist asked as he
stood looking studiously at the card in front of him. *Managing director of
Shell, goodness gracious*, he thought, impressed by the dignified man before

him. He turned his attention to Jawad. "And your name, sir?"

Chris answered for him, "Ruud Gullit. Now is Dr. Ghufran here?"

"Let me check, but could you please sign in for me?" He pushed a ledger on the countertop towards Chris, but the guard behind the reception noticed something and got the attention of the receptionist. They both gazed outside to another part of the parking area, staring at three men who were walking quickly towards a small, white Daihatsu van.

The receptionist pointed at the men in the parking lot. "I'm sorry, sir, but Dr. Ghufran is just leaving."

Chris turned quickly and saw the vehicle. Both he and Jawad quickly exited the facility, Jawad two steps in the lead. As they did, the van sped past them.

It wasn't part of the plan, but Chris yanked the driver's side door open. "I'm driving; slide over," he shouted at Guy who was revving the engine in anticipation of a chase. Chris had already selected a gear before Guy even got comfortable. The Land Rover bounced out of the parking lot and back onto the main road with tires squealing for mercy. Chris caught up to the smaller vehicle quickly and lined himself up, slightly offset, behind with his right wheels running over the white markings on the center of the road. Having first learned to drive on the left side of the road in the United Kingdom, he adapted quickly to the Pakistan roads. The small vehicle was moving fast. Fortunately to accommodate Karachi's heavy industry, this part of the city's roads was well maintained and built for heavier traffic, so the going was good. Chris however, was worried that they didn't have long as they traveled westwards and closer to the sprawling suburbs of the overcrowded city.

"There's a sharp bend in the road and a bridge coming up. He's got to slow down. We have to take him there," he shouted so that Guy and Jawad would be prepared. Just as Chris spoke, a man in the rear of the chased vehicle made his way to the back of the transporter and produced an AK-47.

"He's trying to get us to back off. He would have shot at us already if he knew who we were," Guy blared.

The bridge was rapidly approaching, but the man with the gun pointed it directly at Chris, who responded by tapping the brakes quickly to let the transporter get ahead slightly and then drove his foot hard into the accelerator pedal to regain the momentum he lost. The heavy Land Rover responded well to the new demand for more speed and caught up to rear of the van just in time for it to slow down to navigate the upcoming sharp bend in the road. Chris didn't slow down but did not touch the gas pedal too much either. He jerked his vehicle to the right into the oncoming lane, drew parallel to the hunted vehicle, and put his left front fender into the right rear wheel of the transporter. When Chris felt the connection, he turned his steering wheel inwards towards the collision, not away from it, forcing the rear wheel of the smaller vehicle to lift enough for it to lose traction and spin in front of the Land Rover. Chris continued to drive away and to safety towards the left of the other vehicle but watched the transporter spin, hit the curb on the other side of the road, and flip onto its side.

Chris brought the Land Rover to a stop at a safe angle on the side of the road, but Jawad, the only one armed, got out and sprinted towards the wrecked van. Chris opened his door, left the engine running, and looked on as Jawad moved forward. The Arab stopped within feet of the crashed vehicle and pointed his weapon in readiness of a retaliatory attack. As he got close, he crouched down to get a closer look. He was expecting to see a few trapped bodies in the wreckage but was surprised to see only half of the driver's body in the vehicle; the top was missing. It was obvious he had not been wearing a seat belt and was thrown partially out with the weight and energy of the crash killing him.

Jawad took a cautious step forward and looked through the cracked windshield and saw the man with the AK pointing it at him. He jumped back and, in his excitement, fired two shots. He regained control of the pistol, then climbed up onto the side of the vehicle, and managed to wrench open the sliding door. When he did, he let loose with all the rounds he had in his magazine. Even when he finished dumping all the lead he had in the gun, he reloaded and shot five more times into the vehicle.

Chris seeing that there was no further threat, went to join Jawad on the van. But by the time he got there, Jawad had already gone into the passenger area and retrieved a brown leather satchel. Chris looked down on the carnage. "Did you get him?" he asked sarcastically, looking at the bullet-riddled corpses of the two men below. Jawad gave Chris a scowl but did not reply. He threw the satchel to the ground and climbed back down. Chris knew the effort was futile, but climbed into the cab and checked to see if there was any sign of life. He checked pulses but received no signals in return. He wiped the blood off his hands on one of the dead bodies and climbed out. The stench of death was but minutes away. By the time he hit the ground, the engine was revving again. Guy had the Land Rover sitting straight on the road. Chris looked back at the mess they had just created. If he had any reservations about Jawad's commitments to go after terrorists, they were now quashed.

For the first few miles, nobody in the Land Rover said a word. Each was concentrating on his assigned arc of responsibility: Chris to the rear, Jawad to the front and left, Guy to the front and right. To everyone's relief, there was no chase or police sirens following in their path. As much as the group preferred to have no witnesses at the site, it could not have been avoided with such a huge population in such a large city. Chris only hoped that whoever saw the spectacle didn't write down a plate number or take a photo of Jawad in action. But he knew time was limited as soon rumors and gossip would be spreading that westerners were involved in a shooting incident in the industrial part of the city.

Chris looked at the back of Jawad's head and thought him lucky. Being a Saudi, he could pass as Pakistani or at least a Muslim brother. If a horde of pissed-off Pakistanis descended upon them, he and Guy would be lynched.

Chris told Guy to pull off the main road to find a relatively quiet street to park the vehicle. "Jawad you need to drive," Chris suggested. "You can pass for one of them. It will look better if you are the chauffeur." During the swap, Chris got out the map and began figuring out where they were, turning the map three different ways to get it oriented and then relying upon his memories of all the twists and turns they took to get to where they were.

Guy looked at the brown satchel that Jawad had retrieved and found nothing of importance. However, he ascertained that the contents required a much closer look at a later time. Once finished, he and Jawad got back to watchmen duties looking for potential threats to their momentary safe haven.

"I think we are in the Sweepers Colony," Chris remarked to his companions and then shuffled the large fold-out map to get a better view. He looked for a decent landmark outside the window but didn't find anything worthwhile. "We were heading west. If we carry on, we will get back to the center of the city. If we do that, we'll get a better feel of where we need to be."

"Which is where?" Guy asked sharply. He seemed unimpressed with the situation and was feeling the tension of the moment. "Our great plan failed. We agreed that we were going to take the chemist in. Once we did that, we could get the assistance of the Paks to go look for the clothing warehouse."

"We can't undo it, Guy," Chris replied. "I don't think we had much choice. Jawad showed some balls by going in. There was a guy with a gun. He took action, and it forced us to change, and here we are."

"We made a fucking mess of it."

"I don't see it that way. You know the drill—the person who adapts the quickest will succeed—and that's what got us here. It could have gone a completely different way—us dead and the chemist alive. If you don't like those types of options, then perhaps you should go back to the hotel. Jawad and I can take care of the rest of this."

Jawad strummed his fingers on the steering wheel and continued to observe his surroundings. He didn't add anything to Chris's comments but held back a smile; he liked the man.

"We killed three men. It didn't need to happen that way . . ." Guy continued to whine.

"We haven't got time to go sappy on this shit." Chris wasn't impressed with Guy's after-action meltdown. They still had a second mission to conduct; there was no time to waste sharing feelings and warm hugs. "We adapted to a fluid situation and came out the other end in one piece. Was it to plan? No . . . but we are wasting time talking about it when we need, instead, to focus on what's next."

Guy nodded in submission. He knew there were things still to take care of; there would be time later to have a deep-dive debrief on what happened. He sighed heavily. "Where do we go from here?" he asked Chris resignedly.

"Well, if we go to the Paks now and tell them we had a bit of a party on the road back there, they will lock us up and ask questions later. That will only give al-Qaeda time to consolidate their operations. We don't know where the chemist was being taken to. Could it be the clothing warehouse? I don't think so . . . they were probably trying to get him out of the city, which to me means the warehouse is still a viable target."

Jawad threw his opinion into the mix. "Yes, but it needs to happen soon, Chris. If we have indeed taken out two al-Qaeda operatives, then whoever is expecting them will be waiting for them to return. I agree the warehouse is probably not the location where they intended to take him, but do they need to destroy any evidence there?"

Chris responded pragmatically, "First, we need to find it, then figure how to get in, and then get out . . . Guy you still up for this?"

The small team found the Essa Textile and Trading Company in the Mauripur district of Karachi and near Sewage Water Treatment Plant No.3. While Jawad surveilled the area, Guy made the mistake of opening his window, which made him gag from the stench of the nearby facility. While Chris and Guy waited, they told each other war stories and silly British jokes to alleviate their discomfort; each was itching to get out of there.

Jawad returned to the Land Rover as the last natural light faded over Karachi. He used the back of the map to sketch out what he had found in minute detail. He and Chris went over a dozen what-is-this, what-is-that, and then some what-if scenarios as Guy once again resigned himself to being the duty driver. Once they all agreed on a plan of action, they left the area in search for food and an appropriate lay-up area.

Five hours later, Chris and Jawad were on foot heading towards the Essa facility hoping the cover of darkness and the poor street lighting would disguise their purpose. Jawad had done well in finding his way, which was not a direct route and did not cross any other properties, thus preventing alarm.

When they reached the two-story building, they walked down a pedestrian walkway that ran down the side of the facility. The pathway was used as a dumping ground for material that Jawad assumed came from Essa as large bins full of waste clothing materials, cans of dye, rolls of cotton, and other such things were spread in front of them. Halfway down the path, Jawad stopped in front of a pile of wooden pallets. Without saying a word, both he and Chris grabbed hold of it, carried it twenty feet further down the path, and stacked it on the ground beneath a second-story open window. They repeated the exercise five more times, and then Jawad climbed on top of the stack and peered gingerly into the opening. Satisfied with what he saw, he extended his hand to Chris and helped him up to the top of the pallets.

Within a couple of minutes, both men found themselves in the rear of a storeroom. The space was mostly dark. Small slivers of light appeared from gaps in the ceiling where the main lights of the facility crept through, but at ground level, there was nothing to give them a direction or indication of danger. They both crouched, reaching out to touch their immediate surroundings and then waiting in silence for their night vision to kick in.

Chris was the first to move. Though he stood upright, he walked carefully and slowly, reaching out with his hands to feel the large objects that got in his way. The only thing that gave them a sense of security was that there were no loud or humming machines in their way that could cause injury or give their presence away.

They finally found a door, which was first on Chris's what-if scenarios. Jawad had no idea of what was behind the open window he had found or if it was a room that was locked from the other side. Jawad tried the door handle as both men willed it to release and open the door quietly. Chris fell back to the shadows of the room as the door opened, letting in dim light from the corridor. Jawad listened intently and then peered through the small opening that he had made. Satisfied there was no threat, he stepped out with Chris following close behind.

They crept along the narrow silent corridors of the second floor of the factory, checking each door that they passed but did not enter any on the first pass. Having a better understanding of the layout, they were able to map out an emergency route if they needed to make a quick getaway. They cracked open a door slightly at the end of the corridor they found, revealing the brightly lit fabrication plant of the facility below. One or two loom machines were running, but from a quick glance, Jawad couldn't see anyone operating the devices or present in the direct vicinity. Realizing what they were looking for was probably not on the shop floor, they retraced their steps and began a search of every room that they had previously encountered.

They eventually found the windowless cutting room. Jawad turned on the lights and saw that the walls on each side were plastered with sketches and drawings of all manners of fashion design. In the center were a few computers, tailor's dummies, and various fabrics of all colors strewn across large tables as if someone had somehow caught a rainbow and spilled its contents on to the counters.

Without hesitation, Jawad began to rummage through a few drawers while Chris made for an office to the rear of the space. He turned on a table lamp, sat behind the office desk, and started to open whatever he could. Not finding much to shout about, he turned his attention to a tall wooden file cabinet in a corner and started yanking at one of the drawers. It wasn't budging, but Jawad interrupted him as he held up a pair of leather gloves with a single port on the right hand.

"Bingo . . . help me with this," Chris whispered to him.

Jawad picked up a large pair of tailor's scissors off the desk and wedged it into the file cabinet drawer. As Chris pulled the drawer, Jawad pushed the scissors deeper to cause the wood to splinter allowing Chris to finally break the lock.

Looking inside they found multiple paper files, most of which were difficult to understand and useless to the pair of thieves. They continued going through each drawer until they reached the bottom where they found a number of CD cases. Taped to one was a piece of paper with the symbol of a glove.

"Take them all, Chris," Jawad ordered.

Chris found a nylon bag with the company's logo on it and stuffed what he could inside. "What's the chance there are more gloves around here?" Chris asked.

"There has to be a shipping area or storage around here somewhere." Jawad replied as both men spoke in hushed tones; the area they were in was deadly silent.

Both Guy and Chris had undertaken the mission, voicing their opposition to the speed they were moving, as covert entry to gather intelligence was normally a well-thought-out and practiced event. Chris had been on such missions in the past, and the workup for such an action took weeks, if not months of solid surveillance of the premises, its day-to-day operations, its security, and the behaviors of the workers and the neighboring properties. This ad hoc, fly-by-your-ass undertaking had more holes than a colander. No element of the operation was sound, and for all the two men in the factory knew, Guy Trimble could be outside right at that very moment talking to a cop and explaining a lame-ass story for why he was there in the middle of the night. They had no real escape plan and were pinning their hopes that Guy could hold his nerve and still be waiting outside when they needed him. Sticking around to go through a mountain of clothes in a warehouse was not part of the plan.

"Do you smell that?" Chris asked.

Jawad shook his head.

They both left the office and made their way through the cutting room.

Midway through, Jawad caught Chris's sleeve and held him back for a second. "Smoke!"

Just as he said it, they heard the horn of the Land Rover bleating out SOS. On the third communication, the pair knew Guy would be moving to a new pickup location and away from the building. It was time for them to leave.

Chris looked up to the ceiling. "No sprinklers. If there's a fire downstairs, we are in the shit." He looked around the room for a fire extinguisher and found one. As he pulled it off the wall, the rust of the frame and plaster of the wall fell off with it. He gave it a shake only to find it was empty. He threw it to one side and made for the door five steps behind Jawad.

When they opened the door of the cutting room, they were greeted by thick black smoke clawing its way across the ceiling of the corridor. They dove back into where they came from and slammed the door behind them.

"You thinking what I'm thinking?"

"We were right to come here, Chris, but we may not be the only ones with the same idea."

"Al-Qaeda covering their tracks the easy way, burn the place down."

Jawad nodded and looked for an escape from the cutting room. They rushed around looking for something that would give them hope, but there were no doors or windows to find. Chris looked over to the door and watched as the smoke slithered underneath.

"How long, Chris?"

"Fire-rated door in most countries . . . thirty, sixty, or ninety minutes. This place, direct flame, five minutes."

Jawad walked back in the office where they found the CDs. He looked around hastily. His eyes were trying to panic, but his mind was telling him to remain calm and find a solution.

Chris came in to join him. "Door's going up. Not much time, Ja-wad."

Jawad looked left, right, down, and then up. As he did, he spotted a skylight they missed before. All they saw was the blackness of night, so it was easily missed.

Chris started an impression of Michael Jackson's moonwalk. "My feet are getting hot, Jawad. The floor below . . . holy shit."

Jawad jumped up onto the desk. "The chair, Chris, the chair!"

Chris passed it up to him. Jawad placed it on the desk, jumped up on to it, and reached for the skylight. There was no way to open it, no mechanism or switch, but it was wide enough for them to fit through.

"I need something to break it, Chris. Find me something," he shouted.

Chris raced to the cutting room and grabbed a tailor's dummy, which was mounted on a heavy wooden pole. He tried in vain to get the mannequin off the pole as he rushed to give it to Jawad. Jawad snatched it from him and bashed at the glass as hard as he could. It took four hard blows from the Arab, but it smashed open. He cleared the debris around the frame with the pole, discarded the dummy, and then climbed through to the roof with Chris pushing from below. Once Jawad was through, he reached his hand down only for Chris to pass him the bag of evidence. Jawad took the bag and turned his attention to find a secure location for it, lest it slide off the roof. Once satisfied, he reached back down to grab Chris but heard a tremendous crash, and then there was nothing to grab on to.

———— ✷✷✷ ————

Chris was awake, but he did not have his eyes open. He searched the inside of his eyelids to warm up his senses, and the first things he felt were a headache and an aching right elbow. He remained as he was for a few minutes assessing his situation and then, as a robot, sent messages to his extremities to see if things were still intact. Receiving positive responses from all his bits and bones, his only query was about an unidentified weight at the end of his feet. He cracked open his eyes a smidgen, enough to look down his body to see something orange. "Am I in your spot again, Mango?"

The cat looked at him with disdain and did not budge.

Chris received a kiss on his cheek. "Good morning."

"Hi, how are you? Been awake long?"

"A while," Sandy responded with a smile on her face. "I've been watching you sleep."

"Sounds like a soppy line from a chick flick."

She gave him a playful push. "Hey now, you said you liked that movie we watched last night."

"Well . . ." He searched for a distraction. "What do you have there?"

Sandy was sitting up straight in the bed next to him. On her lap were a stack of photos. "I haven't had a chance to tell you about this." She handed him a few snaps of a pretty vista on farmland. "It's my uncle's place in Washington State."

"Why does everybody call it Washington State? Why not just Washington?"

"I guess they don't want people to confuse it with DC. I don't know. Anyway, it's near Seattle." She gave him some more of the pictures of the emerald-green pastures, forests, and mountain views.

"I've heard about Seattle. Isn't that where people don't tan; they just rust?"

"You're funny. It doesn't rain that much. It's a gorgeous state, one of my favorites."

"You going on vacation or something?"

"Actually, I was thinking . . . my uncle owns this farm, and he has asked me to go out there . . . to move there permanently. I can carry on with my veterinary studies at the University of Washington."

"Oh . . ." Chris mumbled. He'd only been back in the United States a few weeks after leaving Pakistan, and after his debrief, he was allowed a few weeks' vacation. He had no particular place to go, so he ended up back in New Jersey in a woman's bed who was kind to him one night a long time ago. It didn't take them very long to connect again, although they didn't know each other very well. He was chivalrous and stayed in a hotel near where she lived for the first few days. After that, they were inseparable, and she even took time off work just to be with him. It was turning into a whirlwind romance, but Chris had not put much stock into being very serious about it. It was early days in his opinion, and anything and everything could change; no harm, no foul.

"How soon are you thinking of going?" he asked, trying to be positive for her. He could tell it was a dream opportunity.

"Pretty soon . . ." She stopped looking at the pictures and tilted her head towards him. "Will you come with me?"

Chris sat up, blinking his eyes a few times giving away his surprise. He was about to say something when his cell phone rang. He reached over to grab it, and Mango sprang off his legs as if he had just been hit with a Taser.

"Hello."

"Chris, it's Gene. When are you coming back to work?"

"Gene, can I call you back? I'm in the middle of something important."

"Don't make me wait too long. I see a plane ride in your future. Unless you've had enough."

"Gene, I don't want to do this now. I told you I will make a decision about my future, but I don't want to get a decision made for me with the threat of a flight plan. Give me a break, and I will be in touch when I am ready."

"Make it soon, Chris."

Chris hung up the phone and looked at Sandy. She was waiting for an answer too. "It's a bit sudden, don't you think?" he said.

Although Sandy had been unsure how he would react, she was saddened by his reply. But he was right; they were moving pretty quickly. She hesitated before saying anything else and pretended to concentrate on her photos, all the while watching him in an effort to figure out his answer.

"Are they alpacas?" Chris asked looking at one of the pictures with genuine interest.

"Yes, he raises them, makes a small business from the wool."

She was about to carry on the discussion when his phone rang again.

"Goddammit, I'm on vacation," he half shouted and then leaned over to look at the number on the screen that he didn't recognize but knew it wasn't Gene. "Yes," he answered rudely.

Sandy got off the bed and headed to the bathroom. She didn't like his outburst, and his business phone calls were ruining the mood.

"Hello, Chris. Guy Trimble."

"Hello, mate. How are you" he replied with enthusiasm. "How are things?"

"All shipshape and above-board, old chap."

"Have you heard from our bearded friend?"

"Yes, yes, Jawad's fine and in good spirits, recovering well from his injuries. You?"

"I'm tip-top. My wrist is still a bit sore from when he yanked me out of that hole. Otherwise not feeling too shabby. I'd like to catch up with him some time. I still need to thank him properly."

"I know, I know. We will all have to get together one day soon, but listen, I don't have much time. I'm at the airport on another jaunt, but I wanted to ask you something before I go . . . I've been chucking your name around here in my office, and we were wondering that if you are unhappy with your current employers, perhaps you can come over to our side. All is forgiven and all that . . . I will be in DC next week to chat with your boys, so if you're interested, we can go over the details when I am there. What do you think?"

Chris looked at the phone, remembering a conversation he'd had with Guy while waiting for Jawad to complete his surveillance of the clothing warehouse in Karachi. Chris had mentioned that he was frustrated at the CIA as he was often thought of as just a driver or bodyguard by some of his peers and not a bona fide CIA officer. It seemed like now someone had listened. He thought of Guy's proposition, then Gene's earlier request, and then he scanned around the apartment for Sandy.

He put the phone to his ear, but before he could open his mouth, a tear ran down his face as he thought of his friend, Richard Nash.

—∞∞∞—

END

AUTHOR'S NOTE

The work presented here is fictional; however, the impetus to write such a story comes from factual information related to Osama bin Laden/al-Qaeda efforts to carry out chemical attacks against the West before or after the invasion of Afghanistan in 2001. Though these plans never came to fruition for various reasons, the threat was quite real.

Thank you for your interest in *The Next Cell*. It has taken me over 130,000 words to get to this point. If you could spare a few words of your own to let me know your thoughts in a review, it would make this author very happy and realize it was not in vain.

Made in the USA
Lexington, KY
06 November 2019

56664238R00203